THE FALLEN

HELL'S REDEMPTION: BOOK 3

GRACE MCGINTY

ALSO BY GRACE MCGINTY

Hell's Redemption Series

The Redeemable

The Unrepentant

The Fallen

The Azar Trilogy

Smoke and Smolder

Burn and Blaze

Rage and Ruin

Dark River Days Series

Newly Undead In Dark River

Stand Alone Novels and Novellas

Bright Lights From a Hurricane

The Last Note

The Castle of Carnal Desires

Treasure

Hunting Isla (Coming Soon)

Cover by DAZED Designs

For The Triptych of Terror.
I love you guys.

THE FALLEN

PART I

CHAPTER ONE

I woke to an angel standing over me, a dagger pointed at my chest. I smiled, well, at least I tried to. The searing ache in my jaw told me it was probably broken.

Azriel. I spoke into his mind and he stilled, his dagger still pressed to my chest. I took a quick inventory of my body. I was one solid mass of pain, and it felt like they'd kicked me into the room. I was chained to a bar, like a side of beef. I was naked.

Azriel, I whispered again. This time he reared back as if I'd struck him. *I guess it makes sense you're here.*

I couldn't draw breath, a rib must have broken and punctured my lung, and my heart was beginning to feel sluggish.

"Who are you?" Azriel hissed, finding his voice at last. His dagger was still pressed firmly to the space above my heart, indenting my skin. "What are you? No human should be able to speak into my mind, Witch."

I'm Hope. You know my mother and… I struggled to

define my relationship with Ace. It was part maternal, part bad influence. *And my Ace?*

Again, he pulled away as if I had struck him. He had such a beautiful face, achingly perfect even when he was gaping like a codfish.

His dagger slipped to his side. "You were one of her children. The aberrations."

Hey! I protested, but it wasn't as forceful as I'd have liked. I was dying, quickly. *Finish it. I hurt.*

He just stared at me, at the ruins of my face, the length of my bruised and broken naked body. But he didn't leer. It was like he was cataloguing me, as if I was a puzzle that looked complete, but he still had an extra piece left over.

Luckily, he didn't grant my request immediately. In the next flash, Luc, my twin Estrella and Memphis sifted in.

"Azriel, no!" Memphis shouted, lunging toward us. Azriel looked between me and the pair of Fallen angels, his face scrunched in confusion as he disappeared.

Estrella was beside me in the next breath. Blood was beginning to spill over my lips and down my chin. Estrella was pale, her beautiful blue eyes huge and wild in her face.

Rella, I whispered. I wanted to tell her that I loved her, and that she had to be strong. We were twins, but we had a connection greater than any other. My death would break her.

"Shh. I'm getting you down and then we'll get you to a hospital. I got you now. It's okay." She was fiddling with the chains and Luc came over, snapping them quickly. Memphis was there to catch me in his arms. I caught a quick glimpse of the naked rage in his eyes before a pain so intense swept over me that I screamed through my broken jaw. Everything in my body twisted, and sadness chased away the rage on Memphis' face. My empathic abilities were swamped with the depth of his pain, almost drowning out my own. He knew I was dying, that I wouldn't make it to hospital. I looked around desperately for Rella, wanting to send her one last reassurance, but my eyelids closed heavily, my body desperately trying to heal. Too late.

When I managed to open a single eye, we were no longer in dank basement that was to be my tomb. Instead, sun burned hot against my naked skin.

"Mephistopheles! What have you done?" I turned my face toward the beautiful voice that spoke. If I could have drawn enough breath, I would have gasped.

An angel stood before me, more beautiful than any I had ever seen. More beautiful than Luc or Memphis, who weren't actually beautiful so much as awe inspiring, or maybe terrifying would be more accurate. He was even more beautiful than Azriel.

"I didn't do this, Raphael." Memphis sounded hurt that the other angel had even suggested it. The cold note of vengeance had threaded its way back into his emotions. "Humans did this. You must heal her."

"Must I?" Raphael almost seemed amused, his hand reaching out to stroke my face. I turned my face into his palm. "Ah, you are one of Acerezeal's progeny." He gave me a warm smile, and it felt as if my body was healing itself from the strength of his gaze alone. That, or it no longer cared about dying.

"It is too late, old friend. She is the domain of Azriel now."

I couldn't even feel mad that this beautiful Archangel had just sentenced me to death, as long as he didn't stop stroking my cheek. His touch chased away the pain.

"Azriel came and left again. He rejected the call. Isn't that proof enough? Please, Raphael." I'd never heard any of the Fallen beg before, but I knew without a doubt that Memphis was begging for my life. Kinda gave me the warm fuzzies. Or that might have been the beginnings of my nervous system shutting down. At this point, I didn't care which.

Raphael was pondering Memphis' words. "How unusual. Well, I guess if she isn't slated for ascension by the Angel of Death, there's no harm in healing her a little. Most unprecedented, though."

He pressed a hand to my chest, inches from my exposed breast, and a healing warmth spread through my body. I grimaced as my ribs realigned, and my jaw snapped back into place, but the Archangel was buffering me from my pain. I knew this because he took it into himself. I could feel the waves of pain hitting him through my empathic senses.

My breathing became less labored, every movement no longer an agonizing torture.

"There, still broken but not beyond repair. Sometimes the human body needs to heal itself."

I tried to speak, but the pain in my jaw was still intense.

Instead I spoke into his mind. *Thank you.*

Raphael raised his brows. "You are welcome, little one." He turned to Memphis. "Does Michael know she can mindspeak?"

Memphis shrugged, jostling me a little in his arms and I grimaced.

"Sorry," he grunted at me. "I assume Michael knows. He knows all."

The Archangel Raphael laughed. "True. But he isn't as omniscient as some people wish to believe."

I summoned enough energy to look around. Wherever we were must have been somewhere in Africa, poor and rural, because out the window there was an abundance of children with big smiles but heartbreakingly thin limbs. There was a Red Cross on the door. Some kind of clinic maybe?

Where are we?

"Malawi," Raphael answered, his eyes watching me closely.

The gaunt faces broke my heart. *What do they need?*

Raphael gave me a smile that threatened to light up my world. "I see you inherited your mother's warm heart and inability to turn your back on suffering. They need what all these countries need. Food, water and infrastructure. Access to consistent healthcare services. A stable, uncorrupt government and a good influx of funds to help lift themselves above the poverty line." His emotions threatened to overwhelm me, and I mentally locked them in the box with all the other shit that needed to be processed later. Estrella had always stressed the need to keep my empathy a secret from everyone.

I gave a tiny nod. I'd make it so, or at least try my best.

"You must go now. She will still need someone to set her bones and she has lost a lot of blood." Raphael turned back towards the door. "Ah, your cavalry has arrived, Hope."

As he said the words, Luc popped into the clinic with Estrella.

Raphael smiled warmly at the devil. "Lucifer! You look well. I see having Acerezeal back has healed your wounds."

Then Luc did something that I wouldn't have believed possible if I hadn't seen it for myself. He hugged Raphael, a full blown smile on his face. "Hello, old friend."

Rella's jaw dropped open, and I wished mine could do the same. I'd never seen him hug anyone except Ace. Hell, I'd never seen him give anyone anything more than a handshake. Even as children, we would climb over him like our own personal climbing frame, but acts of tenderness were never offered, and definitely not expected. To see him being openly affectionate almost defied belief.

Luc turned to Memphis and scowled. "A little warning next time. Hand her to me."

Memphis scowled back, and held me tighter. For a moment I thought he might refuse and then they'd have a tug'o'war over my battered body, but eventually Memphis shifted me to Luc.

Luc held me safe in his arms, his large onyx wings curling around me protectively.

"Ace would have my balls if anything happened to you," he said, then sifted. I knew what he really meant. It was hard to hide your emotions from an empath. He'd been worried. He felt an affection for us that stemmed from his love of Ace, at least in the beginning. Now, I think he cared for us because we became the surrogate children that they would never have. Though neither of them would ever admit that.

Luc sifted us back to my apartment, Memphis and Rella seconds behind.

I could read Raphael, I told Rella as soon as she regained her land legs, and her eyebrows rose.

As she processed my thought, her forehead crinkled deeply. *Secrecy is more important than ever now. You'd be a threat to them all. Even if they aren't Fallen, it doesn't make them the good guys.*

I didn't respond. My body throbbed and it was a lecture she'd given me once a week since we were three. It was an issue for another day. Today, I just needed to heal from near death.

Minutes after we arrived, and Luc had laid me on my bed, Ace sifted in. She took one look at me, a little less broken but I'm sure I still looked like crap, and sifted back out again.

I curled into a ball and Estrella came over and pulled a sheet over my body, covering my nakedness. Probably too late for modesty. She laid on the bed and curled herself around me. We'd slept like this often since we were babies. I was always smaller and weaker, and

Rella was always my fierce protector. I petted her hand. She would have been terrified.

I'm okay now, I said soothingly. She let out a shuddering breath, and tension slowly seeped from her muscles.

Ace returned less than a minute later with Mom and Eli.

"Hope!" Mom raced to my bedside, stopping with a horrified look on her face when she took in my broken face, the bruises on my neck and chest. The blood drained from her cheeks and I thought she was going to pass out. Ace must have thought so too, because she shifted a few feet closer.

Eli stood beside me. "What happened?" He'd gone into doctor mode. Although he'd retired from being a neurosurgeon a few years ago, centuries of habit died hard.

I couldn't answer him, the pain in my jaw was intense. Estrella filled them in as Eli began to do triage, checking the severity of my injuries.

"She was jumped outside the Summit. Abducted. JJ is dead, executed professionally. Luc and I only found one guard, but he was just protecting the door. A grunt. He told us who paid him and that was it before Luc…" she made a tearing action with her hands, and I winced, as did Mom. Ace just looked satisfied.

Estrella recounted the whole thing without emotion, her own training kicking in. She'd become a cop for the Boston P.D. A damn fine one at that. She'd assessed the scene with cool efficiency. "I felt her go down. I called for Luc. We got there just as Azriel was going to…" This time her voice hitched, a single crack in her professional facade.

Ace let out a hiss. "I'm going to kick his fucking ass."

Not Azriel's fault. He was just doing his job, I defended to Estrella, who begrudgingly passed it on. Ace scoffed, and so did Memphis.

I hadn't realized Memphis was still here. He'd drifted into the shadows in the corner of my room. I tried to get a read on him, and flinched back. His emotions were still a torrent of darkness that scared me. I didn't know why he'd come for me. Memphis, or Mephistopheles as he'd never invited us to call him by Ace's nickname, didn't leave Hell often. Ace called him a Hellbody. She had a weird sense of humor.

Estrella must have picked up my loud thoughts. *He was with Luc when I called. Luc brought him for back up. Overkill, in my opinion. Nothing on the human plane could take on Luc, let alone Luc and Memphis together.*

I could only agree. Luc was petrifying on his own. With Mephistopheles in tow, they were your worst nightmare made flesh. And they'd come for me.

I looked at the dark Fallen angel, his almost midnight black skin making the startling blue color of his eyes all the more intense. His wings sucked up the light in the room, casting him in shadow. His face was perfectly smooth, but it was so hard it may have been marble.

Thank you, I whispered. He inclined his head, and I tried to shift past the anger in his emotions, delving deeper. I was rewarded with the hint of something softer, though I couldn't quite reach out fast enough to grab the emotion. It was like a scent on the breeze, barely a hint before it was swirling away beneath the churning rage.

I was pulled from my analysis by Eli's growl of frustration. "She needed to go straight to a hospital. She's going to need surgery to pin some of those fractures, and she has lost far too much blood. I'm calling an ambulance." He whirled away, a phone to his ear.

Estrella looked guiltily at Mom. "I didn't know how I could explain us sifting into an American hospital with her naked and bleeding. The tabloids would have been all over it, considering she was very publicly in Geneva a few hours ago."

Mom stroked Estrella's hair. "I know, love. It's okay. You did what you thought was right. Eli is just worried. He loves you two."

We knew. We might have seven fathers, but each of them loved us unconditionally.

Eli must have still had some serious clout at the hospital, because the paramedics were there in minutes. Or maybe it only seemed like minutes, because Raphael's healing was starting to wear off and my thoughts were getting slower and slower.

The Fallen went invisible as the paramedics walked through the door. "We'll go collect the rest of your seven," Ace said to Mom. "Lux must be going nuts." She sounded amused. "Memphis will help."

The large angel scowled. "I'm not a taxi service," he grumbled, but he threw me another inscrutable look and nodded. Luc, still invisible, leaned close despite the fact the paramedics were loading me onto a stretcher. "You didn't call me." He sounded hurt.

"There wasn't time." I wanted to reach out and touch his cheek, but that would look super strange.

Luc just growled. "You will call me if you have need." His tone brooked no argument and I smiled.

The Devil had my back. Always.

CHAPTER TWO

I woke up sobbing. Tears dripped down my cheeks until the pillow beneath my face was uncomfortably damp. It was a little from pain, though the pain medicine usually kept me comfortably numb.

Every time I closed my eyes, I saw the shiny barrel of the gun, felt the hot splatter of JJ's blood against my skin as my abductors, dressed as Valet's executed him. I felt every cut, bruise, broken bone all over again. In the true depths of the darkness, my mind made up stories about how I got my injuries while I was unconscious.

I was alone, everyone finally going home to get some rest, though there were still police officers outside my hospital room door.

"Why are you crying?" a voice asked from the darkness, with the almost innocent curiosity of a child. Except he wasn't a child. He was the Angel of Death.

"I hurt," I said, my voice muffled because my jaw was still healing. Even in the darkness, I could see him wince

"You're healing. You aren't in any real physical pain. When I saw you in that warehouse, you hadn't even shed a tear, and you were in far more physical agony than you are now."

I wanted to smile at him then, but that hurt too.

"My pain isn't physical, Azriel." My face scrunched up in pain as I spoke.

"Mindspeak. You are injuring yourself more." His voice was cold, as if he didn't care I was hurting. But then, if he didn't care, why would he have said it?

I'm sad, and scared, I clarified for him. I had a suspicion that Azriel wasn't the most emotionally intuitive of angels.

"You have nothing to fear from me now." He sounded almost offended.

A little laughter bubbled from my throat. *It's not you I'm scared of,* I answered, then laughed again as his face got even more offended.

"How could you not fear me? I am the Angel of Death," he huffed, like he hadn't just told me not to fear him. I think I just hurt his angelic pride.

I raised an eyebrow at him. It was basically the only movement I could do that didn't hurt. *One word. Lucifer. You're scary, Azriel, but he is downright petrifying. Only if you don't know him, though. Once you get to know him, he's basically a huge teddy bear.*

For the very first time, I saw Azriel's lips curl into a small smile. "I'm sure he'd love to hear you say that."

I don't know why that small expression meant so much to me, but it made my heart swell. I tamped down the feeling.

"Not that I don't appreciate your visit, your Angelic-ness, but why are you here?"

The smile dropped from his face. "I wanted to see the aberration up close. You are... different to what I expected."

Oh? I resisted the urge to punch him in the nose for calling me an aberration again. Only the fact he didn't seem to be saying it in a derogatory manner prevented me from kicking him out. *What did you expect? Horns and a forked tongue?*

"I expected more of Acerezeal's influence. But your aura is almost," he hesitated, "angelic."

I raised my eyebrows high. *You've obviously never met my twin.* I couldn't help my smile at the mention of Estrella, despite the pain it caused to my face. *She is a lot like Acerezeal. The apple of forbidden knowledge didn't fall too far from the tree with her, if you get my drift.*

His eyes crinkled, and I could have sworn he was going to smile again, but instead his face turned granite hard.

"Hmm, he's coming. There is something about you that is wrong, because I have never seen him act this way. You've bewitched him."

Then Azriel was gone and I was alone again. Though, as the Angel of Death had suggested, I wasn't alone for long. I felt the swirling discontent before my eyes could even find him in the darkness.

"Memphis." I muffled it out loud, because I wanted to hear him answer me.

"Hope." His voice was cold as he stepped from the darkness, his blue eyes glowing eerily.

He looked like the Angel of Death, not Azriel. Azriel was almost pretty in his perfection, a teenage girl's version of the perfect man.

Memphis looked like a demon, with his black wings and his hard eyes. Why was he here? His huge black wings took up all the space in the room, his hard face sending waves of fear through my body. Or maybe it was lust? Maybe I was fucking losing my mind.

I tried to speak again, but Memphis lifted a hand. "Don't speak. I find I'm disturbed by your pain." He sounded perturbed by the admission too. "I just came to, well, check on you. I do not like you here alone, unprotected."

There's police right outside my door, I reminded him, but he rolled his eyes almost like a teenage girl.

"And your previous bodyguard was from your human armed forces."

The stab in my heart at the reminder of JJ's death made me whimper, and Mephistopheles stepped forward, laying a hand on my shoulder. He loomed above me, and my hindbrain thought that perhaps I should be scared, here alone in the dark with the very embodiment of a nightmare trying to console me.

"I apologize. That was heartless of me. Please don't get upset."

You are a fool, Mephistopheles. With his hand on my shoulder, I heard his thought as clear as my own. I resisted the urge to console him for his faux pas. It was still important to keep my empathic abilities a secret. I just nodded, blinking back my tears furiously.

"I will guard you the night." It was a statement, not

a question. Who would guard me from Mephistopheles, though? I eyed his dark shirt, it's fabric shining unnaturally under the artificial hospital lights. He was handsome, but it was a harsh sort of beauty; you admired him in the same way you admired a well-crafted blade. He drew the eye and held it, and before you knew it you were broken on the floor at his feet. No, he might be playing nice, but Memphis was trouble.

"No need," I said out loud, but he ignored me, going to stand in the darkened corner, wrapping his large black wings around his body until he disappeared into the darkness, as if his huge six and a half foot frame no longer existed.

"Sleep," he ordered. I rolled my eyes, and found that I couldn't resist his command, the darkness of sleep like waves, pulling me under and keeping me safe as I drifted off into oblivion.

THERE WAS no such thing as uninterrupted sleep in a hospital, and at an ungodly time of the morning, someone was there, thrusting a tray on my lap table, the clattering of silverware loud enough to wake the dead. My eyes flew to the corner where Memphis had been keeping watch, but he was gone.

I choked down a jelly and some juice, flicking the tv between morning shows. I wanted to go home now. Hospitals and forced inactivity weren't my forte.

I needed to be at the office, or my home office or with Marinette, JJ's wife, or something.

I sat up, shifting my legs over the side of the bed,

glad that my hospital gown tied on the side so no one had to see my butt. I ignored the pain in my ribs, but the throbbing in my jaw made me hiss through my teeth.

"Should you be out of bed?" I turned too fast at the sound of another person in the room, and my body protested. Quite vehemently. I yelled and grabbed at my side, but my eyes watered with relief.

"Dad."

My father was there in a second, grabbing me in a gentle hug.

"God, I was so worried."

Oz was my biological dad. He loved me with every ounce of his being. They all did, of course, but Oz treated Rella and I as if we were the greatest gift he'd ever been given, and he was determined to cherish us with everything he had. We were his second chance. Being with him was like being cocooned in love, like a balm on my empathic abilities. No matter how bad we screwed up, wave after wave of love just flowed from him.

"I'm okay now," I soothed. I looked over his shoulder, knowing there would be others with him. Mom was the next through the door, closely followed by Lux, who trailed after her like a bodyguard, his eyes always searching for threats. When his eyes rested on me, his whole face softened. Tears slipped from my eyes, and I vigorously tried to blink them back.

I didn't have to be tough with Lux, I didn't have to put on a brave face, soothe his nerves. Lux was a protector. He would make everything better, either with diplomacy or the threat of violence. Usually the latter. He and Rella were a lot alike, despite the lack of actual shared DNA.

He reached out and wiped away my tears with the pad of his thumb. "You are okay."

It was a reassurance, and a promise.

Valery and Ri were there next, and I laughed when I saw Valery had Ri loaded down with bags.

Oz stepped away from me and Ri swept me into his arms, a little less gently than he probably should have, but I gritted my teeth.

"Fuck, Kid. You aged me a hundred years."

"Does that make you a thousand now?" I laughed, though my words were garbled. He pulled back, and his eyes were shiny. I probably shouldn't have spoken. Apart from being a pretty patchwork of bruises, none of my more threatening injuries were visible. But it was hard to hide the fact that I was speaking like a drunk.

Valery ran a hand over my hair, whispering something in French. "Never again, *oui*?" I tried to smile. Valery always switched to French when he was upset. I just nodded.

"Let the poor girl get back into bed," a voice said from the door. I looked up at Sam standing in there. His smile lit up my world, his handsome face ageless. When I was a kid, before I grew boobs, I wished Sam had been my dad. I would have been a stunning. Or maybe I would have been one of those ugly duckling throwback kids that beautiful people had sometimes.

He came over, leaning down to kiss the top of my head, and then held my elbow as I walked the three steps toward my hospital bed.

"Where's Tolli?" I already knew where Eli was; harassing my doctors. I would have bet the family fortune on that one.

"He's outside. He blames himself for you getting hurt."

I raised my eyebrows high. "How?"

Sam shrugged. "He believes he should have been there, not you. If he hadn't asked for you to stand in, this never would have happened." He waved a hand at my battered body.

I snorted in a very unladylike way. "Tolli is formidable, but not even he can control a hurricane. What happened was no one's fault. Except, you know, them."

Talking about it made me uncomfortable. Except with Rella. But I'd made her go home. I needed to be alone with my thoughts for a while, and I couldn't do that with her in the same room. At least if she was in Boston, there was a chance of blocking each other without giving myself even more of a headache.

"Make him come in here, Sam. I need him too."

Tolli and Sam were kind of a package deal. I was closest to Sam and Tolli, because of my position in the family company. They had mentored me. They trusted me as an adult, where the rest of my parents still saw me as the tiny baby they'd almost lost.

"Tolli!" I yelled, and screwed up my face in pain.

Sam's brow crumpled. "Tolliver, get your ass in here before she does something dumb like yell with a broken jaw again," he shouted, sending me a disapproving look.

I tried not to grin because it hurt, but I doubted I was hiding my mirth well.

Tolliver strode into the room like he owned it. It was just his natural bearing. It made him good at business, and once upon a time, had made him a great model. But I could see the small things that were off. He didn't look me in the eye and there was tension in his face that aged him. Not by much, but it was noticeable to me anyway.

Finally, he looked at me, and the tension seemed to leave his shoulders. The roiling guilt was still there, you couldn't hide emotions from me, but the lines of his face eased.

"Hope…"

I interrupted the apology he was about to give me. I didn't need it, and it changed nothing. "It isn't your fault. Come and tell me what's going on with the company. I've been gone for three days and it feels like an eternity."

He came over, pulling up the blanket and fluffing my pillows. The space was packed now, and I was glad I had a private room.

"Should you be talking with a broken jaw at all?" Tolliver asked, his eyebrow raised.

"It's only a small fracture now. Raphael fixed it that much. It hurts but at least it didn't need surgery." Though they'd had wired it shut to keep it supported while it healed.

Everyone tensed at the mention of the Archangel Raphael, the way they did at the mention of any of the Archangels. It's been twenty-odd years since whatever went on with them and Luc and the Angels, but they were still on-guard. Like they expected their lives to be recalled at any moment. It was my mom that spoke. "We are grateful for what Raphael did."

Lux nodded from where he was leaning against the wall. He was well into his fifties now, his formerly dark hair now streaked with grey.

Tolliver filled the awkward silence, telling me about how the NRH Foundation was functioning without me.

It was a testament to how injured I was that his words pulled me into sleep.

When I woke again, they were gone, though traces of my family remained; a thermos of soup that smelled amazing, extra pillows, a huge bouquet of flowers, a terrified beat cop that now physically checked on me every ten minutes like clockwork.

I squealed when I saw my laptop. I could work. Or binge watch Netflix. Maybe a week in hospital wouldn't be so bad. Just like a forced holiday.

CHAPTER THREE

"Hello Hope. I'm Villette, the welfare officer here at the hospital. I'm here because you've suffered a traumatic event, and your doctors would like to assess your emotional wellbeing."

I tried not to physically cringe. Therapists were the worst on my empathic abilities. They either cared too much or not enough, but both types were jarring to my nerves.

"I'm fine, really. I don't remember much and I'd really just rather go home." I smiled sweetly at her, praying she'd just agree and leave.

Unfortunately, Villette fell into a third category. The type that hated me because I was rich. I could feel her disdain as she looked around my private room, at my top of the range laptop, and the huge bouquet of roses.

"It is okay to admit that your… situation has caused you emotional distress. There is nothing shameful about PTSD." She stared at the colorful bruises on my jaw, her tone professional but her emotions anything but.

I sat up in bed, wincing as my ribs ached. Villette's corresponding glee at my pain made me feel ill. She was feeling superior now. She must have seen the disgust on my face, because she reached out to touch my hand.

"Tell me what you do remember."

I didn't pull away fast enough, and I got her thoughts as well as her emotions.

Her kind deserves to be brought down to the real world. Fucking trust fund princesses.

I didn't always pick up thoughts. Only sporadically or if the thought was really loud and believed with overwhelming conviction. I jerked my hand away.

"I think you should leave," I said, my voice as cool as the ice princess she thought I was.

Now it was Villette's turn to rear back. "Excuse me?"

I narrowed my eyes at her. "If you have such hatred in your heart, perhaps it's best you find a different career path."

The welfare officer sat there gaping like a fish. Then her face twisted in a sneer. "Are you threatening me?"

I sighed, suddenly feeling very tired of everything. "No. But I do not need or want your help." I wished I could threaten her, but what would I say to the Hospital Board? She was perfectly professional and outwardly concerned. It wasn't as if I could show them her heart.

"She may not be threatening you, but I am. Leave," a dark voice said from behind her, and Memphis stepped from the shadows. I hadn't even felt him come in.

Villette took one look at Memphis, his wings gone

but his expression one that promised pain and death, and left as fast as she could.

"Back again, Mephistopheles?" I raised my eyebrows, and hoped he didn't notice how relieved I was to see him.

"Yes. Call me Memphis."

I huffed. The disdain of the the so-called Welfare Officer lay across my skin like an oil slick, and it was making me testy. I didn't want to deal with this ancient angel bullcrap. I hated that I had to second guess everyone's intentions. Why could no one just be straight up? Except Rella and Ace. They really were a lot alike.

"Why? Why are you here? We don't know each other. I've met you like twice in my entire life. I know you and Luc are friends, but seriously, Luc and Ace are a whole lot more than acquaintances and they don't see the need to babysit me. So why are you really here? Or did Luc ask you to guard me?"

I tuned into his emotions. It was cheating, but fuck it. He was complicated, in the way all the Fallen were complicated. They felt so much, yet it was buried deep. A millennia of experiences all stuffed deep down into their psyches. They didn't taste the way the Angels did, even Raphael. They all felt overwhelmingly of loss. A loss so profound that I wasn't sure I'd be able to describe it to another person.

But warring with the loss and the anger that normally colored Memphis' emotions was that soft feeling again. Not quite love, or passion, or respect. It was something shinier than that. It almost felt like hope.

"I am here because I want to be here. That is all."

His deep voice rumbled through my bones, and down to some of the happier parts of my body. Memphis had a voice that could tempt you into sinning.

I closed my eyes and relaxed back into my pillows. "That's not really an answer," I grumbled, but let it go. The less time I was alone with my thoughts, the better off I would be. "If you are going to loiter around the place, you should tell me about yourself."

Memphis walked to the darkest corner of my light drenched room. "There is not much to tell."

"Well, I refuse to let you stand there in dark corners like a floor lamp, so make something up," I argued quietly. Last thing I needed was for the nurses and the beat cop thinking I was going nuts, talking to myself.

"What would you like to know?" he said, leaving his place to sit in the chair beside the bed. His emotions told me he was annoyed, probably from being compared to a piece of interior decor.

Hmm, what did you ask a Fallen angel? I knew the general story of how they fell. The Hell version. They got kicked out for questioning the status quo. Ace always painted them as revolutionaries for the rights of every being to have a choice. Luc didn't talk about it. I had a feeling there was more to it than either side let on.

Actually, when Ace told the story, it was always her and Luc, Gusion and Memphis against Heaven's legions. She made them sound close, inseparable appendages of the same being.

"You and Ace were a thing?"

Memphis actually looked embarrassed, which meant his brows lowered and he shifted to stand primarily on his other foot. Nothing in his visage actually changed. Empathic abilities for the win. "A long time ago now. We have thousand of years of friendship behind us. Of companionship. But there is never any doubt that Acerezeal loves only Lucifer. Their relationship exceeds the human concept of love. We were merely diversions to waste away the years. Hell can be lonely. And that ended decades ago," he qualified in one long rush, and I put my hands in the air.

"That's your business." I was glad I was the only empath in the room, because I felt a strange mish-mash of jealousy and relief. "Want to ask me something? A tit-for-tat kind of thing?"

Something about Memphis' stern control made me want to tell him things, to shock him into feeling something.

"How long have you been an empath?"

"Since I was born," I answered automatically, before slamming a hand over my mouth. Then belatedly realizing my jaw was broken when waves of pain shot up and down my face. "Fuck!" I screamed. Memphis was on his feet, looking down at me helplessly.

"Should I call the nurse?"

I let out a low moan. "No. There's no antidote from stupid unfortunately." The pain started to ebb excruciatingly slowly. "What I should have said was that I have no idea what you're talking about. But how did you know?"

Memphis curled and uncurled his hands, and my eyes were drawn to the gesture, to his length and shape of his fingers, to how shiny his nails were. Each hand was divine perfection. "It is my," he hesitated over the

words, "ability to know people's darkest secrets. It is
what makes me such a horror to humanity. Their souls
are laid bare before me." His old world pattern of
speech was so soothing that I momentarily missed what
he was saying.

"Wait, you know everyone's deepest secrets?" I
thought my ability was kind of scary. But knowing the
closest held secret of every person alive? That sounded
like a kind of horror show I never wanted front row
seats to see.

"Secret. Singular. Only their deepest, darkest, secret.
Quite frankly, your empathy is a balm after the normal
depravity of humankind."

For some reason I didn't want to investigate too
closely, my mind went to Azriel. "Even the secrets of
other angels?"

He nodded solemnly, loneliness emanating from him
in a steady pulse. I reached out, and placed my hand
over his huge, clasped ones. "I'm sorry."

He waved away the platitude, though his eyes held
warmth. I worked hard at blocking his emotions. I found
that I didn't want to take more than this man wanted to
give.

I heard voices in the hall, voices I knew, and my face
split in a grin. "You might want to go invisible right
about now. We have incoming."

Memphis' brows swooped down over his eerie blue
eyes, but he did what I asked, just as the Mulligan
women swarmed into my hospital room. All talking at
once, they sounded like an angry flock of geese with
distinct Bostonian accents.

"Hope!" Granny Mulligan said something completely unsavory in Gaelic as she saw my face. Aunt Clary was around her in a flash, and pulling me into a hug. She looked me over, inventorying my wounds, my dressings, my machines. Nodding once, she stood so she could look at my chart. Clary still worked as a nurse in Boston, and she was as no-nonsense as she was loving. Granny Mulligan wrapped me in her arms, still tsking, as she kissed my head.

"What kind of evil would do this to my sweet Hope?" she asked the room, though it was rhetorical.

"Johnnie, you tell Colin he needs to fix this," Aunt Bea said, waving a bunch of flowers around like a scepter. "To a soul as sweet as Hope's at that. The devils work!"

Memphis stepped from the shadows, and I froze. But apparently he was still invisible to everyone but me. Angels couldn't hide from me or Rella. Another oddity of our DNA.

"It wasn't the Devil who did this. Pretty sure the Devil is going to flay the skin off whoever did do this to you, though" he said, and only I could hear. "They are an interesting group, these Mulligans. I've met many of their kin over the years," he said conversationally. "Their deepest secrets are… intriguing."

I internally groaned. I desperately wanted to know now. Way to wave a red flag in front of a bull. But that was a massive invasion of their privacy, right? Whatever, I'd read their emotions every day since I was three. Probably too late to worry about privacy now.

"Oh?" I said, directing it to Granny Mulligan, but

looking at where Memphis stood behind the completely oblivious Mulligans.

He pointed to Aunty Bea. "Hit a man with her car and never stopped." Then to Clary. "Smuggled a family out of Africa on fake passports, their pockets stuffed with pilfered blood diamonds." He looked at Granny Mulligan and grinned. "Tempted a Priest into sin in a confessional." He raised his eyebrows, a small smile on his face. "Granny Mulligan, I am shocked and awed!"

Granny banged her cane on the linoleum floor. "Stop fussing like a bunch of old hens. Hope, my sweet child, we have brought you a gift on behalf of the Family. Your accident does not sit well in the hearts of any of us; you know how much we love you. I heard your former protection was killed, may God bless his righteous soul. We have brought you a replacement. Blue!" she yelled, and another person entered the room.

I'd tuned out most of the emotions in the room, but his hit me like a wave of nothingness. Not because he had no emotions, but he seemed to be purposefully blocking them. I knew they were there, I could feel them circling beneath the surface like fish trapped in a barrel. Physically his face was impassive, but his ice blue eyes all but simmered. They were like steam off a frozen lake.

I looked at Memphis, and his eyes were narrowed, his face scary as he looked at the newcomer.

Uncle Johnnie stepped forward. "Hope, this is Blue Halloran. He is the best in the family at what he does."

I swallowed hard. "And what's that?"

For the first time, the man spoke. "Whatever is necessary."

The words sent a chill down my spine. "What's your darkest secret?" I asked him, my eyes on Memphis though.

Blue answered. "You don't want to know."

Memphis' face was granite. He didn't say a word.

I couldn't drag my eyes from the killer. Because there was no doubt in my mind, that was what he was. He was a strongman. An enforcer. A hitman. A murderer.

CHAPTER FOUR

The hitman wouldn't leave. Or more exactly, when the Mulligans had all headed back to Boston, and I'd asked him to leave, he'd sat in the hard plastic chair with a blank look.

"The Family are scarier than you are," was all he said, and then promptly pretended to go to sleep.

I wasn't going to lie. Blue Halloran petrified me. His compressed emotions felt like a grenade that I was holding in my hand. Even the slightest fumble would have catastrophic circumstances for us both. He was all edges, dressed down in a pair of blue jeans and a perfectly ordinary white tee. He looked like someone you'd find sitting in a sports bar, drinking beer with his buddies and yelling at the umpire. Until you got to the eyes. The eyes gave him away, like fragmented ice, cold and deadly.

He ignored me unless someone walked into the room, then he was casually alert. Nothing about his outwards appearance changed, he still looked bored as hell, but there was a subtle tension in his shoulders. Whenever the beat cops changed shifts, every single one eyed him like he was a rattlesnake curled in the corner of the room. When the nurses asked, he'd just say, "I'm her bodyguard," and they'd leave it at that. Because I was a goddamn heiress. Why wouldn't I have live-in bodyguard?

For some reason that defied logic and self-preservation instincts, I didn't protest too much about his presence. Despite the fact he was obviously a criminal, and his emotions were buried so deep that I'd need the mental equivalent of an excavator to get to them, my gut said that he was okay. That should the cast of my recurring nightmares appear, he would get rid of them, once and for all. On the flipside, my angelic visitors didn't return overnight either. I wasn't sure how I felt about that, but I'd had enough self-reflection to last me a lifetime.

His stony silence was starting to get to me by the following day though. It had been twenty-four hours since he'd arrived and he'd said a total of twelve words to me. Seriously, I counted. Silence was something that totally unnatural to me. Even if someone's lips weren't moving, to me they were always saying something. But not Blue-freaking-Halloran.

"Seriously, don't you ever say anything? Hum a tune, or whistle, or move a little louder, or something. You are driving me insane," I complained. Hospital was driving me insane. I wanted to go home.

"Grumpy today." It wasn't a question. He said it like

it was fact. It made me want to punch him in the nose. Such violence was usually Rella's domain.

"I'm bored. I should be working. Last week I was talking to world leaders. Now I'm napping in the afternoons while you watch me sleep like a creeper."

His cheek twitched. "I do not watch you sleep."

I rolled my eyes and turned over, giving him my back. I could hear the rustle of him standing, and the quiet whoosh of the door open and closing.

Great, I'd offended the hitman. And now I felt bad. Great.

I wished Rella was here. She was great at dealing with people. It wasn't always with the best of manners, but she made friends easily and she usually got what she wanted. I'd always envied that. She'd know what to say to Blue. Unfortunately, it would probably be, "You have the right to remain silent."

I stared at the cheesy rom-com for what seemed like an eternity, not absorbing any of it, when the door opened again. Blue strode back in, a paper bag under his arm.

He put it on the tray table at the bottom of my bed and sat back in his chair in the corner. "What is this?" I asked quietly, staring at the brown paper bag like it might contain a bomb. I mean, it was a possibility, right?

He just grunted. "Open it and see, Princess."

I kind of wanted to tell the tightly wound bastard to take it back, but my curiosity won out. Dammit. Opening up the brown paper bag, I pulled out a magnetic travel chess set. It was actually kind of pretty.

One side was glittery gold, and the other a polished black.

"You play?" I asked, and he raised a single eyebrow at me.

"I have hobbies that don't involve cracking skulls."

My cheeks flushed. "I didn't mean to imply-"

He cut me off with a wave of his hand. "Just set up the board and save the apology." He pulled the chair toward the bed. "You play right, Princess? I'm pretty sure chess is a part of your private education."

I guess I'd started with the gross generalisations, but I still scowled at him. However, I was so bored, I resisted the urge to tell him to take the Queen and stick it. Instead, I set up the board.

"They didn't teach chess. They taught polo. My father taught me chess."

Not even asking, he twirled the board so he was black. "Which one?" he asked, but it wasn't snide like most other people. He seemed genuinely curious.

"Tolliver. He said mastering chess would teach me how to do business. Not sure how getting beaten for twenty years has helped me in the business world though."

Apparently, we'd exhausted our quota of conversation, because Blue just stared at the board and made a move. I found my concentration consumed as Blue countered my clumsy attacks, putting me on the back foot. He was good. His moves were considered, and even the random ones made sense five moves later when he took my bishop and then my knight in consecutive moves.

"Maybe we should have played checkers," I grumbled, as he took another one of my pieces. I was holding my own, but it was hard work. I moved, and grinned.

"Check," I crowed. I was finally going to beat someone other than Rella. Rella did not have the patience for chess. She was more of a 'charge full steam and consequences be damned' type.

Blue took a pawn. "Checkmate."

My jaw swung open. "Shit." I reached out to shake his hand. "Good game."

He wrapped his hand around mine.

Why does she have to be so fucking nice? So fucking perfect all the time?

I frowned as his thoughts echoed through my brain, ignoring the stab of hurt that appeared somewhere near my heart. What the hell did that mean?

"Good game," he muttered. "Another?"

I shook my head. "No. Thanks for getting the board. I'm kind of tired now." Nodding, he packed up the board silently. I laid down in bed, rolling over so my back was to him and he couldn't see the emotions on my face.

The room was painfully quiet once more. I couldn't take it. "Why do you dislike me so much?" I asked, but I didn't turn around because I was a coward. I wasn't scared to admit it. I didn't want to look at his apathetic face as he told me all the reasons why he held me in such low esteem. So if that made me cowardly, then so be it.

For the first time since I met him, a trickle of feeling slipped through Blue's emotional wall. Regret.

"You are everything I can never be. You don't even realize." And that was it. Like that explained anything. I sucked in a shuddery breath and pushed the hurt down deeper. This time it was me who pretended to sleep. Another cowards act; burying my head in the sand and not examining why the words of a criminal, a killer, actually mattered so much to me.

I heard his deep sigh. "You are a princess and I am a junkyard dog. It's my problem, not yours."

I ignored him, but his emotions were burning so bright that they all but seared my nerve endings. For a while, I sat in silence, just letting the wildness of his feelings brush along my skin. So much pain. I would fix him whether the stubborn asshole liked it or not.

"It's eleven in the morning, I know you aren't tired."

"I'm convalescing."

"Maybe you are just a sore loser. Did you want me to hand you the victory, Princess?"

I rolled over and sat up, ignoring the roaring pain in my ribs. I wouldn't give him the satisfaction.

"I'm not a princess. Stop calling me that. And I've worked hard to be the woman I am today, not everything was handed to me."

He shrugged, wheeling the tray over to me. "You are basically a deity to the Mulligan Family. You are more than a Princess. You are a fucking way of life to them."

I scowled. "That's not true." I watched as his fingers deftly reset the chessboard.

He just raised his eyebrows, and moved his pawn. "Isn't it? I'm their best enforcer, their greatest tool, and they took me off all my jobs to come and babysit you in

Manhattan for an undetermined amount of time. If that doesn't sound like paying tribute, what does?"

I made my move, and stared at those unflinching crystalline eyes. "Maybe you aren't as good as you think you are. Besides, they love me, they just want me to be safe. If I had my way, you'd be on the first train back to Boston. Back to your girlfriend, your six illegitimate irish bastards and your killing spree. Your move."

He made a derisive noise in the back of his throat. "You aren't my owner. I might be a junkyard dog, but you aren't at the other end of my chain, Princess." He moved. "Checkmate." I looked down. Fury rose up in me, and I swept my hand across the board, pushing all the pieces onto the table, some rolling of the edge and onto the floor. "Fuck!"

We both stared as the golden queen bounced across the floor, spinning in useless circles. I sucked in a deep breath, calming my emotions. I never lost control like that. Something about Blue Halloran, actually this whole damn situation, was twisting me all up. I needed to go home, get back to my normal life where Fallen Angels didn't brood at my bedside and contract killers didn't say things that hit too close to the damn truth. I took a deep, calming breath.

"I'm sorry," I said, sliding from the bed and bending to scoop up the scattered pieces. I sucked in a breath as my abused muscles protested.

"Stop, I can do it," Blue growled, grabbing the pieces from my hand.

"I can do this," I growled back, snatching the pieces back again.

He shook his head, opening his hand and dropping all the pieces back on the floor. Asshole. I scowled, but I bent down and continued picking them up, glad he couldn't see my face as I gritted my teeth against the pain. Finally, I'd picked them all up except the gold queen.

Blue walked over, scooping it up off the floor. He held it out with a flourish, like a magician revealing the coin he'd pulled from your ear.

I took it from him, careful not to touch him, and placed it in it's spot in the box.

I handed the box back to him, and he took it, shaking his head. I crawled back into the hospital bed, suddenly exhausted.

I felt a wave of love. I looked at Blue. Well, it definitely wasn't coming from him. Then I picked up the comforting probe of Rella's thoughts.

I smiled brightly at Blue, and his eyebrows rose at my sudden shift in mood. Oh, this was going to be good.

I'd just settled myself back in bed when the door opened and my twin, my strong, beautiful twin, ran into the room, throwing herself across my body and hugging me tight. Too tight. I sucked in a breath as my poor abused ribs got battered for the second time in ten minutes.

"It's so good to see you. You look like shit though. What have you been doing? God, I've missed you," I said into her hair, though I didn't think she was listening. That was okay. It was just nice to feel the warm safety of her familiar emotions. The blanket of love that surrounded us both whenever we were together.

She pulled back, and I could see the exact moment she remembered my ribs. "Don't worry, they don't hurt too bad anymore. Besides, I needed that too."

Blue scoffed, and Rella reared back. She was up, a gun pulled from god-knows where, pointed at Blue's face with an almost inhuman speed. Blue, for his part, looked completely unfazed about having a gun trained on him.

"Hope? Why is Blue Halloran sitting at your bedside?"

CHAPTER FIVE

The day after Rella's visit and meeting her, uh, new friends, the hospital released me. Adnan, Aunt Clary's adopted son, Mulligan golden boy, and proof that the Mulligans were moving into the 21st century, hustled me into the car. He barely spared a glance for Blue, which lent credence to Blue's feelings that he was merely a tool to the Family. However, Blue just slid into the back of Adnan's sporty convertible coupe like he'd been invited.

"Ah, Hope. The apartment hasn't been the same without you. Liesel was just saying yesterday that the apartment was just boring without you."

I shifted to buckle in my seatbelt, but Blue's hands were there, clipping it in with cool efficiency, then sitting back in the cramped coupe, his long, muscular legs up under his chin.

I looked over my shoulder. "Thanks, Blue." I glanced at Adnan in the driver's seat. "Do I know Liesel?" It was sometimes hard to keep up with Adnan's dancing friends, almost as hard as keeping up with his boyfriends. They all seemed to have a rapid turnover, both friends and lovers.

"No, but she can tell your aura is missing from the apartment." I rolled my eyes. "Don't roll your eyes at me, Miss I-Can-Read-People's-Emotions."

I whipped my head to him, giving him my best quelling look. "Seriously?" My eyes shot to the mirror and I looked at Blue. Maybe he'd missed that. His eyebrows were raised. Maybe not.

"Pssh. He's your bodyguard, right? Duty bound to protect your body day and night? You were going to slip eventually." What Adnan meant was that he was going to slip eventually. Adnan was not good at keeping secrets. Unfortunately, we hadn't known that when we were five and Rella and I let him in on our biggest secret.

I decided that the best course of action was to ignore Adnan's verbal nip-slip and move on. I told Adnan about the doctor ordering rest, and that I had to take another week off work, maybe two, and I had to get my pain meds on the way home.

I listened half-heartedly as Adnan went off on a tangent about the dangers of pain meds to dancers, which was apparently grave in his opinion, and instead appraised Blue in the rear view mirror as he looked at the streets of Manhattan.

He really was attractive, but it was in an unusual kind of way. His icy blue eyes were a shade that was unsettling rather than pretty, and they were set under low, straight eyebrows that made him look serious, almost cruel. His body was nice though, all hard lines and edges. It was lean muscle, and while he didn't look like he could bench press me or anything, he moved with an elegant sort of grace that told me he was consciously aware of everything around him and his place in the room.

He was dangerous. Self-assured. And sexy as hell.

I sighed, and tried to tune back into Adnan. I did not need to lust over my reluctant bodyguard, especially one with a kill count.

The empath and the murderer, a love affair doomed to fail.

Luckily, with little to no input from me, Adnan wrapped up his spiel just as we came to our apartment buildings underground garage. Adnan swiped his pass, waved to the gate attendant and drove to our spot.

My little Prius sat where I'd left her. As I gingerly stood from the car, I ran a hand over her bonnet. It had to go. Even looking at it was making my heart pound. All I could think about were the men climbing out of the car, the shiny metal gun matching the paintwork almost perfectly in the Geneva sunshine. Logically I knew that my car and the rental Prius were completely different, but my heart didn't seem to care as it thundered in my chest.

A hand reached out and wrapped itself in mine, pulling me away from the car. The subtle wave of Blue's muted emotions cascaded over me, and I dragged my eyes from my Prius to our clasped hands. But as soon as he had tugged me from between the cars, he let go of my hand, his eyes alert. I tensed, but couldn't sense any malice or ill feelings from the carpark. I guess Blue was just doing his job.

We walked to the elevator, Adnan holding my bags. "The place is a bit of a mess, but the cleaning lady is coming in tomorrow," he said as he swiped our key. "I just haven't had time, you know?"

I rolled my eyes. Adnan was also a bit of a slob. It wasn't that he was dirty, but he was creative. His mind lived in a constant state of organized chaos, and as a result, so did our apartment.

I shook my head at him as the doors slid open and he glided from the elevator with all the aplomb of royalty. Looking at him move, you would never guess he was missing a leg, a casualty of a bomb blast that almost killed him when he was a boy, living in Aleppo. His entire family had died, except his older brother Nazir who he adored but didn't see much of, and in a story no one really talked about, somehow Ace managed to move them both to US, and Aunt Clary adopted them and raised them like her own flesh and blood. Aunt Clary was the reason the Mulligans accepted their adopted, Middle Eastern, gay, one legged dancer relation with such ease. To treat Adnan with anything but love and respect would incur the wrath of Clary. I'd only ever heard rumors of Clary's infamous temper, but it kept everyone in check when it mattered.

Adnan hadn't been lying when he said the place was a mess.

"Has your apartment been ransacked?" Blue asked, and it didn't sound like he was making a joke. The place did look like it had been tossed. But I knew it was just Adnan.

I shook my head at Blue, who raised a single eyebrow but said no more.

Adnan cleared off the couch and fluffed some pillows. I walked over and slumped into the seat, exhausted even though I'd done literally nothing but walk to and from the car.

"I'll run downstairs and get you your pain meds and a doughnut," Adnan kissed the top of my head. "Will you be all right with…" he didn't finish, but he didn't need to.

"We'll be fine," I said reassuringly. He hadn't murdered me in my sleep yet, so I thought I was pretty safe.

Picking up his keycard, Adnan swooped from the room with as much grace as he'd entered.

Blue continued to stand in the middle of the room, taking in my home. When it wasn't covered in Adnan's crap, it was usually quite nice. It had a comforting, homey feel. I snuggled down into the plump couch cushions, pulling the soft grey afghan over my knees. It was good to be home.

"What did the Little Prince mean about you reading people's emotions?" Blue said with feigned casualness, as he walked around straightening things.

"You must have misheard," I said, picking up a magazine that had been wedged between the couch cushions and pretended to read.

Blue just raised a single eyebrow again.

I sighed. "Exactly what it sounds like."

Straightening the coffee table books, he looked at me. "Elaborate."

"No."

Icy blue eyes stared at my face, as if he was mining my brain for his answers, and I squirmed beneath his gaze. I wondered briefly if this was how people felt when I spent too long trying to read their emotions.

"Fine. I can read people's emotions. Like right now, you aren't straightening everything to be polite, though I didn't need to read your emotions to guess that. You are straightening because this level of disorganization makes you anxious. It goes against your need for everything to be ordered, perfect. I imagine that can only be a good thing in your line of work."

Blues hands halted. "And now?"

"Confusion. Disbelief. A little fear that what I'm saying is actually true and I'll see all the murky, dark parts of your soul."

He stilled. Like he was unnaturally still, as if he was no longer even breathing, as if his heart had ceased to beat.

I was a little relieved when his breath whooshed out. I was worried I would have to give him mouth to mouth. Yeah, worried, right.

"That's untrue." He moved away from me, as if standing on the other side of the room might dull my other sense. It was wishful thinking. If I tried hard enough, I could feel the emotions of every person in this apartment building.

"There's no need to be frightened," I said quietly. This was why I never told anyone about my abilities.

Our emotions were really the only things that were truly ours. People could tell you what to think, but no one could tell you how to feel. To know that I could get inside their emotions and poke around would freak out anyone. Except Rella and Adnan, but they'd had a lifetime to get used to it, and besides, kids already wore their emotions on their sleeves. It hadn't really felt like a big deal until we hit thirteen and I realized that Charlie, Rella's best friend, had a huge crush on her. It was the first time that I realized I'd be privy to information that could effectively change peoples lives.

"I'm not frightened," Blue growled. I winced. I knew differently. The shock had obliterated his normal wall against his emotions and I was getting everything. It was a deluge of pent up anger, sadness, loneliness and rejection. I wrapped my arms around my stomach and groaned. I couldn't slap my hands over my ears, or cover my eyes to make it stop. The only thing that would make it better was distance, but I couldn't tell him to leave. He hurt in a place that couldn't be healed by bandages and medicine. He hurt down to his very soul.

I stood up, moving closer despite my instincts. He didn't move away, even though he looked like he needed to bolt.

I placed a hand on his arm first, and when he flinched from my touch, I stepped into his space, wrapping my arms around his waist and hugging him to me as tightly as I could. I wanted to take his decades of hurt and pain and suck it into myself, but emotions didn't work like that. I couldn't heal them with a wave of my hand. But I could let him know I had his back, well his front right now, if he wanted it.

Step out of her arms you dumb fuck. You don't deserve her absolution. You made your bed, and she isn't going to warm it for you. Now move. For fuck sake just move, you aren't worth the shit on her shoe! He stepped out of my arms.

"That's not true, Blue. I'm no better than you!"

"What?" He took another step back.

"You're worth just as much as I am," I said, stepping back into his face so he was forced to look at me.

"Are you a mind reader too?" he yelled, his hand moving to his hip, where his gun was. I stilled.

"No. I mean, sometimes but only if I'm touching them and they are feeling really loudly."

He was at the door, and I could feel his rage. "You had no right." Despite his words, I couldn't feel any hatred emanating from him towards me.

I'd fucked this up so bad. I wanted to go to him, soothe his barbed emotions that poked at me like a crown of thorns. But I was very aware of the gun at his hip. A gun so like the one that killed JJ and haunted my nightmares.

I felt a presence flutter in behind me, and I turned. Memphis was there, his eyes promising pain. I raised my hand to still him, though judging by his huge wings, he wasn't visible to Blue.

"Blue," I said again, softly. A plea for forgiveness.

"You had no right," he repeated, opening the door and slamming out.

I looked at the door for a moment, calming my hammering heart.

"He's not coming back, is he?"

Memphis was silent, so I turned. He was staring at the door too, his brows creased. He made himself visible and walked toward me, his wings dragging softly across the polished wooden floors.

"He will be back. But not today." He put a hand under my elbow and directed me back toward the couch. "Please sit. I can sense your exhaustion."

I wanted to tell him it was mental not physical exhaustion, but I kept my silence. When he sat down next to me, I gave into the strange impulse that lingered at the edge of my brain. I crawled onto his lap and rested my head on his chest, appreciating the warmth of his skin, the steady staccato beat of his heart. And when he wrapped deep onyx wings around me, sucking out the light, leaving me with only warmth and comforting darkness, I let the fear seep from my veins. I let the thump, thump, thump of his heart lull me to sleep, and the black of night soothe away the hurt of the day.

CHAPTER SIX

Memphis came back the next day, and the day after that. Usually he would just loom in the corner, choosing to keep himself from Adnan for whatever reason. It wasn't as if Adnan hadn't ever met Luc and Ace. Ace loved Adnan's adoptive mother, Clary. Mom used to tell stories of girls nights out just after we'd been born. I'd shut that down quick. You don't want to know what the Consort of Lucifer and the daughter of one of the biggest mob families in Boston got up to when there was copious amounts of vodka and no restraining influence. My whole body shuddered.

But for whatever reason, Memphis never appeared in corporeal form until Adnan had left for the day. His feelings confused me. Hell, I was pretty sure his feelings confused him. He wanted something from me, but I wasn't sure what it was. It wasn't my body, obviously, because it was still battered and bruised, though I did get the odd hint of lust when he thought I wasn't looking. He guarded his emotions from me, and it was as close as I got to silence. But no one can guard their feelings all the time. It wasn't natural. Emotions seeped out as subconsciously as breathing.

He held so much yearning in his heart when he looked at me. Like I was the answer to a question he had waited a millennia to discover.

Today, he appeared as soon as Adnan had slipped from the door, not even bothering to hide his wings, though he held them tightly to his back. He held a small gold box in his hand.

"What's that?" I said from the kitchen. I made his coffee. Black. No sugar. I screwed my nose up. It would be like drinking tar. I put it in the extra large mug that had *coffee bowl* written on the side because he'd drink it straight from the pot if I'd let him.

"Chocolates, from Peru," he said softly, handing me the box. "Apparently humans enjoy it."

I put my mug down with a thud, coffee splashing over the side and burning my hand.

"You don't like chocolate?" I briefly wondered if I could eject him from my home for such sacrilege.

"I have never tasted it," he said, shrugging in a distinctly human gesture.

I sucked in an outraged breath. "Never?"

My face must have looked comical, because the corners of Memphis' mouth tilted up in a smile. "Never."

This just wouldn't do. Love it or hate it, you had to try it at least once. I snatched the coffee out of his reach.

"Nope. No. No coffee until you try this. I don't want the coffee killing your tastebuds for this."

I grabbed the box of chocolates from his hand, and then led him over to the couch. "Sit."

He let out a low chuckle, his eyebrows raised. But he sat.

I thumped down on the coffee table in front of him, and opened the box. Inside were four small round chocolates sitting in a bed of tissue paper like jewels. I lifted the box and sucked in the rich aroma of cocoa. Oh, this stuff was good.

"You should close your eyes," I said, moving closer. His startlingly blue eyes held mine, and I flushed, swallowing hard. But he closed his eyes.

"Now open your mouth," I said, picking up one of the chocolates. It began to melt on my fingers immediately in the warmth of the apartment.

Eyes closed, Memphis parted his lips, and I was suddenly transfixed by the pinkness of his tongue against the marble blackness of his skin, a color not seen amongst humanity. Of all the Fallen, Memphis looked the most other. Like he was carved from the the deepest shade of Lapis Lazuli, more black than blue. The night sky an hour before dawn. Shaking myself, I leaned forward, placing the chocolate on his tongue. He closed his mouth around the chocolate that was already melting on his tongue.

I watched his face. His brows drew together as he chewed, and if I hadn't felt his pleasure, I would have thought he hated it. He let out a low little hum and opened his eyes.

"It is very sweet."

I nodded, holding still as he leaned forward.

"And velvety smooth," he said, his lips inches from mine.

"Yes," I whispered.

He closed the gap between our lips, kissing me gently. I tasted the chocolate on his lips as they pressed against mine, his tongue flicked out, tempting me to open. His fingers brushed against my cheekbone gently, like I was made of porcelain.

I deepened the kiss, and his wings spread wide over the back of the couch. I didn't want him to kiss me like I was fragile. I wanted him to kiss me like it was our last time, not our first.

His tongue slid into my mouth and I stood so I could straddle his lap. Two huge hands banded my waist, pulling me close against his hard body. My hands ran over the firm planes of his chest beneath the black button-down shirt that felt softer than silk.

"Well, looks like I got assigned the wrong job," a voice said from behind us, and Memphis was on his feet, his wings spread wide to buffer me from the intruder. I looked between his feathers and recognized Gusion. The final Fallen.

He was so fucking beautiful. If Memphis was darkness before dawn, then Gusion was a sunrise. Everything about him was golden.

"What are you doing here Gusion?" Memphis sounded scarily pissed off. He took an ominous step toward his fellow Fallen angel, but Gusion didn't seem overly concerned.

"Cock blocking your ancient ass, obviously." His grin was infectious, and I felt myself smiling even though he was technically cock blocking me too. Memphis made a terrifying noise deep in his chest, and Gusion laughed again. "I see how it is. You can stop with the wing erection, man. It's not like she was naked, and it's not like I don't know what she looks like."

Memphis muttered something in a language that sounded like Latin, and whatever he said didn't sound very complimentary. Gusion continued to laugh.

"But seriously, Memphis, I need a favor. Luc has me watching Uri- uh you-know-who, but he keeps doing his business at night and I stand out like the fucking Flaming Sword of God at night. Unlike you, my very favorite stealth agent. Luc wants you to follow you-know-who for a couple of nights, see what he gets up to. I promise to take care of your girl," he winked at me, and laughed when Memphis lunged at him. "I'm joking, man. I know, alright. I know. I'm just fucking with you."

What did he know? I felt like I was missing something important, but they'd moved on before I could ask.

"He's up to something shady. How that bastard gets away with half of what he does without getting the wrath of the Father all over his ass is beyond me. Luc says we can't just smother him in his sleep. It wouldn't kill him but it'd hurt like hell. Literally."

He laughed like he'd made the funniest joke ever, and I grinned along with him. Memphis looked between us.

"Her human bodyguard is gone. She needs protection."

Gusion crossed his heart. "I promise to guard her with my body."

"That's what I'm worried about," he grumbled.

I took in Gusion now that he wasn't obscured by Memphis' wings. His skin was golden, not like a Californian surfer, but more like the sands of the Sahara. And it shone like someone had dipped him in body oil and then rolled him in glitter. Like a stripper at 3 A.M. Actually… "You don't happen to pole dance, do you?"

His eyes widened with surprise. "No, but I would be willing to give it a try if you would return the favor?"

"Stop, Gusion. Remember to whom you speak," Memphis said, his voice pitched menacingly low.

Gusion stepped closer, so he was in Memphis' space. I tensed. Was I meant to break up an angel fight? Did I get the hell out of the building? Should I pull the fire alarm as I got of the splash zone?

Gusion stepped close until he was chest to chest with Memphis. Then he wrapped his arm around him in a hug that would have crushed the bones of a mortal. "I know exactly who I'm talking to, Mephistopheles. I'd never do anything to jeopardize your future. You know that."

Memphis wrapped his arm around Gusion, and thumped his back just below his wings.

"I know, Old Friend. I am sorry. It's just…"

"I know."

I was mesmerized by their embrace, their arms and bodies wrapped around each other, light and dark, like an angelic yin and yang. A few more back thumps and they pulled apart. Memphis turned to me.

"I must go. But Gusion will be around to ensure your safety. I shall be back in a week." He put a hand on my cheek, and I looked up into those startling royal blue eyes and for the first time in my life, tried to figure someone out without any extra help from my empathic abilities. Maybe having someone able to block me wasn't so fantastic after all. It was like going temporarily blind.

"You guys know I don't need a babysitter, right? I'm fine here. I'm a world away from my abductors. This building has great security. I'm fine," I repeated.

Memphis said nothing, but his eyes still stared directly into my soul. I sighed. "Fine. Be safe. Don't do anything dangerous."

Gusion laughed. "Oh Sweetness, we are the danger."

UNLIKE MEMPHIS, Gusion didn't bother to hide his presence when Adnan arrived home, although he did humanize himself, thank goodness. Adnan's response to Gusion was almost humorous. He was like one of those silver screen damsels who faints at the sight of a handsome man. Except, instead of fainting, he stood there, his mouth hanging open, uncharacteristically mute. I should have snapped a picture, blown it up and framed it.

"Adnan, this is Gusion, my new, uh, bodyguard."

Gus smiled a smile that was a little too bright to be fully human, his perfection almost retina searing. "Please, call me Gus." He put out a hand to shake Adnan's, but Adnan was too awestruck to notice.

I couldn't blame him. Even without his angelic oomph, Gusion was almost unbearably pretty. His face was perfect in a way that defied description. He had strong broad shoulders that tapered to a trim waist and muscular arms. His long, blonde hair was like a shining river of gold that swung down to the middle of his back. I had a sudden, and very vivid image of wrapping that hair around my hands as he drove his body into mine.

"Hope?"

Gusion's question shook me from my Adnan style fugue. Whoops.

"Sorry, come on, let's have a glass of wine," I strode toward the kitchen. A glass of wine was definitely in order. Maybe ten. I put two bottles under my arm and Adnan grabbed three glasses from the cabinet.

The apartment was back to being orderly, thank goodness. Standing in the living room would no longer make Blue anxious.

Thoughts of Blue made me sad. He hadn't returned, even though I expected him too. I'd talked to Granny Mulligan yesterday, and she'd made no mention of Blue. In fact, she seemed to assume that Blue was still here, being my mildly aggressive lapdog. I didn't correct her. Wherever Blue was, he didn't need the wrath of the Mulligans for abandoning his post. It had been my fault anyway.

I twisted to sit on the couch, and for the first time in a week, it was almost pain free. I breathed a deep sigh of relief. I was healing.

"Do you still dance, Adnan?" Gus asked as I poured him wine.

Adnan got the deer in the headlights look again, but this time managed to shake it quickly. "Yes. First amputee dancer in the Manhattan Dance Company."

"You'll do big things if you can look outside yourself." Gus looked into the middle distance, and I narrowed my eyes at him. I was at my quota of weird angelic behaviour for the day, so I let it go.

Unfortunately, letting things go wasn't in Adnan's wheelhouse. "What do you mean? How did you know I was a dancer anyway?"

He flashed that megawatt smile. It was almost blinding. "I knew you mother. Nice woman. Also, I was around when you arrived in the US."

Adnan froze like a statue. We didn't talk much about how Adnan and his older brother Nazir had come to be in the family. It was a traumatic time for Adnan, and when he thought about it, his emotions were ragged and raw, even after twenty-one years. While he didn't remember *before* with the same clarity as Nazir, he remembered enough about all the angelic interference that he hesitated to ever speak about it. It had been the Archangel Raphael who'd amputated his leg after an airstrike had brought down his family's apartment on their heads. It had been Ace that had soothed him when he'd turned up on my parent's doorstep, orphaned and in need of serious medical care.

Nazir hadn't coped, instead running off to military school and then becoming a mercenary. The one time I'd had to shake his hand after one of Adnan's concerts, his emotions had almost crushed me. The anger, the fear, the self-loathing had swamped sixteen-year-old me like a tidal wave. If Rella hadn't been there, I probably would have broken apart.

Now Nazir was with Rella, exacting revenge. The idea terrified me. I never told her how much I depended on her. If she knew, she'd never live her own life. She protected me with the fierceness of a lioness, but I wanted her to enjoy her life for her.

I realized Adnan had found his voice. "You're, you know…"

"An Angel? Well, a former one anyway. Now, I'm Fallen."

I realized belatedly that I couldn't feel Gusion's emotions. Nothing. Not even the brief hints I got with Memphis. I placed a hand on his arm.

A moan bubbled from my lips, the only sign I could give before I dropped my glass and blacked out.

CHAPTER SEVEN

"**S**he must be pushing herself too hard. She is on bedrest. If she can't manage that, I'll move in myself and ensure she rests."

I blinked awake to the sound of Eli's voice. "Dad."

"Hello, Little One. How do you feel?" Eli was in full doctor mode, checking my obs now that I was awake, probably for some delayed brain damage or something. I could have told him my fainting spell had nothing to do with my injuries, and everything to do with my sixth sense. But we didn't talk about it within the family. I was sure they knew, but no one mentioned it. It was safer that way. If we didn't acknowledge it out loud, then no one could use the information against us.

"I feel fine. My blood pressure must have dropped or something." I sat up, and saw Mom fussing at the end of the bed. She came over and gave me a hug. "Seriously, Mom, I'm fine."

"Have you been working too hard? You're meant to

be on bed rest. Do I need to move in and make sure you are taking care of yourself?" she repeated.

I winced. I loved my parents, so much, but the last thing I wanted was any of them moving into the apartment.

"I promise I'll relax more. I'll even tell them I need another week off from work. What are they going to do? Sack me?"

Eli scoffed. "I wouldn't put it past Tolliver. He's very serious about that Foundation."

"So am I, but I know I need more recovery time."

Appeased slightly, they sat on the bed and filled me in on the family gossip. I listened with half an ear about their holiday to some deserted island where they no doubt did "things" I don't even want to contemplate between jet skiing and sunbathing. They told me that Oz had created a new translation system that didn't require internet connection for use by aid workers in refugee camps. Lux had started a gym for disadvantaged youth. Valery had managed to create a twelve foot high croquembouche.

By the time Gusion sifted them away, I really was exhausted. Adnan brought me a glass of water with a slice of lemon.

"You scared me," he murmured, fluffing my pillows needlessly. "You keeled over, then Gusion stood and he had wings and he was so damn beautiful, then he was gone and Eli was here. And then Gus went back and got your Mom, because she threatened to tell Ace if he didn't. You wouldn't wake up. I figured you weren't dead, because Rella would have been here quicker than you could say 'holy sexy angel balls'." He leaned forward and scooped me into his arms. "Don't do that again. You scared ten years off my life."

I rubbed circles on his back. "Sorry Ads." I felt Gusion's presence, and looked over Adnan's head to see him standing in the corner, still incorporeal. "I'm tired. I might try and get some sleep, okay?" I murmured distractedly against Adnan's shoulder.

"Sure thing," he said, leaning forward and kissing my forehead. "Sleep tight. You are at your quota for drama this year. No more fainting or anything, got it?"

I smiled. "My pleasure."

As soon as he left, shutting the door softly, Gus became visible. He walked over and slid into bed beside me. His wings took up half the bed, and tickled my arm. "What happened? I've been around long enough, and had enough mortal wounds to know that wasn't caused by your current injuries."

"No."

"You know, when I was an angel, my ability was to determine a person's past, present and future. Even my fellow angels. But you, you are a blank to me. A mystery. It's like your future is your own. As if God has no divine plan for you, because you weren't meant to exist. You are outside natures plan."

"You sound like Azriel. Next you'll be calling me a soulless abomination."

"Azriel?" Gusion's eyebrows got impossibly high. "What do you know of Azriel?"

"Long story. So, is that what you are saying? That I have no soul?

Gus waved a hand in the air above us. "No. Obviously not. I can sense it in there, glowing with angelic light, wrapped around your humanity like a protective shield. No, what I am saying is that there is something about you that makes you different. Something that made you literally lose consciousness when you touched me." He looked at me with deep whiskey-colored eyes. "Yeah, I didn't miss the cause of your fainting spell."

I couldn't tell him why I'd passed out. I'd felt *him*. Gusion had been the reason they had all fallen. He was so, so desperately sad. And guilty. The guilt of their circumstances, of their fates, ate away at him like a festering wound.

"Maybe I was just overwhelmed by your sheer attractiveness? Or maybe it was low blood sugar. It's fine, either way."

He made a rude noise, calling my bluff, but I stuck to my explanation. It was better than the alternative. *Sorry, you are so fucked up emotionally that you literally shut down my system.*

Apparently, I was collecting the damaged, the self-loathing and the angry. Some people collected Beanie Babies, but not me.

"Fine. You will tell me in your own time. But do not be mistaken, you will tell me eventually." His voice dropped. "Because I'm irresistible."

I laughed even as I rolled my eyes. "Annoying, maybe."

"You should sleep," he whispered, his own eyes already closing.

"Sleeping in bed with me is a little presumptuous,

don't you think?" I asked, though deep down I was glad he was there.

"I am meant to be guarding your body." I raised a single brow. "I find I don't want to be alone tonight," he said, his voice muffled by the pillow as he rolled onto his stomach. His wings slid over me, almost like a downy blanket. He was probably right. I should sleep.

Instead, I gave into the same curiosity that made children poke things in power points even when they knew it was dangerous. I reached out and placed a hand on his shoulder and tried to read him again.

I was better prepared for it this time, for the unrelenting wave of sadness and guilt. Touching him, I couldn't hear his thoughts like I could a human, but I could get a clearer read on his emotions. There'd been a woman, that much I could tell, because he mourned her still, millennia later. Another angel, maybe? I could feel all the emotions snarled together like invasive vines tangling around his heart. He still felt guilty for defying his Father's orders. But there was still love, so much love, but it was a faded love. Anger, grief, guilt. They were like nesting dolls, all inside each other, a wound that wouldn't heal. I wished I could take some of his pain, give him a moment of real happiness. His happy face hid the deep, soul-rending pain.

"What are you doing, Child of Acerezeal?" Gusion's voice was husky. I realized my hand was rubbing up and down his bicep as I read him. Whoops.

"Trying to chase away your sadness," I said, hoping he would take it at face value.

"I'm in bed with a beautiful woman, why would I be

sad?" he asked, sounding genuinely confused. I bit my tongue to stop myself from spilling my secret. Again. I trusted the Fallen. Ace and Luc loved me, and Memphis was already keeping my secret. Gusion loved his fellow Fallen, there was no other reason he'd feel so much guilt otherwise. But I still couldn't tell him.

So I smiled at him instead and moved my hand away. "Just a feeling. Sleep well, Gus." I rolled onto my stomach beneath his wing, and listened to his breathing slow. I watched his face relax into the inno- cence of sleep, and I hoped I was chasing away his nightmares.

Several hours later, my leg was numb and I still wasn't asleep. I hadn't told anyone, but I was still having trouble sleeping. Every time I drifted off, I saw that last moment. The smoke from the gun, JJ's body going down. But now, when the smoke cleared, it was Blue holding the gun, not the nameless men who actually abducted me.

About midnight, I'd had enough. I was uncomfort- able and I was more awake than ever.

Gus had curled his wings against his back again, so I slid from the bed.

Maybe a glass of warm milk with a dash of vanilla might help. Papa, Valery I mean, would make it for me when I was a kid and couldn't sleep. Val was always up early making bread. I didn't make it often now, but when I did, it was as nostalgic as it was comforting. It was like I was home again, listening to Papa's French accent as he told me stories or recipes or sang me anti- quated French nursery rhymes. I turned on the light over the stove and got out a saucepan. Filling it with milk, I set it to gently simmer.

"It's the witching hour, so it seems fitting you'd be awake."

I let out a little squeak, dropping my bottle of vanilla extract. Azriel darted forward, catching it before the glass bottle smashed on the tiles of the kitchen floor.

"Jesus fucking H. Christ, Azriel! What the hell were you thinking, sneaking up on me like that?" I whisper-shouted at him. I didn't want to wake Gus or Adnan.

"I didn't sneak. I appeared. I announced my presence."

I wanted to strangle him as my heart thudded in my chest. What kind of Neanderthal snuck up on a woman alone at night after she'd been through a traumatic experience?

"To what do I owe the pleasure of your visit, Azriel? My apartment must have moved onto the Highway to Heaven and I just didn't realize." The fear was making me pissed off.

"You've bewitched another one, I see?" He was looking through my open bedroom door at Gus spread out on my bed. Great bodyguard, that one. "And in your bed already. Fitting, that Gusion of the Fallen would find his way into the bed of an abomination."

Rage surged up in my chest. "Look, you bag of dicks, I'm tired, hurting, and I don't have time for your holier than thou bullshit. Why are you here?"

"I like watching the animals in their natural habitat."

Oh.

Oh no, he didn't.

"Get out of my apartment, before I wake Gusion and he kicks your ass."

Azriel laughed. "I can take the former Angel of the Fate."

I crossed my arms over my chest. "Fine. Get out of here before I call Ace. She is not your biggest fan right now."

This time Azriel blanched a little. I didn't blame him, Ace in a rage was scary as, well, hell.

"I am sorry. I did not mean to offend you."

I let out an unflattering noise. "Oh? Is calling someone a zoo animal some kind of angelic version of flirting?"

A flush lit his cheeks, and I raised my eyebrows. He was a disco ball of anger, confusion, and something I couldn't quite label. I thought I had every emotion known to man catalogued, that I'd felt it all.

I needed to remember I wasn't dealing with a man. I stared at the snowy white wings on his back to reinforce the thought. Azriel was the enemy. He wasn't one of Luc's Fallen. He had literally tried to kill me at birth. I should kick his ass out the door, and never let him back in. Call Ace like I threatened.

Instead, I poured half of my milk into a second mug, adding a drop of the rescued of vanilla. I stirred it gently.

"Why are you not asleep?" His voice was soft, losing the arrogance that grated against me so badly.

"Nightmares." I handed him the mug, and he looked at it like it was a rattlesnake. I took a sip of mine, proving that I hadn't poisoned it, though I wasn't sure you could kill an angel with arsenic, or whatever people used to poison their husbands.

He took a sip, then looked into his mug as if there was a mystery at the bottom. "I don't understand."

"It's warm milk," I said slowly. "Oh, and there's a hint of vanilla."

He rolled his eyes at me, and I resisted the urge to laugh at the human gesture on all that angelic perfection.

"I understand the beverage. I do not understand your nightmares."

I moved toward the living room, away from the hall to the bedrooms. Azriel followed behind me, his wings held high and tight to his back. His perfectly porcelain skin should have made him look feminine, but instead her just looked unerringly majestic. Almost luminescent in the soft light of the living room. He shone with the soft glow of what I assumed was probably angelic light, but it seemed all a bit fluffy.

I settled onto the couch, but Azriel continued to stand. "Explain."

I sighed. "Please."

"What?"

"Explain, please. Good manners is not a concept reserved only for humans, especially when you want me to do something for you."

His head tipped a little to the side, and then he nodded. But he didn't say please. That was a battle for another day.

"I have nightmares because I have post-traumatic

stress disorder." I winced saying it out loud. I know it shouldn't, but it made me feel weak.

"It is over, yet it still hurts you." I nodded as he repeated my words back at me. The fact he listened to what I had said back in the hospital made me feel almost proud.

Azriel was silent as he contemplated my words, sipping occasionally at his warm milk. I tried to hide my smile. I let my thoughts drift to everything and nothing, to Memphis and our kiss, and Gus and his tragicness. To Blue, the Lost Boy. To Rella, and her crusade that was literally keeping me up at night.

"You have humans for that."

Azriel's voice startled me from thoughts. "What?"

"For your traumatic post stress disorder. You have humans that help with that."

I thought about the welfare worker at the hospital and screwed up my nose. "I don't do well with therapists."

"There is no one you can talk to about this? Family? Friends? The Father?" His lip curled. "Lucifer?"

I couldn't help it. I honked out a laugh before slapping a hand over my mouth, sucking in deep breaths. "Did you just suggest I talk to the Devil about my feelings?" The ridiculousness made me laugh harder, and Azriel's disapproving face just compounded the problem.

"He is a kind of parental figure, is he not?" He sounded peevish now, and I did my best to rein in my giggles.

Clearing my throat, I took a deep breath, but the

smile refused to leave my face. "Sure. But he's the kind of family that you talk to about having someone killed, not about your feelings." The idea was a little ridiculous really. Luc, and to a lesser degree Ace, were creatures of action, not emotion. They were the spirit of vengeance, the judge, jury and executioner for your immortal soul. Not someone to hold your hand and kiss your boo-boos.

"You have me for that now."

Now it was my turn to look confused. "To have someone killed?" He looked at me like I was stupid, his lips pursed as he shook his head. "You mean to talk about my feelings with?"

He nodded, and I held my breath in fear I would say the wrong thing. This was a fragile kind of connection. I had a feeling that what I said next would forever change the immortal creature in front of me. I wanted it to be for the better.

"I'd like that," I said, even though the idea of sharing my deepest fears with an angel who had the emotional range of an eggplant seemed insane.

His lips twitched. "He wakens." He looked longingly at the bedroom, and I felt the overwhelming wave of sadness from him. What had gone on with the Fallen and the Angel of Death that caused so much pain and anger on both sides? I looked toward the door, and Gusion stepped out, jeans slung low on his hips, gold dipped wings dragging on the ground like a sleepy child. When I turned back toward Azriel, he was gone.

CHAPTER EIGHT

"**G**et up."

I looked away from my TV soap opera and at Gus.

"But Sophia is about to tell Stephan that she loves him, and that baby is really Slade's," I whined, and he gave me a disgusted look as he switched off the television.

"You aren't sleeping."

I said nothing, picking at my nails.

"You refuse to leave the apartment to even go to the office."

Shame welled up in my chest, but still I said nothing. What could I say? That the idea of leaving the apartment fills me with dread?

"We are going to the movies. And then wherever else I feel like going, until we get back the confident woman that seems to have gone on hiatus." He knelt down in front of me, forcing me to look at him. "I know you are scared, and the others might be happy to just let you wallow and wrap you in cotton wool to keep you safe. But they are suffocating your light. And I refuse to let that happen. So get some pants on," he sighed heavily. "I didn't think I'd ever say that to a beautiful woman, but this is what we are reduced to, me begging a woman to get dressed."

He pulled me to my feet, and I grimaced at the sight of my pajama pants and my sweatshirt with a cute kitten on it.

"It's already one in the afternoon. Maybe we should go to the movies tomorrow."

"No. Now go." Gus pushed me toward my bedroom. "Fifteen minutes, and then I'm coming in to dress you myself. Actually, take your time," he winked, and I blushed even as I rolled my eyes.

But I still hurried, I didn't trust the Gus wouldn't be good to his word. There was something dangerous and wild in his eyes today, and a little part of me that I didn't know existed thrilled at the idea of being a little wild with him.

I threw on a pretty green sundress that skimmed mid-thigh and left my arms bare. It made my hair shine like burnished garnets.

Sliding my feet into simple gold sandals, I was ready in fourteen minutes. I laughed when I walked out and saw Gus staring at our wall clock. He looked over his shoulder and pouted. "Dammit." He grinned and it was like a punch to the chest. "Let's go. I have plans to help you recover your inner BAMF."

"BAMF?"

"Bad ass motherfucker. Grab your ID. And maybe a

trench coat, because damn you look hot in that dress." He made an mmph noise and I laughed. His enthusiasm was infectious, but still, I hesitated at doorway. He took my hand and pulled me across the threshold and into his arms. I was acutely aware that I was pressed along the rigid length of his body, the hard muscles of his chest under my hands. "I've got you, Hope. I won't let anything bad happen. Memphis would kill me, have Luc resurrect me, just so Ace could murder me again." He tucked an errant strand of hair behind my ear. "Besides, I'm kind of fond of you when you aren't watching crappy daytime television. Now, let's go."

He must have called my car service while I was in the shower, because Reggie, my regular driver was waiting for us in the carpark.

"It's good to see you, Miss." Reggie's emotions pulsed with sincerity, and I teared up. Then he looked at Gus, and sadness colored them blue. He thought Gus was JJ's replacement. I felt guilty all over again that I'd never even gone to see JJ's wife and kids. I'd just forgotten my friend in the wake of my own problems.

"Enough, Hope. Today is not a day for self-loathing and survivors guilt. Today is a day for reconnecting with your old self." He nudged me through the car door, and slid in after me. Reggie drove out of the car park and into the mid-afternoon traffic with ease.

"Where to first?" I asked, smoothing down my dress. Gus's eyes followed the motion.

He cleared his throat. "First stop is the movies. Nice and simple."

The look in his eye made me wonder if anything he

did was ever nice or simple. We sat in silence for the car ride to the local cinema, and as I slid from the car, I felt a little overdressed for the movies in the middle of the day on a Tuesday. The soccer moms and the old age pensioners were certainly casting me strange looks. Or maybe that was just the effect of Gus, with his long hair and overt masculinity. He was a bit of a contradiction to the average person.

We picked the latest rom-com over the action movie, and Gus got two large popcorns and drinks the size of a barrel. I didn't know where he was getting his cash from, none of the Fallen worked in the traditional sense, and I wasn't sure I wanted to know.

As we slid into the back row of the cinema, Gus pulled a huge flask from waistband of his jeans. "Whiskey?"

"In here?" I hissed back, and he grinned. Yep, he was the poster boy for hell, alright. "I'm pretty sure it's against the rules."

But I grinned and popped the lid of my cup. He poured a very liberal amount in, and swirled it around with a straw.

I leaned in close, and tried to ignore how good Gus smelled. "Ten bucks says couple right down front are on their first date, but she feels guilty because she still loves her former lover," I whispered.

He laughed but didn't take my bet.

I pointed to the couple in the back-left corner, just opposite us. Gus half smiled as he joined in my game.

"Presently, they are here to have sex in the cinema,

but eventually they will get married, have three kids and he'll die at 54 of a heart attack."

Ouch. Poor guy. Poor Gus. I couldn't imagine knowing everyone's end game.

"The couple down the front. Do they have a second date?"

The incredulous look on Gus's face told me everything I needed to know. I pointed to a woman in the middle of the cinema. "She looks lonely, but I bet she's just glad no one wants to sit beside her." I could have told him I wasn't guessing their backstories anymore. That I knew because I was an empathetic. But it wasn't the right time.

I looked at the last person in the cinema. "That guy is... not good."

Gus frowned too. "You are right. But he will never enact the fantasies he spends so much time creating, but it will be due to interruption, not lack of intention. He will go to jail, but not for very long."

I sighed. It was times like this I wished that I was Rella, or Ace, or Lux or anyone other than soft, gentle Hope. Weak. They could just walk up to the guy, and threaten him until he believed they would cause him irreparable bodily harm unless he changed his ways.

But I couldn't. I could walk through a crowd, and feel everything from the most beautiful joy and the darkest malice, and I couldn't affect any of it.

Sometimes, when I was feeling discontented, I used to walk up and down the George Washington Bridge, trying to make a difference, trying to be a hero. Now they put up bigger railings, which was good, but I felt redundant again.

The huge wave of lust made it clear that our row neighbors were getting to the climax of their movie. Gus grabbed a handful of popcorn and lobbed it over his head at the amorous pair. Their heads whipped toward us, well his head, hers was otherwise...occupied.

"Don't look," Gus laughed, wrapping an arm around my shoulder and pretending to be engrossed in the storyline of an average man who was in love with his adorably dorky but secretly a cover model neighbor.

Gus leaned close so his lips were a breath from my ear. "Your turn. How about we spice up the first date down there?" He handed me the box of milk duds. "They're further away. You'll need long range ammunition."

Sprinkling some of the duds in my hand, I took aim. And missed miserably.

"I can see why you work in an office, you aren't about to be called up to play for the Sox." Gus chuckled. "Try again."

I closed one eye, and took aim. The screen lit up the dud like a beacon as it flew through the air, nailing the guy in the back of the head. I looked intently at the screen as the guy looked around at all the patrons of Cinema Number One.

"I think you fluked it. Ten bucks says you can't do it again," he murmured under his breath. Picking up another dud, I took him up on his bet. Closing my eye, trying to recreate the perfect trajectory, I threw again.

And missed. On the plus side, I got his date and it rico-cheted off her head and into his.

I turned to look at Gus, and his face was so close to mine that I could see the golden flecks in his eyes, the perfect cupid's bow of his lips. I could cut myself on the sharp line of his jaw. "That's twenty bucks," I whispered huskily, and his eyes crinkled at the corners.

"Oh?" He leaned forward. Shit. He was going to kiss me. And I wanted him to kiss me, I was almost sure of it.

"Uh huh," I said intelligently.

"You'll have to convince me." The smooth tempta-tion in his voice made me want to strip my clothes off in the cinema and make love to him right now.

His lips had hardly brushed against mine when I was blinded by the light of god.

Or maybe the flashlight of the cinema usher. I looked past him to the horny couple, who were giving us the stink eye.

"There's been a complaint."

I MANAGED to look contrite at least until we left the cinema, when I doubled over with laughter. I laughed so hard my ribs hurt and I began to cough a little.

"Go easy, or you'll bust something."

I stood up and sucked in some deep breaths. "It's your fault. I was enjoying that movie," I said as we walked down the sidewalk, weaving in and out of people talking on their phone.

Gus scoffed. "You don't even know what the movie

was about. Don't try and guilt trip me, Sweet Pea, I invented it."

Squeezing in close to fit between two couples having a conversation in the middle of the sidewalk, I elbowed him in the ribs.

"I do so. It was about unlikely love."

He cast a look at me from the side of his eye, but said nothing. He didn't mention our almost kiss. "Okay, this way to the next stop the re-BAMF-ication of Hope," he said, pulling me down a side street.

"I hate to break it to you, but I was never a badass to start with."

Gus raised both eyebrows, but didn't slow his stride. I was basically trotting to keep up now. "You have family dinners with Luc and Ace. You're a badass whether you mean to be or not."

I shrugged. I couldn't argue with that.

We stopped. "Oh, no. No," I said, looking at the sign on the front of the dark building in the side street. "I don't think so."

Gus grinned, and it made my heart stutter in my chest. So pretty. I found myself walking toward the entrance of the building, before I snapped out of it. "Don't smile like that at me. You'll give me a heart attack or something. I'm only human."

"Are you, though?"

Why did people keep asking me that? Of course I was. I'd been nearly dead in a hospital bed a week ago. I just had a little extra oomph, as my dad, Sam, liked to say. I looked up at the sign that announced the shop as a tattoo parlor. I definitely had a thing about needles, and getting one jammed through my flesh repeatedly sounded like some kind of torture Luc would cook up in hell.

"Why not? Are you afraid?" He didn't say it in a taunting way. He legitimately wanted to know if I was scared.

"A little," I admitted.

He leaned a hip against the plate glass window of the parlor. "I can't get tattoos. We heal too unnaturally and it would be gone in hours. But I have always been fascinated by the idea of taking something that God considered perfect, and making it more beautiful. Like he gave humans the ability to create art, but he denies them his most perfect canvas?"

He seemed genuinely perplexed, and it was selling me on the idea, dammit. "Okay. Something small. Tiny. Like a cow from an aeroplane small."

"You want a tattoo of a cow jumping out of an aeroplane?"

I stared at him. "What?"

A smile curled his lips again, and I realized he was teasing me. Again.

I rolled my eyes and held back my own grin as I pushed through the doors. The doorbell tinkled, and the interior was delightfully quaint and even a little retro. The total antithesis of the huge tattooed man that walked through the curtain and up to the counter.

"Yeah?"

He eyed up Gus, then me, and convinced he could pulverize us both, went back to looking bored.

"I'd like a tattoo, if you have time? It'll just be small." The big guy stared at my face, and then at Gus.

"Fine. What do you want?"

I went blank. Shit. What did I want? I blurted out the first thing that popped into my brain.

"Angel wings. One wing black, and the other white."

The big guy pulled out an odd purple marker, and sketched something right there on the counter. I stood riveted, as the wings came to life, breathtaking in their miniature perfection, like he'd seen the wings of an angel before.

I must have let out a sound of appreciation, because while the big, bald tattooist didn't so much as crack a smile, I could feel his pleasure at creating something that caused my appreciation.

"It's perfect," I breathed when he was finished.

"Maybe they should be outlined in gold, the white ones at least. Perhaps blue for the black ones. Just to make them pop."

I rolled my eyes. He was about as subtle as a sledge-hammer. White with gold tips? "Why don't I just tattoo your name on my ass?"

Gus laughed. "I wouldn't be opposed to that."

The big tattooist, seriously, he fit the stereotypical biker/tattooist image perfectly, grumbled low under his breath. When he looked at Gus, he felt nothing but disgust. "Do you guys know each other?"

Gus gave me a precocious grin. "Unfortunately, we haven't." He thrust out a hand. "I'm Gusion. And you are?"

"Cain."

The laugh that Gus let out came from somewhere deep in his soul, and it was tinged with bitterness. "Of course it is."

"Are we doing this or what?" Cain said in a low voice.

I was a bit torn. I didn't understand the tattooists anger toward Gus, when he felt absolutely nothing for me except maybe pity? I had no idea why. People were confusing.

"Sure, let's go," I said, following Cain behind the curtain. He turned as Gus tried to follow. "You stay there. Too cramped."

Gus just smiled and saluted. I walked into a little cubicle in the back and sat down on a black pleather chair. Everything was as sterile as a dental office.

"Where do you want it?" Cain's voice sounded a little like a bass drum. A deep rough burst that you felt in your chest.

I didn't need to think about it. Stretching my arms, I reached the tab of my zip and slid it down peeling my dress down to my waist and prayed that tattooists were like doctors and seamstresses. They weren't allowed to laugh at you in your underwear.

Preparing myself for the a pulse of lust, I was shocked when I got an overwhelming wave of rage. My eyes shot to Cain's face, and he was staring at my ribs, at the green and yellow bruises that patched my torso and made me look a little like I was wearing camo.

"Did he do that?"

I looked at my bruises as if I would see a name written there. "Who?"

"The pretty boy out front."

If there had been a lightbulb over my head, it would have gone off. I rubbed my jaw. I'd forgotten the bruises there too. Cain thought Gus beat me.

I felt an overwhelming affection for this near perfect stranger.

"Oh, no. Gus didn't do this. I had an accident." I didn't think I could explain I'd been abducted by Estonian human traffickers to a perfect stranger.

"My mother had a lot of accidents too. If you need help…" he trailed off as he prepared the tattoo gun.

I sat up and wrapped my arms around this huge beast of a man who was willing to help a complete stranger in need. He stiffened in my arms, and I remembered I was just in my bra. Whoops.

Sitting back, I beamed at him. "Thank you, Cain. You restored my faith in humanity. But Gus really didn't do this. I got caught up in something bad, but I'm okay now. I've got lots of people to watch my back, Gus included." Cain snorted, and I didn't have to have a tap into his emotions to sense his scepticism.

"Don't let the pretty package fool you, he's more dangerous than he looks." He was dangerous on a level that would probably make Big Cain cry.

He gave a non-committal "mmph", and set everything on the tray by the chair. "Lay back. The ribs hurt, and there's a little bit of bruising but I think it is old enough that it won't affect the ink too badly."

Cain was not kidding. It hurt like a bitch. Not as much as a broken rib or two, but enough that I wondered why anyone would get tattooed more than once. Cain didn't speak at all, focused on his task, and I enjoyed the white noise of the tattoo gun. I needed the silence of Cain's simple emotions, and the pain of the tattoo needle, to finally zone out. All too soon, the big tattooist was straightening.

"Finished. Mirror is over there." He pointed over his shoulder to a door mirror that seemed to be adhered directly to the wall. I didn't bother trying to cover up. Cain had literally had his head inches from my boob for an hour, and he'd been nothing but purely professional. Somehow, Cain had made the wings almost the perfect counterbalance to the other, while making both unique. How he'd managed it was a mystery to me, but my eyes misted up a bit at the perfection of each wing. Two halves of a whole.

"You are a true artist, Cain. Thanks." He waved away my words with a grunt, but his emotions glowed again. He dressed it with some kind of ointment and plastic wrap. "No pools or baths for a week. Rub this cream on it every day. Try not to wear anything too tight 'til it heals."

I pulled my dress up over my shoulders, and Cain pulled up the zip at the back. "Thanks," I said, looking over my shoulder at the man that must have been as wide as I was tall, and at least be six and a half feet tall.

I followed him to the front of shop, and Gus was sitting on the hard bench seats, looking through flash books. He stood and smiled when he saw us emerging from behind the curtain.

"How'd it go?" he looked me over. "Where'd you get it?"

I blushed. "I'll show you later."

He grinned but there was a heat in his eyes that seemed to be simmering all day. "Sounds promising."

Cain stepped in front of me. "She says it wasn't, but if I find out you marked her body like that, I will rip your limbs off and feed them to my dogs," his deep voice made the threat seem all the more ominous.

"I'd tear my own limbs off before I hurt her, but I promise you, she can take care of herself."

I wasn't so sure about that, but I smiled at the compliment anyway. I paid for my tattoo and happily accepted Cain's business card. I didn't think I would be back, because what kind of sucker does that twice? But I liked Cain.

Strolling out of the tattoo parlour, the sun was starting to slip behind the taller buildings. The tattoo stung as I moved, but I liked the grounding sensation. I wrapped my hand through Gusion's offered arm and smiled.

"Thanks for today. I had fun despite myself."

He led us around the corner, in a direction that was opposite to the way home. "Oh, the night's just getting started, Sweetheart."

CHAPTER NINE

The music thumped through my chest like a defibrillator. I'd never been to a club like this before, and I had to admit, I was pretty awed by their athletic prowess. And their shoes. Damn I loved the shoes.

"Does that one have gold love hearts dangling from the back of her shoes? Look, Gus, they are so pretty. I want a pair."

Gus sighed heavily. "I think strip clubs might be wasted on you. Also, no more margaritas. Damn, you are a lightweight. I'm going to have a serious word with Ace about your complete lack of corruption."

I snatched my margarita out of his reach and cradled it to my chest protectively. "I'm a badass moth-erfucker, you said so yourself."

"I'm reassessing," he deadpanned, but then ruined it by smiling. When he smiled, there was an audible sigh around the bar that I could hear even over the thumping music.

There were way more women in here than I'd thought, and every single one was transfixed by Gusion. The topless bartender even gave us free drinks. Probably bringing a new meaning to getting a Slippery Nipple.

"Well, my taste doesn't really swing this way. Though, that one might have me reassessing my preferences. Did you see that thing she did with her leg?" Some of the dancers defied the laws of physics and human biology. People weren't meant to bend that way.

"Just wait, Sweetheart. Have I led you astray before?"

"Yes. Three times today and I've only known you less than a week."

He raised a finger and tapped my nose. "Fair point. Oh, here we go."

The music switched to something slow and sexy. The double doors at the end of the stage swung open, and four well-oiled guys strode out.

"Who are they?" I whispered, as my drunken brain frantically tried to count all the visible abdominal muscles. Could four guys have more than thirty abs between them, or was I getting double vision?

Gus looked just as interested in the guys as the women. "They're from the male review next door."

"There's a man strip club next door and I've been in here the entire time? What the hell?" I screeched, earning myself some dirty looks from the people around us. Gus waved me away, and made me watch.

Three more female dancers moved onto the stage, skimpily dressed, err, undressed maybe, in lingerie. The guys were in various pants, some in tailored dress pants and suspenders, some in jeans that hung so low on his hips that I saw the fuzz of hair at the bottom of one guys V. One guy had gym shorts and the other one was in a thong. He was packing and I was a little worried that if he stepped wrong his balls would fall out the side. The slow thrum of bass filled the room, and the dancers all paired up. Each pair played out a different scenario. Sweet tender lovemaking, dancing in a club. One couple was doing what I could only assume was the aerial gymnastics version of having sex.

But it was the blonde with the bedazzled heels and the guy with the suspenders that had me transfixed. They were barely touching, though the guy had her backed up against the pole. He was prowling around her, his eyes appraising her body like he was imagining all the ways he could make it sing. Then he reached out and grabbed her hand, then the other, pressing them both above her head. His hands were so big he could anchor them around her tiny wrists and against the pole with one hand. She curved her body around the pole, sliding downwards and then up again. He ran a hand down her naked ribcage, whirling around her as his body undulated against hers in an imitation of... well, you know. The whole time their bodies were flowing to the music, but I forgot they were dancing, caught up in their story. She shook his hands off, and danced around him, the glee on her face letting the crowd know that what was about to come was going to be delicious. He grabbed her by the wrist, whirling her into his arms, her ass pressed against the tight zip of his pants. He leaned close enough to kiss her, then spun her around so she was facing the pole, pressing her hard into it, his hand sliding down her spine in a proprietary way. Then he smacked her on the ass, a large handprint taking up her entire butt cheek. I sucked in a breath. Heat pulsed between my thighs.

"Like what you see, Sweetheart?" Gus's voice in my ear made me shiver, and I turned. I got caught on his eyes and couldn't look away, not even to look back at the story that was playing out on stage. Fire burned in them, something wild and dangerous that I just knew in my soul was going to scorch me. But I didn't care. What was this crazy feeling consuming me, threatening to undo everything I thought I knew about myself?

I don't know how long I sat there, trapped in his gaze, but the spotlights flicked to the crowd. I turned toward the lights, like a deer, and the MC strutted onto the stage. She let out a theatrical sigh as the dancers walked past her, every single one smiling.

"That's my favorite part of the night. So fucking hot, am I right?" Cheers sounded through the audience. "Well, maybe not my favorite part. This is my favorite part. For the chance to win a cool two hundred dollars, we are opening it up to the amateurs. If you think you could get up here and give us something just as hot, now is your time to do it."

There were whistles, and a few couples standing. A college boy was trying to convince a drunken bride-to-be to try it with him but she laughed and shook her head.

"Hang on now, there's rules to ruin your fun. No nudity. Seriously, for the health of everyone's eyeballs, keep your clothes on. No filming either, people. Put away your phones or Big John will smash it for you. And yes, you can spend the money at the bar. Okay, let's go people. Up on the stage. Two hundred dollars and bragging rights are calling you." She fanned the cash at her face.

Gus was on his feet and pulling me behind him in a second. "Woah, no freakin' way, Gus!" I yelled over the steady pump of music.

"Trust me," he yelled over his shoulder, and the crowd just parted for him, like he was some kind of biblical deity.

I climbed the stairs behind him, and the MC appraised us both. "Oh boy, I just know you are going to be good. Honey, are you looking for a job, because, oomph," she said to Gus, who gave her the panty-dropping smile.

There was Gusion and I, and two other couples. "I don't think this is a very good idea," I hissed, but Gus pretended not to hear me. I felt every single emotion up here on stage, like I was standing in the center of a swirling abyss of feelings.

The MC lined us up, and made a spinning motion to the DJ.

"Gus, I don't know how to dance," I whisper-shouted.

As the music changed to something slow and sensual, Gus grabbed me and pulled me into his chest. "You don't have to know how to dance, Hope. You just have to know how to feel."

I laughed, though the joke would be lost on Gus. I knew feelings better than any person in this room.

"Just let go," he whispered, his body moving around mine.

"Let go of what?" I mouthed back.

He stopped, his body pressed against my back. I could feel his warm breath on my neck. "Control." His lips brushed my ear, sending shivers of pleasure down my spine.

His hands found my hips, gently swaying me against his body to the music. "Keep the beat," he whispered again, backing me up against the pole, just like the dancers earlier. I undulated my body to the music, and Gus reached two hands above my head and gripped the pole. And lifted himself horizontal without so much as breaking a sweat. He slowly stepped on the air, and I stopped, staring. Twisting his wrist, he spun back around and dropped down in front of me.

"Uh-uh, no stopping," his hands were back on my hips as we slowly moved together, our bodies pressed as close as they can be with our clothes on. I met and held his gaze, transfixed by the pure mischievousness in his eyes, mixed with a heavy dose of lust.

"I thought you said you didn't pole dance?" I whispered.

He grinned and spun, climbing the pole like a monkey, then he wrapped his feet around the pole and flipped upside down.

The crowd was going nuts. Absolutely insane, but I couldn't look away from him. His face was inches away from me now as he held himself perfectly still. I couldn't help it. I leaned forward and kissed him like he was Spiderman. My tongue delved into his mouth, one hand on the pole, and I realized it was me spinning around the pole, not the world tilting on its axis.

He folded himself in half, breaking our kiss as he turned the right way up again, and deepened out kiss. He picked me up, and I wrapped my legs around his waist, my arms around his neck as I gave over control. In that moment I no longer cared what was right or wrong, that we were making a public spectacle of ourselves. I cared about the feel of his body against mine as he pressed my back against the pole, slowly spinning us as he climbed the pole. I cared that beneath the showmanship, he was making love to me for all the world to see.

I pulled back to breathe, and realized we were at the top of the pole.

"Time for the climax, Sweetheart. Hold tight," he whispered.

I didn't think he was kidding, so I did what he asked even as I said, "What?"

Then he let go of the pole with his hands, just the pole between his thighs and his impressive core strength stopping us from hitting the ground hard as he laid us out horizontally in the air.

Slipping slowly to the floor, we laid there, his body between my thighs, hardly breaking a sweat as I panted like I'd run a marathon. But it wasn't from physical exertion. The want I felt pulsed in my body. And he felt it too.

"Gus." It was a plea. I wanted him. Needed what he could give me.

"Yes," he answered.

The wave of rage shocked me, the roar of the crowd suddenly deafening. I knew the taste of that rage. I looked to the side, and I saw Memphis. The look of betrayal made my heart hurt.

"Uh oh," Gus said, his eyes glued to Memphis.

Yeah. Uh oh.

CHAPTER TEN

Gus humbly declined our winnings, and we hightailed it off the stage. Memphis' eyes never left me, and I felt guilty. I just didn't know why I felt guilty. Memphis and I weren't a couple. We'd kissed once, that was all.

Repeating that to myself, I stiffened my spine and held my head high. I had done nothing wrong. We stopped in front of him, and I found I couldn't meet his piercing eyes for too long.

With supernatural speed, his fist shot out, hitting Gusion in the face with a sickening crunch. And then he was just gone.

Gus gushed blood into his cupped hand. "I deserved that. Time to go before the humans notice how well I heal." We walked down a darkened hall, and stepped into an unlocked storage cupboard. I made sure not to touch anything. I can't imagine any dark space in a co-ed strip club was going to be particularly sanitary.

Gus sifted us back to the apartment, and I realized we'd been walking like Average Joes all day. I was thankful, because angel porting around was disorientating as all hell.

"Is your nose okay?" I went to the freezer to get out peas or something. I was staring into its icy depths before I remembered that we didn't cook, so we weren't going to have peas. We did have a bag of frozen vodka slushies though. I pulled it out, and Gus just raised his eyebrows at the silver bag. I shrugged.

"It's fine, but I'll take some of that in a glass if you're offering." I grabbed a tumbler from the cupboard and poured him a healthy dose of the fluro pink frozen cocktail. Gross.

"Do you want to explain what the hell that was about?"

Gus sighed, and spread his wings wide, stretching them before folding them delicately against his back. He took a gulp of his drink and winced. Apparently it didn't taste any better than it looked.

"That's really something you should ask Memphis." He flopped down on the couch, suddenly looking exhausted, less luminous. Like his millennia of life was crushing him. I hated it. I hated the loneliness and despair that sat in a fog around him.

I reached out, touching his cheek with the back of my fingers. "What happened to you?"

His brows furrowed, as he pulled back. "What?"

I took a deep breath. Rella was going to kill me. I'd kept this secret for two decades, and now I'd blurted it out three times in a week. "I can sense your emotions. I feel your wounded heart, your hopelessness. It's tearing me up inside."

I waited for the Blue style meltdown. But all I felt was surprise. "I guess Acerezeal's children were a little more angelic than everyone let on. Any other secrets I should know about?" He raised his eyebrows high, seeming more bemused than angry. Though, I guess he wasn't a societal reject with a career in murder, like Blue. He also wasn't human. His secrets ran so deep, they were basically part of his physical makeup, like he was comprised of blood and bones, sinew and secrets.

I can mindspeak. We are a blindspot to most angels, even Luc.

"Even Michael?" He sounded almost awed. I shrugged. I'd never met the Archangel Michael, and if I was lucky, I never would.

He downed the rest of his fluro pink cocktail, and stood. "I should go and smooth things over with Mephistopheles. He can seriously hold a grudge."

I put my hands on my hips. "So can I. You really aren't going to tell me what that was about?"

He gave me a sheepish look, leaning forward to kiss me gently on the lips. "See you soon, Sweetheart." Then he just disappeared. So rude.

THE NEXT TWO days were almost blissfully Angel free. No Memphis, no Gusion and surprisingly, no Azriel.

I also didn't leave the house. I didn't open the front door when anyone knocked, or order in unless Adnan was here too. I didn't open the blinds. I knew I was slipping down a hole that was going to be difficult to claw my way out of, but I couldn't seem to catch myself.

Rella didn't help. I could feel her turmoil from hundreds of miles away, her heart pounding anxiety, worry and fear all compounded with my own. I was a wreck.

Then she'd come to visit, and I finally understood the weird emotions she'd been sending. She had changed. She was no longer my twin in every way. We were different now in a way that seceded my silly little tattoo. She was immortal and I was...me. She was a Gargoyle Queen, and I was scared of standing in front of windows.

Now, I listened to her and Adnan fight in the other room, sitting beside Charlie, who held my hand, and under the watchful eyes of her new Gargoyle consorts? Conquests? Boy-toys? Whatever.

Charlie's hold on my hand was both comforting and excruciating. So much turmoil. He loved Rella, he hated them, he liked them and hated Rella. Well, her choices anyway. I knew there was no way he could ever hate Rella. She was a part of his soul, much like he was a part of hers. They were just too dumb to work out what that meant yet. They'd get there.

So much hurt and rage flowed from the hall, where Adnan was acting like a child. But that was just Adnan. Blue Halloran hadn't been wrong when he'd called Adnan the Mulligans Little Prince.

Rella strode out of the hall, and I was surprised to see Naz right behind her.

Well, maybe not so surprised. Naz had changed, more

than just being turned into some weird Gargoyle/Human hybrid. He was no longer the swirling vortex of despair and depression I'd sensed long ago. He had purpose, and it glowed around the edges of his depression like dawn break.

Rella kissed me on the cheek, and I resisted the urge to pull her to me and never let her go, like a security blanket. I pushed the thought right down so she wouldn't be able to skim it from my mind.

"Be safe," I murmured, and she left, her men flanking her like the Queen she was now.

I kissed Charlie's cheek. "Her heart is big enough, and so is yours, Charles Mulligan. Don't throw away something amazing because it doesn't fit with your boyhood dreams."

With that, I pushed him off the couch. He threw me the Charlie grin, to which I was impervious, and followed the rest of his pack. His family, if he'd just let them be.

I laid my head on the back of the couch and closed my eyes. The steady hum of Adnan's rage and disbelief echoed through the house like a discordant noise. I knew he wouldn't just go and brood in his room, that wasn't Adnan's style. I was waiting for the inevitable confrontation in five, four, three, two…

"I know she's your twin, Hope, but she's gone too far this time." I didn't bother to open my eyes.

"What was her alternative, let him die?" I repeated the words that Rella had used.

Unfortunately, that only made Adnan madder. "How about you leave him out of your freaky fucking world altogether. I should have said no when you asked me to talk to him. I should have known it could end nowhere but bad with your family."

Oh. Oh no, he did not. My eyes snapped open and I leapt to my feet. "My freaky fucking family is the only reason you are here in this lavish apartment, and not scrabbling in the dirt in a war-torn country. My freaky world is the only reason you didn't bleed to death when you were five. I know you're hurting, so I'm going to let it slide, but show some damn respect."

He got right up in my face then, his finger pointed at my nose. "You guys think you are better than the rest of us because, why? You have the ability to sense my feelings? Well, what am I feeling now?"

He sent a huge pulse of disgust and it cut me like a knife, just as he knew it would. Adnan was my best friend, and he knew all the best ways to hurt me.

Adnan was wrenched away and held against the wall by a blacker than midnight hand. "You would do best to watch your tongue, child, before I remove it."

Adnan turned his head to look at me, his eyes burning with righteous anger. His look said, "This is what I mean" but his emotions told me that he was scared under all the bravado.

"Memphis, please put him down."

Memphis did something that I could only assume gave him his stellar reputation. He pulsed his wings wide, sucking the light and some of the oxygen from the room. His face was the scariest thing I'd ever seen, and when it was mixed with his spiked brand of rage, he became the scariest being I had ever seen. Scarier than Ace in a rage, and even scarier than Luc.

"Leave." That single word made the hairs stand up on the back of my neck. He dropped Adnan to the ground, and my best friend disappeared into his bedroom. I stood there, silently contemplating the huge angel in front of me. What did he look like before he fell? Were his wings the snowy white of Azriel's?

Adnan strode back through the room, a duffle bag slung over his shoulder. He grabbed his wallet and his phone and slammed out of the front door.

As the sound echoed around the room, only to be replaced by silence, I crumbled.

CHAPTER ELEVEN

F alling to my knees, I put my face in my hands and tried to suck in a single breath that was large enough to fill my lungs. But it felt like there was no air left in the room, like there was a hand around my throat threatening to choke the life right out of me.

I pulled at the collar of my sweater, trying to give myself more space to breathe. But nothing helped.

Memphis scooped me up into his arms, holding me against his chest. "I can't breathe," I gasped, sobbing at the same time. "I can't breathe." Panic raced through my veins like wildfire.

He sat down with me still clutched against his torso, and grabbed my chin, forcing me to meet his brilliant, bright blue eyes.

"Look at me. Now breathe." It was a command. "You are okay."

His eyes held me. Waves of strength and reassurance pulsed between us, and I wrapped my arms around his neck, burying my face in his throat and did what he said. I just breathed. I breathed in the scent of Memphis, a scent I couldn't describe. It wasn't anything as basic as human cologne. No, he smelled like something earthy, but not of the earth. Ugh. Whatever it was, it was delicious. Maybe even addictive.

Sucking in gulps of air, eventually my breathing slowed, my sobs calming.

I wanted to pull away, but I wasn't ready to return to life just yet. Instead, I brushed my lips against the steady, slow thud of his pulse. I sucked gently, tasting his skin on my tongue, feeling his pulse quicken.

I shifted against his body, straddling his lap. He groaned, and I felt the vibration against my lips.

"Hope…" it was a question, or a lament, I couldn't tell. But I didn't want someone to tell me no. I wanted to take what I needed, and I wanted Memphis to ignore right and wrong for a moment. I kissed up his jaw, until my lips hovered over his.

"Memphis. Be quiet."

I felt his lips curl against mine, but he didn't speak. I kissed him, tracing the soft curves with my tongue, devouring his moans. His hands roamed up my back, the gentle pressure of his fingers massaging the stiff muscles on either side of my spine.

I moaned against his lips, and felt the hard press of his body between my thighs. I moved, grinding our bodies together, making him let out an involuntary moan. There was something thrilling about dragging pleasure from this giant of a man, so I did it again. His hands stilled, spanning the width of my back.

I kissed him harder, exploring his mouth with mine, tempting him, teasing him into kissing me back.

I knew I was out of control, I knew that if I let him take a breath, Memphis would tell me so. But I didn't want to be in control, I just wanted to *feel*. Not other people's emotions, my own. I spent so much of my time digging my way through everyone else's feelings, my own got buried beneath the weight of the world.

I grabbed the bottom of my sweater, pulling everything off in one swift movement. My nipples pebbled as they hit the cold air.

His eyes went black as he watched my breasts. His wings spread wide and he ran his hands up my back, and over my ribs.

I hissed as he hit my tattoo. I'd forgotten about it.

Moving my body back, he stared down at the dual coloured wings, rubbing the skin beneath the tattoo with his thumb.

Deciding there was time to stare at my new ink later, I dived back into our kiss. Grabbing his silk shirt, I gripped the lapels and pulled. Tiny black buttons scattered across the room as I stared down at the hard expanse of his body. He was like a statue made of some kind of precious stone. Hard ridges of his midnight black skin shone under the apartments downlighting. I ran my hands down his torso, and hissed in a breath. So perfect.

"Hope," he started, his voice strained as I reached the waistband of his black linen pants.

I dragged my eyes from his abs, seriously I think he got an extra set or something, and back to his face.

"Memphis. Take me to bed. Please." It sounded a little more like begging than I would have liked, but I couldn't find it in me to care. "Please."

Memphis stood, with me still in his arms, and I wrapped my legs around his waist, my arms snaking back around his neck.

His hands under my ass, he hiked me up until our noses touched. And then he kissed me. I mean really, really kissed me.

The world tilted, or maybe that was just Memphis moving us toward the bedroom, I didn't know or care. I wanted to just consume him and let his fire consume me.

He pressed me against the wall in the hallway as his mouth devoured mine, biting my lower lip until it was my turn to moan. Tearing his mouth away, he kissed down my neck, biting softly down my collarbone before he found my nipple, sucking it between his perfect lips. Holy shit. I arched against him as the sensation pulsed pleasure through my body like he was electrifying. My yoga pants were wet, and he grunted as his hands shifted to my thighs and he pressed the tips of his fingers against the seam.

He made a feral noise around my nipple and pulled away, clutching me against his body as he moved to my room with inhuman speed, his wings bumping into the doorjamb with a painful thud. He didn't even wince. Instead, he placed me on the bed, and peeled me out of my yoga pants.

I laid on my comforter, naked, and he stared down at me like I was an actual gift from God. He stared so long, his eyes roaming over every inch of my body, it was like he lost time. Feeling unnaturally bold, I let my knees fall apart, baring my most intimate parts to his eyes.

He sucked in a harsh breath, then his eyes were back on my face and his clothes were just gone.

Fuck.

I forgot how to breathe.

Fuck. He was...

There were no words.

I didn't get much time to stare, because that beautiful body was over mine and Memphis was kissing me with all the skill and passion the Fallen Angel in front of me possessed. I could no longer think of him as a simple man.

He kissed me until I could no longer think at all, his hard length pressed against my core, making us both moan.

His hand moved down between our body's and stopped where my pussy dripped. His fingers skimmed over my clit, making me writhe, and making him grin. Like really, full on grin. I was so dazzled for a moment that I forgot his hand was between my thighs.

Then he slid a finger inside me. Holy hell. He stroked me like he'd had a millennia to work out what made a woman sing. I whimpered as he stroked me. Then he added another finger. I let out a little scream as I rose higher and higher on his clever fingers. I was so close, my climax just out of reach as he drew his fingers away. I let out a desperate noise, but he caught it on his lips as he positioned his body between my thighs.

Whispering to me in a language that no longer existed, he kissed me deeply and slid his big cock inside.

I sucked in a breath and held it until my lungs began to burn, waiting for him to move, my body adjusting to the size of him. Then he thrust hard, burying himself in me and it was so damn beautiful. My climax crashed over me, but Memphis wasn't nearly finished with me. Lifting my leg over his shoulder, he slid in and out of me in slow, controlled movements. But I didn't want control, no matter how exquisite it felt. Pushing on his shoulders, I leaned up and bit his lip. Hard.

"My turn."

He let himself be pushed onto his back, his wings spread across my bed. I slid back down on him, seating myself. And just stared. He looked divine, the pale milkiness of my skin contrasting so beautifully with his midnight darkness of his. He thrust up and all thoughts of aesthetics disappeared as I moved.

"Oh God." It was hardly a whisper as I moved faster, Memphis holding my hips but not restricting my movements.

He let out an amused huff, but didn't comment as his fingers slid around to brush my clit. My moans were coming out in gasped pants now. He sat up, pulling my legs around his waist, going even deeper. His shallow thrusts hit pleasure zones I didn't even know I had.

"Come for me, beautiful Hope," he whispered against my ear, his eyes holding mine as we moved as one, our bodies entwined. I was helpless to resist. I came in huge shuddering wave, crying out over and over as pleasure lit up every nerve ending. Letting me lean back,

Memphis watched me cum like a starving man, thrusting harder and harder inside me, milking my orgasm until his own rocked his body, making him shudder and let out a groan that was half pleasure, half pain.

Pulling me down against his chest, he wrapped his arms and wings around us both. The hammering of his heart was a staccato against my cheek. We sat there for a moment, completely connected, as I calmed my breathing.

"That was..." I flapped my hands around a bit, hoping they'd portray what my words were failing to describe.

Memphis kissed the top of my head. "Yes," he said reverently. "Come, I'll run you a shower."

I smiled against his chest.

"Will you join me?"

A low rumbling laugh vibrated beneath my cheek.

"Always."

I COLLAPSED BACK onto the bed. The shower had been invigorating in every way possible. I laid in Memphis' arms as he spooned himself around me, his wings relaxed behind him. They really were beautiful. Dark and wet, they glistened an electric blue under the soft lights in my room. I also discovered that if I rubbed the undersides, it drove Memphis wild.

I grinned at the memory of making the cool angel lose his control. I was enjoying my brief stint of being irresponsible. First with Gusion, and now with

Memphis. I didn't know what kind of woman that made me, but I was finding I didn't care.

But that reminded me...

"Why did you hit Gus?" The question had gotten lost under the caresses and the embraces. But it pushed its way back into my conscious now like a freight train. Memphis stiffened slightly around me. I could almost hear his mind turning. This close, it was weird that I couldn't hear his thoughts. But since discovering my little secret, Memphis had become very good at blocking my abilities. Perhaps even better than Rella. I enjoyed the silence. Well, most of the time. Now, I'd really like to know what he was thinking.

He let out a long sigh against the nape of my neck, and I briefly wondered if angels could lie. Especially Fallen angels. Something to ask Ace next time I saw her.

"Gusion saw something a while ago. He is the Angel of the Past, Present and Future, and it makes him privy to certain information. However, he is still a Fallen Angel, and our scruples aren't what they once were."

I rolled in his arms so I could see his face. "I'm not sure I understand."

"He told me, a very long time ago, that I would find someone to love again. A true love, if you will. A soul deep connection with another person." My heart stopped beating, or maybe it was still going because all I could hear was the blood whooshing in my ears.

"And that other person is...Gusion? Ace?" I said, in vain.

Memphis shook his head.

"Me?"

He nodded, just once, and suddenly the last few hours took on whole different meaning. It was too much. I moved away from him slightly. I needed space to process what he was saying.

"You think I am your soul mate or something? That's probably something you should've told a girl before we had sex, you know."

I threw back the blanket, suddenly very glad I couldn't read his thoughts. Just seeing his face morph back into its neutral mask hurt enough. Guilt swept in to temper my anger.

I pulled on my clothes, and when I was no longer naked and vulnerable before him, I knelt back on the bed.

I put my fingertips on the sharp angle of his cheek-bone. "I'm not, I don't know, saying no. If this is even something you can say no to. I just need to process, okay?"

I pulled on my shoes, and stopped at my bedroom door. I looked back at Memphis, lying as still and expressionless on my bed as the statue I'd compared him to earlier. "Don't leave?" I asked, the words escaping my mouth totally at odds with my brain. My brain was telling me that this was too much. I already carried the weight of others emotions. I couldn't carry the burden of being Memphis' last chance at love.

I left before my wayward tongue could say anything else. Picking up my keys, I rode the private elevator up to the top floor and the rooftop garden that would hope-fully be empty at this time of the night.

Stepping out into the cold night air, I went and sat

on a lawn chair, stretching out beneath the stars. Well, one or two stars, the rest were obscured by light pollution. It was odd for me to feel alone, but I did. Rella had gone to Geneva, and Charlie with her. Adnan had left. While I'd never been alone, the sensation that settled in my chest was one I was far too used to. I felt lonely.

I pulled at all the emotional threads in the apartment building, wrapping them around myself like a blanket. I let everything in, the hate, the happiness, the jealousy, anger and joy. But especially the love.

I knew what I should do, and I knew what I wanted to do, and the problem was they were two wildly different things.

But when it came down to it, there was only one road to take. I just had to hope it wouldn't come back and bite me in the ass later.

I fell asleep on the uncomfortable plastic lawn chairs, and woke when the bitter cold of predawn froze my limbs. Stumbling back down to the elevator, I wondered what I'd find. Would Memphis still be there? Would Adnan be there?

I stared at myself in the mirrored walls of the elevator. I looked like shit. Huge dark smudges made me look a little like a corpse. I'd lost weight too, which definitely added to the skeletal thing I had going on. My auburn hair was a rat nest at the back of my head, and my clothes were crinkled. I scratched at a crusty spot on my face that looked suspiciously like dried drool. I didn't look like the love of anyone's life.

I'd never been so thankful for a private elevator. I

was going to go into my apartment, fall into bed, and not come out for a year.

The first sign that wasn't' going to happen was the smell of freshly brewed coffee in the apartment. The second sign was the huge onyx angel cramping up my kitchen. He was perfectly attired again, and I sent a small thanks to...whoever one thanked for fully clothed Fallen angels in your kitchen.

He turned at the sound of the door shutting. I raised a hand before he could speak.

"Before you start, I have something to say. Firstly, you should have told me, but that is neither here nor there now. I'm willing to give the idea of an *us* a go. But I want it to be organic, I guess. So, we are going to pretend that yesterday never happened. We are going to be friends. And if something builds from there, then that's great, but if it doesn't, then so be it. Because I refuse to be peer pressured into something to protect your feelings or anyone else's. My life is my own. Got it?"

Memphis' tense shoulders seemed to relax an infinitesimal bit and he nodded. "I agree to your terms."

"Also, no more hitting Gusion, or anyone else for that matter, out of jealousy. If anyone knows that love isn't necessarily linear, it's me. I will love who I like, and make my own decisions."

He nodded again, if a bit more begrudgingly. I honestly didn't think I'd end up with a relationship like my parents, but I wasn't ruling it out. My childhood had been mostly happy, if not always smooth sailing. There'd been fights, and disagreements, and all the other things that went with being in a relationship with another person. But then you times that by eight people, and it could be a little tricky. But there had never been a lack of love. That was always given easily and received thankfully. Love had saved them, and they all knew it.

I thought about Rella, and the guys. I didn't know if polygamy was hereditary, or if you were just destined to follow in the footsteps of your parents in general, but she seemed to be happily waltzing down the same path. I smiled at the thought. She was going to have her hands full.

Memphis held out a coffee like a lifeline, and I took it thankfully.

"So, how do you feel about the classic cinema channel?"

CHAPTER TWELVE

I winced as the doctor told me for the tenth time how miraculous my recovery had been. Little did he know...

I'd been on death's door. Literally. Now, I could probably run a marathon. It wasn't the physical scars that remained, though I did have a pretty impressive one on my jaw. The injuries that persevered were harder to treat.

"She needs a referral to a therapist. She has PTSD," Memphis said, and my eyes shot to him, as did the doctors. Well, the doctor's eyes had kept drifting to the big angel naturally. Even in his more human form, he had a presence that pressed down on you like a great weight.

I narrowed my eyes at the big traitor. Logically, I knew he was right. But I was dealing with it already, in my own way. Kind of.

The doctor dragged his eyes back to me. "Would

you like a referral to see someone? You went through a violent and traumatic event."

I shrugged. "I didn't mesh very well with the last welfare officer. If you have someone you trust, then I'd appreciate it."

I was going to kick Memphis' ass later though.

We went over a few more things, and then I was officially discharged from the doctor's care.

As we walked to my car, a Tesla because I could no longer look at my Prius, I elbowed Memphis. "What the hell was that? You were my ride, you didn't have any right to interfere in my consultation."

Memphis looked completely unapologetic. "I waited for you to say something, and deduced you were not going to tell your healthcare professional about a potential health issue, so I intervened."

I clenched my jaw, because he was right. I had no intention of mentioning it. Still, it irked. I pointed a finger at him. "You don't get to decide things for me. Not now. Not ever."

He looked at me with his usual neutral mask. I huffed and slid into the driver's seat. I peeled out of the parking lot, and merged into traffic. The silence was deafening, but eventually he puffed out a breath. "Okay."

I raised my eyebrows. "It took you that long to decide to do what is right? No wonder they kicked you out of Angel School."

He laughed, and I let the sound wash over me. He had the best laugh, all the better because it was so rare.

"I am sure it's blasphemous to call Heaven 'Angel School'."

"Is it where you learn to be an angel?" I didn't let him answer. "I rest my case."

He laughed again, but I watched it slip from his face. I felt like an asshole, making a joke about something that forever altered how he'd live his immortal life. Apparently, if I didn't have twenty-four/seven access to someone's emotions, I became an insensitive jerk.

"Gusion is the reason we fell." I sucked in a breath through my teeth. I knew that from Gusion's own emotions, but I didn't know the why. I stayed silent. I didn't want to press, but I was dying to know why.

"He fell in love with a daughter of man. They had a relationship, and then a child was conceived. Only Luc had done such a thing beforehand, but all his children had ended up purely human. I do not know why. It was as if the power of his Archangelicness could not be contained within a mortal body. But it was different with Gusion and his child. The babe possessed the traits of the angels as well as humanity, even in the womb. Afterward, the Father made us all infertile, barren. We understood. Even Gusion." He frowned, as if he were reiterating the point to himself.

"But then Michael, on the orders of the Father I suppose, had Gusion's lover erased, his child in her womb. The entire village. Just to protect the image, I guess. Gusion was ruined." He sucked in a ragged breath. "A broken shell. Luc loved so deeply, and he loved us most of all. His cadre. Acerezeal, Gusion, Azriel and me. Gusion's pain swept through us all and those few decades were dark, dark days. Then Luc did the unthinkable. He questioned why? Why did she have to be killed? We could have forgiven the child, just a tiny spark, none of us would know what such a creation would result in. But Gusion loved her so, so very much. That very love that the Father wanted us to spread through the world. Michael would not give him an answer. So he did something that went against everything we had ever been taught. The vanity of assuming that what the Father did was wrong."

He sighed deeply, the kind of sound that dragged you back millennia to the source of a raw wound that still festered. It was a tragic noise that broke my heart. "The rest you know. It was the first and only divide in the Heavens. But balance was necessary, so perhaps the whole thing was preordained," he finished, and it had a rehearsed quality of frequent repetition.

"Memphis…" I started, but my phone ringing cut me off. Clicking the accept button on my steering wheel, I went into business mode instinctually.

"Hope Jones speaking."

"Hope, it's Rouen. We met the other day."

I scrambled around in my brain for my connection to Rella. It was faint, because she was across the world, but it felt blissfully happy. She was safe. "What can I do for you, Rouen?"

"How quickly can you get to France?"

I looked at Memphis, who nodded. "I'm only a thought away. Why?"

I could almost feel Rouen's happiness through the phone. "There's going to be a wedding, and I know a beautiful woman who'd love for her twin to be there to see her marry her best friend."

I swerved onto a side street, shocked to my very core. I slammed the car into park. "No fucking way. Charlie?"

Rouen's happy laughter thundered through the cars speakers. "Totally fucking way. It's kind of to all of us, but Charlie needs this formal bit the most."

"When?"

"Tomorrow."

My emotions were a tangle but happiness is what prevailed. "I'll be there. I'll bring pastries."

"You don't happen to have a Catholic preacher lying around?"

I turned to stare at Memphis, my smile so huge, it might've actually cracked my face. "I know a guy."

SO MUCH LOVE swirled around the small clearing in the Middle-Of-Nowhere, France, that I was tempted to cry again. Rella looked beautiful. Like an angel. Well, maybe not an angel; there was also enough lust in the clearing that I was going to need a cigarette and a gatorade after I took my leave. I looked at Memphis talking to Romanus, the big one. Well, they were all pretty big. Apparently, the Gargoyles and Memphis knew each other, from, uh Hell. Sometimes my life was just the strangest thing.

Maybe Adnan was right, maybe it was us.

"What's going on with you?" Rella asked, basically inhaling another pastry. I pasted a grin on my face. It wasn't hard. I was genuinely happy for her.

I locked my thoughts down tight. "Nothing. I've got it all under control." Liar, liar pants on fire. "Actually, we should go. Memphis?" He looked up and smiled, and it was like someone cut off my oxygen every single time. Why did he have to be so pretty? With all the lust up in here, I was seriously rethinking my 'just friends' policy.

Rella stood, and I wrapped my arms around her. I hugged her close. I tried to keep a lid on my emotions, just for a little while longer. But I was happy, and scared, and amazed and a little jealous. I stomped on that last emotion. Rella was never going to be *my* Rella forever. She had a husband, er husbands, now. We were adults with differing lives. She would always be my twin, the other part of my soul. And now, they were connected to me too. I poked at their connections in my mind a few more times. At least the Gargoyles and Naz's connection. I looked over Rella's shoulder at Charlie. I had no doubt there would be another thread soon enough.

"Love you, Rella. Be safe."

She hugged me tighter. "You too, Hope."

Memphis came and wrapped me in his arms tightly, the look on his face unreadable. "Home?" he whispered. I nodded once, smiling. Home.

The swirling disorientation of my cells being moved half a world away made me want to vomit. It was worth it to see Rella get married, but it was like seasickness times a thousand when you stopped. And doing it twice in one day made it twice as bad on the way back.

I slipped out of Memphis' arms and bolted for the bathroom, losing the better part of my brunch. Memphis appeared in the door of the bathroom holding a bottle of sparkling water. I took it thankfully. "I don't think I'll ever get used to that. Give me a fifteen hour flight any day," I grumbled, rinsing my mouth at the sink before taking a sip.

"Your body is not really made for it, though your angelic ancestry allows you to do it without killing you. Otherwise, you would quite literally explode. With some exceptions, of course. Your parents for one. Their stint in hell has made them a little more than human. Raphael can transport humans as long as they are encased in his healing light. Sometimes, there is exceptional wisdom in our creation. Other times, our powers feel more like a curse."

I remembered what he said, about knowing everyone's darkest secret. It sounded like a terrible burden to bear.

"I don't know what you're whining about. Try knowing how everyone is going to die. That's a pain in the ass."

I whirled around, but I still hadn't gotten my land legs, so my ankles tangled and I pitched toward the floor. Two strong hands reached out to grab me simultaneously.

"Gus!" I said, unable to help the high-pitched excitement in my voice. I mentally covered my eyes with my hands. *Way to play it cool, Hope.*

"Hey, Sweetheart. Been to a party?" He looked down at my pretty green tea dress. "Hey, Slugger," he said, grinning at Memphis. I felt Memphis' hand tighten on my arm, but he quickly let it go.

"Asshole." His voice was a scary growl, but it just

made Gus grin wider. "Aren't you meant to be some-where, doing something else that isn't hitting on Hope and annoying me?"

He laughed. "What could be more important than that?"

I realized we were all crowded into the bathroom, which was spacious, but not big enough to house two huge angels, their wings and me, without us all being pressed nice and close.

For once, I was glad that I was the only one who could sense emotions, because I was lusting, hard. I was one heated look away from throwing myself on the bed and saying 'Come get me!'

"Let's, uh, go sit in the living room, hey? It's a pretty tight squeeze in here."

Gus looked me up and down. "I'm okay with a tight squeeze. How about you, Memphis?"

Memphis mumbled something incoherent, and his finger slid down my spine. "We should move to the living space. It would be more comfortable for every-one," he sighed begrudgingly.

Gus raised both eyebrows so high they nearly touched his glorious hairline. "Well, that's interesting. You guys been playing Seven Minutes in Heaven without me?"

"Seven minutes is all the heaven your conquests get, Gusion, not mine. Don't insult me."

I turned to stare. Did Memphis just make a joke? By the way Gusion was bent over laughing, I guessed he had.

Gus backed out of the bathroom, still laughing, and I followed him out.

"So seriously, why the fancy clothes? You guys been to a ball or something?"

"A wedding, actually."

He reached out and hugged me close, ignoring Memphis' growl. "You got married to the grumpy old bastard? Congratulations." I knew he was teasing me and Memphis, but I paused at the thought. Memphis would look great in a tux. Could angels even get married? Why would they?

Memphis rolled his eyes, but his lips curled upwards. "This calls for a drink. Champagne?" Gus asked, clapping his hands together decisively.

My stomach revolted at the idea of more champagne. "I'm good thanks. I might just head to bed."

Gusion sighed heavily. "Well, I usually demand to be wined and dined first, but if you insist..." he pulled off his shirt and headed toward my bedroom.

I was momentarily stunned by his perfection. Right down to the two little dimples either side his spine, just above his ass.

"Very humorous. She means alone. Shouldn't you be watching Uriel?"

The Archangel Uriel?

"Ace is watching him."

The comical horror on Memphis' normally stoic face had me sucking my teeth to keep from laughing. "Luc trusts she won't just kill him in his sleep?"

Gusion shrugged. "I guess so. She's too smart to go

after Uriel by herself." He didn't sound as confident as his words would suggest.

I sat there silently, on the off chance they would forget I was there and spill all their secrets. Maybe talk about their feelings. Have a bro hug at the end. Wouldn't that be nice?

"Weren't you heading to bed, Hope? I bid you a goodnight," Memphis said as he shot me a knowing look. Busted.

Gusion blew me a kiss. "Are you sure you don't want me to come? I can promise you a good night."

Memphis' death stare bounced straight off the golden Fallen Angel. I shook my head, because I did not trust my mouth to say what my brain said it should. I waved and walked into my bedroom. As I stripped off my dress, I headed straight to my ensuite. I needed a cold shower.

CHAPTER THIRTEEN

eep breaths. In. Out. In. Out. I stood in front
of the modern glass and steel building that
housed the corporate offices of the NRH
Foundation. My first day back at work was not off to a
good start. I couldn't force my feet across the threshold.

I knew Sam and Tolli were upstairs. They'd taken
over again while I'd be recuperating. But as soon as I
walked in there, I'd have to field a million questions,
weather a million pitying looks, steel myself against the
bombardment of emotions that ranged from curiosity to
downright hatred. Any one of them could have a gun.
Any one of them could finish what Geneva had started.
The call from Rella in the middle of last night replayed
over and over in my head.

"Maximoff Richards was the person who organized
your abduction. He's part of a bigger, evil organization,
but it was Richard's that wanted you dead and gone."

It had rocked me to my very core. I'd kept the nightmares under control by assuring myself that the bad

guys weren't here in Manhattan. They were on the other side of the globe.

I'd been so wrong.

Maximoff Richards hated me, I'd always known that. When the NRH Pharmaceutical wing decided to produce and essentially give away life saving medicines to impoverished countries, we knew we were going to get resistance from the other Pharma companies. We were taking a huge chunk out of their profits. It would put pressure on the execs; from disgruntled stockholders to the public pressure to follow our trend. We'd been prepared for that kind of hostility. No one had been prepared for murder plots.

Part of me wanted to stay in my apartment, the part of me that remembered the immense pain. The more stubborn part of me, the part that got a dash of Ace's craziness, and Mom's sense of right and wrong, decided I wouldn't be held prisoner in my own home anymore. My boogeyman had a name, and now I had some of the power back.

I hadn't told the guys. The last twenty-four hours had been almost like bliss. Their emotions were blocked, and it was like being disconnected from the world for a day or two. We watched more boring TV, I listened to the guys talk about the past. And when they talked about the forties, they meant the 40's B.C. I wanted to get out my notebooks and just mine their brains for stories. I loved every minute of it.

Yeah, they knew where Atlantis was.

They knew what lay at the bottom of the Bermuda Triangle.

The depths of their knowledge defied description. And they were happy to share it with me. They gave me as much knowledge as I could humanly take in, and when I was at capacity, we'd watch mindless daytime T.V. in comfortable silence. They respected my boundaries, even Gus. Well, to a degree. He flirted outrageously, though I think he just enjoyed getting emotion out of Memphis.

I didn't know if I was happy or frustrated that they took me at my word. The two of them, wandering around my apartment without shirts on was torture. The best kind of torture. Sometimes, when I lay awake in bed, I'd imagine what it would be like to have both of their hands on me at once.

"Are you ready, Hope?" Gus whispered in my ear, shaking me from my dirty thoughts. At least my breathing was normal again.

Both Gus and Memphis were with me today. I mightn't have told them about Maximoff Richards, but they were still intuitive enough to know that I was petrified. Especially Memphis, who'd been privy to my little anxiety attack/meltdown last week.

I nodded, wrapping their presence around me like a shield. I stepped over the threshold and stopped in front of security.

The slightly pudgy security officer behind the counter jumped to his feet. "Miss Jones. It is good to see you back." He looked at Memphis and Gus, and blanched. "I was sorry to hear…"

"Thanks, Mike," I interrupted. He was genuinely sorry. I gave him a sad smile. I missed JJ too. "This is my, uh, security. Memorize their faces. They can come and go as they please, okay?"

"Yes, Miss."

I walked through to the elevator, and felt every set of eyes in the building glued to my back. I felt like a moving target. Memphis and Gus closed ranks around me as we stood at the bank of elevators.

"Okay?" Memphis' smooth voice slid over me, steeling my spine. I nodded. I was always on public exhibition, this was no different. Smile for the cameras, Hope.

The elevator doors slid open and the car was thankfully empty. As we stepped in and the doors closed behind us, I let out the breath I'd been holding. That was just the lobby. The worst was still to come.

Gus leaned forward, and kissed me hard. Bruisingly hard. He swallowed my little yelp of surprise, and soon I was kissing him back. I moved my lips against his, trying to give back as good as I got. The man could kiss. He kissed better than I breathed.

Finally tearing my lips away, I stared. "What was that for?"

"You looked pale. You needed a little color in your cheeks," Gusion said, grinning unapologetically. I slid a look at Memphis, but he seemed more exasperated than angry.

"You know, I have blush in my purse for just that reason," I huffed out, but I wasn't really annoyed. No red-blooded woman could be angry after a kiss like that.

"My way was more fun."

Well, touché.

The elevator dinged at the top floor and I straightened. Shoulders back, chin up. I was fierce. I was kind. I could do this.

I stepped into the marble tiled reception area, and breathed a sigh of relief. I'd spent so much time here, it was as familiar as my apartment.

The receptionist looked up, and then nearly dropped her coffee mug. "Miss Jones. You're back! We weren't expecting you. Let me call Mr Mateo. Mr Sigursson is out of the office at the moment, he's across town at an early meeting, but I could call?"

I waved a hand at the secretary. "It's fine, Annalise. Just call Dad and tell him I'm here. I know my way to his office," I said, giving her a warm smile, which she returned. Then her eyes swung up, and hit the wall of angelicness behind me. I was pretty flattered that she'd been so glad to see me she momentarily overlooked the men behind me.

This time she did drop her mug. I grinned. Yeah, that was a fair response.

I had ears. I heard how the women in the office spoke about Tolliver and Sam. Silver foxes was a term that was whispered around the water cooler more often than I found comfortable. And when we had Gala's and all my parents came, well, it was a bit crazy. But Gusion and Memphis, especially Gusion, had an otherworldly beauty that shocked your system.

"I'll just go this way, yeah? Come on, you two."

"I'm not sure I'm ready to meet the parents, Sweetheart," Gusion teased. I rolled my eyes.

I strode down the halls of NRH like I owned them,

halls I'd walked as soon as I could toddle on two chubby little legs. The huge corner office at the end of the corridor overlooked the city on both sides, and both Sam and Tolliver had their desks in the space. I'd often wondered if they ever got sick of each other, living together, working together, being committed to the same woman, but they showed no signs of discord.

I knocked, and a muffled voice told me to enter. I poked my head around the door jamb. As expected, Tolliver was in front of his computer, not even looking up as I entered.

"Hey Dad."

His head snapped up at the sound of my voice and a smile bloomed on his face. "Hope!" He stood and moved around the desk, coming over to wrap me in his arms. He smelled of the exact same cologne he'd worn since I was a child and it soothed my frazzled nerves.

"You are looking so much better," he said as he stepped back, appraising me for any residual injuries. When he met my eyes, his almond shaped ones narrowed. "How are you feeling?"

He'd always been the canniest of my parents; not as instinctual as Lux, or as naturally brilliant as Eli. But he could always, and I mean always, tell when I was lying. He could read me like every word I thought was written across my forehead. When I was a teenager, I was almost convinced that perhaps he was psychic too. But he'd helped raise me, and could read my body language like the keen businessman and attentive father he was.

"Physically, I'm great."

A single dark eyebrow rose. He didn't even ask.

"Emotionally, it's going to take a little while to stop seeing bogeyman wherever I go. I've got an appointment to see a professional about...it."

Tolliver looked over my shoulder. "I wouldn't worry too much about monsters under your bed with the company you seem to be keeping. Gusion. Mephistopheles. Interesting to see you here, with my daughter."

It might have been my imagination, but there was a not so subtle warning in those words. As a child, I'd tried hard to block out the emotions of my parents, much the same way I did with Rella and Adnan. As soon as I knew their emotional frequency, so to speak, I could block it out unless they were feeling high emotion or I was in physical contact. It was a survival technique. I would have gone mad without it.

Even now, I didn't know if I'd emerged from my teens fully sane.

"Luc..." Gusion said as Memphis said, "Hope-"

Tolliver raised a hand. "Stop."

I'd never seen either of them even a little bit flustered. But right now, they seemed at a loss.

"Hurt her, and Ace's wrath will seem like nothing in comparison to the pain that we will rain down."

These were Fallen Angels, who spent their time poking people with pitchforks and torturing wrongdoers. The idea of Tolliver threatening them should have been ludicrous. But both of them nodded solemnly.

I raised a hand in the air. "Uh, hi? This isn't the 7th century. You don't get to make decisions for me like I'm not here. Besides, I'm pretty sure Rella, Mom and Ace together and out for blood is legitimately the scariest thing in or out of Hell." There was a small chorus of agreement. I turned back to my father. "I just wanted to know how the Foundation was getting on without me. I'm sorry that I have been so absent. I hope the soft support from Geneva didn't fall through?"

"Quite the contrary. We've had even more support than you initially projected…"

My heart stopped.

Tolliver's lips were still moving, but there was no sound. A high pitch whine rang in my ears and darkness clouded my vision. Until my heart thudded back online, but it was uneven. Wrong.

Rella.

Rella.

Then half my soul was ripped away and I screamed. I screamed and screamed until I could feel it burning in my chest where my heart used to be. I fell to my knees, pain spearing through my head like a hot poker. Or a bullet.

"Rella!"

She was dead. My twin was dead.

CHAPTER FOURTEEN

Their emotions felt like whips against my already raw soul. I stared at the hole in the ground where they'd lowered the other part of me. I wanted to climb in there after her, curl myself around her like we did when we were young. But instead, she was going to be cold in the ground, alone. We weren't made to be alone. We were two parts to a whole. One couldn't survive without the other. I couldn't survive.

This was wrong.

I could hear them speaking behind me, but I ignored them. Mom sobbed softly into someone's chest, I could tell because her cries were muffled.

"She won't eat. She won't speak."

"She won't look me in the eye. It's like she…" Sam stopped whatever he was going to say, but I could almost hear the rest of the sentence. It was like I died too. I wanted to. It was too much. It had all been too much.

Charlie and Nazir's funerals yesterday, the barrage

of grief-stricken Mulligans like a tornado of sadness, and I sat alone at its center. I wanted the pain to eat me up. Maybe if I felt enough of everyone else's grief, I could forget the emptiness inside me. The connection that was missing.

"Bring her away," someone said, but Memphis stepped in to stop them. Memphis hadn't left my side, nor had Gusion. Even as I lay curled on my bed for hours on end, they were there, silent protectors.

"Leave her. She needs time. We will watch her, I promise. I swear this on my immortal soul. I will let no harm come to her."

I looked to where he was speaking to Lux, who was staring at me with more emotion than I'd ever seen on his face. Such jagged pain.

"Please," Memphis said. He almost sounded like he was begging. "She needs to be alone. This emotion," he waved at the group, "it is pushing her into the darkness. I am not sure we can catch her if she falls much further. Please." This time I was certain he was begging. For me.

Lux was conflicted. I could feel his need to grab me, to take me back home and never let me leave again. To never feel this grief again. He stared at me, and I must have looked like death, because eventually I heard them move away. I was alone again, with that white box. With my twin.

"Rella," the single word came out on a sob, but I sucked it back down. What did I do now?

I slumped to my knees in the soft dirt, ignoring the grave diggers waiting to bury my sister. Rella had always been the invincible one. I was the one who was made to break.

A hand touched my back, and a huge wave of something that felt suspiciously like love came through the contact. I looked over my shoulder, and if I still had the capacity to feel, I would have been shocked.

Luc knelt beside me, his large hand almost spanning my back. His face, his usually hard, scary face, was twisted in something that looked like compassion. And love.

I took one look at his face and wailed. I dove into his chest, and let him wrap his arms and his huge onyx wings around me. He blocked out the world, all the pain and grief, and I sobbed against him as my eyes cried my heart's blood against his chest.

"Hush, little one. Hush. It is okay," he whispered in his deep voice, the voice meant to strike fear into mortals, instead of soothe their wounds. "It will all be okay."

"How?" The word came out jagged and angry. "She's dead, Luc. Bring her back to me. Please. I need her."

He mumbled something low and Latin, but shook his head. "I cannot."

"You can! I know you can, because you've done it before. Please. Please. Please," I begged, my fingers digging into his forearm.

"I'm sorry. But you will see her again, Hope. This I swear. I can promise you she is happy. She is not alone. It is you who must draw strength to go on."

I sniffled as I looked up into his bottomless black

eyes that assessed my very soul with a glance. "She's in Hell?"

Luc inclined his head. "They probably weren't being the most virtuous of people these last few weeks. Romanus and Rouen, and Nazir, were already in my purview. They are all fine. Ace is setting them up a beer pong table in my grand dining hall, of all places." His normal scary mask slipped back into place. "Estrella is sad, but it is because she knows how you will have taken her death. You must pull yourself from the abyss, and live for the both of you now. That would make her after-life truly happy."

I nodded, and then Luc was standing. He helped me to my feet. I didn't bother brushing the mud from my knees.

I wrapped my arms around his waist, and hugged the Devil close to me. He loved me. He loved Rella too, this supposedly Fallen Angel, who was storied to have no capacity for love, but had proven the stories wrong over and over. Unlike my parents, he had never aged. But he was ageless.

"Thank you, Luc."

He let out a scary rumbling noise. "Do not thank me. I failed you both. You are the beloved children of my consort. And I let one of you die." The last part came out in a scary, inhuman voice that made the temperature around us drop. The hairs on my body rose.

I dropped my arms, but I didn't step away. "That's the thing about us pesky humans. We never do quite what you expect." I looked up, meeting his eyes again. A bold move, even for me. "I want them all to pay. Every single person who had anything to do with Rella's death. I want them to regret ever being born."

Luc groaned. "Please. Not another plot for vengeance where you go in with guns blazing. The last one did not end so well," he gently reminded me.

He didn't have to tell me though. I wasn't Estrella. But I was no longer the Hope of last week either. I wasn't the Hope who could rely on the love and protection of her twin any longer. Something was now a little broken.

I shook my head.

I wasn't Estrella. I couldn't shoot, or kick ass.

But I was going to raze their world to the ground. For Rella.

And for me.

PART II

CHAPTER FIFTEEN

"Where is she?"

I felt more than heard Memphis' booming voice over the top of the pounding music in the club. Everyone turned, though I doubt they knew why. His voice was a compulsion, and if they knew which 'she' he was talking about, I had no doubt they would have served me up to him like a sacrificial virgin. Well, it was probably a little late for the virgin thing, but I could definitely be a sacrifice.

I didn't care. I tipped the shot glass in my left hand into my mouth, and then chased it with the shot glass in my right. The tequila was coursing through my veins like an anaesthetic, numbing the feelings. Well mine, not everyone else's. But in a huge group like this, the pulses of emotions became just another muffled element to the atmosphere.

I swung my hips, letting my long, loose curls swirl around my bare shoulders. A guy, well a boy — how did he get in here without being carded? — danced up beside me, and I gave him a fragile smile. I let him dance beside me, until his hips were moving with me and he was trying to be an extra from Dirty Dancing. I rolled my eyes, but I was too drunk to care. I put my hands in the air and pretended he didn't exist. Pretended no one existed. Pretended I didn't even exist.

I felt a hand on my hip. "Get lost kid, otherwise your night is going to get real bad, real fast." I looked up, and the group of people standing in front of me shocked me despite my drunken haze. Blue Mulligan was standing there, his body unmoving amongst the sea of writhing partygoers. He was flanked by Gus and Memphis. They were an odd trio.

Blue held out his hand, his fist curled around something in his palm. He opened it up, and inside sat the gold queen from his chess set.

I stopped moving, ignoring the people jostling me. I reached out and took the queen, my fingers brushing his palm. Tears leaked down my cheeks.

"I want to go now."

Blue nodded, and Memphis plowed through the crowd. Everyone moved or they were moved bodily. Some brave people reached out to brush their fingers on the Fallen Angels as they passed. They might look human, but your hindbrain knew they were more.

We emerged through the club's fire doors, and the security guard opened his mouth to protest, but one look at my escorts and his mouth snapped shut. Clever move, I could feel the simmering rage escaping through Memphis' emotional shield. He must be really pissed.

We slid into a Range Rover. "Who's car?"

No one answered my question. "Why is Blue here?"

Gusion turned, and even he looked a little mad. "We couldn't find you. We can't track you. You are the only fucking human on the planet we can't find, and you are the only human on the planet I even give two shits about." He sucked in a deep, calming breath. "Memphis thought your friend here might have better luck tracking a wayward heiress than us. He talked to some contacts, tracked you down." I could tell the admission that a human could find me easier than he or Memphis burned a little.

Normally, they could have asked Rella. Rella always knows where I am. Knew. Now I was completely untethered from the world.

"You came back?" I asked Blue, my thumb stroking the golden chess piece in my hand.

Blue nodded. He didn't say he was sorry for my loss, or sorry for storming out. But he looked at me, his crystalline blue eyes unblinking. He reached out a hand, and I placed mine in his. He knew this was how I could feel his emotions, read his thoughts.

I was scared. Confused. I'm sorry… for everything. I felt everything in that touch. His sadness, his fear, his sympathy. His desire. He could tell me things in the silence that he could never say out loud. I squeezed his hand hard and let go. I unbelted my seatbelt, and moved across the bench seat in the back of the car.

He tilted his head, a little line of confusion knitting his brow. The back of the car spun, the last two shots of tequila hitting me hard. I shifted until I was so close to

Blue that I could feel his breath on my cheek. I moved quickly, if not elegantly, straddling his lap.

"What the hell is she doing?" Gusion asked, but he sounded muffled. Memphis let out an inhuman noise.

I ignored them both. I leaned forward and kissed Blue, kissed him with all the force of my feelings, hoping I could pour them from my lips into him. He sat perfectly still, not moving, not kissing me back, but I could feel the flare of his desire.

"Kiss me back, damn you," I raged.

"I like my dick attached to my body, Princess. Your friends wouldn't be so happy if I put any appendage of mine anywhere near you when you're this wasted."

"Watch your mouth," Gusion, my normally good-natured friend, snarled out.

Blue just quirked a brow. I laughed, and then I sobbed. I put my face into Blue's neck, and let my tears run down his skin. His hands ran up and down my back. He didn't try to soothe me with his words. He just let me cry my tequila tears as we sped through the streets of Manhattan.

"When does it stop hurting?" I whispered against his throat.

"Never, Princess. We just learn to smile through the pain."

I WOKE up with a mouth so dry, it felt like it was filled with sand. As I moved to the left, the room spun and pain speared my brain.

"Argh."

A soft chuckle came from beside me. I opened my left eye, and saw Gusion's laughing face.

"Sore head today, Sweetheart?"

I slapped a hand over his mouth. "Unnghh. Need. Water," I whispered.

He shook his head. "I'm mad at you. You can get it yourself."

I tried to sit, but the thudding and nauseating spinning increased seven-fold. I moaned and laid back on the bed. I would rather die of dehydration.

Gusion tutted me, and rose. It was then I realized he was in nothing but tight boxer briefs. I lifted the blankets and breathed a sigh to see I was still in last night's dress.

I watched his ass as he walked into my ensuite, filling a glass I kept on my nightstand with water from my sink.

Someone should write an ode to his ass, because it was amazing. He switched the light on, and I winced as someone stabbed me in the brain again.

"Why are you almost naked in my bed?" I asked. Last night was a bit of a haze after the fifth tequila shot, but I did vaguely remember being in the car. And maybe Blue?

"You passed out on Blue Mulligan's lap, and then vomited on me in the elevator."

I sucked in a horrified gasp. "I didn't?"

"Yep. Then I drew the short straw and got to sit in here and watch you sleep so you didn't choke on your own puke like some kind of eighties Rockstar."

I covered my face with my hands, all the blood in my body rushing to my face.

"I'm so sorry," I groaned. Gusion knelt by the bed

and pried my fingers from my eyes. He lifted me up a little, strong hands supporting my back, and gave me a sip of water.

"You have to stop, Hope. Everyone is worried. Your folks are beside themselves. You're giving Memphis a stomach ulcer. You can't party away the pain. It's still there the next day, but you've also got a massive headache as well. Doing this to yourself won't bring her back."

I closed my eyes against his words. When I was drunk off my ass was the only time I could forget, at least for a little while.

"Estrella would be appalled you were trying to kill yourself one drink at a time, making stupid decisions, putting yourself in dangerous situations. You need to cut it the hell out."

I rolled away from him, giving him my back, and my nauseous stomach rolled as well. "You don't have to be here to watch it. No one asked you to stay."

He grabbed my shoulder and rolled me back to face him. "No one had to ask me to stay, Hope. I stayed because I care about you, and don't want to see you dead in the river because you are being a careless child. It hurts. I know hurt. But this isn't the way to fix it."

I ground my teeth together. "What is the way to fix it? Divide the armies of heaven and incite a war that would have my friends cast into hell for eternity?"

He flinched back at my words, and I did too. What a fucking asshole thing to say. "Gus...I didn't mean that."

He sighed and stood. "Yes, you did. And you are

right. But learn from my mistakes. Don't destroy the lives of everyone around you because you are hurting."

He turned and left, and I felt like a bitch.

I dragged myself out of bed and shuffled to the ensuite. Reaching in, I turned on the water and set it to boiling. Every morning for two weeks I'd done this same routine. My body was feeling its punishment now.

I stood beneath the scolding water and pictured Gus' hurt face. I banged my head against the tiles.

"What have you done, Hope? Who have you become that you put that look on Gusion's face? The same man who has held you in his arms as you cried these last weeks?"

Azriel's angry voice made me jump. I made a little window in the steam, to ensure I wasn't hallucinating.

"Azriel, I'm showering! You can't just walk into a bathroom when a woman is naked!"

He shrugged. "Why not? The steam has hidden your naked form from me. I can merely see an outline of your body. I am the Angel of Death. I have seen the human form in every way. I can assure you, yours is no different." His emotions felt otherwise. They weren't overwhelmingly colored by confusion any more, though there were still hints of it around the edges. No, he felt like desire, and lust and all sorts of carnal needs. I wondered if he knew what the feelings meant. I'd bet the family farm he did. He might be confused by his feelings for me, but he wasn't stupid or a child. He'd recognize what lust was; he had seen it in Gusion before he fell. Witnessed true passion in the form of Luc and Ace.

Azriel narrowed his eyes a little. "Besides, you seem to have little regard for the feelings of others. Perhaps I am just following your example."

I was being chastised by Azriel. My behavior had been so appalling, even the Angel of Death thought I was being a dick. He seemed truly offended on Gusion's behalf.

I remembered what Memphis said about Azriel and the other Fallen being friends once. I wondered if those feelings still existed, even just a little.

"What do you care how I made Gusion feel? He is now a denizen of Hell. It's none of your business," I snapped. I could feel the spike in the Angel's annoyance, his sadness, his confusion. I had no urge to help him figure it out. Well, not today anyway.

"Why are you so..." I saw him wave a hand in an expansive way, "fractious about this? You know that your sister's soul still exists, she still lives in happiness with her consorts. As far as souls go, your sister has, what's that human saying? Hit the Jackpot?"

I sighed. I didn't bother responding, but Azriel wasn't finished.

"Her end was quick and painless, her transition to hell without the ordinary soul confusion. It was a good passing."

My body jolted as if I'd been shocked. What was he saying...?

"Were you there? Did you take my sister's soul to Hell?" I asked carefully.

Azriel's face scrunched in confusion. "Of course."

Of course! I threw the door open on the shower,

uncaring of my nakedness. "You sent my sister's soul to Hell instead of taking her to help, and you are standing in front of me, daring to chastise me? Get the hell out of my apartment!"

It was Azriel's turn to look incredulous. "She was far beyond the human capacity for healing, Hope. Not even Raphael could have healed her. It was time for her soul to move on."

He kept talking, and my rage began to spiral out of control. I threw the shampoo bottle at him through the open shower door. He dodged it easily.

"You should have… I don't know. I don't know! But she didn't need to die." The fight fled as quick as it came, and I resisted the urge to slump on the floor of the shower. I could keep some dignity. Well, as much dignity as I could have standing in front of an angel. Naked.

He tilted his head in that way he had when he was listening for the other Angels. "Here come your bewitched suiters, Witch." He looked me up and down, and his confusion grew. An unfamiliar sensation colored his emotions. Not lust, or desire. I knew those colors intimately now. Something different. The mood in the room shifted, the heated anger in my chest dissolving and spreading its way further, uh, south.

Reaching forward, he ran a finger down my collarbone, chasing a droplet of water. I held my breath as his touch jolted through my body like a lightning bolt. He was mere inches from my nipple, and I forgot how to take a breath. A tiny part of me wanted him, a part that ignored the logistics, and the fact that I should loathe him right now, because he took my sister's soul to Hell. If I thought about it really hard, at one point he'd even put a dagger through my mother's heart. But despite all that, there was a tiny part of me that wanted him to climb into the shower with me and explore every inch of my body like I was the universe's greatest mystery. With his tongue.

"Your body looks much healed from the last time I viewed it," he said matter-of-factly.

"Would you like to join me?" I wasn't sure what I was offering. A shower? A lifetime? But it felt right.

Azriel stared hard at my face, and I couldn't breathe. So much indecision, so much turmoil.

"Yes." With that, he disappeared.

Memphis and Gusion burst into the room, looking for the threat.

"We heard yelling," Memphis asked, searching for bogeymen in the shadows of my bathroom.

Blue strolled in behind them. He eyed me still standing naked, and handed me my fluffy white towel, his face impassive. Our fingers touched as I grabbed the towel, and caught the flash of desire, and the memory of our kiss. Oh shit, I kissed Blue.

It came back to me in a whoosh from the night before. My cheeks turned bright red.

What a hot mess my life had become. I wrapped the towel around my body.

"It was Azriel. He'd come to reprimand me for my appalling behavior." If I wasn't so embarrassed, I would have smiled at the comical looks of shock on the faces of my Fallen Angels. I looked between them. Yeah, my

Fallen Angels. We were friends, maybe more, and that made them mine. Blue looked confused, as he searched the room for possible points of entry. I wasn't going to clarify. I'd let him puzzle that one out himself.

I took a deep breath. Azriel was right. Enough was enough now. But I had some serious apologizing to do first. "Okay. Look. I'm sorry I've been such an epic pain in the ass the last two weeks. I'm going to try to be better now, it's just..." I shrugged.

Memphis nodded. "We know."

I looked at Gusion. His face was still stony. I walked over to him, and wrapped my arms around his waist. He let out a deep sigh and wrapped his arms around my shoulders.

"I'm so sorry for what I said. That was cruel of me. There's no excuse for cruelty," I murmured against his chest.

"I understand, Sweetheart. You weren't wrong."

I had been wrong. But I meant what I said; I was going to be better.

And that meant finishing what Rella started.

I turned from Gusion's arms and faced all the guys in the room.

"What do we know about Rella's killers?"

CHAPTER SIXTEEN

Blue was on the phone, standing still in my kitchen, the only indication he wasn't a robot was the odd grunted affirmation. Normal people, well as normal as people in my life got, paced when they talked. Gesticulated. Nodded.

Not Blue. He stood so still, sometimes my eyes passed right over him. His finger stabbed at the end button on his phone.

"The Family sent their second-best enforcer to France. Lux is with them."

My heart broke for Lux. Of all my Dads, he would be feeling the guilt of Estrella's death the most. He took his role of protector very seriously, and he'd loved Rella with all his heart. She was his little warrioress. I still remembered watching them spar with swords as a child, her speed inhumanly quick back then. She was no match for Lux, but she held her own for a five-year-old. I'd been happy to watch, relishing in their joy. I didn't need to learn to fight. I had Rella.

"What did they find?"

"Charlie wasn't stupid. He checked in with the Uncles regularly, kept them informed of any updates. A safeguard in case anything happened." Sadness bled from him then, and I remembered that he and Charlie were cousins. Sure, Blue Halloran was the illegitimate son of one of the Mulligan daughters, but he was still a Mulligan.

"Were you and Charlie friends?"

He shook his head. "Not really. But he was...good. He didn't treat me like some mutt. We talked at gatherings. He didn't want the life." The life of a mobster, a Mulligan criminal. Like Blue.

Tears welled up in my eyes at thoughts of Charlie. My mind had to admit that Rella was gone, because I felt it deep down in our soul. But I couldn't comprehend the fact that Charlie was gone too. Rella, Charlie and I had been inseparable growing up. Best friends. Along with Adnan, we'd been united outcasts. But Charlie was gone now too. I lost a sister and a best friend and I wasn't sure my heart could cope.

Blue cleared his throat, his eyes assessing me, as if he was the one who could read emotions. I gave him a crooked smile, and motioned for him to continue. I could finish mourning in the relative privacy of my bedroom.

"The whole thing is something out of a B-grade action movie. Secret organizations. Corrupt politicians. I don't know exactly what is going on, but they said it's big. As for the person who pulled the trigger, they've found him. Some arms dealer who was a source for

Nazir. They tracked him on traffic cameras on the roads outside the camp. They've got him in their net, he just doesn't know it yet. He's gone to ground, but he can't hide forever."

Gusion leaned closer. "There's no hiding from the Devil himself."

Blue nodded, but I remembered that Blue had never met Luc. I guess he thought Gus was being metaphorical. Or maybe that he meant Lux. I loved Lux, and he was a scary badass when he wanted to be, but Luc made him look like a kitten.

"Right. I have my own sources, and I heard that the threat to you had a name," Blue said into the tense silence. The eyes of the angels suddenly snapped to my face. In all the drama, I'd forgotten to tell them that Rella had given me a name.

"Maximoff Richards."

His name seemed to bounce off the walls, ricocheting back at me like a stray bullet.

Blue nodded. "I've been watching him."

My eyebrows rose high. "That's where you've been?"

He shrugged. "Among other places." I was pretty sure that was the best explanation I was going to get from the cagey hitman today.

Memphis huffed out an impatient sound. "Get on with it, Human."

Blue turned to the other two men in the room, his head tilted as if he was trying to take their measure. I needed to tell him that they were angels, but I was scared he'd run again. Why Blue leaving mattered to me was something I didn't want to examine too closely right now.

It would help if the guys would stop referring to everyone not angelic as 'humans'. They were too used to Adnan.

Fuck it. We had to get it over and done with, like ripping off a Band-Aid. I wanted him here, and I wanted to trust him.

I looked between Gusion and Mephistopheles. Yeah, maybe I'd ease him into it with Gus.

Gusion, the intuitive bastard that he was, was watching my thoughts play out on my face. He quirked a brow, and I gave a nod.

"Blue. Don't freak out, but there's one more thing you should know." I waved a hand to Gus, who dropped his glamor. Wide white wings that looked as if they'd been dipped in gold dust spread out behind his back, the tips catching the light and making the glow. My breath caught in my throat, the way it did every single time he stood before me in all his glory, and he grinned at the look on my face. Cocky bastard.

"Gusion and Memphis are angels. Well, Fallen Angels. Princes of Hell."

"I hate that title," Memphis growled out, but stood, letting his own wings out. They sucked the light from the room, and I realized I'd never seen them both with their wings out together. Again, I thought about what it would be like to have the light and the dark caressing my body at once. Memphis' midnight blue eyes drank me in as if he could read my mind, Blue completely forgotten.

Shit, Blue.

I tore my gaze from the angels to look at Blue. I was prepared for a freak-out. I mean, he'd lost his shit at the idea that I could sense his emotions. Two denizens of Hell should have him running for the hills.

But he looked perfectly blank. His emotional cap was firmly in place, though I could feel the muted sensations of awe mixed in with his usual pain and rage.

He nodded. "Okay, anyway Maximoff-"

I held up a hand. "Hold up. What the hell? I tell you I can catch a few of your emotions and you turn into a hysterical housewife, but faced with two angels you're all blasé? Are you serious right now?"

Blue's pale eyes grew wide. "I did not turn into a hysterical housewife."

At any other time, I would have found his indignation funny. But right now, I was oscillating between amazed and annoyed.

He rolled his eyes, totally contradicting his hysterical housewife denials. "The angels are basically Mulligan family lore now. I've seen your Ace at Family gatherings when I was running security. You only have to take one look at her to know she is something more, something beautiful and scary and terrifying and not of this world. And her boyfriend..." The hair on his arms stood on end. "He is the scariest thing I have ever seen, and I don't mind admitting it.

"Luc." I nodded. "As in Lucifer. As in the Devil." The color drained from Blue's face, but he sucked a deep breath through his nose and nodded again.

He motioned to the two angels in front of us. "The wings are new, but they had the same feel about them.

Like they're predators and we are all as helpless as lambs."

"Smart human," Memphis growled. "Now continue."

Blue's jaw tightened at the perceived order, but he wisely picked his battles. "As I was saying, Maximoff Richards is a giant piece of shit. As a human, he has no redeeming features. Beats his wife, his kids, his dog. Harasses his secretary. Intimidates his underlings."

"Orders hits on his competitors," Gusion added quietly.

Blue nodded solemnly. "Yes." His eyes found mine, and their magnetic hold was soothing. "He is the worst kind of wealthy. Richer than god and entitled as hell. Believes he's untouchable."

"No one is untouchable," Memphis grumbled, and I wanted to walk over and crawl into his lap as the rage slipped through his shields again.

"Agreed," Blue seconded. "He's a challenge though. His personal bodyguard is as twitchy as he is deadly. He'd shoot his own granny if he thought he was a threat to Richards. He's rabid. Luckily, I'm better."

"You're unnecessary when we can just sift around on a thought, Mulligan."

"I'm not a Mulligan." As they argued the logistics of killing someone, I was surprised that I felt nothing. Mostly because the men around me were so fucked up that they'd buried their feelings deep in their psyches, but even my emotions seemed to be absent. Shouldn't I feel something, considering they were talking about killing a man, someone's husband and father?

But I didn't. I felt a well of cold nothingness for Maximoff Richards. He was going to die, and I wouldn't feel a moment of regret.

If it wasn't for the waves of lust that seemed to be rocking my body lately, I'd be worried that I'd lost my ability to feel. Could you be a sociopathic empath?

A knock at the door startled us all. The Angel's whipped their heads around in eerie unison. Blue pulled a gun from a holster at his back. I hated that gun. I hated everything that gun represented, but now was not the time to protest about weapons in my apartment. The Angels bracketed me between them, a huge wall of feather and muscles, determined to keep me safe.

Blue opened the door, slowly. Then he dropped his gun. The sound of the metal clattering to the floor sounded like a death knell. The Angels crushed me between them, and Gusion's body tensed to spirit me away.

Then Blue turned back to me, his face so pale he seemed almost sepia toned.

"It's for you. It's your sister."

Rella's head peeked around his shoulder. "Hey Sis."

The blood drained from my face and my heart leapt into my throat, suffocating me. Estrella.

Black spots danced in my vision, and I sucked in air. But it wasn't enough. I fell into the darkness of Memphis' back, and let the world go as dark as his wings.

CHAPTER SEVENTEEN

I woke to the smiling face of my twin. She was looking down at me, a bright smile on her face, though I could see the creases of worry around her eyes.

"You're dead."

Rella rolled her eyes. "Come on, Hope. You can be less cliché than that."

I sat up, fury coursing through my blood. "Cliché? I watched them lower your fucking coffin into the ground, Estrella Jones. You do not get to taunt me because I don't have something witty to say when you suddenly reappear at my door like you went to the freaking store and not Hell!"

Rella looked pained. I was so relieved she was here, the fire in my blood extinguished quickly. I wrapped my arms around her.

Well, I tried. They went right through her. I was hugging air. "What the…"

Rella grimaced. "It'll take me a little longer to have

the strength to be corporeal. I worked hard just to be able to travel up here. But I had to come. I had to see you. I knew you'd be hurting."

"Hurting?" I stood then, stepping around her although I could have stepped right through her. I noticed her two Gargoyles loitering right behind her. Beyond them, whispering quietly to Gusion and Memphis, was Ace. I whipped back around to face my twin. "Hurting! You tore my fucking heart in two. I wanted to die too," I yelled. I was flip-flopping between relieved and anguished, and I couldn't deal. I couldn't breathe. I choked off a sob, and realized angry tears were rolling down my cheeks. Rella lifted her hand to stroke my face, but paused. Because she couldn't soothe my hurts anymore.

Two arms curved around my shoulders, turning me into strong arms and a broad chest. For the second time in twenty-four hours, I cried on to Blue Halloran's shoulders, but this time I did it through gritted teeth. I didn't want to be weak anymore.

Filling my lungs, I straightened. I brushed the tears from Blue's shoulder, but he stepped away. "Leave it," he said, but his voice was gentle.

When I looked up, Ace was looking disapprovingly at me. She always reminded me of a goddess. A blood-thirsty, battle hungry goddess, but something completely not of this world. A fitting consort for the Devil. And I loved her.

Ace ran a hand down my hair, cupping my chin and stroking a thumb across my cheek. "I know you're in pain. But don't be a bitch. She's the one that's dead, so cut her some slack, okay?" She leaned forward and kissed my cheek. "I have to go. Some of us haven't abandoned all their responsibilities for a pretty face." Her tone was disapproving, but she was smiling at the other two angels in the room. She looked over at Rella. "One of these guys will take you back."

And then she was gone.

I looked back at Estrella. "Sorry. I didn't mean..." It was a lie. I did mean it.

She smiled, but it was a sad, desolate expression. "Yes, you did. But it's okay. I deserved it." One of her Gargoyles stepped forward, placing a gentle hand on her back. It didn't slip through her body like my arms had. Seeing where I was staring, Gus stepped forward.

"They are soulmates, pack mates. Their connection anchors her to them."

An odd stab of jealousy poked holes in my heart, but I just nodded. Then I noticed it was only the Gargoyles here with her. "Where's Charlie? Naz?"

Sadness wafted from the group, the sadness of the Gargoyles. I didn't pick up anything from Rella. My heart stuttered. "They're okay, right? I mean, they're dead, but they are with you?"

Romanus spoke. "They don't have the strength to move to this plane of existence. It can take centuries to move between the veil of life and death. Estrella's angelic heritage helped her break through more quickly than a normal soul. Nazir and Charlie will take another century, at least."

They were really dead to me. By the time they were able to cross the veil, I would be an old woman, dead in the ground. Everyone they'd ever known and loved would be dead and turned to ash.

Grief hit me all over again, and I cursed. They were no less dead than yesterday, but seeing Rella at my door had made me hope that maybe the end wasn't the end.

I stood in the center of my living room, surrounded by people but I was more alone than ever. As if he had a direct line to my dark thoughts, Memphis stepped forward, and pulled me back against his body, anchoring me. I looked up at his brilliant blue eyes and gave him a crooked smile. Words weren't necessary.

Estrella looked between us, her eyebrows raised in an expression so familiar I wanted to cry.

I wanted her to ask her questions in my mind, through our connection, but it was burned away. Instead, she waved a finger between my face and Memphis.

"When did this happen?" She looked at him suspiciously. "If you took advantage of her hurt..." She didn't finish, but the threat was there.

Memphis looked pained. "No. We have been here making sure she doesn't do anything she will later regret, due to the emotional toll of your death." The undertone of disapproval was there.

Rouen stepped forward. "You better watch your mouth, Mephistopheles." The big, golden Gargoyle knocked the dining chair over, proving he was fully corporeal and unimpressed by the judgement in Memphis' tone.

"You did not see her. You weren't here to see the

results of your bloodthirsty crusade," Gusion said, coming to stand shoulder to shoulder with Memphis.

Romanus let out a rumbling growl. "She was protecting Hope. Protecting the vulnerable. Shouldn't you respect that, Angel?" He said the last word like it was a curse word.

Blue stepped forward, the fragile human in between the collective might of the immortals. Right in that moment, he seemed like the bravest person in the room.

"As much as I'd like to know who wins in a fight between Fallen Angels and," he looked at Romanus and Rouen, "whatever the fuck you two are, it's neither productive to our mission or Hope's health. So fucking shut it."

Rella stared at Blue. Then she bent over and laughed, the loud, guffawing laugh that I knew as well as my own. Fuck, I missed that sound. I never thought I'd hear it again. For a moment, I just basked in the noise, and then my lip curled. I didn't know what she found so funny, but the sound of her laughter was like a balm to the broken parts of my soul.

She sucked in some air, even though I guess she technically didn't need to breathe. "The irony. Blue Halloran, the Mulligan Family's pet enforcer-slash-hitman, breaking up a fight between demons from hell." She started giggling again. "What even is my life right now?"

Memphis raised a brow as he looked down at her. "Are you quite done?"

She nodded, though she was still chuckling. She

waved us toward the living room, and that when I noticed we hadn't gotten too far past the front foyer.

I turned and walked toward my couch, trying not to remember the last time Rella was here with me. And Charlie.

I sunk down into the cushion, and tried not to think about why Rella didn't sit beside me. "Do you know, about everything? Tenebrae. Uriel?" She looked at Gusion, and he shook his head a little. Rella frowned. "She needs to know."

He stepped forward and sat beside me, cuddling me into the side of his body. I knew they weren't keeping it from me; they'd talked about it often enough in front of me that I knew they weren't trying to hide it. "I agree. But Lucifer insists on secrecy. You understand what this would mean if word got out."

Rella's eyes narrowed. "She deserves to know."

Gus nodded. "Agreed, but we cannot tell her. Or him," he lifted his chin toward Blue. "Gag order, you know. And while I usually enjoy a good ball-gag, Luc does not play."

"Who would be wearing the ball-gag? You or Luc?" I teased.

Gus leaned forward, until his lips brushed the shell of my ear as he spoke. "You, Sweet Hope. I'd love to hear your muffled screams of pleasure around the gag between those pretty lips," he purred.

Holy hell. My pussy clenched at his words, and the visual. Would I even like that? Heat pooled in my abdomen. Yes, yes I would.

My cheeks were probably on fire, but I ignored it.

Now Rella's eyebrows were basically at her hairline. "Him too? Next you'll be telling me you want to bang Blue-Goddamn-Halloran next."

My eyes shot to Blue's face. He was looking at me with that unflinching gaze. There was no embarrassment on his face, nothing but that intense, clear eyed stare that saw into my soul.

So I shrugged. Maybe.

Blue's lip twitched. "It's Robert, actually."

Now, Rella was staring at Blue. Actually, everyone was. "What?" Rella asked a little dumbly.

"My middle name isn't Goddamn. It's Robert. Irving Robert Halloran."

I blinked. And blinked again. Just when I thought the ghost of my dead sister was going to be the weirdest part of today. I cleared my throat. "Would you like me to call you, uh, Irving?"

Blue, uh Irving, visibly shuddered. "No."

Rella was subtly shaking her head, just slow blinking at the hitman. Then she turned back to me.

"I know a little. Why don't you tell me?" I prompted.

By the time she was finished, I wished I hadn't asked.

CHAPTER EIGHTEEN

I stared at the ceiling, contemplating the depth of the information Rella had just pushed on me. Rella.

By the end, she'd begun to fade in and out as she spoke, her energy waning after being away from Hell for so long. Fear gripped me every time it happened, as if I was going to lose her all over again. Eventually, Memphis made her leave, transporting the ghost of my twin and her Gargoyle pack mates back to Hell. There's a sentence I didn't think would ever cross my mind.

Her words echoed around my head. A society so wide-reaching and evil, that it was global. I corrected myself; not evil. It was started and run by a freaking Archangel. Uriel was the reason my sister was dead. He might not have pulled the trigger on the gun that stopped her heart forever, but I had no doubt that he felt some glee at the news. Even I knew that Uriel and Lucifer didn't get along.

I wasn't Rella. I couldn't take on an entire corrupt

organization of thousands of extremely powerful people. I didn't even know where to start. I was a broken doll in her Princess Dream House.

Could you kill an Archangel, anyway?

I wondered how many people at that last conference in Geneva, where I stood on stage and talked about the need for the rich to aid the poor, how many of those people were Tenebrae? If Rella's information was right, dozens of them were benefiting off the suffering of the very people I was trying to help. How many knew I was to be kidnapped, possibly tortured and killed. Maybe even sent off to a fate worse than death.

The idea made my blood boil. Gusion opened the door to my ensuite, and stepped into the darkness of my room, the light of the bathroom and the clouds of steam haloing him like an angel. His white wings hung down his back, heart wrenching in their perfection. His torso was bare, and a pair of shorts hung low on his hips. His body was completely smooth. His perfection left me breathless.

"You have to stop looking at me like that, Sweetheart. I fell for a reason. I have poor impulse control," he joked as he prowled toward me. His long golden hair was loose around his shoulders. I never thought I'd like long hair, but I'd be damned if I didn't want to tangle it around my fingers.

I thought about the attraction that had been simmering between us for weeks. Maybe I had poor impulse control too. "I like looking at you," I said, barely recognizing the husky quality of my voice.

He stood beside the bed now, staring down at me.

"Do you want to play?" he teased, but there was an edge to his voice and it promised pleasure that could change a person. Did I want to play?

Hell yes.

I nodded. Gus' answering grin was like a two-by-four to the head. I saw stars.

"Your hitman is about to get out of the shower, so you will need to be quiet." He leaned in close. "Can you hold back all those pretty noises? Or do you want him to hear?" he taunted, his finger running down over my collarbone, until it ran into the barrier of my camisole. I sucked in a breath, and when he knelt on the bed, straddling me between his arms and his thighs, I sucked in a ragged breath. He slipped his hand up my shirt, scraping his nails along my flesh, leaving shivering skin in its wake. He brushed his fingertips on the underside of my breast, making my nipple pebble.

"Are you emotionally attached to this piece of intimate-wear?"

I blinked as his words tried to penetrate my foggy brain. He shrugged. "I will buy you a new one, I promise."

With that, he took the delicate silk of my camisole and tore it in half. Angel strength. Or maybe it was horny guy strength, I don't know, but it shredded in his hands like tissue paper. And then his golden eyes were staring hungrily down at my breasts. Leaning forward, he swirled his tongue around one aching peak. My body bowed toward him, begging for more. He chuckled, and blew a cool stream of air across the dampened skin. My nipples hardened painfully tight.

"Look how prettily they ache for my touch," he murmured, more to himself than to me. "I could taste them all day, just to watch you writhe under me like this." He swapped breasts, giving the opposite nipple the same treatment, but this time he sucked the aching flesh into his mouth.

I moaned long and loud. Oh god.

He pulled back, the nipple passing from his lips with a pop. "Remember, quiet, Sweetheart. Or would you like me to find a gag to put in that mouth? I think I'd like to hear you screaming my name around it."

I gave into the urge and wrapped my fingers in his hair, pulling his mouth back toward my aching breasts. He chuckled, and leaned down to nip my nipple. I gasped in air.

He shook my hands from his hair. "Uh-uh. You aren't in control right now, Hope. Give it up to me, and I promise to make you feel really good." He looked at my padded velvet headboard.

"If only I had some cuffs, or rope, so I could keep this delectable body just where I want it," he said too loud and then winked at me.

I was confused by the gesture, until Memphis stepped from the shadows of my room. "Perhaps I could be of assistance?" The cool rumble of his voice made a shiver run across my body. Heat radiated from my core. Gus chuckled, as his hand slid between our bodies, cupping my pussy.

"I think she would very much like that, Mephistopheles. But we should ask, anyway. Consent is what separates us from the animals, no?" He stared down at me, all mirth gone from his face. "Would you like Memphis to join us?" He leaned forward, and kissed me softly on the lips. He tasted of heaven. "Give me control for tonight, Sweetheart, but the choice is always yours. You say yes or no. You say stop, we stop."

Memphis was looking down at me, his blue eyes dancing like the hot center of a flame. "Yes."

Gusion's answering grin promised pleasure, but it held a hint of mischievousness too.

"Okay, remember the rules. Quiet, so our prudish human housemate doesn't hear, or perhaps Memphis has something you can put in your mouth to muffle the sound?" He waggled his eyebrows. "I'm the boss, tonight, Hope. You do as I ask the first time, or there will be consequences. But I promise you nothing but pleasure."

He nodded his head at Memphis, who stripped off his clothes slowly. Inch after inch of smooth, onyx flesh was revealed and I forgot how to breathe. I remembered the taste of his skin and the feel of the cock. He stood there, completely naked, as I tried to memorize every curve and angle. Then he climbed on the bed and rested his back against the headboard. Tugging at my arms, he lifted me as if I weighed nothing until I sat between his thighs. He was already hard, pressed against my back.

Gusion stood at the end of the bed, his hooded gaze taking us in. "No. That won't do at all. Lay down, Mephistopheles." I was pressed right along Memphis' body now, my head against his chest, his dick pressed between the cheeks of my ass. Well, I would be if my silk PJ shorties were still on. "Now that is a fucking symphony," Gus moaned, wrapping his hand around his dick. I wasn't sure when he lost his shorts, but I couldn't drag my eyes away from his hand stroking his long cock.

"Arms up, Sweetheart. Memphis is going to hold you nice and still for me." He crawled up the bed until he was poised between my thighs. I lifted my arms, wrapping my hands behind Memphis' neck. I felt one of Memphis' huge hands grip my wrists, holding them gently captive against his skin. The dark curtain of his hair was like silk against my fingers, and I curled my fingers through it. A small contented sound echoed through his chest. His other hand came down to grip my hip, his fingers spread wide, anchoring my lower body to his.

Gus reached out and peeled my silk shorts and panties from my body, leaving me deliciously bared to them.

Gus' gaze feasted on me like a starving man, and I squirmed beneath the heated look. Unfortunately, or fortunately, the movement rubbed my bare ass on Memphis' cock. His fingers pressed into the soft skin of my hip and he moaned.

The look of pure glee on Gus' face told me that he was working us both. He was in control of us both, and he loved every second of it.

"You better keep it down, old friend, or I might gag you too," he laughed, and Memphis gave him the finger.

Gusion knelt in front of us, the smile permanently etched on his face as his eyes blazed. He ran a golden hand up my thigh, nudging it wider, and my other leg followed suit. He leaned forward, putting my thighs over his shoulder and his hands either side of Memphis' hips. He pressed forward, bending my legs up and pressing my ass tight against Memphis and then ran his tongue in one long lap up my slit.

"Fuck," Memphis breathed against my hair.

Ditto. But I kept as silent as I could, as Gus lapped at my pussy again, circling my clit. I writhed again, as pleasure shot to the swollen nub and Gus' tongue electrified my body. Stroke after stroke brought me higher and higher, his clever tongue knowing the right pressure, the right pace, the right everything to make me want to scream his name. But I kept my lips stubbornly closed as he pressed his tongue inside my core.

"Oh my…" I whispered as he swirled his tongue one more time. My fingers gripped Memphis' hair painfully tightly as wave after wave of pleasure rocked my body, and I came all over Gus' face.

Gus pressed up, watching me cum, his tongue swirling around my clit, prolonging my orgasm.

I panted but I didn't make a sound.

Gus made a happy noise. "Well done, Sweetheart. You deserve a reward for doing as you were told." Gus' smile was a reward all of its own. He moved further up my body, until we were face to face. I was pressed between their hard chests, like the meat in an unholy sandwich. I was fairly sure this was actually heaven right now, trapped between the Princes of Hell.

"Ready for your reward, Sweetheart?" I arched toward him, wanting to make him hurry. My hands were still trapped behind Memphis' neck. He slid the hard length of his cock inside me, and I forgot not to moan. Holy fuck. He was big, but perfectly big. I shouldn't be surprised; he was like a wet dream, from head to toe.

He palmed one of my thighs, and thrust himself home, that delicious burn making me scream. Luckily, the sound was muffled as Memphis' hand moved from my hip to my mouth. Gus withdrew, then slammed inside me again, pounding me into Memphis. A disembodied part of me wondered how that could be comfortable for him back there, but then Gusion was moving again, a slowed control pace pushing me up and down Memphis' body.

I felt Memphis' hands on my wrists tighten, as he let out a long low moan.

"I thought you had more control," Gus teased, his pace never faltering.

Memphis threw his head back harder against the pillow. "You are the one with the control issues," he said, his voice low and husky.

Gus just smiled and inclined his head, increasing his pace, his eyes focused on my face. I wished I had a mirror on the ceiling, just so I could see for a moment how we looked. My dark prince, my golden angel and me, with my pale Irish skin and my cheeks flushed. Did they feel this too, this overwhelming feeling of rightness?

"I want to feel…" I gasped out.

Gusion pushed deeper into me. "You don't feel me, Sweetheart? How about now?" He rolled his hips while he was deep inside me, and I swear, my eyes rolled back in my head. One of Memphis' fingers slid between my lips, and I sucked it into my mouth.

"Jesus-fucking-Christ," Memphis groaned, now rolling his hips softly in time with Gus'

Gus' low chuckle made me wetter. I didn't think it was possible to be wetter, but damned if I didn't feel my juices running from me and onto Memphis, making as both slippery. I was so damn close.

"That's a bit blasphemous, Brother," he teased, his body stilling above mine. I let out a protesting cry around Memphis' finger.

"Fuck blasphemy and move you asshole," Memphis growled, his hips pushing us both upwards, until my pussy was grinding against Gus. "She wants to feel your damn emotions. Let down your shields. I want to feel her come apart."

I felt Memphis first. It was a shockwave of lust, and I moaned deep. I didn't doubt he was enjoying it now, his awareness of every curve of my body on his. He wanted to taste every inch of my skin.

Gus hesitated, indecision in his eyes. He remembered last time. I gave him a reassuring look.

He dropped them, and another wave of lust hit me. But it was more. The sadness was still there, but it was overlaid with power, contentment. Happiness. He was truly happy here, buried inside me, bantering with his oldest friend.

He leaned down and kissed me hard. It was a branding kiss. This was going to change something. "Ready, Hope?"

"Mmpphh" I said against Memphis' palm as it recovered my mouth. The owner of the hand peeled it back.

"Yes. A thousand times yes. Now move, *please*," I begged, squirming as much as possible, pushing him to just get me there. I was so damn close I could reach out and touch it. That is if Memphis didn't have my wrists trapped in his fist.

Gus let go. He let go of his control and just moved. His hips thrusting in time with Memphis, so I was pressed back again and again into his unforgivingly hard body. I loved it. Their emotions crashed into me like their own kind of foreplay, and feeling their pleasure made me so hot I was sure I was going to turn into an inferno.

Suddenly my wrists were free, and Memphis was moving his hand down my side, slipping in between my soft flesh and Gus' punishing hips. His fingers found my clit like it was magnetized, and the smallest pressure made me fly apart. My hands clutched at Gus' shoulders beneath wide spread of his wings, as my orgasm surged through my body. My pussy clenched tight around his cock, and I felt the echoing burst of pleasure. He continued to rock into me; short, sharp thrusts that milked my orgasm for all its worth, giving my first ever multiple orgasm.

As my orgasm wrung me out, I felt hot bursts of Memphis' cum shoot up my back. A smile twisted Gus' lips, as if he'd been waiting for Memphis to reach his peak. He dropped his head to my shoulder, and pounded into me, his thrusts finally wild and out of control. I was making crazed noises as each thrust sent an exquisite combination of pleasure and pain through my body. With a final roar that I was sure Blue must have heard, he came hard, his lips taking mine in a punishing kiss that was a clash of teeth and tongue.

Rolling off to the side, Gus laid on his wings, his chest heaving as he tried to draw breath. I knew the feeling. I was boneless, still pressed against Memphis. I looked up, feeling the burning gaze of those blue eyes. I gave him a small, contented smile. He smiled widely in return, and lit up my heart like the Fourth of July. He slid me off his body, and he was over me in a second, bracketing me beneath the canopy of his dark wings. He leaned forward and kissed me, and the first touch of his lips on mine transferred the most glorious sensation I had ever felt. I wished I could describe it. It was like happiness and hope and pure, unadulterated joy. I smiled back, happy tears sliding down my cheeks. I didn't know if it was my happiness, or theirs, but at that moment, it didn't really matter.

Gus let out a heavy sigh. "I made her orgasm, and you made her cry. This is why you've spent the last few millennia alone, Brother." He'd rolled onto his side, so he could watch us both, looking perfectly contented. "Now we'll have to make her cum again, just to dry her tears."

Memphis grinned down at me. I hoped Blue had headphones.

CHAPTER NINETEEN

"Get dressed. I'm long overdue to rip off the Band-Aid."

So much for angelic protection. Gus and Memphis were still sound asleep, a mash of legs, arms and wings that was as beautiful as it was hilarious.

Gusion opened a groggy eye, and rolled over, slapping Memphis in the face with one white wing. Memphis groaned, reaching out a long, muscular arm and shoving Gusion all the way to the other side of the bed. Maybe I was going to need a bigger bed if this was going to become a regular sleeping arrangement. I paused at the thought. Did I want it to become a regular arrangement?

Everything south of my naval screamed a huge, resounding yes. I was still walking on Jell-O legs, even after a long, hot shower. Last night had been crazy. Crazy wonderful. Crazy pleasurable. Crazy scary. Because I'd let go and just lived in the moment. I got a brief flash of just before dawn, where Memphis woke me up to thoroughly make love to me, the easy rhythm of his movements winding me up until my muffled moans woke Gus. He'd watched me come apart in Memphis' arms, and it was so freaking hot I was probably going to self-combust thinking about it.

Gus' hooded gaze told me he knew the nature of my thoughts, so I gave him a quick grin and left the room before I ended up back in bed.

I needed to do something before this whole thing changed me forever. I had an errand that only the Old Hope could complete. I'd do it myself, except I didn't think the guys would let me out of the house without a full contingent of bodyguards.

My steps faltered when Blue was in the kitchen, drinking coffee out of Adnan's favorite mug. I sucked in a huge, fortifying breath, and stepped into the kitchen.

"Good morning," I said, trying not to sound too upbeat, or like a person who'd just engaged in an all-night ménage with two ridiculously hot, and talented, Fallen Angels.

I wasn't sure exactly what that would sound like, but I did my best. Maybe I would be lucky, and he'd slept like a log and was completely oblivious to our midnight shenanigans. Maybe he went out, and I didn't notice. I mean, he wasn't a prisoner here. It was completely plausible.

He mumbled something, but didn't meet my eyes.

Okay, so maybe oblivion had been too much to ask for. "I have to run an errand today, out to the suburbs. I think I'll be fine, if you don't want to come."

This time, he lifted his eyes to mine, and I winced at

his expression. Completely neutral. Not a hint of how he felt, like a perfect Blue Halloran mask, looking like the killer he'd been the first time he'd stepped into my hospital room. I hadn't realized how far he'd come until that moment. Like it had been such a slow, gradual thing, like your hair growing, or the five pounds you put on over the holiday season. Even after he'd returned after our fight, he hadn't reverted back to this Blue. Murderer Blue. Dead inside Blue.

"Look-" I started, but Blue stopped me with a look.

"None of my business," he cut me off. "I'm your bodyguard, not your chaperone. Your attack dog on a leash, nothing more."

Why did those words make my soul hurt?

"That's not true."

Now emotion crept into his expression. Anger. Hurt. Why? Apparently, self-delusion didn't sit well with me. I knew why.

"You like me." It was a statement, not a question. I could feel it in the betrayal that was wafting from him like acid.

He just stared. He didn't need to verbalize it. We both knew that I *knew*.

"Do you like the idea of me, the Princess on the Mulligan pedestal? Do you see this playing out as some kind of Aladdin story where the street kid makes good? Or do you actually see me?" The words were harsh, but I needed to know. I was already knee deep in someone else's unholy redemption, I didn't need a second. I just wanted someone to want me for me, not for what I represented. He stayed stubbornly silent.

"Answer me!"

He took a menacing step forward, and grabbed my arms, pulling me into his body until we were nose to nose. Then he kissed me.

Blue's shields weren't as good as Gus and Memphis', so the moment his lips touched mine, I got everything. Thoughts. Feelings. He was a swirling vortex of lust, and self-loathing. He was on his third cup of coffee because he'd stayed up all night, hard as a rock, listening to the Fallen Angels making me cum time after time.

What am I doing? Last night she was kissing angels. How can I compete with fucking angels? Is she comparing us now, judging my technique with theirs? I should pull away. Cut my losses. I'll go back to the Mulligans, get them to change my job. Tell them I have feelings for her. They'll send me across the fucking ocean to get me away from her. God, she tastes good. So soft. That noise. Fuck, I'm so hard right now.

He nudged me back into the bench, his hands drifting down to my ass, kneading gently.

I'll make this moment count. Never again. I wanted to answer his thoughts, but I'd learned from my mistakes. But I wasn't comparing. I could barely remember to breathe let alone do a complete analysis, so I kissed him harder. I let my fingers run through his short soft hair. Maybe I could pour my assurances through his lips. He lifted me onto the kitchen bench and I wrapped my legs around his waist. I felt the solid length of him against my core, and moaned gently. I knew he wouldn't let it get that far though. His doubt was a dark thread of emotion in his mind, even as he lost himself in the kiss. I felt his shoulders tense as he prepared to pull away. I let him.

"I don't want you to go," I said quietly, gauging his reaction from beneath my lashes. Now we weren't touching, I wasn't privy to his thoughts, but I could see the indecision in his eyes. Finally, he nodded once and left the room.

Gusion walked into the room, his face solemn for a change. Stepping between my thighs as I sat on the bench, he looked down at me, his gaze measured but he remained silent. I rested my forehead against the steady thump of his heart.

"What happens in the future?" I asked, not lifting my eyes to his. Asking felt like cheating, but I wanted — no, needed — to know.

"I have three more cups of coffee before I can even feel remotely alive. Memphis has a pastrami and swiss on rye for lunch. Blue Halloran falls in love with you, but you knew that already, didn't you?"

All the breath left my body.

I WALKED past the white minivan parked in the driveway. The grass along the edges of the pathway was a little overgrown, and the sight made a lump form in my throat. I stepped over a bright yellow toy truck, and if I'd been the Hope from before, I would have jumped down the hopscotch grid that looked like it had been painted on the footpath a decade ago. It probably had.

But I wasn't in a hopping mood. I walked up the

porch steps, and knocked on the screen door, my heart in my throat.

A young woman, still in her teens, opened the door, a fussing toddler on her hip. Her mouth swung open and her eyes narrowed. "What are you doing here? You are a month too late. Dad's funeral came and went without even a card from you. Turn around and go back to your Manhattan tower, Princess."

Each word was a stab through my heart. She meant each one too. In that moment, she hated me. It rolled off her in thick, dark waves. But beneath it was overwhelming, shuddering grief and that was an emotion I could relate to. Not even the looming presence of Gusion and Memphis eased her hatred.

Claudette, JJ's teenage daughter, stared me down with pure wrath.

"I'm sorry." I was more than sorry. I should have come to see my former bodyguards family sooner. He was my friend. They'd treated me like family and I'd abandoned them when my presence was needed the most. The baby on Claudette's hip began to fuss more, and my eyes dragged to his little face.

Claudette had gotten accidentally pregnant at sixteen, a fact that had stressed JJ out so bad, he went grey almost overnight. But he was nothing but supportive to Claudette, reassuring her that despite her mistakes, he loved her and he would love the baby. Claudette had adored her father, so I understood the malice she was throwing my way. I deserved it. Now John James Junior would never know his granddaddy, and Claudette had lost the one person who had her back at all times.

"Who's at the door?" A voice yelled from inside the house.

"A ghost," Claudette yelled back, her nose scrunched up in a sneer.

A second figure appeared in the doorway. Marinette was small and delicate, more like a doll than a woman who would be married to a former spec-ops marine. Her light voice was made even more sweet by her slight French accent. I took one look at her, and burst into tears.

"I'm so sorry," I said between sobbing breaths. Marinette strode forward, bending me so somehow, until I was crying on her shoulder. She whispered to me in French, platitudes that I knew because Valery would murmur the same words when I was little and scraped my knee.

"It's all my fault, and I wasn't even here." The words were garbled by tears.

"Tsch, it is okay. JJ, he knew. He knew every day when he got out of bed to go to work, that there was a chance he would not come home. It has been that way since he was a young man. It is not your fault, *ma petite.* I have been prepared for him to die in the line of duty since he joined the military." Claudette made a disgusted noise, and strode back in the house. Marinette sent an exasperated but sympathetic look at the retreating back of her daughter. "Will you come in?"

I shook my head. I wanted to, but I couldn't. I couldn't face her empathetic face, her understanding. I needed her anger. Her accusations that it was my fault. It was my fault. And in the end, JJ's death had been for absolutely nothing. "I can't."

Marinette nodded. "We all need time to grieve, and you, you have had a pain worse than anything these last months. You always have a sympathetic ear here, *ma petite*. JJ, he thought of you as a third daughter. You are family."

Her words made me sob harder. Gusion put a supportive arm around my waist, making Marinette smile. "It looks like you are in good hands." She leaned forward, her eyes sparkling. She fanned her face and made a high pitch whistle, making me smile through my tears.

I reached out, grabbing her hand and wrapping it in mine.

"Do you need anything? The girls? JJ Junior?"

Marinette shook her head. "No, child. You Papa's been around, set everything up. Made up some lie about a pension fund that JJ was supposed to get and now shifted to his widow. I am not silly, the only person who gets a pension that size, is the President, no? But I will take it, for the girls, and Junior."

"Lux came here?"

Marionette nodded. "*Oui*. And Tolliver. And Sam. Also, the handsome French one brought us a ratatouille that reminded me of home. Your Daddy came and hugged me so tight I thought my bones would crack. He felt JJ's loss. He told me what you looked like in the hospital. If my husband had any regrets, it would be that he could not have saved you from that pain."

A tear slid down Marinette's cheek then, and I was lost. Gus reached out a hand, catching the teardrop on his finger.

Memphis crossed his arm across his chest, his right hand fisted over his heart. He bowed low at the waist. Marinette stared at my dark angel, a little awed. Memphis had that effect. "Thank you," he said solemnly. Marinette merely inclined her head. I wiped my tears on my arm and reached out to hug the beautiful French woman one more time.

"You need anything, anything at all, you call me? I owe you everything," I mumbled. She patted my back soothingly.

I said my goodbyes, and we left. I slid into the back of my Tesla. Memphis and Gusion together in my small car was almost laughable. Even with the seats all the way back, it was like a clown car.

"Where to?" Gusion asked from the driver's seat.

I stared out the window as we pulled away from the curb. I memorized the house, the shape of Marinette in the doorway, the face of Claudette in the upstairs window staring daggers at me. I pictured JJ on the porch with Marinette like he had been so many times before. I memorized it, because I knew I wouldn't be back. Despite Marinette's assurances, I would forever be a scab that wouldn't heal. Sometimes a clean break was better.

I sat in the back and let the tears flow easily. They were cathartic. Sometimes tears were the only way to cleanse wounds to the soul.

"Hope?" Memphis prompted.

"I need something deep fried and smothered in chocolate."

Gusion's golden eyes met mine in the rearview mirror. "My specialty, Sweetheart."

I gave him a tentative smile. "I thought your specialty was sex and sin?"

He grinned, and I wished I could take a picture of his face in that moment. It was like sunshine in a thunderstorm. "It is, Princess, and it's even better with chocolate sauce."

CHAPTER TWENTY

We were in the elevator when Memphis' phone rang. This was surprising for two reasons. One, I didn't realize either Angel had a smartphone. Memphis muttered about new technology when he was driving my car, or trying to figure out the microwave. The idea of him having a state-of-the-art cellphone was a little amazing, frankly.

The second reason it was surprising was because the name on the screen read 'Luc'.

"They have cell reception in Hell?" I mouthed at Gusion. He rolled his eyes, but the corners were crinkled in amusement.

"He's in Mexico," he whispered back. Ah, that made more sense.

So far, Memphis hasn't said anything, just made small grunts of affirmation.

"Yes. Okay, we shall be there momentarily once we secure Hope. Yes. Of course. No, I trust the Mulligan, she will be fine."

With that he hit the end button. The doors slid open onto the penthouse floor in silence. I took the three steps forward into the foyer and waived my key-pass. I then typed in the eleven-digit code on the keypad. Yes, eleven digits was overkill. Tell it to Lux.

"Making plans for me again, Memphis?" I asked, walking into my apartment, my eyes involuntarily searching for Blue.

"Unfortunately, we are needed in Hell. We shall be gone for an indeterminate amount of time as time moves differently in the underworld. It is not predictable. That being said, we shall return as soon as possible. I estimate less than an earth week."

Gusion raised a brow. "We've been summoned? Must be important."

Memphis' eyes held mine. "Lux and the Mulligans caught up with the arms dealer that dispatched Estrella. Unfortunately for him, he made his way to the afterlife in pieces. His ending was not swift or painless. Lucifer would like us to ensure that he knows that his afterlife will be as painful, and never ending. He is otherwise occupied." This time he looked over my head at Gus. "Ace had to talk Azriel from casting his soul into purgatory."

Gusion's eyes opened wide. "Daddy's little death dealer wanted to break the rules and put this man's soul into the abyss? Why?"

Both eyes turned to me. Gusion waggled his eyebrows and Memphis looked annoyed. "What? It had nothing to do with me," I argued.

Gusion stepped forward and swept me into his arms,

bending me backwards as he nailed a playful kiss on my lips. "Oh Sweetheart, it has everything to do with you, and you know it. Azriel, the Mighty Angel of Death, has an angelic hard on for a pretty mortal." He kissed my nose and straightened me. "It would be funny, if I didn't have a hard on for the pretty mortal too," he said, adjusting himself in his jeans. "I better go tell the hitman that we have to leave. Threaten his life if you so much as get your feelings hurt, that kind of thing. I'll channel Memphis." He winked and walked further into my apartment.

Memphis looked like he wanted to thump Gusion. Or maybe hit him in the balls with a baseball bat.

"We should go." He stepped forward, pressing a tender kiss to the corner of my mouth. "Try not too…" he trailed off and sighed. "Just, be safe, yes?"

I winked at him, patting his cheek. "No getting drunk and bar hopping. I got you."

Gusion reappeared, Blue in tow. Memphis shot the shorter man a steely eyed look that would have made a normal mortal man shudder. But not Blue. I was beginning to think that perhaps he was more broken than I thought.

Then Memphis and Gus were gone. I was left alone in my living room with a flint-eyed Blue Halloran. I didn't know what to say. He didn't leave. But he didn't seem happy he stayed.

I was emotionally wrung out. For just one day, I desperately wanted to be able to push my own emotions down the way Blue did.

Blue didn't speak. He just stood there, his gaze

unflinching, his face filled with judgement. "Do you have a problem?" I was tired. So fucking tired.

"Yes."

That was it. Just yes.

"Are you going to do something about it?" I taunted. "Or can you only do what you are told? I know you don't like when life gets messy. But guess what, fuck-head? I am one giant mess, and I am done with your bullshit." I glared at him, and then purposefully turned my back on him. Something about Blue was primal, driven by his animalistic urges. I could feel them there, under the cracking wall of glass that held down his emotions. I wanted to take a sledgehammer to that wall. I walked back toward the front door, but a hand grabbed at my elbow.

"No."

I whirled around to face him. "Stop me, asshole. Maybe you'll have to use more than one syllable sentences. Or can't your simple little mind handle that? Do I need to spell out what I want to you? Is that what you need, someone else to be in control?"

"No."

I lost it. I leaned forward and screamed in his face. His hand was still gripping my arm. He yanked me forward, and my mouth crashed into his, his lips silencing the shrill noise coming from my throat.

He wrapped his hand in my hair, twisting it tight around his fist and held me there as his mouth nipped at mine, demanding. Plundering. He was such a taker, Blue Halloran. He took what he wanted, consequences be damned. Women, money, lives. He took them all and apologized to no one. I moaned against his mouth as I pressed myself closer to the hard edges of his body.

"I'm always in control."

I pulled back, ignoring the pain, my eyes defiant. "Not of me."

He dragged me back, kissing me harder until I was struggling to breathe. "Especially of you, Princess."

He loosened his grip on my hair, and stepped back, his feet spread wide, his stance completely in control. But he was still. He was giving me an out. If I turned away now, that would be the end of this. But I didn't want it to be the end.

Blue eyed me like a predator, but I no longer wanted to be prey. I wanted to be a predator too. I wanted to fuck, and fight, and be conquered.

I quirked my eyebrow and grinned. Then I ran.

I feinted around him, running through the apartment, hurtling the couch in one long stride. I could hear Blue's footsteps as he thundered over the floorboards after me. I spun, eyeing the man on the other side of my couch. His cool eyes were suddenly on fire. Oh, he liked this. A twisted part of me did too.

I should have known he'd be about the chase.

"Is that all you've got?" I prodded, my chest heaving with excitement. He dodged left, and I ran right. But instead of following through, he cleared the couch. I let out a squeak, that could have been a laugh, and took off toward the kitchen. Rella had been the sports star in high school, but I was no slouch either. I was fast on my feet. I launched myself over the breakfast bar, expecting him to stop on the other side like he did with the couch.

Instead, he slid across with me, landing on me and dragging me to the floor. His body was pressed along mine, his breathing fast. I didn't think he was out of breath either.

I tried to push him off, but he just grabbed my hands and slammed them down beside my head. Ouch.

"What are you going to do now, Puppy?" I prodded. His eyes alight, his lips crashed down on mine. I bucked him with my hips and he slid down, straddling my hips, his mouth never leaving mine as his tongue plundered. I could feel the hard press of his cock against my stomach.

He dragged his mouth away. "Whatever the fuck I want, Princess." His body weight pressing down on my arms, he moved downwards, licking my collarbone, biting the upper swell of my breast. Yeah, that was going to leave a mark.

"Do you submit?" His dark voice sent shivers straight to my core.

"No." I threw his word back at him, grinning like the Cheshire cat. Using his teeth, he pulled down my tank top, exposing my lace bra. He sucked in a breath, the only outward sign that he liked what he saw except the hard press of his dick.

He sucked my nipple through my bra, the sensation hot, wet, rough and completely delicious.

"Do you submit?" he asked again, repeating the gesture on the other side, my aching nipple desperate to be out of the restriction of my bra.

"No," I said again, but it was more of a moan. He bit my nipple hard, making my body arc off the ground, my brain not able to decide if it liked, or hated the sensation. My lady parts knew though, as my juices coated my thighs. Blue shifted, moving one of his knees between my thighs. He kicked my legs wider, pressing his hard thigh against my aching pussy. I pushed up against the hard muscle, rubbing my wet core against the roughness of his jeans, my yoga pants offering little in the way of resistance. He moved the other thigh in, and shimmied down, until now the bulging seam of his jeans was resting against the apex of my thighs. I arched into him, and the eyes that watched me were wild. He thrust against me hard, making me moan.

"Do you submit?" His voice was a little more strangled. His eyes that were almost devoid of color they were that pale blue. He thrust one more time. Dirty trick.

"Yes," I moaned.

"Thank the fucking heavens." He moved his hands from my arms, sitting back on his heels, and flipping me onto my stomach. He pulled my yoga pants down with rough, impatient hands and then sucked in an involuntary gasp as my dripping wet pussy was bared to him. He rubbed his hand along my folds, his finger brushing my clit.

He plunged two fingers inside of me, and I pushed back against his hand, burying them deep in me. He thrust them in hard again, and again, until my moans were echoing around my kitchen. I heard the zip of his jeans, and I turned. I wanted to see. But his fingers were back in my hair, holding it close to my scalp, turning me back around. I felt the head of his hard cock press against my entrance, his hand on my hip keeping me steady, giving him control.

Finally, he pushed into me in one hard thrust, burying himself so deep his balls slapped against me.

"Yes," I whispered. Or maybe it was a scream. I was beyond caring as he drew all the way out, and buried himself again. He released my hair as he moved both hands to my hips, moving my body like it was made for his own personal enjoyment, slamming into me in a punishing pace. My arms gave out and I dropped my head to the hardwood floor, burying him even deeper.

I was so close to coming, it was just there, waiting to turn me inside out. Blue scraped his nails up my spine, sending shivers through my body, my moans getting more desperate.

"Yes. Yes," I repeated over and over. He reached around and flicked my clit with his fingers, and I moaned as the sensation rocketed through my body like an atomic bomb.

I was fucking done. My strangled screams were barely muffled by my arms as I came on Blue's cock, its hard length still buried deep inside me.

Letting me ride out my orgasm, he waited with inhuman control for me to collapse in a heap. Then he pulled out, flipping me over so my shoulder blades hit the floorboards, driving back into me. I let out another involuntary moan and wrapped my legs around his waist, holding him tight against me. Oh damn. He pushed up my shirt until it tucked under my breasts, exposing my stomach, and he slid his hand up my torso, along the creamy whiteness of my skin.

He grunted something unintelligible as he leaned forward, kissing me hard as he pistoned into me like a man dying of thirst, his strokes a little ragged and finally out of control. I tried not to smile in triumph. He pulled out and sat up, his hot cum spurting over my stomach like a branding iron.

Resting on his heels, his jeans around his thighs, he stared at me with an impenetrable look. I'd blocked his emotions, but now I reached out a hand to touch his arm.

So fucking beautiful, like the fucking Madonna. Why does she undo me like this?

He whipped his shirt over his head, and used it to wipe his cum from my body. He stood, tucking the balled shirt under his arm. He reached down a hand to help me to my feet. I wasn't sure I was ready for this little interlude to be done. To go back to incriminations and angst.

Sighing, I took his hand and let him haul me to my feet. I felt oddly exposed, standing in front of him in nothing but my tank top.

Still silent, he brushed a hand down my face. *That was...thank you.*

His face didn't even twitch. Still impenetrable. Still stoic. Still in complete control.

He reached out, wrapping his arms around my back and one around my knees, and hoisting me into his arms like I was a freaking princess he was always accusing me of being. I let out a girlish squeal, but didn't protest as he walked me down to my bedroom as if I weighed nothing. Skipping the bed, he walked me into the ensuite and set me on the long marble vanity.

He ran the water, peeled off his clothes and stepped in. He looked at me, a slight rise of his brows the only sign he wanted me to join him.

I slid from the vanity and removed the last remnants of my clothing. Stepping into the shower, I let the hot spray massage my aching muscles. I leaned forward and rested my head against his chest. The rapid beat of his heart was the only physiological indicator that he was as worked up as I was.

"What do we do now?" I asked over the sound of the pounding water.

Blue ran his hands over the tops of my shoulders, and the up further to cup my cheeks. His eyes gave nothing away. If the eyes were the window to the soul, then he'd bricked up the windows, with Blue Halloran trapped inside. His thumb ran over my cheekbone, almost tenderly, as he said, "I think we should go and kill a man."

He pressed me against the wall and fucked me until my horror at the easy way in which he said those words no longer mattered.

CHAPTER TWENTY-ONE

Apparently, the trick to being a contract killer was not to be stealthy, but just to pretend to be so ordinary, you are basically like a fire hydrant on the sidewalk. I had my hair wrapped in a low bun and hidden under a baseball cap. Apparently sunglasses and a ball cap was the fedora and trench coat of years gone by. If you pushed a baby stroller and had a tan, you were basically invisible.

Blue and I sat in a cafe across the road from Maximoff-Fucking-Richards' apartment complex, drinking tea and rocking my imaginary baby. I'd almost swallowed my tongue when Blue had insisted we stop at a thrift store and stepped out looking like a boy scout in beige chinos and pushing a baby carriage. In the crook of his arm was a doll, dressed in bright pink newborn wear. From a distance, it looked pretty lifelike.

I wasn't going to fool myself, the sight of Blue holding that baby doll made me feel... disconcerted.

Yearnings I wasn't ready to admit to myself, and definitely not to Blue Halloran, crept their way into my chest.

It was all part of our cover. Happily married with a baby was basically an invisibility cloak.

"Smile at me like I'm charming," Blue said, grinning happily at me. It was the freakiest expression I'd ever seen on his face. I shuddered a little.

"I can't while you're making that face. You look like a wax doll or something. Stop." I rocked the pram, which was draped in a muslin wrap, hiding the pseudo infant from general sight. Beneath the doll was Blue's gun. I tried not to think too hard about that little fact. I was going to need some serious therapy. If only I didn't hate therapy. Maybe I just needed to talk to my mom.

I looked at Blue, who was schooling his features into polite attentiveness as if his face was made of putty. I hated the fake expression. He had dark sunglasses, and I knew he was looking past my shoulder at the building behind me, but his head was tilted as if he was the perfect young husband listening to his wife. It made my heart do funny things.

"Do you actually want kids?"

"Beside Blue Junior there?" His lip quirked.

"It's a girl."

"Bluella?" he suggested.

I huffed out a laugh. "Stop avoiding the question."

He looked at me. I still couldn't see his eyes, but I could feel the weight of his stare on my face. Maybe it was a bad question to ask a man with whom I'd just had kind-of angry sex. He might get the wrong idea that I actually wanted to reproduce with him. Which I didn't.

I shook my head. No, definitely not.

"Maybe one day. I'm not in the right profession for ties. A family is a weakness in my line of business."

I sipped my latte. That made sense. When a normal husband brought work home, it meant manila folders and a locked office door. If Blue brought work home, it meant drive-by hits and mortal wounds.

"How about you?"

My attention snapped back to the subject of my thoughts. "What?"

"Do you want kids?"

I thought about Memphis and Gus. They couldn't have kids. Angels were sterile. If I was Memphis' fated love, or whatever I was, then I probably wouldn't have kids. I was too young to mourn the loss of something I'd never considered.

I shrugged. "Maybe one day. I never really thought about it."

He looked from my face, to my hand that was still rocking the pram. "You'd make a good parent. I think you should. You've taken better care of that doll then my own mother took care of me."

I blinked, not even knowing how to respond to that statement, when his mouth tightened. It was the only outward sign that anything had changed.

"Time to move." He stood, throwing a few bills on the table to pay for our coffee. "The driver is pulling the car around." He grabbed the pram and started walking down the sidewalk toward my car. We'd parked right in front of Richards apartment building. Blue popped the boot and folded the pram with practiced ease.

I held the swaddled doll in my arms, opening the back door and placing it into its imaginary car seat. I was really unwrapping Blue's gun from the swaddling.

I held the heavy weight of it in my hand and felt sick. My lungs began to restrict, and I couldn't breathe.

No, not now. There were no bullets in it. It was just a hunk of metal. Just for show. It was okay.

Blue's hand grabbed my hip and pulled me from the backseat. He tucked the gun in my hand behind my back, tucking the weapon into the waistband of my jeans as he spun me to face him. He looked down at me through those dark glasses, but I could imagine the icy intensity of his eyes. Then he leaned forward and kissed me, like he was breathing air back into my oxygen starved lungs. I kissed him back, anchoring myself on his lips.

"We don't have to do this. There's no shame in getting in this car and going home. I can get him another day. We can wait until your demons return from Hell," he said, barely shifting his lips from mine to talk.

"They're angels," I protested weakly on their behalf.

"Tomato, potato," he said, his lips feathering across mine.

I kissed him again, tracing his bottom lip with my tongue. "No, I want to do this. He fucked with my world, and I want him to pay."

He pulled back further, staring down at my face. Then he nodded. "Follow the plan. You just gotta drive."

In my opinion, the plan was a little lame. I had to pretend to be a ditzy wife who forgot her phone at the cafe. As the crazy driver-slash-bodyguard moved around to open the door for Maximoff Richards, who apparently was too fancy to open his own door, I was going to slip in the driver's seat while Blue disabled the bodyguard. Then Blue would slide in beside Richards, I'd peel out into traffic, we'd abandon the car two blocks away where we'd get into an untraceable vehicle that Blue had managed to acquire while he was on hiatus from me. Then we'd drive somewhere super secretive and I'd finally get my answers. Or retribution.

Blue bit my bottom lip. Hard! "Focus!" he grumbled. "Ready?"

I nodded, then tilted my head back. I took in the hard curve of his jaw, his high cheekbones. I counted the little scars on his face. Four.

He ran a hand down my hair, and he was looking lovingly into my face. "You've got this." He paused, his face angled toward mine, but his attention on the car the just pulled up beside us.

"Okay, go."

I laughed, and threw him a saucy look, sashaying toward the street. I stood and waited for the oncoming traffic, all the while keeping an eye on the driver. I tilted my head away, pretending to look to the left, so Maximoff didn't see my face. As soon as I heard the door slam, I doubled back, opening the driver's door, and sliding into the seat, the heavy weight of Blue's empty gun in my hand. I turned in the seat, facing Maximoff Richards for the first time since Geneva, and pointing a gun in his face. We'd see how he liked it.

"Hello, Maxie. Give me one good reason to put a bullet in your face." I sounded like a badass. I sounded like Rella. It was all fake. I couldn't kill anyone, but if I could, the man staring at me pale faced in the back seat of his state-of-the-art town car would be the top of the list.

"You wouldn't kill me," he said, all confidence. I wanted to prove his smarmy ass wrong.

"My sister is dead because of you. Try me." My voice was ice cold, devoid of emotion. A little like Blue.

I heard grunting, and the unmistakable sound of a fist hitting flesh. The driver fell through the door and into the back seat. Blue stuffed him into the seat, and slid in behind him.

"Go!" he yelled, and I peeled out into traffic. I looked into the rearview mirror, and noticed that Blue had his gun barrel pressed firmly into Maximoff's temple.

"If I put a bullet into your temple right now, it wouldn't even break the glass. It'd make a hell of a mess of your car interior though." He said this pleasantly, like he was making small talk. Eesh.

I pulled into a lot about a block and a half east. Stopping next to a junker Toyota, I lined up the rear passenger door with the boot. Blue pulled two cable ties from his back pocket, and threw one to me. "Tie up the muscle while he's still out." He motioned to Maximoff with his gun. "You too." He held out the loop of cable tie and motioned for him to put his hands in. Maximoff hesitated, and Blue flicked the safety off his gun and pressed the silencer harder into his head, until his face was jammed between the window and the gun.

"I want to kill you right now. End your shit-eating, entitled existence right now. But Hope wants answers. But she doesn't need answers that bad. Maybe my finger could slip?"

He said it conversationally. It was terrifying to see Blue in his natural habitat, so to speak. Blue wasn't physically imposing, nor did he swear or generally try and intimidate Maximoff. No, the scary part about Blue was that he seemed completely unperturbed by the circumstances. Like he really could kill Maximoff with the ease that a normal person made a cup of tea.

He was doing a job. Checking off task after task, except it ended with Maximoff dead, a bullet between his eyes.

My stomach flip-flopped at the thought.

Maximoff threaded his wrists through the loop and winced when Blue pulled it tight, the shrill noise of the tie grating against me.

"I'll kill you for this," Maximoff threatened, but he only thought he was the biggest predator in this vehicle. Blue undid Maximoff's tie and shoved it in his mouth, dragging him out of the back seat and toward the boot of the Toyota.

I leaned between the seats, and lifted the hand of the unconscious driver. He was big, physically intimidating. Bigger than Blue, that was for sure. But that was just like Maximoff. He wanted to have a big, scary bodyguard as a sign of prestige. Dick.

I threaded one through, and lifted the other.

The bodyguard's eyes snapped open and his hand wrapped around my wrist with bone crushing firmness.

I got a huge wave of his emotions as he ricocheted back into consciousness. Anger, pain, and the recognition.

That recognition was reflected in his muddy brown eyes. Then regret. Loathing, but surprisingly not for me. For Maximoff. The bodyguard hated his boss? I mean, it wasn't a leap, because Maximoff Richards was the worst humanity had to offer. But still...

"Do you know me?" I asked, rather redundantly.

He nodded.

"Do you know why I'm doing this?" Another nod. "Your loyalty is admirable, but that asshole doesn't deserve it. I promise I won't kill him," I couldn't make such a promise for Blue though. "You don't need to die for his ego though. We'll pretend you were out of it," I pleaded. I could read this man's soul. He was all sorts of crazy, but his heart was good. He was loyal to a fault though. I didn't want him to be hurt.

"Are you a religious man?" I asked, and he stared at me, then dipped his chin. "Well, the Devil is coming for Maximoff Richards, and you don't want to be there when it happens. The Devil does not ask questions, and he does not do leniency."

He stared at me unblinkingly, but didn't say a word. Then he lifted his other hand and threaded it through the cable tie. My fingers brushed his wrist.

The Devil will take me eventually, but it won't be for that jerk off.

I smiled down at him and laughed. "Good choice. He doesn't deserve it. I happen to know the Devil, I'll put in a good word for you."

Eyes wide, the bodyguard lifted his fingers to his mouth and shook his head.

I raised my eyebrows. "Oh, you're mute?" Whoops. "I just thought you were the strong, silent type. Well, Marco, it's never too late to become a nun, or have a career change, or not work for douchebags."

I tapped him on the forehead. *Do you need a bodyguard?* He grinned at me. What a damn flirt.

I laughed out loud that time, drawing Blue back from the Toyota. "I'm at my quota for stubborn, alpha types, thanks Marco. But I wish you luck."

But Marco's eyes had drifted to Blue, and now they were back to being hard and slightly murderous.

"You shouldn't flirt with your captives, Princess. It's bad business etiquette. Also, letting them see your face? A big no-no."

I patted the top of Marco's head and tightened the cable tie. But not too tight. He'd work his way out eventually.

"Me and Marco have an understanding. We're cool."

Blue's perfect dark brows lowered down over his eyes. "Is that true, Marco? Do you have an agreement?" he murmured in a low voice.

They had some kind of hitman/murderer glare-off, but eventually Marco nodded.

"See?" I said as I grabbed the keys from the ignition.

"I'm gonna take these; can't make it too easy. Be good, okay?"

Marco grinned again, and gave me a wink. Cheeky bastard.

I gave the keys to Blue, who threw them as far as he could over the fence. Then I slid into the passenger seat, and tried not to think of Bonnie and Clyde. Ride or die, right?

CHAPTER TWENTY-TWO

Apparently, you can never really know a man until you've walked a mile in his shoes. As I stood in the abandoned meat packing plant owned by the Mulligan family here in New York, watching Maximoff Richards swing from a meat hook, I thought I might know Blue Halloran a little better now.

But I didn't know myself anymore.

Faced with a silent, red faced Maximoff, I found myself only having one question, but my conviction that he needed to die was wavering.

"Why?"

Maximoff rolled his eyes and spat at the ground at my feet. Blue pulled back his fist and hit him in the solar plexus, the heavy thud of flesh on flesh making me feel ill. What was I thinking being here? I was caught up in Blue and sex pheromones and survivor guilt. This wasn't me.

"She asked a question," Blue said calmly. There was

a fissure in his personality. Blue the Lover and Blue the Killer.

Maximoff sneered. "Did you know the stocks in my company dropped twenty points within minutes of her giving her speech at the conference. All it took was one world leader tweeting a positive 250 characters in support of her idea, and the stocks began to plummet. I'd heard rumors, of course, I have my insiders. I'd prepared. I know what her type is like, do-gooders that never let it rest. When I heard that she was taking her father's place, I knew I had a chance to destabilize my competition once and for all. Fucking tender hearts. This is business. The fact the bitch would be made into someone's sex slave was just the icing on the cake. I wanted for them to just kill you, but they insisted on it as part of the payment. Valuable merchandise. The Estonians are also businessmen. It's a pity they fucked it up." He gave me a cold smile.

Blue shook his head in cool exasperation. "It's like you just want me to shoot you."

Maximoff sneered in disgust. "She won't let you kill me. Like I said, fucking tender hearts."

Rage bubbled up in me because he was right. I wouldn't let Blue kill him, because I was a better person than the Maximoff Richards' of the world. Except...

"Did you arrange to have my sister killed?" I asked quietly. His life really did hinge on his answer to this question. There was nothing tender about me when it came to Rella's death.

Finally, an emotion past over his face; regret. But not

regret for her death. Regret that he hadn't had a hand in it.

I looked at Blue. "Shoot him."

Blue grinned, such a joyous expression suddenly de-aging him. "Gladly." He lifted his gun and pointed it at Maximoff Richard's head. I turned, throwing up a wall between me and the fear he was emitting. He deserved it. I repeated it to myself again. *He deserves it. He deserves it. How many lives has he ruined? The world would be better without him.* I strode toward the door that led to the rear car park.

Suddenly, with a flash of blue-black wings and a stormy face, Memphis was there. "Not going to stay and see the results of your order, Hope?" He looked...disappointed. "If you order a man's death, you should stay until the end. Taking a life shouldn't be like ordering takeout. It has a toll, on all involved."

I swallowed hard and my eyes welled with tears. I looked over my shoulder at Blue. His gun was relaxed in his hand, his face almost an artist's replica of ease. But his emotions felt dirty around the edges. How hadn't I noticed that? Although there was grim satisfaction, and cool efficiency mixed in, Blue didn't want to be a murderer again.

I noticed Gusion off to the side. His face was grim. "This is not who you are, Sweetheart. Not deep down. This will forever tarnish your soul."

I sucked in a shuddering breath. "You saw what he did, look into his future, can you see anything but destruction and ruination there? Because his soul is black. He deserves consequences."

Gusion gave me a scary smile then. "Oh, there'll be consequences."

Maximoff began to laugh. "Maybe the Estonians did more damage than I thought. The bitch is losing it. Who the hell are you talking to, whore?"

I realized the guys were still invisible to the naked eye.

Blue pistol-whipped him in the temple, but he was smirking as he did it. Blue knew who was with us in this plant.

Memphis reappeared in front of Maximoff. He spread his wings wide, and I lost my breath at the sheer beauty of them again.

I could tell the exact moment Memphis appeared to Maximoff, because the color leached from his face and piss trailed down his leg. He struggled on the hook, like a worm that just realized it was about to be swallowed by a barracuda.

I couldn't hear what was being said, but the terror on Maximoff's face gave me a few clues. Then, Memphis leaned in and pressed a hard kiss to the pale, thin lips of the man who had destroyed my life. The kiss was a promise. A promise of death and pain and torture.

He walked away, heading back to where I was standing, wrapping an arm around my shoulders.

Gusion moved to take Memphis' place in front of the captive, showing himself. Maximoff was gaping like a fish, his mouth opening and closing soundlessly.

"My God was the old testament kind. An eye for an eye." He pulled back his fist and nailed Maximoff right in the jaw. I heard the sickening crunch of bones shattering. I watched in fascinated horror as Maximoff gagged up several teeth. "A tooth for a tooth."

He strode away, a smile on his face. "I love it when I can work something biblical into my vengeance, don't you? Makes me feel like I'm doing my job right."

I just blinked, staring at him until I felt Memphis pulling me away and wrapping his arms around my waist.

Around his bicep, I could see Blue pointing the gun at Maximoff's dick. Maximoff started to scream through his broken jaw. Sighing, Blue dropped his gun a little lower. "A knee for a knee. No, that doesn't work. This is why I don't do cheesy catchphrases," he complained, as the high pitch whistle of the silencer echoed around the empty plant and Maximoff's kneecap exploded into minced meat. I gagged at his high pitch wails, then he passed out. Blue picked up his shell and poked the bullet from where it had buried itself in the concrete floor.

"Always good manners to pick up after yourself when you are a guest." He wiped the bullet on the hanging man's slacks, and walked over to me, where I was surrounded by Fallen Angels. "I just have to set fire to the Toyota. That should get someone's attention before he bleeds to death. But I could use a ride afterwards?"

Memphis growled, and Gusion put a restraining hand on his chest. "Easy," he whispered.

"She should never have been here. You put her in danger."

Blue didn't flinch under the piercing gaze of Mephistopheles. "She needed to take her life back. Violence begets violence. How's that for biblical?"

Another murderous growl bubbled up from Memphis' throat, and before he could do something stupid, like strangle Blue Halloran, he sifted us away and into my apartment. Then he pulled me out of the apartment, into the elevator and through the foyer. He didn't stop until we walked into a tiny cafe across the street from my apartment building.

"Turn so the camera can see your entire face and smile like I said something humorous," he whispered in my ear. He sounded anything but humorous in that moment. He sounded pissed. But I did as he asked, turning slowly toward the counter as I smiled broadly.

Memphis leaned toward the awestruck looking girl at the counter. "We'll have two Reubens on Rye. Extra mustard."

I was fairly certain that neither of those sandwiches was from me. Actually, I had the distinct impression that I was in big ass trouble. The girl made the sandwiches way too quickly. As she handed over the paper wrapped sandwiches, Memphis leaned close again and nipped my ear in what would have looked affectionate but I knew was pure reproach.

"Now smile and say goodbye to your alibi," he whispered and then kissed me on the cheek. I gave the girl a genuine smile and walked back toward my apartment.

Well, at least it was only Memphis giving me a lecture. It could have been way, way worse.

. . .

IF MY LIFE had been narrated by Morgan Freeman, this would have been the part where he said, 'But it was indeed way, way worse.'

A very, very pissed off Luc stood in front of the couch, where I was currently seated and doing my best to look recalcitrant. Blue sat beside me, looking fucking petrified. I kept sneaking looks at him, trying to memorize the expression, because I didn't think I would ever see it again.

Luc rubbed his temples, and his scary 'you will rue the very day your ancestors decided to fuck in a cave and create your whole line of Neanderthals' look on his face. It was a distinct look. It was two parts pissed and one part frustrated.

"You are the last living child of my beloved. Your mother has just put your sister in the ground. You are the only one of us with any purity of soul at all, and you decide to throw all caution to the wind and put yourself in some hare-brained scheme with a fucking Mulligan." He turned to Blue. "Your whole line has been a giant pain in my ass for half a century. I'm tempted to raze your whole twisted family tree to the ground."

His dark eyes bore into Blue's soul like a laser.

I felt like a teenager again, being chastised for staying out late on a date with some kid from senior class. My parents had thought I was dead in a ditch somewhere and I was basically forbidden to date ever again. In all honesty, I'd face Lux's wrath and Dad's bewildered disappointment a thousand times over rather than getting chewed out by Lucifer for one more minute.

"Do you know what I was doing when you pulled away my two Princes of Hell?"

Memphis scowled. "Don't call me that."

Luc went on as if he hadn't spoken. "We were torturing your sister's murderer. Because punishment is my domain, not yours. Their deaths are mine, not yours, despite how slighted you feel. Do you understand me?"

I nodded. Because there was no arguing with him today. "Are you going to tell Ace?" Because Ace was scarier than Luc. Ace would kick my ass. Then she'd tell my Mom. Ugh.

"Yes."

I winced. "Luc..."

He held up a hand. "Unless you promise not to try and murder a man in cold blood, forever staining your soul black, ever again."

I crossed my heart. Geez, I really was reverting to a teenager under the weight of his disapproval. But until you've stood toe to toe with Lucifer, you couldn't judge me. It's not as easy as it sounds.

I tried one more time. "Luc, I know something more is going on here. Something to do with Uriel and the Angels and I want to know what it is. I want to help."

Luc turned a fiery gaze to Memphis and Gus. "Who told her?"

Gus put his hands in the air, but he didn't seem perturbed by the look he was being given. "Not me."

I crossed my arms over my chest. "Rella told me."

Luc heaved a sigh. "Stay out of the affairs of Archangels, little girl. Nothing good can come from you poking your nose where it doesn't belong." His eyes shot back to his fellow Fallen. "Anything happens to her, it is you who will have to tell Ace. I have seen her heart break enough for one lifetime."

With that, he disappeared.

Breath whooshed out of Blue, and he started compulsively straightening everything on the coffee table while muttering "Holy shit, holy shit," over and over again.

Gusion flopped down on the couch beside me, wrapping an arm around my shoulders. "That didn't exactly sound like a no, am I right?"

Memphis shook his head. "Gusion, no."

Gus pulled me onto his lap, ignoring Memphis' admonishment. "I was really disappointed in you today. I understand your need to take control of your life, but abducting a man and beating him in the meatpacking district isn't the way to do it." I thought about pointing out he was the one doing the beating, but decided to let it go. "However, I do have a reasonably low risk thing you can do to help us bring down Uriel, and by extension, the organization he created."

He leaned in close. "Do you own any latex?"

CHAPTER TWENTY-THREE

B lue scowled into the crowd. Then he scowled back at me, at my barely there miniskirt and my lace halter bralette, and then back at the room. Actually, he hadn't stopped scowling since Gusion had made his suggestion.

We stood in the entry of a BDSM dungeon on the lower east side. I'd almost missed it. We'd walked down a back alley, and stood in a dead end. The only door was a heavy metal door with an 'Employees Only' sign beneath the numbers '1028'.

The club had heavy music with a low, slow beat playing, but it wasn't unbearably loud. We hadn't made it very far past the coat check and Blue had gotten another look at my outfit.

"So, who gets the paddle, me or you? Or do I finally get to leash Cujo?" I teased.

I couldn't read his emotions in this undulating pool of feeling. It was like drowning in a sea of white noise. It was actually kind of glorious. Pleasure, pain, lust and hatred all twined together to make the club a heady experience for me.

But I could see the desire clouding his eyes, and I knew this place was affecting Blue just as much as me. His hand slid down the bare line of my spine to rest on my ass. "No one leashes me, Princess. Remember your role. Tonight, you are mine."

Heat flooded me and my heart rate picked up. Tonight I had to give up complete control to Blue. He was in charge of my every move. The idea had me wet between my thighs already and we hadn't even entered the main area of the club.

When Gusion had suggested I do reconnaissance at a club that was owned and operated by Tenebrae and often frequented by Uriel himself, I wasn't sure who protested louder, Memphis or Blue.

But I was the only being on the planet Uriel couldn't 'see'. I could watch in a way Gus or Memphis had been unable to for all this time. I was perfect for this job. I'd put my foot down in a way that I would never do if it had been Luc. But Memphis seemed to want to keep me happy as much as he wanted to bubble wrap me. The weight of his expectations was starting to tug at my nerves, and this whole thing needed to come to a head already so we could work out whether what I felt for him was gratitude or lust or something more.

Luckily, he hadn't seen me in this outfit, otherwise I'd still be in my room, probably being held captive or thoroughly fucked against a wall. It was fifty/fifty with Memphis.

And Blue, well, he was equally as torn. But if the

outfit hadn't won him over, then my absolute stubborn-
ness and his need to control every situation had.

I was brought back to my present circumstances by
Blue tugging on my hand and leading me toward a
darkened corner. He pressed me against the wall, lifting
one stiletto-tipped leg over his hip until he was pressed
so tightly against me all I could feel was the hard ridges
of his body beneath his stiff white dress shirt.

"Here's how it's going to go, Princess. I don't like
this." The bulge in his expensive black slacks said otherwise. "I don't like walking into unknown situations, and I
definitely know we are playing out of our league right
now. So, here are the rules.You don't meet anyone's eyes
but mine, you don't speak unless I say you can. We get in
and out as quick as we can and blend in as much as
humanly possible with you looking like a fucking dirty
fantasy." The last bit was said in an almost pained tone.

My hair was wrapped in a high bun on top of my
head, exposing the slender line of my neck. My face was
over half covered in a stick-on latex filigree mask that
seemed to accentuate the highness of my cheekbones
and the vivid green of my eyes. I was also wearing
barely anything, but I kept reminding myself that people
wore less clothing on the beach.

Groaning, Blue stepped away. "Let's go. I need to
get you home. Remember, Princess, eyes on the floor."

"But how am I..."

He held up a hand. "And no speaking. Tug on my
hand if you need something, like you want to leave so I
can..." He cut himself off and took another deep, shud-

dering breath. The lust was now rippling from him in waves.

As he walked off, I frowned, already struggling with these invisible restrictions. But at the same time, there was something freeing about not having to worry about anything past the front of Blue's shoes. I slid my eyes to the side, my face still downcast, and took in the room. An assortment of spaces occupied the walls. Women, and men, were restrained in various ways. A woman was trussed like one of Valery's racks of lamb, except the woman was also suspended from the ceiling.

A man was tied to a Saint Andrews cross, and just a little up from him a woman who was bent over a pommel horse, her hands tied behind her back, being flogged with a mean looking whip. I winced every time the knotted tips hit her flesh, but she didn't seem to mind the pain. In fact, if her emotions were anything to judge by, she really, really liked it.

A man stepped between me and Blue, and I had no time to stop, instead plowing into his body. The man's hands reached out to steady me, but they landed on my ass and he pulled me close. His emotions were a complicated mixture of lust, and sadism, but not in the good way. He wanted to see me hurt, but for his own pleasure, not mine. I made the mistake of looking up into his dishwater brown eyes. They were hungry and lascivious and made me feel gross.

"Eyes down," came Blue's cool voice. Gladly. I dropped my eyes to the floor and prayed the guy would disappear.

But I didn't need an angel to make my wish come true. I had Blue-Fucking-Halloran.

"Your hands are on my property. Move them, or I'll remove them permanently." His voice was congenial, but there was no mirth in his tone, no hint he was joking.

The man laughed. Apparently he couldn't read tone the way I could. "She is beautiful, but in need of a little more training, I think. I'd be happy to help you break her in?"

My body rippled with a shudder.

"I do not want or need your help. Now take your hands off her before I cut off your cock and stuff it into your obnoxious mouth," Blue said in a voice pitched so low, no one else could hear it. I broke the rules and looked up again. The stranger looked almost pleasant, but his eyes were dead. The man removed his hands from my skin and backed away.

"Keep her, man. There's plenty of willing flesh here tonight."

I watched the man's back as he walked across the crowded floor, towards a raised alcove where several men lounged and at least a dozen women sat bolt upright, like ornaments spread across a mantelpiece.

I was distracted as Blue leaned close. "Okay?"

I nodded, but didn't look up. See, I was learning already. Another set of feet entered my field of vision. They wore huge, clunky boots that wrapped right up the man's calves. He had on a pair of tight latex pants.

"You handled that well. You are new here." It wasn't a question, and the soft voice made me want to look up.

Blue made an affirmative noise. "She's new to the lifestyle. I thought she might enjoy something a little more public."

I could see a lanyard around his neck, which seemed a little odd considering the rest of his outfit was criss-crossing straps of leather. The lanyard was splashed with the letters DM, and in smaller writing underneath, Dungeon Monitor.

I couldn't help it. I looked up into the kind eyes of a huge, golden skinned man. He wasn't good looking, or horrendous. He was just an average looking dude, like the kind you'd see in the deli section of a bodega. Or at your kids soccer match. Or doing construction. He smiled down at me, and I dropped my eyes again.

"Very new. I kind of like them at this stage. Watching them fully immerse themselves in the life. Just know, if you need anything, or are uncomfortable at any time, let one of the DM's know. We are here to keep everything and everyone happy and having a good time." He addressed Blue, but I knew the words were for me.

"Thanks, man," Blue said, and put his fingers under my chin, lifting my face up so I could meet his eyes. "You broke the rules, Princess. Go to the bar, and come back when you can follow the rules," he ordered, and I nodded, acting chastised. Hell, maybe I was even feeling a little chastised.

Blue continued talking to the DM as I made my way through the bodies to the bar. There was a dance floor, and people gyrated around in the imitation of sex. Actu-ally, a few of the couples may actually be having sex.

I blamed all the excess energy in the room for almost tripping over an Archangel before I felt his angelic signature. I sucked in a breath at the golden haired angel sitting at the bar. He was watching the alcove, his eyes intent.

He tilted his head in my direction, though he didn't shift his gaze to me. "Hello, Hope. It is odd to see you here."

I blinked, gaping at the Archangel's blazing aura. How could others not see him? I frantically tried to recall what Uriel looked like, but the man in front of me didn't seem to match. That left...

"Michael?"

The man gave me a beatific smile. "Indeed. Come, sit." He indicated the seat beside him. I just stared. I looked down at my outfit. I was about to sit next to the Archangel Michael, practically naked, in a BDSM bar. This was so wrong.

I sat on the very edge of the stool, and Michael finally looked at me. "You are changing things."

It wasn't a question, or an accusation. It was a statement of fact. As if it were an inevitability.

"I'm sorry?"

"Don't be. Change is at the very center of nature. Without change, there is only stagnation. Stagnation leads to death." His eyes switched back to the alcove, and my gaze followed his. I caught a flash of fiery red hair, as the creepy man from before moved away from the low slung couches and towards the women lined up like items at the grocery store. He picked one and led her from the VIP area. She stunk of fear that was acrid even all the way over here. She was being sold. I knew it deep in my soul.

The hair belonged to the other Archangel in the room tonight. Uriel. He was exactly how the guys described him, right down to the 'douchebag expression that makes you want to put your fist through his skull'.

"He's selling those girls, Michael. Can you not stop it?" I pleaded to the almost omniscient being beside me.

He shook his head sadly. "I cannot. He is following God's law for the Angels. Finding and punishing wrong doers."

I scoffed. "I may have never read the bible, but I'm pretty certain there is no 'Thou shalt sell the unwilling for profit' clause."

He gave me a sad smile, and shook his head. "No, look closer." Then he placed a hand on my forehead, and my eyes blurred, like someone had spiked my drink with acid. Only I hadn't had a drink yet, and there was no way acid made everyone look like a technicolor rainbow. Hell, maybe it did, but the fact I was seeing everyone haloed like a 1970s discotheque was seriously tripping me out. "What the…"

Michael was looking at me, the sad expression finally leaving his eyes. "You are even more special than I thought. At the time, I wondered. But now I can only think that maybe there is a plan, something greater than those known to me."

"Do I even want to know what you are talking about?" I asked, trying not to look at him too hard because his light was making my eyes water. "Am I seeing people's auras right now, because this is seriously giving me a headache."

Michael nodded and then gestured toward the raised alcove where Uriel was holding court. The colors varied, some even in shades I'd struggle to describe. I watched a man with a violet aura walk up to Uriel, shaking his hand. The pale blue of his aura suddenly turned red at his hand and partially up his arm. Then he walked over to another official looking man, who's aura was a horrifying shade of sewer brown and the same red, except it had spread from his hand until it encapsulated almost all his body, eating away at his natural poop brown aura. The red all but oozed around him. The pale blue aura guy gave him some cash in the guise of a handshake, then walked over to the line of mannequins, I mean women, lined up on the couch. He picked one and her aura flashed an alarming grey color. The color of fear.

I watched for a little while longer, and saw the pattern repeated. Except it wasn't all men. Or singles. No matter what the color of their aura initially, as soon as they touched Uriel with the purpose of buying a woman, their auras changed irrevocably.

"He's marking them."

Michael nodded. "They know that the women are being sold, but they do not care. He is marking evil-doers. The mark eats at them, turning them to God. But it doesn't stop at loving thy neighbor. Mostly people marked by Uriel become zealots. Extremists."

I wanted to yell and scream at the injustice of it. I

wanted to make Michael do something. But I was meant to be keeping a low profile.

He is the reason these women are even here to be sold! How can he be doing God's purpose if he is the root of all this suffering? I shouted in his mind. He winced.

"You can mindspeak? That's interesting. Anything else?"

I thought of Rella, of all her warnings about the good guys not necessarily being good just because they came from heaven. Uriel proved that. But Michael, with that tragic look on his face, well, I didn't think he was a bad one. I wouldn't tell him I could read angels though. That would be bad.

"I'm empathic, and sometimes a little telepathic."

He raised his eyebrows, and smiled. "You are very special. I told Acerezeal that she did the right thing, but I didn't realize how intrinsic you would be."

Angels talked in riddles, and Archangels were officially the worst. What I did know was that Michael could put a stop to this, right now. He was the Hand of God, he could squash this shit in a heartbeat. I reigned in my anger.

"You could fix this. Why don't you just go over there and send him back to whatever hole he crawled out of?"

Michael threw back his head and laughed. The sound turned heads and made my heart sing. "That 'hole' as you so aptly called it, is Heaven. And I haven't been told that he needs to be reigned in. The Hand of God I may be, but I am just the Hand. I can't operate without instruction, and I just have to trust he has stilled me for a reason."

I stood, my eyes drifting to the ground in case he saw the fury and disgust in them. I heard him chuckling beneath his breath. "You have no awe for me at all, do you, Child of Acerezeal? Perhaps you will do what I cannot."

And with that, he was gone.

CHAPTER TWENTY-FOUR

I felt sick. Perhaps I'll do what he can't? Was he telling me to bring down Uriel for him? He was the fucking flaming sword or something. I could no more bring down Uriel than I could bring down Luc. I walked back to where I left Blue, who was still chatting to the Dungeon Monitor, almost companionably. I wondered if the DM was gay, because he seemed enthralled by Blue.

"Have you been suitably punished, Princess?" he murmured just loud enough to be heard above the music.

I nodded in what I assumed was a docile manner, looking up just enough so I could see the DM's lanyard. I stiffened. His aura was green. Which wasn't such a bad thing, it seemed like a 'good' color. No, my problem was that I was still seeing auras. Holy shit. Michael didn't take it back. My panicked gaze shot to Blue's face. He was pink. I mean, his aura was pink. I blinked, stunned

by the warm color. Deep down, I worried that he would
be the sludgy brown of the man in the alcove with Uriel.

The DM laughed. "She's a stubborn one, but they
are the best. I like spirit myself. No one is fun when they
are broken, you know? Maybe she's a brat." He smiled
at me. Dammit, I was meeting people's eyes again. I
looked back down, but I had a feeling it was too late.
Blue gave a choked laugh, but the DM just continued.
"We have a cross available if you want to do a scene?
Perhaps she will learn better with a stronger punishment?" The question was inherent in the man's tone. He
wasn't presuming that was what I wanted. He was
leaving it up to us. Consent, it's key.

"Hmm, I think you might be right. What do you
think, Princess? Do you need to be punished more thoroughly?" Blue's voice had dropped low, and I could feel
his lust. Now, I could see his lust as it tinged his aura.
This was so fucked up.

But despite my new 'ability,' I wanted what Blue was
offering. Just once. I just wanted to know how it felt
once. So I nodded.

The DM saw my movement, and I knew he'd been
waiting for my consent before he led us across the room.
I looked up toward the alcove, but Uriel and his blind-
ingly white aura was gone.

"The rules aren't revolutionary, they are the same for
most dungeons. Consent only, we insist on safe words.
Green, Yellow, Red. No sex on the equipment. There
are rooms in the back for that."

Blue made some sound of assent, and I stood before
a huge X that had leather buckles on all points. I gaped.

I couldn't help but draw comparisons to my abduction, the restraints that tied my wrists and the way I was suspended to the ceiling. I sucked in a deep, shuddering breath as my heart hammered in my chest. I could do this. I was badass. This was another step in regaining control of my life, by trusting enough to give it up. I could do this.

Blue leaned in close, his hand possessive but gentle on my hip. "Are you okay? We don't have to do this. We can go home right now, no matter what we came for."

I didn't tell him I'd already gotten all the information I came for, and then some. I was intrigued, and more than a little aroused by all the pheromones and emotions that were pouring through the room. My anger, the weight of Michael's words, made me desperate to lose control just for a moment. To just be free. To feel something for myself.

"I'm good. Let's do this," I whispered back, and gave him a crooked smile. Heat flared in his eyes, and I wondered not for the first time tonight, if he'd done this before. Was this Blue's thing, or was he just caught up in the moment?

He pressed a kiss to my lips, a soft, tender touch. "Turn around and face the cross, Princess."

Doing what I was told, I put my hands up toward the restraints and spread my legs. My skirt rolled up my thighs a little, and I could feel the air cooling the wetness of my lace thong. Blue restrained me with gentle hands, his fingers stroking across my flesh as he moved from my left wrist to my right, leaving goosebumps in their wake. Then he moved both hands down my sides and dropped to his knees behind me. Running his hand down my left thigh to my ankle, I sucked in a breath. Then the he moved over to my right, securing it and tracing his fingers up the back of my knee before curling around my thigh to brush my center. I moaned. Loud. He hooked his fingers under the bottom of my skirt and pulled it up, baring my ass to the entire room. I tried not to feel embarrassed. There was just the two of us in this moment.

He stepped away and I looked over my shoulder at him. He was standing a few feet away, staring at me as if I was the most beautiful piece of artwork he'd ever seen. He picked up something that looked like a multi-headed whip with a smooth black handle, the tiny metal studs that tipped each leather strand shining under the soft lights. Holy shit.

Blue tucked it under his arm and stepped close again. "Eyes forward, Princess." He ran his hand down my spine until he reached my ass. Cupping my cheek in his hand, he gave it a rough squeeze and then pulled his hand back and spanked it. Hard. I sucked in a breath, but didn't let out a peep. Heat flooded my body and I felt like I was on fire. He pulled his hand back and smacked the other cheek, rubbing it soothingly afterwards. This time, I couldn't help it. I moaned long and loud, and I could feel the wetness drip down my thigh. I wanted to rub my thighs together to get some kind of relief, but I was trapped. And I loved it.

The handle of the flogger moved across my ass, dipping down to tease my thighs, so close to where I needed it. Then he pulled it away, but it wasn't long before I felt the studded flogger across the back of my thighs. He wasn't landing it hard; it was more like a kiss of leather. Except the kiss was all teeth. Holy fuck.

I didn't realize I'd sworn out loud until I heard Blue's dark chuckle. He pulled back and laid the flogger on the other side. He wasn't doing it hard, just enough to sting, all the blood rushing to the area. He knelt behind me and licked the tender skin. Then he blew a soft gust of breath across the raised flesh. I dropped my head forward and shuddered. Down there, on his knees behind me, I knew that while he was in control, he was worshiping me as well. Like I was some kind of deity, just like he once accused me of being.

Time after time, the flogger came down, criss-crossing my ass and thighs with red marks that he lavished with his tongue, or brushed with a feather light caress, just using the tips of his fingers. Panting, I turned my head to the side, trying to see his face, even though I could feel the absolute pleasure he was getting from our little scene. I wanted to see the heat in his eyes, feel his lips on mine as I came. But my gaze caught a different set of eyes.

Azriel.

He strode forward like it wasn't weird for the Angel of Death to be in a BDSM club. Hell, maybe it wasn't; there'd already been two Archangels here tonight. He held himself so straight, his face completely unreadable as he walked up to Blue and took the flogger from him.

"What the..." Whatever Blue saw on Azriel's face stole his words. Blue looked between me and the Angel, and took a step away.

"Color," he growled out.

I stared between them, at the intense look in Blue's eyes and the strange lack of emotion on Azriel's. But I could feel their emotions, and Azriel's were a tumult of desire and confusion and jealousy and straight up lust. The Angel, vowed to chastity by the creator himself, so disdainful of his Fallen compatriots, wanted me with a burning need that stole the oxygen from my lungs.

"Green."

Blue nodded, and came to stand beside the cross, his eyes watching Azriel's every move. I expected jealousy or fear, but he had buttoned his feelings up tight.

Azriel put down the flogger and picked up something that looked like a riding crop. He leaned forward, running a single fingertip down the curve of my shoulder blade.

"What is it that you've done to me?" he whispered quietly, and I wasn't sure if he meant me to hear. Stepping back, he stood further away than Blue had, running the tip of the crop up my thighs. He rubbed the flat leather tongue across my wet, lace covered center and my knees went weak. Moving it again, he stroked it back and forwards tentatively, as if he was learning my body by extension.

I bit my lip, holding back the explosion of pleasure that welled under my skin. I wanted this moment to last longer, to give Azriel more time to explore. Letting out a pained moan, I couldn't hold back any longer, so I just let go.

I came hard as the whip continued to stroke me, throwing my head back and moaning my pleasure, uncaring of the other people in the room who were watching me come apart. Azriel moved to my other side, watching my face as my orgasm made me shudder. He was looking at me like I was a science experiment, leaning so close that if I moved just a little, I could kiss him.

But I held still, allowing him to make all the moves, no matter how much I wanted him to close the distance. He leaned closer until his cheek was brushing the stained timber of the Saint Andrews Cross.

"Saint Andrew would not have approved of this at all," he whispered, and disappeared. In front of everyone. What the hell?

I turned to look at Blue. "You saw all that right? You saw him?"

Blue nodded as he unbuckled my feet, and then my wrists, catching me as I fell.

"I want to go home now, Blue," I said quietly as he held me against his chest, his arms supporting me easily.

He nodded, wrapping an arm around my waist, holding me up as we moved through the crowd. Stepping away from me to briefly to talk to the girls at coat check, he was back in a flash, wrapping me in my hunter green trench coat.

We were out of the club and in the back of a cab with a speed that never happened in Manhattan. It was a night for miracles.

Blue tucked me against his body, his hand stroking my hair.

"Hope..." he started, letting his words trail off. His bright pink aura was still there, mashing against the orange of the cab drivers. I knew what he was going to say. Blue had feelings for me, the type of feelings that scared the shit out of us both.

I didn't push him. Right at this moment my empathy really was a curse.

His voice was gruff when he spoke. "Tonight I am going to make love to you like you deserve," he promised. No, it was more than a promise. It was a vow.

CHAPTER TWENTY-FIVE

I woke to Gusion staring down at me in bed, his head tilted to the side. I blinked sleepily and looked over at Blue, who was still snoring and looking heartbreakingly vulnerable in his slumber. I also realized I was naked, and more than a little sore, not only from the club last night, but from the seriously vigorous sex I'd had with Blue when we'd arrived home.

Then we'd snuggled. It had been equal parts weird and absolutely wonderful.

I think that one looks like an elephant, Gus said in my mind. I looked down to where he was pointing, and noticed a love bite on my breast. *That one looks like an umbrella,* he added, pointing to the other one. They both just looked like angry, red skin to me, but maybe I didn't have Gusion's imagination. Blue loved to mark my skin, and sometimes he was a bit of an artist, I think.

I laughed silently, and shifted out of bed. I didn't want to wake Blue. Gusion's eyes followed me as I moved about the room quietly, throwing on Blue's dress shirt that he'd carefully draped over the back of a chair. I tipped my chin at the door, and tried to ignore how the heat in Gusion's eyes made me want to crawl right back into bed with him. We closed the door softly behind us and moved into the kitchen.

Memphis stood there, holding out my mug, and I felt tears well in my eyes. Which was stupid. Maybe I was PMSing. It was just coffee, not a freaking kidney. But the small gesture burrowed its way into my heart.

I swallowed hard and smiled. "Thanks," I said, taking the mug, and because I was unable to resist, I tilted my face up for a kiss. The first touch of his lips on mine felt like relief. The more I was with Memphis, and Gus for that matter, the more they felt like a safe harbor, like the place I was meant to be.

But then there was Blue. And Azriel... I had a sudden, very vivid flashback of last night. The guy was only one step above loathing me. I mean, we had a tentative kind of friendship, maybe. But what I felt last night, and what he had felt, was so far beyond friendship it wasn't even in the same stratosphere. I was pretty sure the definition of a true friend didn't involve orgasms.

"What happened last night?" Memphis asked, his deep voice bringing me back to the present. I looked between my two Fallen Angels, and smiled to myself. This was going to be good.

"Oh, you know, not much. I just chatted to the Archangel Michael at the bar, he gave me the ability to see auras which I'm still a little pissed about by the way, being an empath was more than enough." I held up a hand when Gus went to ask a question. "Hang on, I'm not finished. I worked out that Uriel is turning bad people into religious extremists and Blue tied me to a rack and Azriel made me come with a riding crop. Now you can ask questions."

The silence in the room was deafening, and their stunned expressions filled me with so much glee I could hardly contain it, letting a smug smile curl my lips.

They both spoke at once.

"Michael was where?"

"Azriel did what?"

I began to giggle until I was laughing so hard I had to set down my mug. "Maybe I should start from the beginning."

By the time I was finished, we were all sitting down, me on the bench top and the angels on the kitchen stools.

"I told you Azriel wasn't far from falling. You wait, he'll lose those snowy white wings that he's so damn proud of sooner rather than later."

The idea of Azriel falling made my stomach churn. Even now, with the happiness both Memphis and Gus felt in this moment, there was still that underlying sense of loss. I didn't think it was something I would ever understand. But for Azriel to lose whatever it was that still affected the Fallen millennia later? I didn't want any part of causing that kind of pain, no matter how I felt about Azriel. I would not let him fall because of me.

Memphis shook his head. "I think you a missing the point here, Gus. The Archangel Michael, the very Hand of God was in a BDSM club. Watching Uriel."

Gus rolled his eyes. "It's Michael. He's basically everywhere."

"What you are seemingly too dense to understand, Gusion, is that Michael *knows*. If Michael knows, then the Father knows. If the Father knows, then he is not doing anything to stop it."

Gus shrugged. "Humans do these things every day. It isn't our purview, or the Angel's for that matter, to clean up the mess of humanity. Only they can do that. It is lazy to ask for divine intervention when there is so much they can do to help themselves. No, my interest in Uriel extends only as far as the fact that his morally ambiguous plot almost got Hope killed, and that is something that is in my purview. Because I-" he snapped his mouth shut, and a solid wall came over his emotions like a bank vault.

"Because you what, Gusion, Fallen Angel, Prince of Hell?" Memphis prodded, almost cruelly.

"Because I feel things for her," he turned to me, his face pained, "that I swore I would never feel again. She isn't only your fated True Love, you obnoxious asshole. She's my last chance too. But because I never wanted to feel the pain of losing someone again, I ignored my own fate. But there is no ignoring your destiny. It doesn't give a fuck about your feelings or your plans."

He disappeared then, leaving me staring at the empty air where he'd just been.

"You guys know how to make a dramatic exit," a voice said from behind us, and I turned to see Blue, his eyes hooded and his hair adorably mussed. He wore only his suit pants, that were still miraculously perfectly pressed. He walked over and pressed a kiss to my lips, basically daring Memphis to say anything. Memphis' face tightened, but he stayed silent when I didn't pull away. We had made an agreement, what felt like a life-time ago, and he seemed set on honoring it.

Memphis stood, coming over so he was between my thighs where they dangled from the kitchen bench. He gave me a branding kiss that I felt all the way to my toes, a blend of reverent and resentful that only Memphis could master. I let out a low whimper as his tongue pushed into my mouth and he deepened the kiss. Woah.

Then he broke off and looked at Blue, who's eyes were blazing with anger and jealousy.

"She is not a possession to be had, human. She is a queen to be honored, a soul to be worshipped. What do you have to offer her except death and pain in your short life?"

Blue got up in Memphis' face, either because he was brave or just plain crazy.

He poked Memphis in the chest, and the way the huge angel looked at the offending appendage, I was worried he'd snap it off. "I can offer her a life. Children. A family and a home. You can offer her the pits of hell."

With that, he turned on his heel and stomped back into the bedroom, slamming the door so hard that the picture frames rattled on the walls.

My heart was hammering in my chest, as I tried to comprehend what the hell had just happened. Did Blue admit feelings for me? Did he offer to have my babies? I ran my hands through my tangled red hair, huffing out a breath.

"I can't even, right now." I shimmied off the bench and padded toward the bathroom. "I'm going to have a stupidly long, hot shower, and then if we are all done beating our chests about who owns me, I know a way to track the members of Tenebrae and maybe do some good in the meantime, yeah?"

I closed the bathroom door gently with a soft click, and washed away my worries under a deluge of scalding hot water.

WE SAT in the parking garage of Maximoff Richards apartment building one more time. Maximoff was apparently still in hospital undergoing a range of surgeries to reconstruct his knee. Somehow, I was going to hold off on the mournful violin music for his struggles.

No, I was watching for someone else this time.

When I saw my mark exiting the elevator, I slid from the front seat of the SUV and walked over.

Marco didn't look any different since our last meeting, far less banged up than his employer, and I smiled in greeting. My smile fell when I saw who was behind him though. A beautifully made up woman, her blonde hair falling down her back in what was obviously a very expensive haircut, a designer bag clutched tight against her body. A boy, about six, with big, sad eyes stood beside her, clutching the hand of a tiny, dark-eyed girl, a stuffed bunny pressed against her chest. The Richards family. Maximoff's wife and kids. Apparently, Marco was the bodyguard for the whole family.

Marco took a step forward, his face a feral kind of

angry, standing between me and the group of people behind him. I held up my hands placatingly. "Hey Marco. We are all good." I searched his aura for the tell-tale red stain of Uriel, but I got nothing but a furious yellow. I breathed out a sigh of relief. However, I couldn't say the same for Mrs Richards, who's aura was stained right up to her shoulder and across her chest. Tenebrae.

I stopped, really staring at the group then. Marco wasn't standing between us, and Mrs Richards. He was standing between me and the kids.

Well, that was interesting. I stared hard at the little girl with her huge brown eyes that looked oddly like Marco's and nothing like Maximoff Richards. I remembered what Blue said about that slime-ball, how he beat his wife and kids, and another piece of the puzzle that was Marco fell into place.

I focused on Marco's emotions, and he had that cold, flat feeling that Blue got when he was working. He was ready to do what needed to be done, to protect the kid. I pushed deeper. Both kids, though only the girl was his. He felt nothing but disdain for Mrs Richards though, although at some point he must have felt something more for her, if my understanding of the birds and the bees was right.

"What's going on here, Marco?" Mrs Richard's high pitched voice was grating. "I'm going to be late."

Marco signed something at the little boy, who translated. "He says that if we would like to get into the vehicle, he'll be a second. That these people are associates of our Father."

I felt the surge of disgust in Blue's emotions, but he didn't refute the claim.

Mrs Richards' huffed, and strode off, leaving the kids to trail after her. Marco signed something else, causing the little boy to smile, and the little girl to sign something clumsily back. The boy held the girl's hand as they walked carefully toward the huge, pretentious BMW.

I put a hand out to touch Marco's fingers as he watched the kids in the carpark.

I was prepared for the wave of love he felt directed entirely at the two departing figures.

"Yours?" the question was a little redundant.

Cara is mine. Sammy isn't mine by blood, but he's still mine, you know?

Apparently, Marco remembered that he could speak directly to me. I'd wondered if he'd write the whole thing off as a concussion induced hallucination.

"Mrs Richards looks like a bitch," I whispered in a low, conspiratorial voice.

He laughed inside my mind, and it made me smile. *She's worse. Not as bad as her husband, but she isn't a good person.* Sadness, frustration, anger all leaked from him, and I could only imagine what would cause such a tightly leashed ball of negative emotions.

"I'm here to fix that, I guess. I want to bring them all down, but especially Maximoff Richards. But I'll need your help. I'll make sure the kids don't suffer any hardship, I swear it. Plus, I know some really good lawyers and some really 'persuasive' people, I guess you could say."

You sound like a mobster. His eyes were on Blue when he said that. Smart man.

"Not the illegal kind of persuasive. More the biblical kind, I guess." I winced at my explanation. I sounded absolutely insane.

Marco regarded me, and then Blue and Memphis behind me. The hitman and the Prince of Hell. Well, the watered down version of the Prince of Hell. He still looked as scary as a nightmare under your bed, though.

I see what you mean. Okay, meet me at Giovanni's Pizza at ten. You know the place?

Uh, yeah, I knew the place. Best pie in the city. I nodded.

Marco turned and left, climbing into the front of the BMW and peeling out of the lot.

"Giovanni's at ten," I told the guys, who were only privy to my side of the conversation.

"Can we trust him?" Blue asked, but the question was almost rhetorical. He came from the old school where you didn't trust anyone.

But I knew a man who could see your darkest secrets. I turned to Memphis. "What do you think?"

He paused, his eyes watching the BMW's taillights disappear into traffic. He nodded, but his face was grim. "Only one way to find out."

CHAPTER TWENTY-SIX

I sat on Gusion's lap as I ate the perfect blend of sauce, cheese and pizza dough. This seriously was the best pizza in Manhattan. Gus had reappeared in the early afternoon, after our visit with Marco the Marshmallow, and went on like nothing had happened this morning. Like he hadn't had a disagreement with Memphis and basically said he loved me and that I was his fated soulmate.

And you know what? I was okay with that. I had enough on my plate without unpacking all that stuff right now.

Gus kneaded my denim covered hip, making happy little orgasm sounds as he chewed his pizza.

"We need to teach the demonesses how to make this shit," he said on a moan. Memphis let out a low chuckle.

"Sure, but you can be the one to tell Ace why those harpies are all up in the palace." I wiggled back further in Gus' lap, making him emit a noise that had nothing to do with pizza and everything to do with the fact my ass was pressed right against the growing hardness in his pants.

"You sure we can trust this guy? How about we just go home right now?" His voice sounded pained, and I smiled sadistically. No prize for guessing what he'd do as soon as we stepped through the door of my apartment.

I shook my head at him and just enjoyed the moment. How long had it been since I'd just taken a moment and really appreciated how lucky I was? Before Rella's death, certainly. Maybe even before my abduction. These guys gave me something, a refuge from the constant bombardment of life that was my curse, or blessing. Each one was becoming more and more special to me, and I was petrified that one day soon, they would make me choose. I thought of Azriel.

Fallen Angels, Death and a Hitman did not share well, even for me. It was a recipe for disaster.

But that was a problem for another day. Today, I was going to enjoy good food and good company and a hard body beneath my ass. I could worry about what-ifs tomorrow.

Marco moved silently for such a big man. He sat down at the empty seat at the end of the table, and picked up a slice of pizza.

I moved my hand toward his, and laced his fingers in mine. Gusion let out a low, ominous sound in his chest.

Aww, he was jealous. "He's mute. It's the easiest way for us to communicate. Unless you know sign language?" I teased.

Gus scowled, but didn't say anything.

I see what you mean now about all the alpha personalities. The big guys are scary as hell.

I laughed. Hell jokes never got old.

"You have no idea. The kids?"

Off at etiquette camp for the week, or some bullshit.

I didn't need to be an empath to sense his disgruntlement on that one.

"Aren't they a little young?" I asked. The girl, Cara, couldn't have been much more than three.

Yes. I sensed I wasn't getting more than that on the subject. *What do you want from me?*

I wished I could speak into his mind the way I could with the angels, but instead I lowered my voice until it was barely a whisper.

"I want to burn your employers world to the ground. I want to take all his associates and any other member of Tenebrae I can find out of the equation for good. I need his contacts."

I didn't know if he just had a good poker face, or if he was aware of the secret society, but he showed no confusion. We all sat in silence for a while as Marco thought over my offer. He didn't ask who or what Tenebrae was, which was either a good sign, or a really bad one. I ate the remaining pizza, because it was too good to abandon. That's my kind of sacrilege.

Okay. But I need your guarantee that the kids will not be hurt, and if anything happens to me, that they are taken care of properly.

"Done," I said, though it wasn't much of a bargain. I had seen those kids with my own two eyes, sensed their trauma. I did not have it in me to make their childhoods worse, and I lacked the ability to sit on my hands while others suffered. I was the tender-hearted do-gooder Maximoff had so scathingly accused me of being. Even if Marco had turned down our offer, I would have helped those children.

Let's get out of here and I'll tell you what I know. Tenebrae have eyes and ears everywhere.

He would have sounded like a supporting actor in a cheesy spy movie, if every word hadn't been completely true.

IF I DIDN'T HAVE the guys at my back, I'd have been really worried when Marco led us to a secluded under-pass. If this was a B-grade movie, this is the part where the plucky heroine dies from her own stupidity. But I felt pretty secure with Memphis, Gus and Blue by my side.

A little voice inside my brain reminded me that Rella had a merc, two gargoyles and the son of an Irish Mafia family at her back, and she still died in the most horrific way possible. My chest suddenly began to restrict, and I sucked oxygen into lungs that refused to work. It happened anytime I thought about the exact circum-stances of Rella's death. Her fear, her grief, her pain.

Gusion twined his fingers in mine, squeezing them tight, grounding me. Now was not the time to have a panic attack. I saw the glint of a gun in the back of Blue's jeans, and it both reassured and scared me.

Marco's eyes bored into mine, and I knew he was trying to speak to me. I stepped forward, but Blue's hand crossed my torso, stopping me.

"Just so you know, you harm a single hair on her head, I will kill you in the slowest, most painful way I know how. Then I'll do the same to every person you've ever loved. And there'll be no rest for you in the afterlife, that is a promise." His voice was cold, but certain. He meant every single word. Warmth for Blue flooded me. I didn't know what I'd done to earn his loyalty, but I was glad I had it.

Marco nodded. It must be rough to be a mute with such a particular skill set. I wrapped my hand around Marco's wrist.

I wouldn't sleep too often around that one. He screams crazy. You should sleep with a knife beneath your pillow.

I laughed. "He is the knife beneath my pillow."

Dropping my hand, he walked to the underpass, lifting rubble out of the way to find a hole that had been chiseled into the wall. Inside the nook was a small leather-bound journal. He handed it to me without flourish, his fingers touching mine.

That's the names and addresses of every person he's ever met, every late-night secret meeting, every illegal activity. The things, the people, he's bought and sold. I was saving it to black- mail him for custody of Cara. But I couldn't leave Sammy behind. These people... they aren't here to fuck around. If they know you are sniffing about, you are as good as dead. They'll not only take your life, but your reputation, leave your family destitute, have your dog put to sleep. Their reach knows no bounds. They have everyone from police to politicians in their ranks.

I flicked the book open and saw names I knew, people I'd been to fundraisers with, voted for, sat beside at society luncheons and some I went to school with. The money was staggering in itself.

Tenebrae paid, and paid well.

"This is perfect. It's all the proof we need."

It won't hold up in court. It's all circumstantial, and the things I did while I was employed by Richards...

He trailed off, but I knew his horror at his actions, his self-loathing. I reached out and brushed his cheek. "Don't worry, Marco. We don't deal in legalities. We deal in justice." I stepped away, feeling like a badass. As we walked back toward our car, I looked over my shoulder.

"If you can Marco, I'd try and get a DNA test done. Cara is going to need her Daddy soon."

I slid into the back seat of our SUV, and Memphis slid in beside me. Blue drove, and Gusion sat beside him. We pulled out from the underpass and back onto the freeway. Using my phone, I sent photos of every page to Lux and Tolliver.

Tolliver would sink the company. Lux would sink the man.

I would take care of the rest of Tenebrae, and I knew just the avenging Angel to help me.

I waited until I was home, in my kitchen, drinking a glass of wine before I called Ace. She was like a hurricane in a teacup and her emotions were so intense all the time. She loved as fiercely as she hated. She only lived in the shades of grey in life. But she was vengeance personified. She believed in punishing those that preyed on the weak.

Ace? Ace, I need you. My entire life, that was all it had

taken. Four words, and she would be there. She loved me so fiercely, almost as she much as she loved Luc.

Ace appeared, speckled with blood on her dove grey wings. She looked like the goddess of war with her long black hair, her lithe frame basically a teenage boys wet dream.

"Are you okay, Hope? I was a little, uh, preoccupied."

My stomach turned at the sight of the blood, but that seemed a little hypocritical considering what I was about to do. I handed her Marco's notebook. She took the book and looked at Gus and Memphis who were reclining on my breakfast stools like they owned the place.

"Did you break the Princes of Hell, Hope? Because, I'm pretty sure Memphis is smiling." She eyed him like he was a clone, or an alien, or something.

I looked over my shoulder at Memphis, who did look content. I smiled at him, and he gave me a warm look.

I shrugged at Ace. "We are taking it slow. We're figuring it out. You aren't, you know, angry or anything?"

Ace made a rude noise. "I want the assholes to be happy. You seem to make them happy. Or maybe Gusion's just constipated. I could never tell the difference between those two expressions."

Gusion laughed and gave her a rude gesture. Ace grinned, and it was one of those completely raw expressions that meant you couldn't help but grin back. She looked over at Blue. "I gotta say though, our family doesn't have a good track record with Mulligans.

Although your sister seems reasonably content with hers if the noises that coming from their wing of the palace is anything to go by."

I slapped my hands over my ears. "Seriously, Ace? That's gross. No more details." I meant it too. I was glad Rella was happy, even in death, but I didn't need details.

She flicked through the pages of the notebook, the mirth slowly leaving her face. "What have you brought me?"

"All your Christmas' have come at once. I'm pretty sure all these people are Tenebrae or people who have done business with Tenebrae. But luckily, I have a system for knowing who is innocent, and who is rotten to the core."

Ace raised both eyebrows. "Oh, have you become an Angel overnight?"

I grinned. "Kind of. I met an Archangel in a dungeon and he gave me the ability to see auras."

Ace's mouth swung open like one of those cartoon characters. "I think you better start from the beginning."

CHAPTER TWENTY-SEVEN

We sat out the front of an ordinary office building uptown, its shiny glass and chrome exterior pretty, but wouldn't win any design awards. It was average, just like the people who exited its rotating front door.

Well, they were average to the naked eye. To me, every single one had an aura, and a good portion of the people leaving the building had a parasite on their aura, a shining red promise of damnation. They varied of course. Some had barely more than a spot. Some were consumed by the red parasite that circled their entire bodies, eating away at their aura, and their humanity in a slow, methodical way.

"Can you see the auras?" I asked Ace, who was sitting in the front seat of an extremely ostentatious mustang that went way, way too fast. I'd learned that the hard way.

She shook her head. "Not with the same clarity that you can, apparently. I can see their auras, but there's no red. There's more like a…" she paused and rubbed her cheek as she struggled to find the word. "Like a smudge over a section. Like a fingerprint on a camera lens. It's not noticeable unless I look at it in the right light. It must be why I never noticed before," she said, more to herself than to me. Ace hated being wrong.

"So what's the plan?" I asked quietly. For the first time in a while, I was without my looming male escorts. Basically, because Ace and her sword were scary as hell.

"I'm going to go in, kill the ones that need killing."

My stomach turned at the violence. Too late to back out now, though. I just pushed the taste of fear that I'd witnessed at the club to the front of my mind. These were not good people.

But still…

"Do you think there's any way to remove Uriel's mark? Give them a chance to turn their lives around?" My family were big on redemption. All of my fathers, each of the seven, had been damned to hell for a reason. But that was a story for another day.

Ace cupped her cheek as she rested her elbow on the armrest, drumming her fingers across her cheekbone. "Maybe. Hang on, I'll be right back."

She slammed out of the car and walked around the corner out of sight. I watched the people coming and going from the office building, mentally sorting them into categories. Tenebrae, Non-Tenebrae, oblivious to anything other than the video-games he wants to play later, Tenebrae, Non-Tenebrae.

The driver's door reopened, and Ace hopped in, stuffing a red-headed kid in before her. He looked at me with huge wide eyes and I noticed he had small brown freckles across his nose. He didn't look much older than me.

"Hope meet… what's your name, kid?"

"Uh, Ben?"

I smiled, and looked Ben's aura over. Wrapping around his right hand, discoloring his sunny yellow aura, was an insidious red spot. Poor Ben.

"Did you kidnap me a test subject?" I asked Ace, who just grinned and shrugged.

She lifted up Ben's right hand. "It's here, right? I wanted to test myself, see if I could pick up even the subtlest of marks."

I nodded, and took Ben's hand. "Ben, how do you feel about human trafficking?"

The kid's face went pale, even his freckles washed out, and his eyes went wide with fear. I probably should have phrased that question better. "I mean, do you think it's a reasonable way to make money. I promise, we aren't about to sell you for parts or anything."

For some strange reason, my words didn't seem to reassure him. Ace shook him a little by the shoulders. "Answer the question, Benji."

"Uh, I don't like it?"

"Sweatshops that employ child labor?"

"Not good."

"Undermining a coworkers' chances at promotion by spreading rumors?"

This time, Ben hesitated, heat flushing his cheeks and his eyes going a little wild. "I only did it once."

I brushed his floppy red hair off his forehead gently.

"Once is enough to ruin a life, Ben." I looked at Ace. "Do you think if we chopped off his hand, that would stop the mark?"

Ace gave a considering look at the aforementioned hand, holding Ben still as he tried to climb over her and back out the car door.

"We could try. It does seem to be confined to his hand. I think if we get it at the elbow, we should be fine."

I could feel the rapid thrumming of Ben's thoughts. His fear, his regret. I rested my other hand on his head, pushing positive emotions toward him, forgiveness, absolution, the promise that he had time to fix his mistakes. It was an ability that worked sometimes, but it was patchy. It always worked best with Rella.

"Well, that's new," Ace murmured beneath her breath, and I looked down at Ben's aura, and noticed the red fading until it was like it had never been there.

Ace grabbed Ben's face, and I felt his fear ratchet up, but the red taint didn't return.

"Listen, Ben. Consider yourself lucky. But if you fuck up again, try and take the easy way up by causing suffering, there will be no second chance for you. I'll cut off your hand and bitch slap you with it, got it?"

Ben nodded, and tumbled out of the car and onto the footpath. He ran so fast, he was basically a blur.

"Well, that complicates things. I was going to sift in and slash anyone who had Uriel's mark, but now I actually have to be picky." Ace pouted like I'd just told her that Santa wasn't bringing her a puppy this year.

She opened the book, mentally ticked off a few

names, then disappeared into thin air. I sat in the car, the sounds of AC/DC's *Highway to Hell* playing through Ace's stereo speakers and I wondered whether this would stain my soul, like Luc had said. I had instigated this after all, even if I wasn't the one, err, slashing.

"This is interesting." I screeched as someone spoke from the back seat of the Mustang. I whipped around and gave Azriel the stink eye. "Seriously? Are you messing with me right now?"

There was a tiny smirk on his lips, and I realized he was actually messing with me. He thought it was funny. I didn't have the heart to yell at him for giving me a freaking heart attack again, not when it made him show open emotion, even if it was at my expense.

"Hello, Azriel."

My voice was huskier than I intended, my mind flicking back to the BDSM club. I saw him swallow, and his face go carefully blank. That was when I realized I couldn't feel his emotions any longer. Instead, the smooth barrier that Memphis and Gus could place over their emotions blocked me. I reached out and touched his hand, but I still got nothing. I wondered if I kissed his lips, whether that wall would crack in two.

"I heard that you have the ability to sense the emotions of others. I suspect it's not just humans though, am I right?" He was looking at my lips, and maybe I imagined it, or it was wishful thinking, but I thought I saw longing in the depths of his ancient eyes.

I gave him my own blank look. Apparently, my empathic abilities were hot news on the Angel grapevine. I wondered how long it would take to get

THE FALLEN   255

back to Ace and Luc. I was going to get my ass kicked for a second time this week. "What are you talking about?"

His lips twitched. "Keep your secrets, Child of Acerezeal." He leaned forward and stared at the office building. "There seems to be an alarming call for my services in there. And here you sit. Care to tell me what is occurring?"

I shrugged, not seeing the harm. "Tenebrae, the organization that arranged my abd-," I swallowed back the word. I still couldn't talk about it without my heart feeling like it was going to explode from my chest. "That arranged what happened in Geneva, operate out of this office building. Ace is doing what she does best. Exacting retribution."

His eyes narrowed as they snapped back toward the building, his face going cold. "I see. You are morally fine with her doing this on your behalf?"

I stiffened my spine, staring at him straight in his beautiful face. "Yes." I dared him to argue, to tell me I was wrong.

Instead, he just flexed his jaw and his hands tightened on the headrest of the driver's seat. "Me too."

Then he was gone too.

It wasn't long until people began to pour out of the building like ants from a kicked nest and I could hear the steady wail of sirens. I contemplated leaving, even though I was in a car park right across the street, as far as you could be from the center of the chaos. I wondered how Memphis and Gus were going holding up our end of the bargain with Marco. I didn't want details. I didn't want to know the end result. I just wanted the whole thing to be over.

I watched the vivid red auras of the first responders screech to a stop in front of the building. They were almost all fire engine red, not the oozing old blood red of Uriel's mark. I hoped Ace would know the difference.

A knock on the driver's window made me jump in my seat. I looked over to see a policeman in an NYPD uniform leaning in.

"Ma'am, I'm going to need you to move this vehicle."

I nodded frantically, getting out of the passenger side and walking around to the driver's side, glad Ace had left me the keys. I tried not to act suspicious. "Of course, Officer. Is everything okay in there?" I nodded toward the building, telling myself that a normal bystander would be interested.

The police officer nodded. "We believe there has been an incidence of bioterrorism." The older Officers face softened. "Go home and lock your doors," he said quietly.

I touched his hand. "Be careful," I said, and sincerely meant it. I trusted Ace not to deviate from the plan, but I was beginning to worry we hadn't planned for the insanity of humanity. People did not think clearly in these kinds of situations. Panic prevailed.

The cop waved me off, and I pulled out into the rolling traffic, everyone gawping at the building. Ace needed to hurry the hell up before she ended up in prison. Again.

With no other options, I drove back toward my apartment.

I was going to get Azriel to take me to see Michael again. Maybe he could petition to the Big Guy on my behalf. This cycle of violence, even though I perpetuated it, couldn't keep going. Uriel needed to be reined in or stopped. Then everything would be okay. We could clean up the insidious violence that had wormed its way into the very fabric of society. Slowly. Cut off the head of the snake, the body will wither and die.

I missed Rella right then. I wondered what she would say about this whole thing. I laughed to myself. If Rella was still alive, I would be nowhere near this violence. She would be kicking ass and I would be sheltered in my own little bubble, trying to help the world while ignoring my own problems.

I breathed a sigh of relief when I saw my building coming up. Pulling into the underground carpark, I parked the mustang behind my tiny Tesla. It stuck out a little, but it would be fine. Ace would come and take it back soon enough, and store it wherever else she stored her worldly possessions when she was living it up in Hell.

I stepped from the elevator that led to the carpark, and crossed the foyer to the private elevator that went straight to the penthouse. I smiled at the doorman. He was young and handsome, and so new I couldn't remember his name. I scanned his aura for a red patch out of habit, but it was a warm orange that seemed to match his fake tan and his big smile so much brighter.

"Hi," I said warmly. "Is my bodyguard back yet?"

The man shook his head. "Not yet, Miss. Would you like me to call up when he arrives?"

I waved him off. "No, it's okay."

Blue was off talking to a contact who could fake a paternity test so well, you'd start seeing the same features in the kid, even if he was completely unrelated. We figured that if Marco could get one legitimately for Cara, then maybe we could give the tests for Sammy a little nudge in the right direction. I kept remembering his big, sad eyes, the flicker of warmth when he signed to Marco, the care with which he held his sister's hand in the car park, taking better care of her than her own mother. I couldn't leave any child in that situation. Especially when it was just some well-placed funds and a guy who knew a guy, and I could provide him with love and a happy home.

Unlocking my apartment, I slipped off my shoes, suddenly emotionally exhausted. I needed a bath, a glass of wine and a huge block of chocolate. Preferably all at once.

But first, wine.

Pulling down a glass, I pulled a bottle from the rack. It was fancy, and I was supposed to let it breathe, but I just poured it straight into my glass, right to the top, and prayed that Valery never found out. He was such a wine snob, and the reason I had so many good bottles of wine.

"Hello, Hope."

I screamed and dropped my glass, the fine crystal shattering and splashing on my feet, tiny shards nicking my skin.

I was blinded by the white light of the Archangel before me, his bright red hair making him look like a candle in a white hot flame.

"You've been meddling in the affairs of Archangels, Child. And I cannot have that," he stepped forward, his words echoing Luc's, making me remember a promise I'd made when this all began. As his hand made contact with my wrist, I screamed to the only being I knew could save me.

LUC!

PART III

PART II

CHAPTER TWENTY-EIGHT

The static of a radio pierced the darkness first. It was fuzzy, like it was just slightly out of range. It was damn annoying anyway. Whatever the announcer was saying was almost indecipherable under the static.

Wait.

I sat bolt upright in the darkness. It was a darkness so thick that you felt like you had to wade through it. The frigid coldness made my lungs burn, but I felt warm. I touched a hand to my face and realized my skin felt like ice. Panic made me suck in huge gulps of the freezing air.

Memphis? Gus? I called into the darkness, panic gripping me. No answer. I called again.

Ace? Luc? I yelled again, tugging hard on my connections. *LUC!* I screamed into the ether.

My hands gripped something beneath me that felt like a thin blanket.

Luc! I screamed again. I felt the call reverberate

around my brain. I blinked hard so I didn't cry. It was so cold, I wasn't convinced my tears wouldn't freeze on my cheeks.

Hope? Luc's voice sounded far away, and I didn't know how that was possible.

Air whooshed from my lungs, and the burning lessened. I wasn't alone. The tears I tried to stop froze on my eyelashes.

Luc. Huge wracking sobs shook my chest. *You were right, I should have listened.*

His relief flooded down our bond, strong despite the quietness of his voice. *Thank the Father, you're okay.* His emotions were palpable, even with the weak connection. *Where are you? I can't fucking find you. Estrella can't find you. I was so...* His voice was hoarse, and he didn't have to say the words. He was scared I was dead.

It was Uriel. He just stole me right from the kitchen in the apartment. My heart thundered at the memory of that serenely cruel face. It should have been impossible, but Uriel scared me more than the Devil. *I don't know where I am, Luc. It's dark and it's so fucking cold. I can't see.*

I stood, putting my hands out in front of me. I reached back and grabbed the thin blanket, wrapping it around my shoulders, suddenly glad I decided to get wine before I took my shoes off this afternoon. Or maybe it was yesterday. How long had I been out for?

I walked straight until I felt a wall, clinging to my connection with Luc.

I followed the wall, until I felt an opening. My heart was thundering, my ears straining for the hint of a sound. Any sound. But there was nothing but silence.

Not the wind rattling the building or the sound of crickets. There was just the cold and dark and that stupid radio. My eyes hadn't adjusted to the dark. There was just nothingness.

I turned left. If I kept turning left, surely I would find a door, or a window, or something that led outside, right?

Hope? Talk to me! Luc sounded panicked, which made me panic. Nothing fazed Luc. Not even being cast into hell.

I'm here. I'm looking for a door, or a way out, or a freakin' light-switch or something, I grumbled, so he wouldn't know how terrified I was right now. I could be strong, even when my knees felt like they were frozen, not with the cold but with fear.

What can you tell me about where you are?

I could tell him that it felt like death. Like the inside of a coffin, six feet underground.

It's cold. And it must be night and somewhere rural because there's not even the barest hint of light anywhere. There's a radio playing but I can't understand the words. It sounds Nordic, or Russian or something. I'm so shit at languages. Why hadn't I paid better attention to my languages subjects, instead of Mr. Rosanna's emotional turmoil over his divorce?

Luc? Are you still there? Are Memphis and Gus okay? Blue? Tell them not to... fuck!

I swore as I tripped over something on the floor. I flew forward a couple of feet, banging into what felt like dozens of hard objects that were basically all corners. I hit my head, felt the hot splash of blood on my skin, before I finally slowed to a stop on my back.

I hurt all over, every bump felt like I was being stabbed by knives because my skin was still so cold. Tears streamed down my cheeks and froze. I was going to die here. I could feel it deep down in my bones.

I wondered if I would go to Heaven or Hell? I wondered if I really wanted to go somewhere that there was no Rella. No Ace and Luc. No Memphis and Gusion. Already, the idea of an existence without them made something inside me whimper.

Hope? Hope? I realized Luc was yelling at me, though it was hard to hear over the ringing in my ears. He sounded fearful. Shit.

I'm okay. I just tripped. I'm going to have to drop our connection for a bit to concentrate, otherwise I'll break my neck in this darkness. I paused, trying to hoist myself to my elbows, and rubbing a forearm against my eyes. *Luc? You will find me, right?*

There was a long silence, and I thought he'd left. I wasn't prepared for the completely desolate feeling that pierced my soul.

I will find you Hope, Child of my Beloved. Child of Mine. I will raze the face of the earth until I find you. Do not despair.

Then his consciousness left mine, and I was really alone. And I let the tears fall freely this time, uncaring if they froze against my eyelids.

Again. I'd been abducted twice in two months. Who had I pissed off that I would be tormented like this over and over? Either I had the world's shittiest luck, or my parents had really ticked the Big Guy off.

I sobbed into the darkness, wallowing in my pity party for one. The rats scuttled about, their breathing loud. It seemed almost wrong. I sat up further, crawling back the way I thought I came on battered knees. I hit a massive pile of downy blankets, piled high, right beside the wall. Well, at least I knew what I tripped over. The blood running down my face was beginning to slow, though I wasn't sure if it was because it was clotting or freezing, but at this point it didn't really matter.

Shifting through the blankets, I tried to find the source of the noise.

Until something grabbed my wrist.

CHAPTER TWENTY-NINE

I screamed, and jerked my hand away, scrambling back in the darkness. The sound of my panting seemed too loud in the silence of this place.

"Help." It was barely more than a whisper, but finally I felt, more than heard, the other person. Even their emotions were almost non-existent. I knew what that meant, had felt that protective fog that numbs emotions and pain right before the end. Whoever was underneath that pile of blankets was close to death.

Death meant Azriel. He would come to take the soul of the unfortunate person, and he would save me.

"Help," the voice whispered again, so weak I couldn't tell if it was a man or a woman.

I could be rescued, and all I had to do was not help. To sit on my hands and let nature take its course. I could be ruthless, just this once.

"Please."

Who was I kidding? I could never do that.

"Hey, I'm here. It's okay, I'm coming back over. You

scared me, that's all," I said as I crawled back toward the pile. Damn, damn, damn. I couldn't do nothing.

I began to peel back layers of blankets until my fingers tangled in long, stringy hair. A woman, maybe? The smell beneath the blankets made me gag. But when my fingers touched skin, it was almost so hot it seared my fingertips. She had a fever so bad, she was probably cooking.

Throwing off the rest of the blankets, I gagged at the smell of infection that wafted from the beneath the blankets. I tried not to think about germs and diseases as I dragged the woman, I decided it was a woman until further notice, away from the spot and to the other side of the room. Not far enough away in my opinion, but at least I wasn't going to puke on her. The smell of infection followed us.

The woman whimpered and I stopped, laying her back down as she shivered. But already her body was slightly cooler. "Where are you injured?"

"Left ankle," the voice was dry and raspy. "Tripped. It's broken. Wrist is broken." She seemed to run out of air or energy or something. She sucked in a painful sounding breath. "Gash, right leg."

Oh shit. In this place, in this cold, it was a wonder she wasn't dead already. I couldn't see her wound, so I moved my hands down her face, to her shoulders and down her arms."Okay. I'm Hope, by the way. I'm just going to try to assess your injuries in this godforsaken darkness so excuse the wandering hands." I felt the swollen flesh of her right wrist, felt the weird angle of the bones. Yep, that was broken all right. I followed down her side and over her hip, patting down her leg looking for the gash. I didn't have to search long, as the radiant heat of the infection travelled up most of her leg, and the oozing pus of the four inch wound was tacky against my fingertips. I was definitely going to puke now.

The woman was making this dry, raspy, wheezing noise, and I realized she was crying.

"Hey, don't worry," I said, lifting my non-pus covered hand to her face and cupping her cheek, sending her reassuring emotions. "It's going to be okay now. What's your name?"

"Sera," it was a cough. "Short for Serendipity."

I couldn't help the choked laugh that came out. Someone had a divine sense of humor. "Sera. Looks like both our parents like inspirational names. Okay, we have to do something about that leg. Do you know if there's a bathroom or a shower or something in this place? We need to get you a drink, clean this wound, and tidy you up a little. We could do it now, or we can wait until morning and there's a bit more light."

"No light."

"What?" I stared down at her, a bit redundantly really considering it was so dark. I couldn't even see the outline of her head. The only reason I could see her at all was because of the fist sized pink ball of her aura near the center of her chest. Shouldn't my eyes at least be partially adjusted by now?

"Never gets light. Always dark." Then she began to cry again.

I cried right along with her, our combined emotions

finally too much. How had she survived the pain and the darkness? I sucked in a deep, shuddering breath and wiped my eyes on my shoulder. I didn't want to risk putting my filth covered hands anywhere near my face.

"I'll get us out of here, Sera. Just wait. But first, we need a bathroom."

Sera grabbed my hand, and squeezed hard. The pressure of her hand in mine gave me hope. Then she uncurled my hand and drew a map with her finger on my palm.

"Stay to the walls. Kitchen and bathroom side by side."

My heart buoyed a little at the idea of a kitchen. Maybe it had food. Maybe I wasn't going to starve alone, well not technically alone, in the dark, if hypothermia didn't get me first.

"Okay, hold on. This will probably hurt a little, but I'll try and be gentle." I put my arms under her armpits and dragged her gently along the wall. I let my blanket fall to the ground. I thought briefly about putting her on it and dragging her that way, but I was loathe to dirty possibly the only unsoiled blanket left in the building.

We had to be underground. The cold, the complete absence of light. It was the only thing that made sense.

Although I tried to ignore it, each whimper of pain that Sera let out pierced my heart. But her directions were good.

"Let's get you in the shower. A warm shower makes everything better."

"Water's cold," Sera said, her teeth chattering.

Of course it fucking was. This was hell. No, it

wasn't, because Hell would have Rella, Memphis and Gus.

What if the water was icy, like the temperature in here? What if it sent her into cardiac shock? Was that even possible? I needed light. I needed help.

The static filled voice continued to play, and if I ever found that radio, I was going to smash it to pieces. The floor switched to a rough stone, so we must have made it into the kitchen. That was a wild assumption, but my gut was all I had to go on right now.

I lowered Sera back to the ground gently, feeling my way around the room for something, anything. A sink. Water. Food.

I bumped into a table, pushing it forward, the sound of wood scraping on stone ear-piercingly loud in the room. I felt my way around it, to the other wall. My hand hit something coarse. I knew this texture.

"It's wood! We can make a fire!" I shouted to Sera.

"No matches," she answered, her voice getting thready.

Dammit, dammit, dammit. There had to be a way, I just needed a little light.

Why hadn't I joined Boy Scouts? Or been interested in anything outside of my mind? If I rubbed two sticks together, would it work?

I wasn't Chuck Norris, able to kick ass and take on anything with just my ginger beard and devil-may-care smirk. The closest I'd ever come to being a survivalist was watching Bear Grylls with my Dad.

I walked forlornly away from the pile of wood, in what I realized was a slightly raised fireplace. A long marble bench, with a sink, ran along the wall beside the fireplace. I turned on the tap, and dipped my fingers in. And then pulled them back as the icy chill of the water burned my already cold fingers.

I swallowed down the scream that was threatening to suffocate me. It was like this place was designed to send you insane. Light deprivation, coldness, noise that was completely incomprehensible. Wood but no matches. Water but no heat. This was a torture chamber of the worst kind.

But I wouldn't let it beat me. I was tougher than this now. I was a BAMF.

There was a kitchen sponge in the sink, and I dreaded to think what germs it had on it, but at least I could use it to wipe the worst of the grossness from Sera.

My fingers brushed on the steel wool sitting on a draining rack. No matches, but a full range of stuff to do the dishes. This was definitely Hell.

Something stuttered in my brain, my fingers stilling on the steel wool. There was something there, some memory that I needed, hiding in my mind. I could have screamed in frustration.

Dad had been watching one of those prepper shows that always made him laugh. I used to tease him that he only watched it for the beard-spiration. I'd seen an episode where they'd used steel wool to light a fire. But it was only if you had something else random. I slammed my hand against the sink over and over again, hoping it would shake the words loose in my brain. I remember thinking what were the chances of being stranded without matches, yet you had steel wool in your pocket and…batteries!

I had to find that damn radio. I moved back around the room toward Sera, my hands sweeping across surfaces.

"Sera, do you know where the radio is?" I said, sounding out of breath. Fire meant light and warmth and hope. We needed this to work.

"In the living room. It doesn't get any other channel or music. Just the same Latin phrases droning on and on, slightly out of tune." The despair in her voice made my chest hurt. How long had she been here for?

That was a question for when we were clean and warm in front of a fire. I followed the wall back through the door, toward the sound of the radio. I was pretty sure it was being pumped into all the rooms through speakers, but who listened to a channel in Latin? Who even spoke Latin anymore?

So many questions but so few answers.

The voice on the radio got louder and louder. I was heading in the right direction, but was getting hopelessly lost in my desperation. I stopped and took a few deep breaths to slow my racing heart. I hoped I could use Sera as a guide to find my way back. I closed my eyes. Instead of struggling to see, I tilted my head and listened. My hands in front of me, I stepped from the wall and into the inky nothingness in the middle of the room. I followed the odd, discombobulated voice. My feet were sure and steady as I moved around unseen obstacles.

Finally, my hands settled on an old, wireless radio.

"Please. Please. Please," I chanted as my fingers felt around on the back of the radio for a battery compartment. "Please," I prayed once more, my nails lodging in a groove in the plastic along the back. I held my breath as I pried open the compartment, uncaring of my nails pulling back painfully. I needed this more. A small, nine volt battery popped out of the back and into my hand.

"YES!" I yelled, hoping Sera could hear me. The radio continued to play. It must have had a secondary power source. I sighed. I would have liked for it to fall silent. It would have been a silver lining.

"Sera? Can you hear me?"

The thready reply was barely audible, but I got a general direction. "Did you ever play Marco Polo as a kid? Who knew that would become a valuable life skill. Ready? Marco!" I yelled, straining to hear her whispery, "Polo."

We did this a few more times until I was back in the kitchen, the cold flagstone floor beneath my feet. I moved toward Sera, leaning down to touch her forehead. Well, I was aiming for her forehead. I got her in the shoulder and then in the eye. She was sweating, but she was icy cold. She smelled like the sour note of death. I had to hurry.

Moving back toward where I thought the sink might be, I grabbed the steel wool and all but ran to the spot where the kindling was. I was never going to take central heating for granted ever again.

Trying to remember how the preppers did it, I rubbed the battery on the steel wool. Nothing. I did it again, only faster. Sparks lit up the darkness and I wanted to cry.

Tears cooled on my neck. Oh, I was crying.

I did it again, and this time, the steel wool caught alight. I blew gently, making the flame build, finally able to see my hands, the brightness of the light hurting my eyes. I placed it underneath the little pile of sticks I'd created. "Come on, come on," I chanted but it still went out. I needed something to act as a fire-lighter. Well, more so than the steel wool. In the bottom of the bucket of wood were tufts of bark. That would have to do.

This time, my pleas were silent as I struck the battery over the steel wool. Sparking, I placed the fine bark hairs on the wool. And they caught.

Thank god.

I slowly added piece by piece, not turning back to Sera, not wanting to take my eyes from the fire in case it went back out, plunging us both back into darkness. Now the tiny flame had spluttered to life, I was terrified that it would go out. Because fire meant hope. Fire meant life. I needed to keep it burning.

After a few minutes, my eyeballs felt like they had frozen solid, but the fire was now burning on some kindling the size of my wrist and I was reasonable sure that it wouldn't go out as I transferred it to what I could now see was a fire bucket in a large open hearth.

I'd burned a huge charred spot into the counter, but I didn't care. What were they going to do? Keep my deposit?

I finally got a good look at my surroundings in the weak firelight. The kitchen was a rough stone building, almost medieval in style. If it hadn't been for the radio, I'd have thought we'd gone back in time. Whatever building we were in was old though. The walls on two sides of the room were rough stone. The other was some kind of roughly assembled plasterboard like they'd rushed to put in walls. The fireplace was one of those big open style ones, a long metal rod running across the top to hold cooking pots above the fire. I focused on the fire until it was blazing, and I was sure it would run for an hour or two without going out if I put one of the big logs on it.

Then I finally turned to Sera, walking toward her and pulling her towards the struggling heat in front of the hearth. I got a good look at her face, and realized she would probably have been beautiful once. Now her face was completely sallow, a skeleton with skin stretched across the canvas. Her eyes were sunken in her face, surrounded by dark shadows. Her body was scraped with hundreds of tiny sores. The measles? Leprosy?

No, they were hundreds of little teeth bites. Rats. She'd been feasted on by rats. I was going to throw up.

In the dim light I could see that the kitchen was pretty well equipped, and I grabbed a large cast iron pot, filling it with water and setting it above the fire. The warmth of the flames made my skin prickle. I couldn't find any clean clothes, so I took off my shirt which was still reasonably clean, and set it in the water to boil as well.

Sera's eyelids fluttered closed, either because she passed out from pain or from sheer exhaustion. Looking at the bites, I wasn't sure if that wasn't a blessing. Her breathing was shallow and ragged as I peeled off her clothes, and threw them into another room. I'd deal with that later. Her ankle and wrist were definitely broken, and by the look of it, they'd been broken a while ago. The bruising was green around the edges.

"How long have you been down here?" I whispered, although she couldn't answer me. The cut on her leg further up was worse. It was hot with infection and oozing pus. It smelled terrible.

I searched through the cupboard beside the sink and heaved out a relieved sigh when I found salt. It wasn't perfect but it would have to do. I tipped half of the container into the boiling water.

I wasn't a 18th century medicine woman. Everything I knew about field medicine I got from reruns of M*A*S*H.

When the water was hot enough, I got out my shirt and used a knife to slice it into strips. I sent a silent apology to Sera, as I bathed the raw, red wound on her leg. I didn't like the look or smell of it. If we didn't get rescued soon, she was either going to lose the leg or die.

I bathed the rest of the wounds on her body, and then tipped the water out and put some fresh water on to heat.

I had a problem, because I couldn't put her back in her old clothes. Venturing down the hall, I found the blanket I'd abandoned on the floor. That would keep her a little warm, and preserve some of her modesty, though it was probably too late for that.

Lying the blanket as close the fire bucket as I could

get without her cooking or the blanket catching alight, I rolled her onto it.

She opened her eyes slightly and sighed at the warmth. "Thank you," she whispered.

"It's okay. How did you get here anyway? Do you know where we are?"

Her eyelids were already drooping, but she shook her head. "Angels. Angels did this. The rats..." The cold terror in her voice iced my veins. But then she fell into a fitful sleep. I placed my hand on her head and tried to settle her pain.

Uriel.

I decided in that moment that I was going to make it my life's mission to make that evil, overgrown turkey pay.

Luc? I called out into the darkness, glad when I felt the answering relief. *I'm not here alone. There's another woman here. She said an angel brought her down here. They fed her to the rats.*

The words that Luc called Uriel probably shouldn't be repeated.

When she wakes, ask her to make a deal with the Devil. I will answer her call.

Of course. Just because Luc couldn't find me, didn't mean he couldn't find Sera. I felt like an idiot for not thinking of it sooner. I smiled for the first time since this whole ordeal began. Luc would find us and by this time tomorrow, I would be home, snuggled on the couch between the protective bodies of my lovers. Boyfriends. It sounded weird, but I didn't care.

Exhaustion overcame me, the adrenaline draining me of any ounce of energy I had left.

I'm going to sleep while I can. I didn't want to sleep too long. I couldn't risk the fire going out.

Luc's voice held a hint of promise. *I will see you when you wake.*

I believed him.

Maybe I shouldn't have.

CHAPTER THIRTY

Whimpering woke me. I felt a smile curl my lips. Maybe Luc had found us while I'd slept. Maybe the whole thing had been a bad dream and the whimpering was just Blue having a nightmare beside me.

I opened one eye, and then both eyes were open and I was scuttling away. An unfamiliar angel was looking down at me, an unsettling expression on his face. I looked at Sera, who had her hands over her eyes, her body was shaking with terror.

"Uriel said he had dropped another here. One of Acerezeal's abominations. And he delivered. Have you come to join the whore in feeding the rats in the dungeon?" A twisted grin curved the slash that he called a mouth. My stomach rolled at the thought. How Sera got those injuries made more sense now. My hand subtly shook, and I hoped the angel didn't notice.

His wings were beautiful white, his aura the blinding light of an angel. But he meant me nothing but harm.

The knowledge crawled along my skin, like his darkly righteous emotions. He was punishing wrongdoers, upholding the only law that mattered.

Some primordial instinct told me I did not want to be in his clutches for long. I kept moving backwards on my hands as the angel advanced. My palm landed on the knife I'd used on my shirt last night. I clutched it in my hand, holding it out in front of me.

The angel laughed. It was a cruel, awful sound. "And what do you intend to do with that, human? I am an immortal."

He made a good point, but having a weapon made me feel better. So fuck him.

I jumped to my feet, circling back around toward Sera. I stared the angel in the eye, like I was way more badass than I was. "I know, but making you bleed would make me feel better."

The angel scowled as he walked forward. "You really have descended from Acerezeal; you have her blood-thirsty nature."

I was so shocked at his disapproval, I almost dropped the knife. "Says the man who locked a woman in a dungeon filled with rats."

The angel looked condescending as he said, "She is a whore, an adulterer. She deserves her punishment. It is law."

"I guess you are one of those Old Testament angels. An eye for an eye, eternal punishment for the audacity to love another person," I said, not even attempting to hide my disgust. I was going to stick my knife in his heart out of principle, even if it was the last thing I ever did.

He walked around the edge of the room, over to the smoldering fire. "Quite clever of you to create fire. Integral in the evolution of Man, but it won't help you now. There is no rescue coming for you here, no hope for you to cling to. Only a slow, and eventual death."

He rushed me then, and I dodged, but tripped backwards over Sera's prone body. I thrust out with my hands, grabbing the front of the Angel's shirt and pulling him down with me. At least if he wasn't standing over me, he couldn't squash me like a bug. We landed in a heap, Sera moaning beneath me, the angel's body crushing my chest, the warm stickiness of blood dripping down my arm.

Oh no. No, no, no. Who attacked an immortal being while holding a damn knife? I was going to die by my own stupidity.

I wondered, not for the first time, if I'd even like Heaven. It was meant to be paradise. I thought about the angel who was going to probably choke the life out of me. I'd prefer Hell.

"Hope?"

My heart stopped at the voice. A voice so familiar I wanted to cry. Because there was only one reason he would be here. I was about to die. Again. At least it was fairly painless this time.

"Azriel."

Hands gripped the angel's shoulders, pulling him off me. I looked up into Azriel's beautiful face. There were worse views to see as I died.

"What have you done, Hope?"

My face scrunched up in confusion. Obviously, I'd actually managed to get myself killed with stupidity.

But he wasn't looking at me. He was staring at the angel with a knife in his chest, a knife that went right through his heart.

An angel that was an impossibility.

An immortal that was dead.

I looked up at Azriel, my eyes wide as I stared at the blood dripping down my arm, and pooling around the body of the angel. It was leaking onto his white wings, turning them pink as the blood soaked into his feathers.

Angel's could bleed. And they could die.

"This is not possible," Azriel said, echoing my thoughts as he stared at the dead angel near his feet. "None but the creator and the Archangel Michael can kill an angel."

"And you," I whispered, but he was shaking his head.

"No, not even I. I can take their soul from their body, but eventually, it will be reborn into another angelic body unless it gets artificially transplanted into a human." That would be a weird statement if you'd never met my parents or Ace. Azriel removed Ace's soul, for reasons I still didn't understand, but Luc managed to recapture it, and kept it until he could graft it to my Mom's soul. It was a whole thing.

He finally looked back at me, his eyes staring into my soul in a way that was almost uncomfortable. "Dalius' soul is gone. I heard the call of his death, even though I was confused at why Dalius would be in Purgatory, and now his soul is gone. Hope, do you know what this means?"

I didn't know what any of this meant. I shook my head as if I could deny reality. "Hold up, did you say Purgatory? I'm in Purgatory?"

Azriel nodded, and he was finally shaken from his shock. He reached down, and I grasped his outstretched hand. He pulled me to my feet, and then did something that I would remember forever, even as I tried to block out the whole nightmare of Purgatory. Azriel wrapped me in his arms and hugged me as if his heart had been broken. I buried my face in his chest and sucked in deep, even breaths of his scent, felt the electricity of his touch where his large hands spanned my back. Felt the wash of relief, of horror, of fear... of love. That strange emotion that played around the edges of his feelings, I knew what it was now. The beginnings of love.

"I was so worried. Memphis and Gusion have turned the world inside out looking for you. Luc and Ace have terrorized the guilty and the innocent alike. I asked Michael..." He trailed off, but his words shocked me.

He didn't need to finish his sentence. He went to Michael to ask if he knew where I was. But I was a blank spot even to the Hand of God. Thank Hades. Because if Michael could see this now, this clusterfuck, I would definitely not be leaving Purgatory. I knew this for sure. I killed an angel; one of his Legion.

"Azriel, I killed an angel."

I said it out loud, and sheer terror ran through my veins. I stepped back. Azriel was an angel of the Legion of Heaven. He was a rule follower. He would have to tell. When I was out of arm's reach, I gave him half a smile.

"Will you take me back first? So I can say goodbye? I know you need to tell Michael about this, but I'd like to hug my Mom one more time."

The conflicting feelings that Azriel usually kept buried deep down played across his face. He was torn. Fearful, but resolute.

"We will go. We will pretend this never happened. I…" He trailed off again, and I didn't need my empathic abilities to know that this conflict went to the very depths of his soul. I felt an overwhelming wave of emotion for the angel who was willing to sacrifice everything he believed in to keep me safe.

He held out a tentative hand, and I took it. I twined my fingers in his and squeezed. I wanted him to know that I knew what his was costing him. That it meant something.

Sera made an odd keening noise as she looked at the body of the angel. "We can't leave her, Azriel."

Azriel looked incredulous. "She is the only witness to what happened here, Hope. She cannot live."

I pulled my hand from his and planted it on my hip. "I will not leave her in this hellhole. No one deserves this, and least of all some innocent pawn in Uriel's game. She comes with us. I'll make sure she doesn't talk."

He stared at the stubborn set of my jaw and shook his head. "So be it, Hope. But let's not dally."

I bent down, placing a calming hand on the trembling body of Sera. I pulled her to her feet, and she was so insubstantial I was worried she'd float away. Azriel lifted her into his arms.

"Wait! Can she even sift? Won't her pieces get all scrambled?"

Azriel shrugged. "I do not know. But she got here, so unless Raphael brought her, then she must be able to sift. Is it a risk you are willing to take?"

Who was this woman with the ability to travel as angels do? As I could? But Serendipity was an enigma for another day.

"She must go somewhere out of the way. Somewhere she isn't going to come into contact with any of the Archangels. Somewhere she can be forgotten."

And protected. I didn't say this out loud, because Azriel would have scoffed at me wanting to protect my loose end. That meant not with my parents, or the Mulligans.

A small smile curled my mouth.

"I know a place."

I sent him an image of the address with my mind. With a nod, I wrapped my arms around his waist, and we sifted away. I kept my fingers crossed that all of Sera would be there when we got to the other side.

CHAPTER THIRTY-ONE

After depositing Sera, and trying to explain to her new guardian why she was there and ensuring she'd get medical treatment, we finally reappeared in my kitchen. It felt like months since I'd been home, but it had barely been a night.

Except when Blue turned, his face was shadowed by a ginger beard that had to be at least a few weeks growth.

"Hope!" He vaulted the coffee table and the armchair, wrenching me out of Azriel's arms and into his own. He curled his fingers in my hair and squeezed me so tight I wasn't sure I could draw enough air into my lungs to take a full breath.

Within seconds, both Gusion and Memphis were there, and Memphis pulled me into his strong arms, wrapping his body around mine and clutching me even tighter than Blue. Gusion didn't try and take me from Memphis, merely pressed into my back and buried his face in my neck.

"We thought you were dead." His anguished voice made my breath hitch. My poor guys. So much of their happiness hinged on me, and I somehow managed to get kidnapped every month.

"I'm okay, I was only gone a day," I whispered soothingly. The weight of their unshielded emotions was beating against me.

"A day?" Blue echoed. "You've been gone a fecking month, Hope. It's been two whole weeks since Luc heard from you."

The Fallen seemed to notice Azriel, but there wasn't any of the old animosity. Memphis nodded once, a solemn expression that held an eternity's worth of weight.

Azriel lifted his chin in reply. "I found her in Purgatory."

The guys reared back as if they'd been slapped. Azriel didn't elaborate how he found me, but the guys deserved to know.

"I killed an angel."

This time, Memphis leapt away like a scalded cat. Or like I was the Antichrist. Even Gusion stepped away, and the weight of their shock and disbelief, their rejection, made my heart hurt. Blue stepped into the space that they vacated, pressing me close to his side. "I hope it was Uriel, that motherfucker."

Azriel shook his head. "Dalius. He was there to torture another soul in Purgatory. To torture Hope. He deserved to die." I didn't know who he was trying to convince, Gus and Memphis, or himself.

Memphis blinked, his face expressionless. Gusion

reached forward and clasped my hand in his, but didn't step closer.

Memphis seemingly came to some decision, because he took a deep breath. "This is going to be a problem. No one should know."

Azriel huffed out an annoyed sigh. "I agree, I said the same thing. But then she went and blurted it out to you three."

They all wore almost identical annoyed expressions, and I let the small smile curl my lips.

I caught Memphis' eye, and held it. "I don't keep secrets from the ones I love."

I saw the tension in his shoulders ease slightly, and he gave me such a meaningful look that it filled the cracks in my heart. If my night in nothingness had taught me anything, it was that I couldn't ignore the little things; light, warmth, my feelings for the men that now crowded my life.

"What do we do?"

Blue sucked in a deep breath, and I was pretty sure it was because he was breathing in my scent. "I think it's obvious. You kill Uriel. The rest is semantics. He was cocky enough to be at the club once." My eyes shot to Azriel, and I found him staring back, a peculiar look on his face, but Blue went on. "He doesn't think there is a single thing on this planet that is a threat to him. But we're here to prove him wrong."

Azriel cleared his throat. "I need to go. This is… treason, at best." He gave me one more longing look, and disappeared. We all stared at the place the Angel of Death had just stood.

"You've bewitched him," Gus said, his words echoing those of Azriel, except he sounded more bemused than accusatory. I gave him a look. Did he know? As the Angel of the Past, Present and Future, did he *know?*

Gus raised a single eyebrow, but didn't say anything. He turned to Blue. "That's a great idea, but the problem is that Uriel will know that Dalius is dead eventually. There are very few beings that can kill an Angel, and one has a pretty sword and the other just left this room. He's going to be on-guard, even if he does believe he's being a righteous asshole."

I shook my head. I was done. I needed a moment. Or several moments. Hell, I needed an eternity to comprehend my life.

Memphis studied my face. "She needs to rest." He grabbed my hand and gently led me toward the bedroom. Fingers grabbed my other hand, halting my progression.

"Woah there, demon-boy. She is not leaving my sight. I don't care who you are," Blue said stubbornly. "I can't…" He didn't need to finish the words, because I saw the same feeling reflected on the others faces.

I squeezed his hand. "How about we all sleep in my room. Just sleep. No angelic threesomes, or feathery orgies, or anything that involves whips, chains or fresh produce," I eyed Gusion, who just laughed. His fingers curled on his stomach, his shoulders shaking. I couldn't help the grin that went all the way to my eyes, and healed my heart in its own way. He had the best laugh.

"Okay, Sweetcheeks. No naughty stuff. Just good old

fashioned spooning with three men in your bed. So vanilla, it could almost be missionary." He leaned forward and kissed my nose, leading the way toward the bedroom. "Do we scissor, paper, rock for who gets to be big spoon and who has to sleep beside Memphis' hairy toes?"

Memphis scowled. "I do not have hairy toes. You are confusing me with the Mulligan. He is the one who evolved from the chimpanzee."

This was true, the angels were hairless. Everywhere from the neck down.

Blue growled. "I did not evolve from a monkey. Besides, you aren't meant to believe in evolution. No wonder you fucking fell," he grumbled.

Memphis shrugged. "Sure, you were made in his image, but every creation has a gestation period. Humanity's just happened to involve fleas."

At the sight of my bed, I almost wept again. I needed a shower first, though. Gusion must have read my mind. He walked into the ensuite, setting the shower to hot. I moved toward the steaming cubicle. I was never going to take hot water, or even warmth, for granted ever again.

Surprisingly, they left me alone to shower, and I washed away the filth of that weird little cottage. I closed my eyes, and the darkness pressed in on all sides. Snapping my eyes open, I turned off the water. I needed the guys, I needed the warm press of their bodies, the steady thump of their hearts.

I wrapped a towel around my body, and walked back into the bedroom. Somehow, they'd figured out the pecking order, and I was surprised to see Blue on the pillows and not cast down to the bottom of the bed. I smiled. I should have known better. Blue wasn't intimidated by being the only mortal in the bunch.

Gusion was at the bottom of the bed, but he was reclining back with his arms behind his head as if he'd chosen to be there. Maybe he had. I stopped by the bed, appreciating the glow of their auras. I would never be in the dark again, as long as I had these three. Four?

I tried to imagine Azriel on the bed too, and failed. But Azriel was a problem for another night. I dropped my towel and crawled into bed between them.

Blue growled. "Damn, Princess. You punishing me for something?" He placed a hand on my hip as I pressed my body right along Memphis' side.

"No, but I just don't want anymore barriers between us. I need to feel your skin against mine, I need to know that I am home, and with you all, and that I'm not there anymore. That this isn't just a beautiful dream."

Memphis leaned forward, pressing a kiss to the strip of skin behind my ear. "You are home. I will never let you go again. I will follow you to Hell and back, because you are mine and I am yours."

My eyes welled with tears, and I wiggled back into him more. Blue grabbed my hand and placed it on his chest, right over his heart. He didn't say anything, just closed his eyes. No one attempted to turn off the bedside light, and that threatened to make the tears fall. Gusion rolled over, wrapping his fingers around my thigh just above my knee, throwing a wing over us all.

"Your wing is touching my junk," Blue said without opening his eyes.

Gus sniffed. "You're welcome. Now go to sleep. Our girl needs rest. It's been a long few weeks."

I reached down and wrapped my fingers in his. It had been a tough twenty-four hours for me, but it had been a cold hell for them for almost a month.

I closed my eyes, and drifted off to sleep, letting the restful moment heal us all. I doubted there would be many more of these moments in the days to come.

"THIS IS SO CUTE, I don't even want to wake you," a voice said, and I drifted out of sleep. For the second time in two days, an angel stood over me as I woke. This one didn't terrify me though, although perhaps she should have.

Ace grinned down at us, and I did a quick check to ensure I was covered. Gusion's wing still covered my lower half, and Memphis had his hand around my left boob, essentially covering me from view.

"Then why did you?" I asked, but I was smiling. The endless waves of relief and love just poured off Ace. And the subtle hint of irritation. Uh-oh.

She crossed her arms over her chest. "Two reasons. One, these lazy assholes are meant to be guarding you. But I waltzed in here like I had a key—"

"You do have a key," I interrupted, but she held up a finger to shush me.

"And I could have been anyone. Maybe they'd guard you better as eunuchs?"

Memphis rumbled low in his chest. "I am attached to my testicles, Acerezeal. Plus I knew you were here, I just didn't care. You'd rather cut off your own wings with a rusted scimitar than hurt Hope."

"Beside the point, *Mephistopheles,*" she said.

I felt Gusion's silent laughter shaking the bed as he pretended to be asleep. Giving up the ruse, he lifted his head, resting on his elbows. "You're in trouble now. She used your full name. Ace always calls you Memphis unless you're in trouble."

Ace narrowed her eyes at Gus. "That's because his name is obnoxiously long. The second reason I woke you is because I had to hear about your rescue from Azriel. Not the child of my heart, or my most trusted, eternal friends. From fucking Azriel, the pompous jerk off Angel of Death."

Even I winced at that one. Whoops. Also, I guess she didn't know that Azriel and I had a, uh, thing? I definitely wasn't about to mention it, and apparently neither were the guys. Ace hated Azriel, but it was a hatred born from hurt feelings and perceived betrayal and lost friendships. Also, he stole her soul and tried to kill her living host. Did I mention it was a whole thing?

Gusion rolled over, his wings tucking against his back and out of the way. Blue was there with a sheet, covering my nudity. I hadn't even realized he was awake.

Gusion seemed oblivious to the fact that he just almost flashed my — whatever Ace was — my privates. "Does Luc know?"

This time it was Ace's turn to look smug. "He's in the living room." Both Memphis and Gusion groaned simultaneously, leaping to their feet and looking for clothes, while Ace sang about how much trouble they were in, but in a disconcerting falsetto.

Ace looked at Blue. "You're off the hook, Mulligan. He doesn't expect much from your family tree at the best of times." I laughed at Blue's scowl, and curled into him. Ace looked at him skeptically, her eyes crinkled with amusement. "Although, I wouldn't let him catch you boning his pride and joy."

I blinked in her direction, momentarily stunned. "I'm his pride and joy?"

Ace rolled her eyes. "Don't read too much into it. The only other thing he's ever created is Hell, the demonesses and the Palace. He's pretty proud of the palace, but you and your sister stand a little above that." She threw me a wink and left.

I stared at the ceiling, small bands of light sneaking in through my venetian blinds. I looked unblinkingly at those beams of sunshine until my eyes began to water. Blue rolled closer, pressing a gentle kiss to my lips. He was completely unguarded with me right now, the soft pink glow of his aura embracing me, the swell of his emotions brushing over my body like fingertips.

"Are you okay? I was so glad to have you back whole, I didn't think about anything else. But not all injuries are physical, are they? You've had a rough few months, Princess."

That was an understatement. I didn't want to dip too far into my psyche right now. But I felt bolstered by Blue and Memphis and Gus, like they were holding together all my pieces until I worked out how to fit them back together.

I thought, that maybe one day, when this shit was all over and I'd grieved for the innocence of my old life, I would be okay. For now, I'd survive, and live every day like I was going to be abducted and possibly tortured the next. Because apparently that was statistically possible.

"Yeah, I'm okay. But I'm more okay with you here." It was a whitewashed version of the truth, but it would do. I kissed him back, a tender thing full of need and promise.

Then I sighed and sat up. I needed some pants, some emotional armor to hide behind, something. Pulling on my favorite jeans, and a pretty top in a deep purple, I walked into the bathroom. I could feel Blue's eyes follow me around the room.

I winced when I looked at myself in the mirror. I looked like, as Ri was so apt to put it sometimes, ten pounds of shit in a five pound bag. I don't even want to know where he got that saying. It's not something a father should say to his child, but it made me laugh every single time when I felt down. I picked up the mascara, but my hands still felt unsteady. I was likely to stab myself in the eye.

"Do you want me to do your makeup?" Blue asked from the doorway.

I felt my chin hit the floor. Well, maybe not the floor but there was definitely an audible click. Did the hitman just offer to do my makeup? Maybe I was still in Purgatory and this was one of those hypothermia hallucinations.

"What?" I'd obviously misheard.

"Would you like me to do your makeup?"

"Uh, sure?" His eyes were intense, but his heart was reflected in those crystalline irises. I couldn't say no. I had a brief premonition of looking like my doll when I was five, when I gave her a permanent makeover with my markers.

He wrapped his hands around my waist and lifted me onto the bathroom counter. He opened the drawer that held my makeup.

Moving between my thighs, he picked up my tinted moisturizer and sponge. He swept it along my cheeks with a practiced hand. Too practiced.

"Are you a drag queen on your days off, Blue? No judgement, you'd make a beautiful Queen. I'm totally cool with that." I let the question run out in one long breath.

Blue rolled his eyes, but his lip quirked. "No. Have you tried running in stilettos? Impossible."

Who the hell was this person that had taken over Blue's body, that cracked jokes about wearing women's shoes and did makeup? I looked at him expectantly.

"Growing up, I lived in an apartment building with a lot of working girls. I spent a lot of time wandering the halls, graffitiing the walls. Eventually one of the girls noticed my meticulous art, decided the skills would transfer to makeup, and when she was too drunk or high to do it herself, she'd make me do it." His lips turned down sadly at the memory. "A hooker's face is her selling point. You'd think it would be her body, but something about the face draws people. Another working girl noticed, and got me to do hers. More girls caught on, realizing they could spend more time getting high, completely oblivious to the realities of life, and still be out in time to work." He shrugged. "They gave me five bucks every time, small change, but by the time I was nine, I had quite a nest egg."

I put my hand against his chest, and pushed him back a bit so I could meet his eyes. "Your mother let you do makeup for prostitutes when you were barely a baby?"

He lowered his chin in a single nod, picking up the contour powder, sweeping it expertly around the edges of my face and below my cheekbones. "I was out from beneath her feet. Sometimes, I think she would have been happier if I was dead."

"But you are a Mulligan!" My protest seemed weak in the face of his memories.

"I'm the bastard son of a good catholic girl who went catting around outside of marriage. I was a taint on the name. It wasn't until I was much older and far more useful that they cared if I lived or died, but it's still in an offhand way. They take care of me in the same way you take care of your tools, to prolong their usefulness. Lower your eyes."

I did as I was told, and felt the eyeliner slide across my lid in one smooth, sure stroke and then the other lid. A gentle puff of air whispered across my face. I opened my eyes and looked at my hands clasped in my lap.

"I care about you a lot, Blue. I know this situation, with Memphis and Gus, isn't what you wanted, I'm not what you wanted, but I just want you to know that my feelings for you aren't going to change."

He nodded again, leaning in to kiss my lips, before pulling back to swipe on a nude lipstick.

"I don't know how to love, Princess. I don't know if I'm even capable. But I'll give you my loyalty. My life. You are exactly what I want, but not what I deserve."

I smiled sadly at him. "I have a lifetime to teach you what love is, Blue Halloran, and I can't wait." I leaned forward and kissed his cheek, leaving a shiny lipstick print on his face.

"You're going to smudge it," he grumbled, but there was so much emotion shining from his eyes that I knew he didn't mean it. I slid off the vanity and turned to look in the mirror. I looked wonderful. Understated, but way less like death.

"You are a man of many hidden talents," I laughed. I shouldn't have been this surprised. Blue did everything with care and precision, from ordering food to completing a hit. Everything was perfect, or it didn't happen. Now I wondered if that was a leftover from his childhood.

I ran a hand over his blonde head, and down his spine. I stepped into his arms, pressing my head against his bare chest, appreciating the scratch of his chest hair against my cheek. He wrapped his arms around my shoulders and pressed me close, and we stood there for a moment, taking refuge in each other.

Eventually, I pulled back, but entwined my fingers in his. "Do you, uh, need a shirt?"

I chanted *no, no, no* in my head in a vain attempt to

sway him with my Jedi mind tricks. I must have been a little more obvious than I thought, because he just laughed and grabbed a shirt off the floor. I think it was Gusion's.

"I'm not meeting the Devil in your living room with my nipples out," he grumbled, and I laughed.

"Does it help that they are very nice nipples?"

He shook his head at me, but his smile was radiant. He dropped the shirt back in the hamper.

When people asked me what kind of guy I would end up with, I would have said someone like Rella's best friend Charlie, but definitely *not* Charlie himself. He was well and truly Rella's from the day she grew boobs. But someone like him; charming, easygoing, loyal to a fault.

Somehow, I'd ended up with a harem of brooding alpha males, where each smile was like getting flowers and chocolates on your birthday.

When I got to the living room, there wasn't just Ace and Luc sitting on my sofa. Rella was there too, flanked by her Gargoyles like always. She looked more solid than the last time I'd seen her.

My lower lip trembled, and I sucked it between my teeth. I could be brave in front of anyone but Rella. Tears rolled down my cheeks and the terror that I was going to die roared back to the surface. She was beside me in a flash, wrapping her arms around me like she was my only anchor in the world.

"Hey now, it's okay. I'm here, I've got you." She brushed my hair from my face. "Don't cry, you'll make your makeup run."

I blinked rapidly, and whispered, "Blue did it for me."

Rella's eyebrows almost touched her hairline. "Blue Halloran. Hitman, mob enforcer, currently half naked in front of the Devil, did your makeup for you?" she murmured in a low voice.

Her incredulity must have mirrored mine. I took a deep, steadying breath. I looked around her shoulder at the huge mountains she called mates. Romanus looked stoic, as always, his disconcerting eyes taking my measure. There was more sympathy in Rouen's, and he gave me a wink and grin. I smiled back, and stepped away.

That's when I noticed the other person in the room. Well, the other two, because they were on opposite sides of the room, just about as far as you could get from another person in my apartment. On one side was my dad, Lux, leaning against my breakfast bar. His sword was strapped to his back, which was never a good sign.

The other was Azriel, standing by the windows. He looked incredibly uncomfortable, and I wasn't sure why he was here, but it would have taken a lot of balls to come into a small space where 70% of the people currently inhabiting it hated you with a passion. I gave him a private smile, hopefully letting him know I was glad he was here, even if everyone else in the room wanted to rip off his wings and beat him to death with them.

"Was there a party I forgot about?" I said, trying to lighten the atmosphere of the room. Lux strode over and pulled me into a hug.

"There was a party. A damn search party. This needs to stop, baby girl."

Lux and Rella were very alike. They both made you feel as if everything would be okay now. They were fixers.

"Sorry Dad. Is Mom a mess?"

"We didn't tell her," he mumbled.

I reared back, looking between him and Ace. "What?"

"She was so stressed from your first abduction, and then Estrella's death, that I was worried about her health. Her heart still isn't a hundred percent, you know that. So Ace convinced her you were shacked up somewhere with Memphis and Gus, getting over your grief."

I winced. I could see why they did it, and in their positions I probably would have done the same thing. But boy, if Mom ever found out, they were going to be drawn and quartered. I would not want to be them.

I nodded, mock zipping my lips. I'd tell her if she ever asked, but I wouldn't go running and telling tales.

"So you are just here to see that I'm okay?"

He shook his head, stepping back so I could take in all their solemn faces. He looked straight at Azriel when he said, "I'm here to help you kill an angel."

CHAPTER THIRTY-TWO

A ce laughed, and took a step closer to Lux, in solidarity or to hold him back if he actually made a lunge for the Angel of Death, I wasn't 100% sure. I assumed they didn't mean Azriel, and moved toward the coffee pot in the kitchen.

If we were going to talk about Archangelcide — it didn't even have a word because it was such a stupid and dangerous proposition — then I needed to be caffeinated. Maybe I'd make it an Irish coffee and attempt to kill those few remaining brain cells that were screaming that even contemplating it was a bad idea. I picked up a pair of sunglasses from the bowl on my breakfast bar. The collective angelic auras in the room were giving me a headache.

Rella sighed heavily, her aura non-existent. It was like a stab in the chest every time I noticed. I turned to her, sipping my coffee. She looked longingly at my cup. "Luc and Ace only have instant. It really is hell down there."

Ace made a rude noise and Luc scowled. Or scowled more. I laughed, glad to have my sister back, even for a moment.

I went over and sat on the couch beside Blue. Memphis and Gus stood like sentinels at either side of my back.

"Will you two sit? Rella already brought the Gargoyles, we don't need anymore fierce statues in the room," I teased, and one of the aforementioned Gargoyles let out a low rumble, even though Rella barked out a laugh that I knew as well as my own. It was probably Romanus; he looked scarier. Gus sat down, but Memphis continued to stand at my back.

"So what do you propose, we walk up to Uriel and say, 'hold still while Ace attempts to dismember you?' Because I can't see that working," Rella said as she just hovered in the same spot with eerie stillness. I mean, I hugged her before, felt the warmth of her body, the physicality of her flesh and blood, but she no longer seemed alive. Her chest no longer moved because she didn't breathe, she didn't even blink unless it was out of habit.

"I will call him out. We will battle in the method of old," Luc said, tilting his head to either side like a prize fighter. He was in peak condition, but then he was immortal, a prime specimen of what perfection could have been.

But so was Uriel.

"Could you take him? Because Uriel is a dick, but you almost killed my wife reuniting yourself and your consort, and I don't want that heartache to be in vain,"

Lux added. My dad had serious brass ones. But he and Lucifer had a long history.

"Lucifer could not. The battle would be bloody, but without Michael's sword, it would just be an eternal battle," Azriel piped up in the corner. Maybe he had brass balls too, but he was more likely to get them lopped off. Lucifer's dark eyes slid to him in a way that wasn't at all human, but Azriel went on. "I'm not doubting your prowess, Lucifer Morningstar." His tone definitely implied otherwise. "But you are both Archangels, and Uriel has nothing to lose. And you have everything to lose. Your life is riddled with weaknesses." He looked at Ace, and then over to me.

Lucifer stepped toward the angel. I wondered if angel entrails would come out of my rug? I stood and hurried over to where Azriel was standing. I somewhat stupidly put myself between them. I was thankful that all the Fallen had their emotions on lock. I would have had a pounding headache otherwise.

"Please, Luc. We all know you are the scariest being to prowl the earth," I placated uselessly. I placed a hand on his chest, stopping his single-minded stride toward Azriel.

Luc looked down at my hand and then quirked an eyebrow at me. He looked amused. I felt a weird combination of terrified and annoyed. I had no time for this posturing.

"Perhaps the Angel of Death needs a reminder of that fact," he said in a soft voice that was no less scary.

I shrugged. "Maybe, but not today, yeah?"

Luc dipped his chin. He looked over my head at

Azriel. "What are you doing here anyway, Angel?" he taunted. He knew. I had no doubt in my mind that Memphis and Gusion had informed Luc of Azriel's interest in me. If he hadn't, he would have plucked the thought from Blue's head with ease.

"What he did to Hope was outside the rules," Azriel mumbled.

Lucifer merely tilted his head at the Azriel, whose snowy white wings were hidden for once. He just looked like an average man. A beautiful, perfect, average man. "Hope is outside the rules. You know this."

They stared at each other, some silent communication borne from eons of familiarity with each other making words obsolete.

"And you are all about the rules, aren't you Azriel? But you are close, my friend," Luc whispered quietly, but he didn't seem gleeful. He looked more concerned. I was getting whiplash from the mood changes in the room. "What do you propose?"

Azriel sucked in a deep breath, but the muscles in his shoulders didn't relax at all. "We petition Michael."

I let out a sigh, turning to look up into his brilliant blue eyes. He was so perfect, but only on the outside. Inside he was as messy and complicated as the rest of us. "I've tried. He said your Guy hadn't said to halt Uriel's organization of immoral assholes. His hands are tied."

Azriel reached out, his face tense as if he was fighting the action. "That was before he was putting unwilling women in Purgatory." His fingers were halfway to my face when he let them drop.

Disappointment rushed through me, but I kept my

face neutral. "He has been putting unwilling women all sorts of places and they didn't care; why would Purgatory be any different?" It was a rhetorical question.

I handed my coffee to Luc as a distraction, who surprisingly took it, and then drank the remainder.

"Estrella is correct. Hell only has instant." His raised eyebrows dared me to protest. Instead I laughed, and threw my arms around my pseudo-parent.

"Thank you for finding me. For giving me hope. I..." I couldn't describe what hearing Luc's voice in the darkness felt like. It had been the most beautiful sound I'd ever heard.

He wrapped his arms around my shoulders and hugged me close. I didn't dare breathe in case I spooked him. Luc didn't hug back ever. Maybe Ace was right, and I was his pride and joy, though his emotions were locked down tight, so I couldn't know for sure.

I could hear Rella talking to one of her consorts. "Luckily I'm not the jealous twin, or I'd be worried he loved Hope more."

Luc stepped back and rolled his eyes. "I do. She is less mouthy." He shook his head, focusing back on me. "Do what you need to, but it will come to violence. It always does with Uriel." His tone had the kind of certainty that spoke of future knowledge. I looked at Gusion, wondering what he had seen, and not told me. I had time to uncover his secrets later.

I stepped into Azriel's space, pressing my body close to his. "Let's do this." Azriel's eyes went wide, his gaze darting between all the people in the room. It was probably a mean gesture on my behalf, but I liked to shock him.

"Do what?" he squeaked, and I couldn't help the chuckle that bubbled over my lips.

"Consummate our relationship, of course. It's a human custom," I said straight-faced, and his eyes got impossibly wider.

Ace was laughing so hard at his expression, she was holding her side. I finally took pity on him. "We are going to say hello to Michael, as you suggested," I clarified, and the relief on his face was hilarious and a tiny bit insulting. "Do you even know where he is?"

Azriel looked offended that I'd even suggested he was anything other than all-knowing, his straight brows lowering until they were slashes across his face. He had nice eyebrows.

He wrapped his arms around my waist, in a completely platonic position of course, and sifted us away. I was prepared for the whirling feeling in my stomach, but perhaps I should have had a bagel first. Your molecules dematerializing and then rematerializing was hell on an empty belly.

We found Michael on a beach, somewhere in the world, I couldn't say where. He had his plain white linen pants rolled up to the knee, his beautiful pale skin almost the same color as the sand. His shoulder length hair shot through with a few silver streaks that somehow made him look young and dignified rather than old. His face was ageless and kind as he stared at the abandoned beach, toward where the waves were crashing onto the rocks.

As we landed, his head whipped toward us, his brows lowered. All of a sudden, I could see the warrior angel that he was, the enforcer of God's Will, rather than the benevolent force I seemed to have consigned him to in my mind.

"Your soul is stained, Hope, Child of Acerezeal. What have you done?" He stood, and I noticed the flaming sword strapped to his back. Well, it wasn't flaming now, but I assumed that was *the* sword.

I stepped back, and right into the chest of Azriel. "Nothing that wasn't just, Archangel," Azriel said, his head bowed low. I did the same.

Michael's presence was like standing in a lightning storm, right beside a huge divining rod. All the hairs on your body stand up and you can taste the ozone.

He stopped in front of me, and shook his head sadly. "Just or no, it has stained her soul. A stain so black that it could only mean one thing. A thing that should be impossible. You have killed an Angel."

Uh, maybe I should have told Luc this part before I got behind Azriel's plan to see Michael. I was so used to being hidden from them, an enigma, an aberration in the world of both humans and angels, that I'd forgotten the true power of Michael.

"If I may interrupt," Azriel said as he stepped in front of me, putting his body between mine and that of the Archangel's, although he didn't posture. He was still completely subservient. Judging by the small smile on Michael's face, he wasn't fooling the wily angel anyway. "Dalius was killed in Purgatory."

Michael gave Azriel a patient look. "I am aware of

that, Azriel. I am the Right Hand of God. There is very few things of which I am unaware." His eyes shifted to me, and an eyebrow quirked.

"His death was at Hope's hand," Azriel continued, and this time it was Michael's brow that knit. Yeah, ponder those ramifications.

"In my defence, he was there to torture a woman. With rats," I added, as if normal torture wasn't bad enough.

The weariness on Michael's face broke my heart. He slumped back down on the rock he had been resting on when we'd arrived, and his shoulders curled in. He was silent, and I wished I could read his emotions.

I missed having everyone's emotions on tap. Who was the stupid idiot that let that one slip? I wanted to rub his back and tell him that it would all work out in the end, but telling an Archangel that he had to have faith seemed a bit redundant. Instead, I sat down beside him in silent solidarity.

"Uriel's taint is spreading," he said to me, or maybe it was to the Big Guy in the Sky, I couldn't be sure. He didn't seem to want confirmation or conversation, so I remained silent. He stared out past the horizon, and I wondered what he saw. What was the true extent of his angelic abilities, if Memphis could see your darkest secret, and Gusion could see your past, present and future, and Azriel could steal your very soul from your body, what could the Right Hand really do?

"I trust in the plan," he said to me, or maybe himself. "I do, but this is wrong. We are protectors, nurturers of the Father's creations. We aren't this horror that Uriel has tried to twist angelkind into. But my answer is still that same, Hope Jones."

I let out a long breath through my nose. I hadn't expected any other answer, despite my support of Azriel's plan.

Azriel gaped at his mentor. "We must."

"Are you questioning?" Michael asked lightly. There was no accusation in his voice, just a sad kind of resoluteness. "You are right to question," he said, looking back at Azriel. "I cannot help."

And with that, he was gone. I stayed seated on the rock, and tried to see what Michael saw. Tried to trust in the plan. But I wasn't made to just lie back and let the tide of fate take me where it wanted me to go. I was a Jones. We were fighters. Emotionally, anyway. Rella was the only real fighter.

"Did he just…" Azriel, the angel with all the answers, looked dumbstruck.

The beach was no longer abandoned. I wondered if the tourists all disappeared so Michael could have his moment. A man walked along kicking at the waves, a small dog at his feet, and his hands filled with fishing gear. His smile was so wide I could see it from where I was sitting. I wondered if I would be ever that happy again.

The man walked up over the sand dunes towards me. I looked over my shoulder at Azriel, realizing we weren't too far from the road. We'd have to wait until the fisherman left to sift back out of here. Azriel still had his wings hidden, and we looked like a touristy couple visiting…wherever the hell we were.

"Beautiful day today," the man yelled as he got closer. He was an average looking guy with a big smile and a torn 'Jesus is My Homeboy' t-shirt, which made me laugh. The character on the front of the t-shirt had a huge cheesy grin and his thumbs up, a knowing wink scrunching up one side of his face.

"Beautiful," I agreed, appreciating the sunny skies, the crashing waves, the small birds that circled the air above us. It was a little slice of paradise. The small dog, which appeared to be a random mix of different dogs mashed into one, from its long hound dog ears to its short stumpy legs, ran in circles around my feet.

I squinted at the guy. Something about his aura seemed off and his face was oddly familiar.

"Do I know you from somewhere?"

The guy smiled, his straight teeth glinting in the sun. "Maybe I was just a stranger on the bus?"

I blinked at him, but he was walking away whistling a familiar tune that I couldn't quite place.

Well, that was weird.

I turned back to Azriel, who seemed to have missed the whole thing as he worried at his bottom lip with his teeth. He seemed anxious or perturbed or something completely un-Azriel like and I was getting a little worried.

"Let's go home. We can figure this all out later, maybe after a bagel."

I stood, brushing sand from my skirt. I grazed my hand against the rock, and I hissed out a breath as something clattered down the rocks and into the sand.

"Holy Jesus fucking Mary and Joseph," Azriel whispered.

It was a sad indicator of where my life was headed that my first thought was 'that's a rather incestuous three-way'.

My second thought was that crazy string of blasphemous curse words coming from Azriel meant either we were about to die, or he'd finally snapped.

I whipped my head around, expecting Uriel or the apocalypse. But he was just staring at the sand.

More specifically, at the sword in the sand.

More specifically again, Michael's sword in the sand, the only weapon capable of killing an Archangel.

"Holy shit," I whispered, looking around for Michael, who was surely on his way back here to collect the Sword of freaking St. Michael. But he didn't reappear and we continued to stare. "Do we leave it here?"

"No!" Azriel yelled, leaning forward to pick the sword up, but hesitated. He shook his head, and reached out, wrapping his hand around the hilt until it suddenly it just...vanished.

"What the...Argh!" I said, as the sword reappeared at my feet. I jumped back like it was a spider the size of a football. Again, I looked for Michael, who hadn't suddenly reappeared.

Azriel didn't look nearly as freaked out as I did, but I guess he was used to things that disappeared and reappeared, considering that's what he did on the regular.

"I think you have to pick it up?"

I took a huge step back, stumbling in the loose sand. "No way. I am not touching that."

"It is merely a sword. It can do nothing unless it is in your hand."

I grinned, because I couldn't help it. "I bet you say that to all the girls."

He blushed, making me laugh. I bent forward, wrapping my hand gingerly around the hilt. If only Gus was here to make a dirty joke.

I expected an immense weight; an item that could wield such a heavy toll ought to be heavy. Instead, it was light as air. It fit in my hand like it was made for me.

Azriel stared. I didn't feel anything. There was no sword in the stone moment, no power filling my veins. No shining beam of heavenly light. Nada.

"Well, that was underwhelming." I looked around, all of a sudden completely paranoid, like I was wearing a hundred grand Harry Winston through the ghetto. "We should go. If Michael needs his sword, he can come to the apartment."

Azriel stepped forward, his body wrapped around mine. I breathed in the scent of him. I wished I could describe it, try to replicate it and bottle it, because it was intoxicating when I was this close to him. He smelled like light and life. Warm summer days, and the scent of that moment when a heatwave breaks. It was completely indescribable and I loved it.

The sword pressed between us, he sifted me back to the apartment, and I resisted the urge to puke all over the carpet. It was my carpet, and coffee colored puke was impossible to get out of the carpet fibers. Adnan had proven that to me on more than one occasion.

Thoughts of Adnan dampened my mood. I missed

him, but he hadn't even reached out when Estrella died. When Naz and Charlie had died. Not even a word as the other Mulligan's rallied around. He'd completely ignored me as if I didn't exist at the funeral. There was a gulf between us now that I wasn't sure could be fixed by anything other than time.

I stood there for a moment, completely surrounded by Azriel, and I wanted nothing more than to leave my head on his chest, listening to the steady thump of his heart.

Azriel leaned close. "He gave me his blessing."

I tilted my head back to meet his eyes. "Blessing to what?"

"To fall."

I stepped out of his arms, my eyes wide. Did I miss that conversation?

Someone cleared their throat behind us, but I couldn't drag my eyes away from Azriel's face, trying to decipher his nearly inscrutable expression. Did he want to fall? Would he fall, for me?

"Hey lovebirds, what did Michael say?" Ace said, and I spun toward them.

There was an audible inhale in the room, and then Luc let out an inhuman roar.

"WHAT HAVE YOU DONE?"

CHAPTER THIRTY-THREE

I sank to my knees as the sound of Luc's voice pierced my brain. I dropped the sword and it clattered to the floor in front of me, and I slammed my hands over my ears. Azriel was in front of me in an instant, his body blocking me from Luc, although I could see Ace in front of her consort, her hands on his cheeks.

"Be calm, my love. It is Hope. She wouldn't harm a soul. It is just a sword. Be calm."

I wanted to fling the stupid thing across the room if it meant Luc stopped making that noise. Gus and Memphis were between us, though they both looked just as haunted as Luc, and torn. I was in pain, but then, so was Luc. He had been their friend, no closer than that, their brother, for more millennia than I cared to count. Their loyalties were divided, and the anguish on their faces broke my heart.

However, Rella had no such qualms, standing in front of me ready for a fight, although the noise didn't seem to bother her. Actually, it didn't seem to be bothering anyone other than me.

"What is he doing to her?"

Ace ignored her, as she spoke in a low voice to Luc, who was clutching his chest. It was Memphis who answered.

"It's the sword. It is the one that tore him from heaven. Hope is succumbing to his pain." I was starting to pant, but I crawled toward Luc. Gus, sensing my intention, bent over and picked me up and cradled me to his chest. I didn't remove my hands from my ears, although I now knew the noise radiated from inside my head. Once we were close enough, I launched myself from Gusion's arms and onto Luc's body, finally moving my hands away so I could wrap my arms around Luc's back.

I pushed every ounce of positivity I could muster from my empathic abilities. Every healing thought, soothing consolation I could think of I channeled through my hands. I channeled the love I felt for him, my gratitude for the fact that he was always there, that his love was all the more special to me because it was so rare. I channeled the love the guys felt for him, the fact that they would follow him to the very pits of Hell because they respected him so greatly. I pushed Lux's admiration, and even Azriel's long buried ties of friendship.

Lastly, I slapped a hand over his heart, and pushed just a fragment of Ace's love for him. I pushed it as deep as I could with my newfound abilities, urging it to spread, this unending well of emotion that Ace felt for her consort. She loved him fiercely, and wading through their emotions felt like free diving in the very depths of the ocean; it was as beautiful as it was terrifying and painful.

I don't know how long we all stood there, me clinging to the Luc's back like a baby koala and Ace whispering to him in Latin. It felt like hours, but was probably no more than a few minutes.

Finally, he shuddered, and stood up straight. It was like seeing a phoenix shake itself and rise from the ashes.

He gave the sword one last haunted look where it laid abandoned on the floor. "We have our plan," he said softly and disappeared from the room.

Ace stroked my hair, kissed my forehead and left too.

I stumbled back toward the couch and flopped down, suddenly exhausted. Blue wrapped his arms around me, and I soaked in his warmth.

Rella came over, a sad smile on her face. "You are truly amazing, Sis. Your strength..." she trailed off. She leaned down, and hugged my head like she used to do when we were kids. It was always an awkward gesture, but it made me smile. "Our ride just poofed out of here like a cat with its tail on fire. You think you could sway one of your bed buddies to drop us back down?"

"I shall take your father home, Hope. He is less... chatty," Memphis added quickly.

Instead of being offended, Rella's lips quirked. Uh oh, Memphis had done it now. He'd shown his weakness. Amateur mistake. Gusion laughed, and shook his head. He leaned down and kissed me softly. "I'll be back, sweetheart. I should-"

I put a finger to his lips. "Luc is your friend. Take all the time you need. You too, Memphis. I'll be fine here with Blue."

Memphis opened his mouth to protest, but Azriel interrupted. "I will stay and watch that Uriel does not return for Hope."

They both blinked at him, and Lux stepped forward, inserting himself in the conversation. He was like that, hiding in the shadows until he wanted you to know he was there. It was a skill he mastered as his time as a Spartan. You know, in Ancient Rome.

Don't ask.

"She can come home until this is all done."

But I was shaking my head before he'd even finished. I didn't want to take this badness home with me. Mom was still reeling from Rella's death, and none of my parents were as young as they used to be. No, they needed to stay out of it. If I could persuade Lux to stay home, I'd have been even happier. But that was extremely doubtful.

"I will be fine here with Blue and Azriel."

Lux's eyes shifted to Blue, and his eyes narrowed. "I am not comfortable leaving you alone with the Angel that killed your mother and the Mulligan's number one hitman, Hope." He used his stern Dad voice, and the urge to agree was almost overwhelming.

But I loved the Mulligan's number one hitman, and Azriel... well. It was complicated.

I gave him my most reassuring smile. "I will be fine.

They'd both rather chop off their hands than hurt me, Dad. I trust them with my life."

Eyes narrowed, he looked between the two of them. "So much as a hair is hurt on her head, and I will fuck you up until you'll wish you were dead and in one of Lucifer's fiery pits."

I resisted the urge to roll my eyes like an errant teenager, but Blue nodded almost immediately. Lux's steely gaze caught Azriel's and they had some kind of weird stare-off until Azriel dipped his head.

Apparently this was satisfactory man-speak, because I was up and hugging him goodbye before I knew it.

Memphis kissed me. "We will not be gone too long, but time moves differently in Hell."

"I'll be fine," I promised.

As Memphis rested a hand on Lux's shoulders, I remembered something. "Wait. Dad, you should take the sword. Keep it safe. I don't want the responsibility." If nothing else, my parent's house had a vault that would make a Swiss bank jealous.

Lux inclined his head, and bent down to lift the sword. But as with Azriel, it just vanished, only to reappear at my feet.

"I do not think anyone is meant to wield it except the Archangel Michael," Azriel said softly, "and now you." I tried not to think of Michael's words back at the club.

He wanted me to do what he could not.

He wanted me to kill Uriel.

I kicked it under the couch, and pretended at least for a little while it didn't exist. The weight of this responsibility didn't exist. Besides, no one would think to look under the couch for a magic sword.

Memphis looked at me like I was being completely sacrilegious, which I probably was considering it was a holy object. Lux shrugged off his scabbard, pulling out his own sword. "You'll need this, I think." He handed me the ancient leather scabbard, and kissed me on the top of the head. "Be safe, Kid. I can't do another funeral." His eyes were bottomless pits of misery. I nodded gently and gave him a reassuring smile.

Gus just winked at me, before disappearing with my twin and her growly yet oddly silent entourage.

Memphis and Lux left too, through the front door though because Lux didn't enjoy the sifting thing. I could hear him protesting that he didn't need an escort home from the hall. It was probably true, next to any being on earth, Lux could still hold his own, even at his age. But against an angel, and especially Uriel, I didn't want to take the chance. Memphis knew that. I loved that Memphis knew that.

I loved Memphis.

The thought steadied me a little, at least until I looked up into the face of a whole different problem.

"You can't fall because of me."

Azriel stared down at me, completely silent.

"Uh, I'm gonna have a shower. I'm only a yell away, okay?" Blue said, as he stood and kissed my cheek.

When had they all decided that Azriel was one of them? Apparently, they'd bonded during my short captivity. Well, short for me.

I grabbed Azriel's hand, and pulled him down

beside me on the couch. "I'm serious, Azriel. A month ago you thought I was an abomination."

"Yes."

Lord save me from monosyllabic men.

I gave him my best withering look, but it didn't seem to phase him. I crossed my arms over my chest and let the silence hang between us. I took stock of his features. Was it because I knew him better that he didn't seem so cool, so inhuman anymore? Or did I have my rose-colored glasses firmly in place?

Azriel let his wings reappear, shifting them so they hung over the low back of the couch. I reached out and stroked the long white feathers, and he shuddered.

"You do not know. There was before you, and there is after you, Hope. I cannot go back to the angel I was before. I cannot forget…"

I swallowed hard. "Forget what?"

"The feel of your skin." He let out a longing sigh. "Your breasts."

I took a deep breath and tried to hold in the laugh that threatened to burst from my chest. Now was not the time to laugh.

"I understand all too well, Azriel. I feel things as well, more than any other person I know. I feel things for you. But I am an empath, I have tasted every emotion, including yours. Including the pain that Memphis and Gus still feel to this day, when they let down their guard and think about what they used to have when they still basked in the light of Heaven. And their pain is heart wrenching. I can't be the cause of that kind of pain for you. I care for you too much."

I put my hand in his, running my thumb over the smoothness of his palm. This was right. It was better to do this now, because it would hurt too much to let it go any further. It already hurt but I would survive.

"No."

"Pardon?"

"I said no, Hope. It is my choice. A millennia ago, I let Lucifer fall, I took Acerezeal's soul, I silently mourned Mephistopheles and Gusion's damnation. Deep down, I wanted to fall with them. I believed what they believed. I had seen Gusion with his Daughter of Man, knew his love was pure and good. I knew that they had cause. But I followed the rules, did what I was told was right." He turned to face me, cupping both of my cheeks in his palms. "This time I choose to do what my heart says. What is the Father's purpose of giving us these emotions, if we are unable to embrace them? Feel the full depth of what the heart has to offer?"

One of his fingers ran along my lower lashes, catching the tears that still sat there. Then he sighed deeply, and leaned forward and kissed me.

It was a kiss that shook worlds, a kiss that I would struggle to describe, but I felt the gentle caress down to my soul. It changed something, that small press of lips, but I couldn't find it in myself to regret it. In fact, as he pulled away, I chased his mouth with mine, pressing one more hard kiss to his full lips. It was a promise of something more. It was a promise that I would catch him if he fell.

He leaned into the kiss hesitantly, like he was cataloguing every sensation as it happened. I sat perfectly still as he sucked my bottom lip between his, ran the tip of his tongue across my teeth, combed his fingers through my hair. I resisted the urge to press my body into his, to rush this moment.

He pulled away, breathing heavily. His eyes were wide and wild. I realized I was sucking in air as well.

"How could I ever go back to believing that these feelings I have for you are wrong?"

I couldn't argue against something I wanted too, despite me playing Devil's Advocate. Heh. I leaned forward, and kissed him hotly. I wanted to show him that they weren't all chaste kisses and gentle exploration. Emotion, sex, love; they were messy and heartbreaking and so wonderful you wondered how you could survive if they were ever gone. And they would be gone. I would die in sixty or so years time, if I was lucky, and Azriel would have fallen for nothing.

I couldn't save Gus and Memphis the heartache of my fragile humanity, and it was doubtful now that I would be going anywhere but down, so it was okay. I could look forward to an eternity with them, in Hell.

But Hell was like the Wild West from what I'd heard from the guys, and Azriel was law and order. He would hate it, and eventually, he would hate me.

But I couldn't stop. I kissed him harder, this time I was exploring him, tasting him. I let out a surprised squeak as he picked me up and placed me on his lap, pressing me against the flat, hard planes of his body. Oh boy.

He let out a happy little hum of pleasure as I strad-dled his thighs, his hands on my hips pulling me closer. I wrapped my arms around his neck, threading them through the pale hair that was so blonde it was almost white. If I only had him for a little while, I wanted to consume him, body and soul.

But I wouldn't let him fall.

I pulled away, and slid off his lap.

"If we are going to embrace the dark side, let's order pizza and eat it in bed while having a Harry Potter movie marathon."

"Harry Potter?"

I shook my head. I held out my hand, and pulled him to his feet. "It's a series that came out when my parents weren't dinosaurs. Prepare yourself for some movie magic, Angel-Boy."

I walked into my room, listening to the water run in the shower. Blue had left the door open, probably so he could hear me easier, and steam was pouring into the bedroom, making the room hazy.

I pulled back the blinds and opened the window, letting the steam dissipate. The water turned off and Blue was suddenly standing in the doorway, a towel wrapped around his waist, his hair wet and shaggy.

"Everything okay?"

I nodded, swallowing hard and trying to think G-rated thoughts. "We are going to order pizza and watch Harry Potter. Want to join?"

Blue let out an audible groan, but nodded anyway. He slipped on some sweats that rode way too low and made my mouth water. I crawled into the middle of the bed and plumped the ridiculous amount of cushion. Then I sat down to watch the show. Not Harry Potter, but the way Blue's abs moved as he pulled his shirt over his head. I was going to get him a bunch of turtlenecks that were two sizes too small, just so the show could go on longer.

What kind of insane woman decided to date more than one man at a time? Apparently, this insanity was genetic. Maybe gluttony for punishment was hitched to one of our chromosomes.

I found the first Harry Potter movie in my computer and sent it to the huge TV in my room. My dad was still a tech geek, and I had all the latest gadgets, usually Oz-ified, which meant they were even better. I could turn on the coffee machine from the shower, and if that wasn't as close to Heaven on Earth, what did I know?

"What kind of pizza do you want, Azriel?" Blue asked, on the phone to the pizza place, Azriel just looked at him blankly. "You've never had pizza?" Blue asked, horrified. I just smiled at his wide eyes.

He finished off the order, getting a pepperoni with extra cheese, and came down to lie down beside me on the bed.

Azriel remained standing, staring at the space on the bed, and at Blue who was pressed right along my right side. I held my breath and tried to look completely casual. This was just another day, no big deal. This wasn't a test about whether or not we could cope as a unit. Because, Azriel might be willing to fall for me, but I would not, could not, give up the others. They needed me, my lost boys.

Seeming to settle whatever internal war was going

on, he climbed onto the bed, a few inches between us, and I let out the breath I'd been holding.

This might just work.

"BUT WHY DID they not use your human guns? I don't understand. It would have obviously hurt them, they are still human after all," Azriel argued, and I rolled my eyes. Blue snored softly beside us, falling asleep sometime after the third movie, though I was pretty sure he dozed most of the way through that one too.

"Because it's a movie made for children," I said patiently, though I enjoyed this outraged version of the Angel of Death, who had consumed an entire pie by himself and then binge watched all eight Harry Potter movies. Even I slept through the fifth and sixth ones. But Azriel could not get enough, and he watched them one after another, wasting twenty whole hours where we did nothing but cuddle, watch movies and eat cereal.

It was oddly peaceful. Also, angels didnt need a lot of sleep apparently. Memphis and Gus tended to sleep when I slept, so I just assumed.

I shifted from my spot at the end of the bed and stretched. I realized Azriel was still arguing about plot holes, but I knew he'd loved it. The Boy Wizard had a new fan, showing you are never too old for Harry Potter because Azriel was a million years old.

Blue stretched, and blinked sleepily at Azriel. "What's he talking about?" He gave me a drowsy smile. "You're hot in the mornings."

I grinned so wide my cheeks hurt. I went to his side,

leaning down to kiss him while he was still in this soft, unguarded mood. "Right back at you," I said close to his lips.

"Why don't you hop bac-"

Whatever Blue was about to say was interrupted by the chirping of my phone. Ugh, I couldn't remember where I left it. I patted down the bed covers, it had to be in there somewhere, and then ripped the blankets off.

"Hey!" Blue protested, and I was mildly distracted about how low his sweats had ridden overnight. They were barely hiding anything.

He grinned at me, his eyes sparkling with mirth. "Your phone?"

Oh shit, yeah. I finally found it poking out from under a cushion and dived for it, simultaneous pressing the answer button.

"Hello?" I sounded a little breathless, and I cleared my throat.

"Marco says you have to come," a childish voice said down the line. What?

"Pardon?"

"Marco says you have to come, that you have a situation. He said he couldn't send it in a text, because phones have beetles." There was a pause. "Bugs. He says phones have bugs."

It was a testament to how Harry Potter fried my brain was, that it took me awhile to connect all the dots.

"Tell Marco we'll be right there," I said. "Uh, bye?"

"Buh bye," the kid said on the end.

Blue was already up and getting dressed, slipping on his cool, neutral, killer face. Azriel was clothed in white linen pants and a white shirt, and I grimaced. Dressed in white, he looked inhuman, even without his wings.

"Uh, we are going incognito. Here, wear some of Gus' clothes, he won't mind," I said, digging around in the drawer that somehow magically started to store Gusion's clothes. There was a matching drawer for Memphis. Blue had just completely taken over the spare room.

I handed Azriel a pair of jeans and a well worn band shirt from some indie band that broke up in the 1990s.

Azriel looked at them like they were rattlesnakes.

I went and brushed my teeth, and by the time I returned, Azriel was dressed. My jaw dropped. He was sexy as hell. I mean, Azriel was beautiful, but he was too much perfection in a pretty package. Gusion's clothes dirtied him up a little, made him rougher, more edible.

"Wow. You look…" I walked over, and stood up on my tippy toes to kiss him. He rested his hands on my hips and pulled me close, kissing me back with enthusiasm. I wrapped my arms around his neck. He was a quick learner in the kissing department, and I squeaked out a surprised noise when he slipped his tongue between my teeth.

Someone cleared their throat behind us. "I hate to interrupt, but that call sounded urgent." There was an amusement to Blue's tone, and I sighed against Azriel's lips.

"To be continued," I whispered, and felt his smile in return. I think I'd move mountains for that smile.

. . .

FOR THE SECOND time in seventy-two hours I landed on Marco's doorstep. This time, instead of a practically dead woman in my arms, I had the sword of St. Michael strapped to my back. Azriel refused to let me leave it behind.

I went to knock on Marco's door, but it opened before my fist had the chance to connect to the wood. An irritated and slightly crazed Marco stood in the doorway.

I automatically reached out and held his hand. Not out of affection, though I was a little fond of the mute but somehow still gruff, gun-for-hire. But it was the easiest way for us to communicate.

You have a serious, serious problem. You have to take her away from here. I have kids in the house.

I stepped through the door, dragging Marco behind me, though I could feel his general dislike at having anyone behind him, especially an almost stranger. Azriel did have an unsettling presence.

"Slow down and go back to the beginning. She seemed sweet enough and as weak as a kitten. How could Serendipity be any danger to the kids?"

If I'd thought she'd be any trouble at all, I would have found a different place for her to lay low and recuperate after Purgatory. I'd never knowingly endanger those kids.

It's more complicated than you thought, came Marco's gruff response. *She's not so weak now. Actually, she healed remarkably quickly. Inhumanly fast.*

He stopped in the living room, where Sera sat between Cara, Marco's daughter and Sammie, Cara's half brother. They were watching a Disney movie on the TV. Marco rapped on the wall beside his head, and Sammie turned around. Marco signed something at him, and the solemn little boy nodded.

"C'mon Cara. We gotta go," he said, standing. Sera looked over her shoulder at us, her eyes quickly shuttering when she saw Azriel.

"I don't want to! I want to see the prince rescue the princess," Cara whined. Sera pressed pause on the remote, and petted the little girl's back.

"Princesses get rescued by handsome princes, Cara. Queens save themselves," she told the girl with a small smile. "Off you go. We'll finish it in a moment."

Sera had a slight accent that I hadn't noticed before, and her skin glowed now that it wasn't covered in rat bites. The bite marks weren't just healed, they were completely gone.

"We have a serious, serious problem," I whispered at Marco. I turned back to the woman on the couch. "Who the hell are you?"

The woman stood, moving, or maybe floating would be a better term, toward us. She smiled and stepped forward to hug me, but both Azriel and Blue were in front of me in an instant. She shrugged.

"Serendipity Smith," she said, jutting out a hand, and I shook it. All I got from her was a fuzzy frequency, relief, pain, angst but overall happiness shone from her emotions.

"Hope Jones," I said, and returned her smile. "You're something else. What are you? Gargoyle?"

Rella said all the other Gargoyles had died off, but

maybe she'd been in hiding. Sera just shrugged. "What are you?"

Well, touché. I wasn't about to spill my secrets to a stranger either. "You aren't human, though." It wasn't a question. I could feel the otherness of her,

"No. But then, neither are you entirely. Let's sit." She signed to Marco, who just scowled at her.

We walked into the kitchen and sat around the table. Well, I sat, and the guys all loomed, even Marco.

"Marco doesn't like you," I said conversationally.

"Marco doesn't like anyone, except those kids. And maybe you," Sera said. She was probably right, but it annoyed me that she thought she knew him so well after barely three days.

Marco gave the woman a rude sign that needed no translation. Sera just grinned.

"How long had you been in Purgatory for? I assume you knew it was Purgatory?"

I watched her face for any sign of deceit. She tilted her head to the side as if she was thinking hard. "Two months, four days, purgatory time."

If my stay in Purgatory for 24 hrs had been almost a month in earth time, then that meant she'd been trapped in Purgatory for five years!

"Why?"

Sera laughed mirthlessly. "It's the same stupid, age old story. Got drunk, slept with someone I shouldn't have." I remained silent. I needed more than that. She blew out a whistling breathe between her teeth. "I didn't realize until afterwards that he was more than he seemed as well. I should have known, I'm just so used to humans, you know? I stopped looking for anything more years ago."

"Did the angel had a name?" It had to be Uriel. Or even Dalius.

"His name was Luc, and he was the handsomest man I had ever seen."

Holy. Fucking. Hell.

CHAPTER THIRTY-FOUR

The chair scraped against Marco's beige tiles as I jumped to my feet.

"That's impossible," I said, and meant it with every fiber of my being. I would have been less surprised if she'd said it was the Archangel Michael himself. But Luc would never.

"You lie," Azriel said, equally as disbelieving. Because he was sane. Any being with two eyes could see that Luc loved Ace, body and soul. He would never cheat on her with anyone, even someone as beautiful as Serendipity.

Blue stepped forward, and sat down in my abandoned chair. "Describe him." The cool voice brooked no argument. It wasn't a request.

"Tall, perfectly built, eyes that saw into my very soul."

My heart sunk into the pit of my stomach.

"And the most beautiful hair, like a flame."

Relief made my body sag. Not Lucifer. Thank god.

"Uriel," Azriel breathed. "He's fallen. No wonder he hid you away in Purgatory," he said more to himself than Sera.

"Do you love him?"

Sera's face morphed into a terrifying mask that made me reconsider whether or not she was a Gargoyle. She looked deadly.

"No, we only had sex the once and then he stuck me in hell. Worst morning after ever. If I see him again, I am going to punch him in the balls so hard that he'll taste them on the back of his tongue."

Well, okay then. I was extremely glad that she didn't have some angelic version of Stockholm Syndrome.

Marco put a hand on my lower back. *That isn't your biggest problem.*

He pointed toward Sera, and my eyes naturally followed the direction of his hand. Right at Sera's torso. Right at the small bump where her stomach was. The very round, pregnant bump.

"No?" Azriel exclaimed, his voice climbing up an octave. "How can that be possible? It cannot be."

Blue leaned around to see what we were all gawping at. "It's either that, or she ate a really big lunch."

"I mean, it cannot be Uriel's. Angels are sterile. Even Archangels. Especially Archangels. It must be the offspring of a human, that is the only thing that makes logical sense," he muttered to himself.

Blue slid his eyes to me. "I think Sera broke your angel."

Azriel was pacing back and forth, and I was worried that Blue might be right, but I had to deal with this first.

I needed to… hell I didn't know what I should do. I was so out of my depth right now.

I used the techniques that my Dad gave me for use in business. I made a list of what I knew, and what I needed to know. I knew that Sera was something not human, and she healed quickly. I knew she had an affair with Uriel, and now she was pregnant, with Uriel's baby. I guess the baby must have gestated at Purgatory pace, and not human time.

"It is Uriel's, right?"

"Who's Uriel? This is Luc's baby, yes."

I cringed at her words. She was going to have to stop saying that, because if the wrong ears heard, it would lead to one hell of a mess. Ace was more of a 'kill first, ask questions later,' kind of person.

I needed to explain. But what if she was a spy? She'd seemed pretty adamant, and her emotions felt truthful, but we couldn't be too careful.

But I'd trusted my gut and my abilities for this long, I couldn't start second guessing them now.

I sat down, and I told her most of it, from the very beginning. I left out a few things, like the fact that Michael's sword was currently chafing my back, or the fact we planned to kill Uriel. But I told her about Ace and my Mom, and Luc's bet with God about the redemption of damned souls. I explained about Tenebrae, and Uriel's hand in all this bad, including the human trafficking. Sera's face got so stormy that I thought maybe she was a Valkyrie. If Gargoyles existed, so could Valkyries, right?

Silence echoed around the kitchen when I finished.

It was an amazing kind of a story, when told from the beginning. I knew only the basics of my parents story, and I'd pieced a little more together from my talks with Memphis and Gus, but everything since I'd been abducted outside UN Geneva headquarters had been a bit of a wild ride.

The silence was interrupted by a small child hedging around the edge of the room, hiding behind the island bench, until she was close enough to duck under the table.

Sera's face softened immediately. "Cara, what are you doing?"

"Hiding."

Sera's chuckle, and the fondness as she looked down at the child told me I'd made the right choice. "I see. And why are you hiding?"

"I want to go back and watch my movie. I want you to come and sing the songs. You sound so pretty when you sing," she cooed, climbing onto Sera's lap.

Sera looked at Marco, who was still scowling, but he nodded his approval for Cara to go back to the television, and the little girl skittered off Sera's lap and out of the room again.

Marco really didn't like Sera. I reached out a hand and fully assessed his emotions. He didn't trust her, but not because she rubbed him the wrong way. Because she rubbed him the right way. He desired her, but she was a threat to the children, to his way of life. He hated being out of control, out of his element. He was a lot like Blue in that way. I wondered if it was a hazard of the job, the constant need for control.

But he was right. Sera did pose a risk to the children.

When Uriel realized she wasn't in Purgatory. If he realized she was pregnant… I shuddered at the thought.

No. She had to be moved, but where?

"What are you thinking?" Sera asked

It had to be somewhere completely unconnected to me, or my family, or the Mulligan's. Somewhere wholly unconnected to NRH foundation.

I could only think of one place, one person, and it was a tenuous connection at best.

"We have to move you. You can't stay here with them." I nodded toward the living room, at the two heads that could only just be seen over the top of the couch. "This changes everything."

The wave of loneliness that washed over me made me choke back a sob. She'd been so lonely for so long. I reached over and wrapped my hand in hers.

"It's not forever. And I am always here. Whatever it is you are, or what you have been through, you won't have to do it alone anymore."

Blue chuckled. "Hope Jones, collector of the broken, fixer of wings," he teased, but the tenderness he felt was like a warm breeze that washed away all the filth of the last few months. "You adding girls to your harem now?"

I gave him a saucy wink. "Maybe," I joked, but we both knew it wasn't serious. Sera was beautiful, but I liked my guys too much. The thought of adding anyone else, either male or female, seemed wrong.

She stood, and I appraised her. She was tall, and her hair was a beautiful golden blonde that hung in a long waterfall to her waist now it wasn't matted and covered in crap. Her skin was a tawny gold, some kind of mediterranean heritage perhaps, and her eyes were a violet. She was a couple of inches taller than me, but still shorter than Azriel. "I will go gather my things," she said quietly, the sadness still coloring her aura. She glided from the room like a beauty queen, and I shook my head. She was definitely something else, and maybe one day I would get the truth of what that was. But until then, she needed protection. I thought back to her ferocious expression. Maybe she only needed a little protection.

I shoulder-bumped Marco. "Here I thought you were hanging out to be the fifth leg in my merry band of men. You've been turned by a pretty pair of violet eyes."

Marco scowled so hard, I thought his face might crack. *She is trouble.*

"Beautiful trouble."

He grinned. *Just like you. I should have known she could bring nothing but misfortune when I answered my door and you were there.*

"Hey, I'm not trouble." Blue let out a strangled cough that was badly hiding a laugh. I shot him a dirty look. "Well, not on purpose. Besides, I think she likes you," I added, and I was satisfied by the small stain of red on his cheeks.

The woman in question reappeared, a small plastic shopping bag of stuff in her hand. She looked at Marco. "I just want to say bye to the kids, if that's okay. I'd like…" she took a deep breath, "I'd like to come and visit them some time, if I could, after this is all over and I'm still alive."

I was close enough to feel the jolt of panic that shot through Marco at the thought she might be killed, but his face betrayed nothing as he inclined his head.

"I won't let anything happen to her. To them, I mean," I said quietly, and Marco just nodded, careful not to touch me. I respected his privacy.

We all walked to the front door, and Blue went out to bring the car around. Azriel had been strangely quiet since the revelation that Uriel had impregnated a woman. Would this change things for him, for us? Had the sterilization ban on angels been lifted?

My heart did a weird flip-flop at the idea at tiny Memphis', or Azriel's or little golden Gus' running around. I squashed the longing. I didn't think it was that easy, despite what Sera said. I think it had more to do with her than Uriel. She was the odd link right now.

Besides, I was happy. Kids were not something I wanted to think about right now. I was way too young and I'd been through way too much shit to be someone's parent.

I grabbed Azriel's hand, and threaded my fingers through his. He looked at me with faraway, haunted eyes, but eventually they softened.

"Call me if you need anything," I said to Marco as the car pulled up. "Take care of the kids, they are your first priority, but I don't need to tell you that."

He nodded.

Sera signed something in his direction, and a small smile broke through his scowl. But it was so fleeting that I might have imagined it.

Azriel slid into the front and I hopped in the back

with Sera. As we pulled away from the curb, she seemed to curl in on herself.

"I want to fight," she said in a low, growly kind of voice.

"You can't," I said, though she was kind of scary, definitely giving credence to my valkyrie theory.

"Why not?" She uncurled a bit, and I could see the steel return to her backbone. I shuffled a little closer to the window and pointed to the roundness of her stomach.

She glared at her midsection. "This is the spawn of evil."

Now it was my turn to get some steel in my spine. "Do you really believe that?" We weren't our parents. Genetics meant nothing when it came to evil. It was the choices you make, the people you surrounded yourself with, that was what made a person evil. Not simply genetics.

Sera curled back around her protruding stomach. "No, I don't. You can't judge a child by their parents. I am proof of that," she laughed mirthlessly. "I will love it, no matter who its father is."

I gave Blue the address, and he raised an eyebrow but didn't say anything about it. We drove through town, through traffic and we were all silent, lost in our own thoughts. Sera was an anomaly, but she wasn't my biggest problem right now.

"Is that a sword in you pocket, or are you just happy to see me?" Sera asked, breaking the silence, and I grimaced. Damn sword.

"It's a sword. Can never be too prepared, for you

know, ninjas and really large steaks and stuff. Oh look, we're here!"

We pulled up in the alley, and parked in front of a hydrant. A parking fine was the least of my troubles now. I was going to hell for stabbing an angel to death. Everything else pretty much paled in comparison.

I stepped out onto the street, and opened the heavy door to the shopfront. The bell above the door tinkled, just like last time.

A familiar figure stepped through curtain that led to the rear of the shop. "Can I help... it's you!" The giant man was genuinely glad to see me.

"Hi Cain, it's good to see you," I said, and I genuinely meant it.

"Back for another tattoo?"

"Tattoo?" Azriel asked, and I shushed him. But he'd drawn Cain's focus, and so had Sera.

"Not today, Cain. I was hoping for a different kind of favor. You see..."

CHAPTER THIRTY-FIVE

Cain had closed up the shop once Blue had emerged from the car, and strolled inside. I expected Cain to take an instant dislike to Blue, who had an air of violence he couldn't shake, but he invited us out back, got Sera a juice from a small mini fridge he kept in the office, and asked for details.

In this case, the Devil was actually in the details, so I painted a story that was close to the truth. Sera had a one night stand, and now the guy was now obsessed with her and had kept her captive for two months. We couldn't go to the cops because he was part of an organization that had spies everywhere. Close enough to the truth that he wouldn't ask questions and hopefully he wouldn't die for the answers.

I'd forgotten how huge he was. Easily taller and wider than both Azriel and Blue, it looked like he swallowed his twin in the womb and they'd both grown together. But his face was soft when he looked at Sera, then at the small roundness of her stomach. He nodded.

"She can stay with me. I have somewhere she'll be safe. But if you just give me the name of the guy, I can make the whole problem go away permanently," he growled, and I almost believed him. Sera smiled at him bemusedly, but she seemed comfortable with the big guy. I was glad she could see his mushy insides, without the bonus of my empathy. Cain looked scary, but I knew in my gut that he was a good person.

"I live above the shop, but I'll close down for a few days. Take her somewhere she can be protected."

Sera began to protest, but he just shook his head. "No. I will lose a few days profit. You could lose your life," he said in a low voice, and I could see the swell of sadness in his emotions.

I leaned over and gave him a hug. He stood stiff in my arms, but I expected that. He was too tough to hug me back, but he still needed the contact.

I won't let another one die. I'll protect her and the baby. It won't be like-

Cain pulled away, and I frowned. The big man had secrets. I thought about the sword still strapped to my back.

We all had secrets.

I stepped back into Azriel's arms. Cain raised an eyebrow. "Done with the pretty one?"

I laughed at his mention of Gusion. "My heart is too big to love just one person."

He let out a loud, booming laugh that scared the hell out of me. Even Sera jumped.

"If you were any other woman, I'd say that was an excuse to cat around. But with you, I think it may just be the truth. You seem to have no trouble finding trouble. You may need two," he looked at Blue, "three men just to fish you out of those tight spots."

I was about to correct him, that it was actually four, but I resisted. It was time to go anyway so I just did my best impression of a Mona Lisa smile.

I looked at Sera, giving her a questioning glance. If she wasn't comfortable, we would find another solution. But she seemed pretty fond of Cain already, not even in the least bit scared. Actually, Cain fussed around her like a mama hen. If she was happy, so was I.

We said our goodbyes to Cain and Sera, and I gave Cain all the details he would need to contact me, just in case.

I hugged Sera on the way out too, but unlike Cain, I picked up no stray thoughts. She was so muted my empath powers were no use. What was she?

CHAPTER THIRTY-SIX

I asked Azriel that very question when we got into the car. But he had even less answers than me. And seemed way more perturbed.

"What, are you worried about another 'aberration' roaming around the planet?" I teased, although I leaned in close to him so he knew I wasn't mad. His eyes got soft, and he wrapped his arm around my shoulders.

He shook his head. "No. I have seen lots of races walk this earth, more that have died out completely. The Gargoyles, the Atlanteans, the Annukaki, the Orisha, the Skinwalkers, the Mer and the dual-natured. All gone. But she fits with none of those. She is not the last relic of a long dead species. She is an anomaly."

I was silent while I mulled this over. Also, I made a mental note to google some of those races. All of a sudden those crackpot conspiracy theories didn't seem so far out. "Do you think she is a risk?"

Probably should have asked that question before I

dropped her off with a perfectly defenseless human man, but you know, hindsight and all that.

"Yes, her soul is reasonably pure. Well, as pure as you can get in modern times. Odd, but not malevolent."

She was just another piece of the puzzle. Sometimes I felt like I was trying to solve the puzzle blindfolded in a hurricane. I sighed and rested my head on Azriel's shoulder. He sat stiffly, like no one had ever rested their head on his shoulder before. Maybe they hadn't. So many firsts with this angel. As much as I wanted all his firsts, I still wasn't sure about what I could give him that would be even as remotely important as his wings.

Yeah, he was definitely another problem.

I tilted my head up to look at his face, and when he moved his head, I caught his lips with mine. He was a beautiful problem though, with the softest lips that I'd ever kissed.

I ran my tongue along the seam of his mouth until he opened and I could tangle my tongue with his.

I desperately wanted to be his first everything.

"Where to now, love birds?" Blue said from the front, his tone gruff but not jealous. Blue had changed. His wall had dropped until it was possible to climb over it if you tried.

And still, I was sitting here, happy and terrified, waiting for the other shoe to drop.

"Home, I guess. We'll have to talk to Gus and Memphis about this. About Sera."

Blue nodded, happy to give control of the issue over to the Fallen. "She did look a little familiar though, don't you think? Maybe she's Tenebrae?" Blue sounded as perplexed as me about all this crap. Actually, he was taking the whole supernatural aspect way better than I thought. Even Adnan, who'd known of this world his whole life, never accepted it with as much ease as Blue. Because Blue was fearless. How scary could the unknown be if you didn't fear death?

I looked down at my watch. Actually, while I was tying up loose ends...

"Blue, I changed my mind. Let's go to the ballet." Blue raised his brow, but did an extremely illegal U-turn and headed back the other way. There was one more festering wound that either needed healing, or cutting out at the root.

BLUE PULLED up at the service entrance of the theater where Adnan was currently dancing. "Want to wait until I park the car and I'll come in with you?" he asked, his expression kinder than his normal neutrality.

I shook my head. "We don't have passes. I'll just get Azriel to sift me in."

With a single nod and a look that I assumed said 'protect her with your life or I'll make buffalo wings with your major body parts', Blue pulled the car around the corner

Azriel didn't ask any questions, even though I could see the burning need to on his face. Look, he was learning. I wrapped my arms around his waist.

"I am not an elevator, you do know that, right?" he complained.

I laughed. "You mean a teleporter. And I know that,

I've never wanted to kiss an elevator until its eyes crossed. Now beam me up, Scotty."

He huffed, but sifted us the short distance to the other side of the door. Maybe it was all the sifting I'd done lately, or maybe all the angel mojo was rubbing off on me, but I didn't want to throw up on Azriel's shoes this time. Maybe it was because we only sifted a ten feet away.

I'd been here enough times that I knew my way around the back corridors of the theater. I could tell from the noises backstage that they were doing rehearsals, and that is where Adnan would be. He was never far from the limelight.

We walked into the main stage area, and I stood up the back, watching the dancers run through the blocking. When the music came on, and Adnan stepped out, I held my breath. He moved with unimaginable grace for a man with a prosthetic leg. He leapt, spun, his body rolling with perfect fluidity it was like he was made of air.

I'd always loved watching Adnan dance. It was beautiful. I looked down at my watch. They'd call lunch soon.

As if summoned by my thoughts, the choreographer called it. I watched the painfully thin but incredibly strong ballerinas stride off the stage. I was going to get a donut on the way home, and eat one in their honor.

I followed Adnan with my eyes as he talked to another dancer, but eventually he looked out into the darkness as if he could feel my gaze. Maybe he could.

When he met my eyes, I raised my hand. I saw his shoulders straighten, and he lifted his chin.

Would he just walk away? I held my breath, but he was nodding at the other dancer and moving towards us. I walked down the stairs to meet him halfway.

His face was casual and polite. The expression you would give a stranger. I smiled, trying not to let my sadness show on my face.

"Hey. You look well." Despite my efforts, my voice still sounded rough.

"Thanks," he said, a tiny smile on his face. We stood there awkwardly, though Adnan's eyes kept drifting to Azriel.

"Adnan, this is Azriel. Azriel, this is Adnan."

Azriel nodded, but stayed silent. Actually, he was acting a little weird too. He was doing his best impression of a marble statue with resting bitch face.

"Hope—"

"Look—" we both started at the same time, but he waved for me to continue. "I'm sorry about this whole thing. You are my oldest friend, and I love you. We've been through a lot, but I'd really like if we could start to, you know, rebuild what we had. Your room is still there, waiting for you."

Adnan's face hardened. "How could you think I would come back, Hope? My brother is dead. My cousin is dead. All because of your family. There is no way I am coming back to live with you."

His words were like knives in my chest. "I know, Adnan. Believe me, I know. I lost my twin sister, and one of my oldest friends."

He took a step closer, and Azriel was suddenly beside me, his blue eyes steely.

Adnan just gave him a scathing look. Maybe I should have told him that Azriel was the Angel of Death. Maybe he'd be a little more careful about who he gives the stink eye.

"There is no repairing our friendship, Hope. Your sister cost me my last living relative, and that is something I can never, ever forgive. I'll be by to get my stuff. I am going to pretend you and your family don't exist. It's better for everyone that way."

He turned and stomped back down the stairs like he hadn't just shattered my heart into a million pieces.

I watched him go, the last piece of my childhood, the last piece of that idyllic time I had before. Before I was abducted. Before sociopathic archangels and shady organizations.

"You know, he could just trip down the stairs. No big deal. He could see his brother sooner rather than later," Azriel said in a low voice.

Despite my pain, I couldn't help but smile. "He's an asshole, but he isn't bad. He'd definitely be going up. Unless the thumpers were right about the whole God hating gays thing?"

Azriel scoffed. "Please. He doesn't care who you love, as long as you don't go around murdering innocent people. That book is only half right."

I was pretty sure there was more to it than not murdering people, but I was glad to hear it anyway. I gave one more look at my past walking away with a rigid, angry posture.

"Goodbye," I whispered as I turned away too. I made it all the way to the exit, pushing out into the daylight, still holding myself together, Azriel behind me with a hand on my back. When I saw Blue leaning against a wall, waiting for us, I lost it.

Azriel looked at me shocked, his bewildered stare taking in my shaking shoulders and the tears tracking down my cheeks as I cried.

Blue had me wrapped in his arms in an instant, and I pressed my face into his chest and breathed in the scent that was just wholly Blue.

I could hear them talking above my head. "What happened?" Blue asked Azriel.

"The Mulligan forgot to whom he owed his life. He broke her heart." Azriel's words were spoken in that impassive way he had, like he was talking about the weather or the rising price of gas, but I knew that deep down he was simmering.

Blue let out a low, growly noise, and turned me into Azriel's arms. I hadn't realized how close he was until that moment. That I'd been pressed between them.

I reached out and just caught the edge of Blue's t-shirt as he marched toward the doors to the theater. "Wait, where are you going?"

"To teach the entitled little fuck a lesson he won't forget," he said, his voice scarily low and full of rage. This wasn't Blue, the calm and apathetic hitman. This was Blue the protector. The man who had let me close enough to care that someone had hurt my feelings.

The thought, and the fiery way he looked at me,

butterfly-stitched closed the hole in my heart, at least temporarily.

"It's not worth it. Let's just go, okay?" Fresh tears rolled down my cheeks, and I swiped at them with my arm angrily. I was sick of crying. Sick of always being some sad damsel.

With one last look of barely contained violence at the theater doors, Blue nodded and started toward the car.

We drove home in silence. Azriel sat beside me, cupping my hand in his, making little circles on my palm with his thumb.

My past might be gone, and my present might be pretty perilous, but my future was full of love. And that was something worth fighting for.

CHAPTER THIRTY-SEVEN

D espite my resolution in the car, the sadness hung over me for the rest of the day. I missed Gus and Memphis, and Azriel seemed at a loss. Blue did what he could, but he solved problems with violence, not with emotions.

I was on my third bowl of ice cream when Azriel stood in front of me, in the way of my Golden Girl's reruns. Right now, I didn't care if the creamy, sugary goodness went straight to my ass. I was dating four guys, so getting a chunky butt from over consumption of ice cream just meant there was just more of me to love, right?

"I do not understand you, Hope Jones." He sounded perplexed.

"Join the club, buddy," I quipped back, but instantly felt guilty. "Sorry. What don't you get?"

He continued to stare down at me like I was a puzzle again, like he had when we'd first met. "How you can be strong and fearless in the face of the Archangel, survive the very place designed to break you, yet you fall apart at the words of a selfish man-child? You are better than that."

I spooned another mouthful of ice cream, holding Azriel's gaze defiantly. He didn't understand, couldn't understand the connections I had lost, the years of memories that would forever be tainted. Unfortunately, in my defiance, I'd completely missed my mouth, dripping ice cream down my chin and all over my t-shirt. Dammit.

I sighed and grabbed a tissue, wiping at the chocolate syrup. That was probably going to stain. "You don't get it. I'm not…" my words trailed off as he leaned forward to lick the ice cream from my chin. Woah.

"You are not what?" he asked, tasting the ice cream from the corner of my mouth.

I held my breath. "Strong. I'm not strong enough to say no."

I wasn't strong enough to say no when desire burned through both of us, Azriel's feelings laid bare to me like an offering. He was so certain, although that certainty was colored by a fear of the unknown.

He pulled back a little until he was staring at me, the desire in his eyes like a punch to the chest. "Then say yes, Hope, and let me be your strength too. Trust in my sureness."

We had the place to ourselves. Blue was out buying milk and coffee and every carbohydrate-laden treat I could fit on the shopping list. This was the moment. The moment where lives changed.

But Azriel was wrong. I was weak and I wanted it all.

I captured his mouth with mine, and suddenly my hands were furiously tearing at his clothes like they'd taken leave of my brain and were acting on their own.

I should take this slow, ease him gently into it, but I was worried if I wasn't totally consumed by him, that I'd start second guessing him and myself. Luckily, Azriel was right there with me, muttering about stupid human clothes as he got my shirt stuck on my chin.

By luck or magic, I managed to get his shirt off. I stilled and sucked in a breath.

He was so damn perfect. The smooth expanse of his chest tapered down into his stomach, the light grooves of his abdominals just perfection above the cut V that led the way into the torn jeans he'd loaned from Gusion. His perfect white wings were spread out behind him, and looking at them took my breath away, halting my frenzied quest to get him naked.

"Are you sure?" I whispered. I wanted no regrets.

He stepped closer, until the warmth of his skin pressed against my hands. "I am very sure, Hope. What I feel for you is…" he frowned as he struggled with the words. "Right. It is meant to be." He unclipped the front clasp of my bra, letting my breasts fall into his hands. His eyes went huge, and if this wasn't such an important moment, I would have laughed at the look on his face.

Even so, I let out a gentle chuckle and led him back toward the bedroom. The first time wasn't going to be on the couch like we were a couple of horny teenagers.

Blue had made the bed and straightened my room after our movie marathon. I don't know when or how, but it was immaculate again. But that was Blue. He needed everything to be orderly, to be in its place.

We stood beside the bed awkwardly. The frantic energy was gone, but the desire and need were still there. For the first time, Azriel looked out of his depth. I stood on my toes and kissed his lips softly, and when he kissed me back harder, I let him take control. I was with him every step of the way, but he was setting the pace.

His hands grabbed my hips, and slid up over my ribs until they sat just under my breasts. He pulled back and looked down as his hands cupped both of my boobs and squeezed lightly.

"Why are these so amazing? My brain knows they are just another piece of human flesh but every other part of me thinks they are the most amazing things I've ever seen. And I have seen a lot of things, Hope," he argued. I wasn't disagreeing. Actually, I was trying not to laugh as he moulded them with his hands.

I ran my fingers through the light blonde strands of his hair. "You know, it's even more fun if you put them in you mouth," I said as he ran his thumbs over the hard peaks of my nipples, making me shiver. He laid me back on the bed, and I giggled at his comical look of delight. But all mirth left me as he wrapped his lips around my nipple and sucked hard. Holy hell.

My giggles turned to moans and his wonder morphed into male satisfaction as he moved from one breast to the other.

Suddenly we were both too clothed. I arched against him as he licked and sucked at my nipple, and when he scraped my the sensitive bud with his teeth, I shuddered.

He grinned, his face still pressed into my breast. He seemed to notice there was more to my half naked torso then just than my breasts and moved downwards, his lips brushing along the slight swell of my stomach, his nose dipping into my navel.

I reached down and stroked the underside of his wings, and was reward with a full body shudder. "That feels very nice," he mumbled against the skin over my hip. He'd reached the waistband of my jeans and stilled.

I hooked my fingers under his chin. "Are you sure?"

He nodded, and flicked open the button. I lifted my hips so he could tug them down and I kicked them off over my feet. Kneeling on the bed, he stared down at me, mentally cataloguing me, his eyes intense as they travelled over every inch of exposed flesh. When he got to my plain black underwear, he hooked them in his fingers and dragged them down excruciatingly slowly.

I had a moment of panic, of self doubt that I wasn't enough. He was perfect, and he was about to fall from perfection. He needed someone perfect. I had scars, both physical and emotional.

He let out a low noise in his throat, his eyes no longer impassive. He knelt between my legs, and began his slow, inexplicably erotic exploration downwards. There was something both arousing and unsettling about another person studying what made you aroused with almost academic proficiency.

When Azriel reached my center he pulled back, staring at the most intimate part of my body not like an angel, but like a man. "Is this also more fun if I put it in my mouth?" he asked, the quirk of his lips telling me he already knew the answer and was just teasing me.

"You can always try it and find out," I said, my voice more of a breathy gasp than teasing.

He took his time, leaning down, studying my vagina like it was a brand new species and he was David-Freakin'-Attenborough.

Finally, he leaned close enough that his breath cooled the wet heat of my pussy. His tongue darted out, rolling over my clit with pinpoint accuracy. *Well, score one for the angels*, I thought as I rolled my hips against his mouth. He was nothing if not thorough, and his tongue went to work, exploring, tasting and teasing me until I was a writhing mess. Maybe a clever tongue came with the wings.

My fingers were twisted in his hair as he continued, and my moans were hitting a desperate pitch.

"Azriel," I gasped out as my orgasm climbed. He made a low growly noise against my clit and that was it. I was gasping as pleasure flooded through my body in waves. I panted as Azriel rested on his elbows, his wings spread wide across the bed as he watched me come.

I grabbed his face and pulled him up my body, hissing as the rough fabric of his jeans pressed into my sensitive flesh. They were going to have to go ASAP. I kissed him hard, tasting myself on his lips, and it was so erotic I felt heat pool low in my belly all over again.

"You need to lose the pants, Angel-Boy," I laughed. He stood, grinning at me. That smile transformed him. Lifting his wings from the ground, he shucked his jeans.

I gasped. Not at his dick, which I wasn't going to lie was as perfect as the rest of him.

On the tips of his wings was a burnt orange color smudging the edges, the color of the last rays of a sunset. It was as beautiful as it was devastating. Subconsciously, I knew his wings would change when he fell. Well, I at least suspected they would. But the physical representation of his falling was a harsh reminder.

Azriel stared at the color staining his wings, and smiled. Actually smiled. Boobs had obviously fried his brain. My Azriel was a rule follower, he didn't smile at evidence of his fall from grace. "Why are you smiling?"

He knelt back on the bed and crawled up toward me, nestling his delightfully hard body between my thighs. My brain fuzzed and I almost forgot the question. "I was worried they'd be an ugly color. Like sewer brown or slush covered snow."

"You aren't sad?"

He looked at me quizzically, then his gaze traveled downwards, between our naked bodies. "I am the opposite of sad." He took a deep breath, his body lining up with mine. Then he stilled.

"Uriel made a child."

Well, that was a completely unsexy thing to say. "Yes?"

"What if I…"

Oh. Well, I guess it was probably something we should consider. But I'd been making love to Memphis and Gus for weeks and I wasn't knocked up by demon spawn just yet. I was reasonably sure that whatever voodoo had made Uriel suddenly fertile had less to do with Uriel and more to do with whatever the hell Sera was.

I wasn't 100% sure, but I was willing to take the risk I was wrong. Would a tiny little Azriel be the worse thing in the world?

"It will be fine. We'll discuss it with Gus and Memphis when they get back," I said, rolling my body against his, because quite frankly, I couldn't help it.

He leaned forward and kissed me. There was no doubt on his face, nothing but carnal desire. I pushed against his chest, stopping him one more time. "Are you sure?" There might be still a way to go back, if that's what he wanted.

In answer, he slid into me in one smooth glide until he was buried balls deep. I let out an involuntary moan, and threw my head back, but I made myself keep my eyes open. I wanted to watch his face as he experienced this sensation, and for a moment, he let his walls completely down. I felt everything; the pleasure, the restraint, the raw emotion he felt when he looked at me. Unguarded passion.

It was beautiful.

He slid back and thrust in again, finding a rhythm that came naturally to even angels. Soon, I was too caught up in the moment, in the sensation of our combined emotions and the feel of our bodies dancing, to worry about whether I was going to go directly to hell for killing an angel and making another fall. It felt too right to be wrong.

I wrapped my legs around his waist, pressing him

closer to me. His thrusts were getting harder, more ragged, and I was climbing.

"Hope." His guttural plea was the best thing I'd ever heard, and my nails dug into his shoulders as I held on, my orgasm sweeping through me, tearing me to pieces and putting me back together again as someone different. Azriel let out a long, low groan as my orgasm coaxed his own, and he buried himself in me, our bodies so connected I could feel every hitched breath and the rapid thud of his heart.

It wasn't the wildest sex, or some kind of marathon. But I felt our souls knit together in a way that scared me.

He buried his face in my neck as he heaved in breaths and I searched his emotions for anything resembling regret. I found none. But there was fear. I hugged him close to me, my arms banded around his back.

"Azriel…" I started, needing to fill the silence. But he lifted his head, and he looked perfectly content.

He leaned forward and kissed me. "I understand."

"What?"

"Why they fell. Why Luc went to such great lengths to return Acerezeal to her place. Why they hate me so."

He rolled so he was lying beside me, and I snuggled into his chest. "There is always time to change. And they don't hate you." He raised a single eyebrow. "Okay, maybe a little, but it is just hurt feelings. And that you stole Ace's soul. And that you stabbed my Mom. It's all water under the bridge now." I looked over his shoulder, and gasped again. "Your wings!"

They were no longer just dusted with burnished gold. They were the colors of a fiery sunset. Deep indigo up near his shoulders, slowly changing into a deep orange color before being golden on the end. They were magnificent.

He looked over his shoulders, his heart thundering against my cheek. Finally, he nodded once and turned back to me. "They aren't bad."

I shook my head. I kissed his chin and tucked myself right along his body.

"Not bad at all," I whispered back, and kissed him again. Maybe I'd introduce him to doggy style.

WHEN WE EMERGED a few hours later, because quite frankly I was starving, I was surprised to see Gus and Memphis were back. They lounged on my couch, watching baseball and drinking beer with Blue. It was the most domesticated scene I'd ever witnessed. They all looked in our direction, and I felt Azriel tense for a fight. Blue gave me a smile and went back to watching the baseball, but Memphis and Gus stood, coming over to kiss me.

"I missed you guys," I said to Memphis, who pressed a kiss to my cheek and then my lips. "How is Luc?"

Memphis shrugged, and let out a long sigh. "There is no cure for those kind of nightmares, Hope. Not even time. But I'm pretty sure Estrella and her consorts have taken refuge, because Acerezeal's version of therapy involves having coitus on every available flat surface."

Gus laughed. "And a few unavailable ones. Hence why your twin has had to barricade off their wing of the palace." He wrapped me in a hug that lifted me off my feet. "I'm jealous, Pretty Girl."

My eyes widened. Of all the men in my life that I thought would be jealous of Azriel, Gusion had been at the bottom of the list. "Gus–"

"I'm jealous his wings are prettier than mine," he interrupted, mock pouting.

"Stop fishing for compliments Gusion, you all have beautiful wings," I laughed.

"Except the Mulligan," Memphis stated.

"I just have a beautiful dick." Blue added. "I've got nachos in the oven. Sorry, I don't know how to cook. I can kill a man in under ten seconds without a weapon, though."

Azriel's lip quirked. "An enviable life skill," he said. He turned to Gus and Memphis. "Did Blue fill you in about the girl?"

All mirth left their faces. The timer for the oven went off and I walked into the kitchen. I got a couple of beers from the fridge, and made a quick garden salad to go with the nachos. Of course, Blue may only make nachos, but it was meticulously prepared. I was fairly certain even the corn chips were symmetrically aligned. Blue wandered into the kitchen, his eyes dipping to the spot where we made love on the floor. Hot images of our chase through the apartment heated my cheeks. We were definitely going to have to do that again very soon.

Apparently, Blue had the same idea, because no sooner had the thought entered my mind, then I was backed up against the island bench, one leg over Blue's hip and his mouth all over mine. He kissed like he fucked; with absolute control and dominating precision.

"Soon, Princess." It was a simple promise, but then I was back on two feet, slightly out of breath and holding myself up with my elbows on the bench. He grabbed the plates down from the shelf and walked back into the living room, but I saw the bulge in his black jeans. Yeah, I wasn't the only one a little revved from out stolen kiss. I grabbed the salad and followed him, and stopped in the doorway. They all sat around the table, all four of them, the angels with their wings hanging over the back of the chairs, and Blue looking completely at ease. This could work. I could make this work.

But first, Uriel had to die.

CHAPTER THIRTY-EIGHT

Eventually, Luc had to return to the apartment. Ace came first and made sure we had the sword well hidden. I'd stuffed it in my laundry hamper, so deep under my dirty clothes and Blue's stinky socks that not even a sniffer dog would be able to track it down.

Memphis watched the whole ritual with a horrified expression. Azriel had to actually leave the room. The blasphemy just kept rolling in my apartment.

Finally, Luc appeared. He looked uncomfortable, almost embarrassed. I wanted to hug him, but that was probably a one-off thing. Instead, I handed him a beer, even though it was only one in the afternoon. The rules of propriety didn't really apply to the Devil.

He thanked me, then looked over my head to Azriel. Because I stood so close, I could hear his sharp intake of breath, but otherwise there was no outward display of shock at Azriel's fall.

He smiled, looking between us. "Welcome, Brother.

It is nice to have you back with us, finally," he looked down at me. "But if you hurt her, I will tear your wings off and feed you to the Specters in the Seventh Circle. Clear?"

Azriel didn't look fearful, he just looked amused. He gave a nod. "I fell for her, Lucifer. I would never harm her."

Ace looked positively gleeful. "Not all harm is physical, Azriel, Angel of... holy crap, who's collecting souls?"

Azriel shrugged, looking uncomfortable for the first time. Happy to fall, happy to be threatened, but at the mention of his dereliction of duties, he finally showed some guilt. That was such an Azriel thing that it made me smile. I walked over and wrapped an arm around his waist, pressing into his side.

Luc was just nodding. "Explains the lack of foot traffic over the last week. I thought the humans had finally managed peace on earth."

All five angels laughed. I rolled my eyes. That was definitely Angel humor.

Luc walked over and slapped a hand on Azriel's shoulder. "Do not stress, they have found someone to do it. The numbers have picked up steadily today. I imagine they've pulled Raphael in to do it for the time being."

Luc and Azriel began to talk shop, about soul distribution and other topics that were unbelievably boring considering they were legitimately talking about eternal damnation.

Ace stood beside me. "I am pissed right now, Hope."

Uh oh. Did she find out about Sera? Not that I was hiding her or anything.

"How come Azriel gets the pretty wings?" Ace said as she looked between her dove grey wings and the rainbow ombré of Azriel's. Who knew Fallen angels were this vain about their wings?

"Don't ask me, take it up with management."

We both laughed. And in that moment I had an epiphany.

Or I was slapped in the face by the brutal truth. "The stranger on the bus. Like the fucking song." My strangled yell got everyone's attention. They were looking at me like I'd lost my goddamn mind, and maybe I had.

"It was him, on the beach. Azriel, how could you not know it was him?" I bounced around, no longer able to stand still. What did it mean?

Azriel was looking at me like I was nuts, and Gus came over, wrapping an anchoring hand around my forearm. "Slow down, Pretty Girl. Who are you talking about?"

I took a deep breath. "On the beach, after Michael left, there was this guy walking up the beach toward the car park. He looked familiar, and when I asked if I knew him, he said maybe he was a stranger on a bus. Like the song!" I whistled the tune and Ace laughed. "He had this awful 'Jesus is my homeboy' shirt on." Ace laughed harder. "And after he was gone, we noticed the sword. The guy was The Guy, with the capital G."

It made so much sense. Michael would never disobey enough to leave behind his sword. Everyone knew that.

And I hadn't magically gotten the power to hold the freaking flaming sword. The Big Guy in the Sky had made his move, but for some reason instead of just getting Michael to shut Uriel down, he gave me Michael's sword.

I still wasn't sure of the why.

"Am I the only one who still has no idea what she's talking about?" Blue asked the room.

Azriel looked shaken. He was staring at me like I was something altogether different. A new creature that he hadn't yet encountered. "She means that we encountered the Father. He gave her the sword of St. Michael. Now would be the right time to cross yourself, Mulligan."

The only person who didn't seem overly perturbed by the idea was Luc. He tilted his head to the side, a huge grin on his face. "Well played, Old Man."

Gus pulled me into his arms, hugging me tightly. I realized my hands were shaking a little. It wasn't just that Michael wanted me to bring down an Archangel, because let's face it, even that sounds preposterous. But the other guy...

"Am I the only one imagining Michael totally freaking out right now? It'd be like telling your dad that you crashed his vintage car," Gusion said, little high pitched giggles sneaking out from between his lips. "That conversation would be worth going back to Heaven for. 'Uh, Father, I kind of misplaced the Sword of Light you gave me to battle Hells enemies. I checked behind the couch and in the pockets of all my favorite linen shirts, but I just can't find it anywhere,'" he mimicked, his giggles turning into full blown honks of laughter. Ace was laughing right along with him, and even Memphis seemed amused.

Blue looked completely bewildered. Pale, he leaned his head on the back of the couch and was staring into space. That was the appropriate response. Falling obviously fried more than a few brain cells in the rest of the people in the room.

Except Azriel. I wiggled out of Gusion's arms, and moved toward him. I touched his face, stroking the tiny frown line between his eyes, marring his normally impassive expression. Well, it was less impassive these days.

"Are you okay?"

He nodded, but I wasn't convinced. "I didn't know him. I always thought if I was graced by His presence, I'd know."

I didn't know what to say to that, so I rubbed circles into his lower back and hoped that it was enough.

Luc drew himself back up to his full height. "As amusing as this has been, it is not why my consort and I have come. The how or why the sword came into your possession matters not. What matters is what we intend to do with it."

That silenced the room.

"We've been over this," Blue said. "You know where I stand."

"Would the sword recognize Estrella?" Ace asked. "No offence to Hope, but killing doesn't come naturally to her."

All four of my guys turned to me. Well, I guess there

was no time like the present. "I killed the angel Dalius in Purgatory, and rescued a woman who is pregnant with Uriel's child."

In that moment I did something I never thought I'd be able to do.

I shocked the hell right out of the Devil.

And Ace, who literally had a witty comeback for everything. "I… well… " She waved her hands uselessly in the air.

"I think you may have some explaining to do, Beloved of my Consort."

Uh oh. I was in trouble now. I think I'd just lost my standing as his favorite.

I hesitantly recounted everything that happened in Purgatory. Well, the finer details anyway. When I got to the part where I accidentally stabbed Dalius with a knife, Ace snorted. So it wasn't as badass as it sounded, but that didn't change the facts.

Sera however peaked their interest. "How sure are you that she is indeed pregnant with Uriel's baby?"

A small smile curled Azriel's lips. "She said it was yours, Luc."

That teasing rat bastard. Ace's head whipped to the side, and the comical look of horror on Luc's face would be burned into my retinas for the rest of my life. I was going to cherish that look.

"We think Uriel used your name, when he uh, picked her up and fornicated."

Luc's cheeks flushed. Nope, that was the image I was going to save in my mind for rainy days when things seemed impossible. If Lucifer could blush like a southern belle, then anything could happen.

"Obviously. I would never." The more he protested, the bigger Azriel's grin grew. Apparently, I wasn't the only one amused by Luc's uncharacteristic awkwardness.

"Obviously," Ace said drily. "Where's the girl now?"

I hesitated. "I've hidden her away somewhere safe." Both of the Fallen angels looked at Blue. Poor Blue. Mentally, he was always going to be the weakest link. By the stormy look on his face, he knew it too.

"Ah. I know of him."

Now it was my turn to look shocked. "You do?" Had I left Sera with a closet serial killer? What if my gut had been totally wrong about Cain.

"Don't fret. Cain may be many things, but he is protective of innocents. She is as safe as she can be among humans." He finally sat, dragging out a chair and then wrapping an arm around Ace's waist and pulling her onto his lap. His thumb stroked up and down the curve of her hip. They had a love I could only aspire to; but I was going to damn well try. "Let us talk about how you will kill Uriel."

I blanched. Ace had been right. I wasn't a killer, and everyone in the room knew it. But I had a lot of anger at Uriel, and that might just be enough.

"I have a plan," Azriel's voice filled the silence in the room. "About how to kill Uriel."

Maybe this really was the End of Days.

MY HEART THUNDERED in my chest, but Blue was

there to steady me yet again. When had I begun to rely so heavily on his steadying influence? I was in a bustier that pulled tight around my waist until I had an hour-glass figure like a burlesque dancer. I was wearing tiny black shorts that had shiny gold buttons up each side and silk stockings underneath them, a long black seam running up the back of my legs from my classic black Louboutin's to the hem of my shorts. My hair was curled wildly, hanging loose around my shoulders and my lips were painted red. I looked like sex.

But I felt like a mouse in a room filled with veloci-raptors.

We were back at Uriel's S&M club, and the room was packed. Blue looked amazing. He was in tight, leather pants which were tucked into chunky, black boots that had probably gutter-stomped half of Boston at one time or another. He was shirtless, and the soft lights made him look dangerous and wild. He was wearing guyliner, and his blue eyes popped so hard that it was like falling into the abyss every time they caught you in their line of sight.

"I got you, Princess. We've practiced this. He won't see it coming. In, out and we are done. We can move on with our lives. Five minutes of bravery for a lifetime of happiness," he whispered.

We skipped coat check, mostly because we wanted to be able to make a quick getaway and partially because neither of us were wearing very much in the way of clothing. Somewhere on his body Blue had his gun, but I couldn't spot where in his tight clothing.

We headed toward the bar, blending into the crowd.

My eyes kept moving toward the St Andrew's crosses on the other wall. I wasn't playing cute little submissive today. I was being a badass.

I ordered two scotches from the attractive and wildly underdressed bartender, and when he slid them across the bar, I downed mine in one gulp. I needed the courage more than I needed the brain cells.

Blue turned me so I was in his arms and kissed me hard. "We've got this." He looked down at his watch and I looked at mine. The plan relied on us being where we needed to be exactly on time. Two minutes.

"I love you, you know that, right? I don't tell you enough. I love you," I whispered as I pressed close, the light dusting of hair on his chest scratching against my shoulders.

"I know. I love you too, Hope Jones. And I don't intend for this to be the first and last time I tell you that, so harden up." He slapped my ass, and I let out a shocked yelp. "God you look so hot right now, these pants are torture."

I laughed and kissed him, uncaring that I was smearing him with red lipstick. I pulled back and took a deep breath. "Two minutes. Let's go."

I squared my shoulders and walked over to the raised dais where Uriel sat like a king over his fiefdom. Girls, and teenage boys tonight, were lined up like prize dolls along one wall of the small alcove. I gritted my teeth at the amount of sludgy red that was smeared across everyone's aura. Blue must have felt me tense, or maybe he just knew me now, because he whispered, "Cutting off the head would make the rest of this scum easier to clean up." He stilled and I resisted the urge to cling to him. He had to wait at the bar, his thoughts mixed up with those of the rest of the crowd. Uriel would pluck our plan from his brain like he had it written on his forehead if he stepped any closer.

I strode toward the stairs to the dais, only to be stopped by security. The guy was huge, and I didn't think he'd been there last time we came. Maybe Ace's little foray inside the headquarters of Tenebrae had shaken them up.

"Let me past." My voice was cool, confident and I was a little proud of myself for my resting bitch face.

The gorilla just stared down at me.

"Let her through," came Uriel's too sweet voice. I gritted my teeth, and pushed past the man mountain only to come face to face with Uriel's smug expression.

Ace was wrong. I might be a pacifist, but I think I could gladly stab this smarmy asshole.

"Child of Acerezeal. How strange to find you here."

I screwed up my nose. "I bet."

I couldn't keep the sneer out of my voice, so I sucked in a deep breath.

"Look. I want to call a truce. I don't want to go back to that place ever again." I didn't have to fake the terror that made my voice waver. "I'll stay out of your... whatever this is." I indicated his small troupe of thugs around him. "Just leave me and the people I love out of it."

I snuck a small glance at my watch from the corner of my eye. Thirty-seconds. Azriel hated that he had to be left behind, to grab Michael's sword. The theory was that if he grabbed it, it would disappear and reappear at my feet. We'd tested it over the last few weeks at different distances, and every time anyone tried to grab it, it would appear by my feet. We were going to use that to our advantage. Just thirty more seconds.

"So be it, human. But first…"

Suddenly he was in front of me, his hand around my neck, squeezing gradually like a vice. "How about you tell me how you killed Dalius and stole the whore from Purgatory? Do you think I am stupid?" I struggled, my feet no longer touching the ground as I clawed at the Archangel's wrists. He was crushing my throat in his huge hand, and I tried in vain to suck in air around my constricting windpipe.

I heard the gunshot, and struggled to look toward Blue, who was suddenly there, gun pointed at Uriel.

HELP! I screamed. I screamed it to anyone I thought would hear. The bullet that had left Blue's gun stopped, turning and thundering back toward him. *BLUE!* I lifted both hands and gouged them into Uriel's sadistically gleeful eyes, loosening his grip just as Memphis and Gusion arrived. Suddenly Luc was there, the temperature dropping as I fell to the ground, Uriel tossing me to the side like a piece of trash.

I scrambled toward Blue, who's white skin was a mess of blood. "Blue. Blue, it's okay." I held my hands over his chest, but the blood was rushing up from between my fingers.

"Hello, Lucifer."

"You will die, Uriel. And I will enjoy torturing your soul for eternity."

Then I was gone, sifted back into my apartment.

Gus held me in his arms, but I struggled out of them. "Blue! Gus, we need to go back for Blue!"

"Shh, Memphis has him. Do not worry. He is fond of your Mulligan, we all are. We won't let him die."

Tears dripped from my face, the image of Blue's chest covered in blood was permanently etched into my mind. My hands were covered in blood. Blue's blood. Why did the word blood keep repeating in my head?

"Gus…" I whispered as the edges of my vision got blurry. I couldn't work out if it was tears or if I was about to pass out. I gritted my teeth, holding onto my consciousness and my sanity. Blue needed me. "He needs me. He needs us. We need to go to him."

My phone rang, and it was my Eli. "Dad…" and then I cried.

"I'm taking him into surgery now. We are at Mount Sinai." He barked orders at someone with enough authority that everyone jumped. "We got him here quick, Hope. I'll do my best."

"I know," I whispered, and then the line was empty.

I sucked in a single, ragged sob. And then I hardened up, like Blue said. "We need to get to Mount Sinai hospital."

Gus nodded. "We should drive. There's nothing you can do until he gets out of surgery, and puking all over the waiting room is not a way to pass the time."

I nodded. I needed the time to compose myself anyway, or I was likely to shatter into a million pieces. I needed Blue's steadying hand right at that moment, but instead he was possibly dying on an operating table because of me.

Tears welled up in my eyes again, but I blinked them back. I grabbed the gold queen chess piece from the mantle, clutching it to my chest like a security blanket.

"He'll be okay," Gus said soothingly as he led me out of the apartment and into the elevator. "Azriel is there now. He will make sure his soul stays exactly where it's supposed to be. Blue Halloran is as stubborn as the Mulligan blood in his veins. He is not going anywhere."

I wasn't so sure. What if this was punishment for killing an angel? Or making another fall. What if this was karmic justice?

We slid into my Tesla, and Gusion guided the car out of the carpark and into traffic. Gusion was not a good driver. He drove like he flew for a living.

I'd never seen any of them fly. Maybe their wings were decorative, like a chicken.

"Can you fly?"

The question seemed to startle Gus, who jerked the car too close to the curb. I winced at the scrape of my hubcaps on the gutter.

"Where did that come from?" I shrugged, the odd tear still escaping from my eye to drip down my cheek. "Yes, we can fly. These things on my back would be pretty useless if we couldn't."

I stared out the window. "Chickens have wings and don't really fly. Or penguins."

Gus forced out a laugh. "Sweetheart, I am neither a chicken or a penguin. One day I will take you flying. Maybe after you marry Blue Halloran, or after you give us all two beautiful children to dote on."

I whipped my head towards him. "Does that

happen?" He's the angel of the past, present and future. "You'd know right, if Blue survives this?"

Gus took a deep breath. "Nothing is ever set in stone. You and your sister were proof of that. Ace getting her soul back is further proof. Life changes every day, and it is in a constant state of flux. You bump into a man in the street, halting him three-seconds in his day, but that three-second delay means he doesn't get run over by a driver whose vehicle is out of control and mounts the sidewalk. That man gives money to an animal shelter, and that animal shelter adopts a cat to a woman who was going to commit suicide until she found the unconditional love of a pet. That woman eventually finds love, gets married and has a baby who cures cancer and saves millions of people for decades to come. Life isn't a straight line, it is a complex web of emotion and interactions and energy and intention."

I held my breath. "But?"

He takes his eyes off the road for a second, just so I could see the sincerity in their golden depths. "I too want Blue to live. You have to understand that. But nothing I say is a guarantee." I nodded. I got it. "When I first met Blue, that is what I saw. I saw him chasing around two little red haired children in the backyard of your parent's house."

I felt like I could breathe a little easier, despite all of Gusion's warnings about the future not being a static thing. But in some universe it happens, and I could only pray it was this one.

CHAPTER THIRTY-NINE

I laid my head on my Mom's shoulder. It had been hours, and I was exhausted. But so was she. No matter how many times I told her to go, she stayed with me, her hand wrapped in mine. All seven of my Dad's came and went, taking turns to sit beside us, forcing coffee into my hands, or a sandwich, or water. We got more than a few weird looks. Mostly because my parents were a hot commodity for the media. Their faces were recognizable, even if they couldn't name them all.

And during the whole five hours, my angels stood like sentinels around the room, invisible to the human eye, but I felt their love all the same. They'd dropped their shields until I was bathed in their love for me, and their respect for Blue.

Eventually, everyone left for the night, leaving only Mom, Lux and Ri. They weren't as young as the used to be, and all night vigils were no longer in their wheel-house. Except Ri, who was used to being up all night because of the club, and Lux who had never lost his battle readiness.

I don't think Lux would leave even if he was tired. He was still angry that I tried to stage an Archangel assassination without him, but he couldn't yell at me because Mom didn't know. It was why I didn't protest too hard when Mom insisted on staying.

Finally, Eli walked into the room, and I jumped to my feet. I ran into his arms, and he hugged me tight.

"It went fine. The bullet hit a rib and shattered, and it was hell trying to get out all the pieces. A couple went worryingly close to his heart, but by some strange miracle they stopped. He should make a full recovery. He is in post-op now. Give it a little bit, and then you should be able to go in and see him. We called the Mulligans, who are listed as his next of kin, but no one would come out. I told the nurses you were his wife."

Then I cried. Again.

Everyone went home, except Lux. He followed me as I walked down the barren white corridors toward the elevator that would take us to the post-op ward.

I was in for it now. "You didn't tell me." I shook my head. "Why?"

It was Memphis who answered, even though he was still invisible. "They are going up, Arcadia and the rest of the seven. You have behaved so well for the last twenty years, you could almost be selected for sainthood. Even I can see it. They are all going to Heaven. You fuck up in this life, and you will be back down in Hell. You didn't fight so hard to be redeemed, only back in

Hell for all eternity for killing an Archangel. It was better if you stayed out of it."

Lux's jaw tensed. "And if she'd died? What good is going to Heaven if both my daughters are in Hell with you assholes?"

He couldn't see Azriel. I didn't tell my parents he was there. It was a drama I didn't need right now.

We reached the nurses station. "I'm here to see Irving Halloran; I'm his wife" I said, ignoring the note of desperation in my voice.

"Bed six. Only one of you though, sorry."

Lux kissed my forehead. "I'll head home with your mother." He tipped up my chin so he could meet my eyes. "I'd happily go back to Hell if it kept you safe. You know that, right? You mean the world to me. So did your sister."

I choked down the lump of emotion that lodged in my throat. I nodded, because I didn't think I could speak.

"Love you, Kid."

I hugged him tight. "Love you too, Dad."

I watched him walk away, and noticed the eyes of the nurse following him down the hall. When she looked back at me, and realized I'd busted her perving on my father, her cheeks flushed red.

I gave her a knowing grin. I was used to it. I got all A's at school the year Mom couldn't make my parent/teacher interview and Lux went instead.

I pushed through the door and into the recovery ward. The guys were behind me, exempt from the one person rule. Only one visible person, right?

I finally found the right bed. I pulled back the curtain and nearly cried. Blue was asleep, his chest covered in a white, square bandage. A tube up his nose gave him oxygen and the steady beat of the monitor told me that he was okay. His heart was beating it there. He was alive.

I walked over, standing beside the bed and wrapped his hand in mine. I felt its dry warmth and finally I could breathe. I kissed his chin and his cheeks and finally his lips.

I'd almost lost him. I couldn't lose any of them. My heart wouldn't survive. It would have been shredded right along with his.

"Hey, Princess," his raspy voice whispered against my ear, and I let out a little sob of happiness. I laid my head on his shoulder. He smelled of antiseptic and iodine.

"You scared me, Blue Halloran. I hate that you scared me. I hate that you almost died. You aren't allowed to do it again, okay?"

"Okay," he said, and he sounded completely serious.

The nurse bustled in, checking his vitals now he was awake. I stepped out of the cubicle into the hall with my guys. She asked Blue a bunch of questions that he must have answered correctly because she wasn't freaking out.

Another nurse walked past me. "Why don't you go wait outside, sweetie? This won't take a moment, but he'll probably be asleep again before you know it. We'll transfer him up to ICU in about an hour. Go get some rest, have something to eat. You look exhausted."

I felt exhausted, fear sapping me of every ounce of

energy I had. I went to tell Blue I was going up to the cafeteria, but the other nurse had been right. He was sound asleep.

I'D FALLEN asleep in the hard hospital chair beside Blue's bed. Voices pierced the blackness, but I just groaned and tried to move into a more comfortable position.

"She's uncomfortable. You should move her onto the bed," someone whispered.

"I would, but your nurse is scary as hell," someone else whispered back, and I smiled a little in my sleep.

"You scared her. You scared us. No more shooting bullets at immortals with powers far greater than anything you could comprehend. Your death would have broken her." That low growl I knew. Memphis.

"He was strangling her. What was I supposed to do?" Blue argued. He had no remorse. His next words proved me right. "I'd do it again if it would save her."

Someone let out an annoyed noise, and I opened my eyes to see all of my angels standing around Blue's bed.

Blue's eyes were bloodshot, but they were the best thing I'd ever seen. I walked over to kiss him, careful where I put my hands. I wanted to kiss every inch of his stubborn, beautiful face. "We have to stop meeting like this, Blue Halloran." I put the chess piece on the table.

He laughed, reaching out for the piece. I put it in his hand and he curled his fist around it. "You've turned the tables, Princess. Now it's you guarding my body. Come here." I leaned forward and he kissed me, his lips dry and scratchy. But I didn't care.

I kissed him back with all the love I had for him. "You scared me."

He nodded. "I'm fine though. Go home, get some sleep. Have a shower. You look like hell. You didn't look this bad after you came out of Purgatory."

I scowled at him. "This was worse than Purgatory, asshole. I thought you were going to die."

He laughed and then winced. "You can't get rid of me that easily, Hope Jones. I'm yours for life. Now get out of here."

I kissed him once more, and stepped back into Memphis' arms. I let him wrap his big, dark wings around us both and rested my head on his chest.

"I fucked up, Memphis. I fell in love. How will my heart ever survive loving you all?"

He planted a kiss on the top of my head. "It won't. We just patch it up with little pieces of our own. We are one unit now. You heart is ours, and you hold all four of our lives in your hands. That's what love is."

He sifted us both back to the apartment, straight into the bathroom. He ran the shower and slowly, methodically undressed me. I always felt like such a weakling when I enjoyed this part. But I figured it was win-win; I got to be worshipped and he got to unwrap me like it was Christmas morning. Once I was naked, and magically so was he, he lifted me up and I wrapped my legs around his waist. He stepped into the shower, and the water immediately began to pool where our bodies were pressed tightly together.

"I love you, Hope Jones. For me, you are life." Then he kissed me like he could prove his words with his lips. He held me effortlessly as I kissed him back, his body rubbing against me in a maddeningly slow but extremely erotic roll of his hips.

"I love you too, Memphis."

He grinned at me then, and it was so fucking beautiful. "Then you better hold on, Heart of Mine, because I am going to make love to you until you forget anything else but pure happiness."

Boy, did he deliver.

Once we stepped out, pruny but well-loved, I dressed in one of Gusion's t-shirts. I wanted to sleep for a week, but first I should probably eat. I padded out into the living room on bare feet, however my plans for toast and a nap dissolved in an instant.

Luc was on my couch, yet again. Gus sat beside him, drinking a beer. Azriel was in the armchair, his eyes closed but his body alert.

"If we keep this up, maybe we'll have to make this Hell's palace," I teased, but it was a fragile sound. Still, Luc smiled. Ace was nowhere to be seen. "Where's Ace?"

Now his grin grew into something wide and fearsome. "She and your sister are out exacting revenge in the bloodiest way possible. My consort has decided that she would like to make it a full-time project to eradicate as much of the Tenebrae as she can. Starting with the people who watched Uriel strangle you in the club. Then I believe they are going to move down the ranks until they get to the 'salvageable' ones." Luc made quotation marks with his fingers. Sometimes Luc was without mercy, and I could see how he earned his crown. He stood, and I gasped when I saw Michael's sword in his hand. I'd left it at the club, forgotten in the face of Blue's injuries.

"You can wield it!" I sounded like a bad extra in a Shakespearean play, but I was that shocked. But the shock was closely followed by relief. I could pass this burden off to Luc. He could squash Uriel like a bug.

He frowned at the look on my face. "No, Hope. I cannot wield it. I can stop it disappearing into the ether. I can hand it back to you. But I cannot destroy Uriel with it. That is your burden to bear, although I would shoulder it for you if I could. Even now, the sword struggles to return to its rightful hand." As if to prove his point, he uncurled his fist and the sword disappeared, landing at my feet with a thud. I was beginning to hate that sword.

My phone rang and I fished around in my purse. A number I didn't recognize flashed on the screen.

"Hello?"

"You need to get down here now," someone yelled down the line. "Now!" The phone got muffled as someone yelled "Jesus, get back in the clubhouse. They are here for her!"

The sound of gunfire echoed down the phone, and I almost dropped it. It could only be one person. "Cain!" There was silence and more gunshots. "Cain! Where are you?"

There was a scuffle and the sound of heavy thudding. I could hear shouting. "Get her back into the office and barricade that fucking door."

Cain's voice came back over the phone. "Damnation MC Clubhouse, in Oakland New Jersey. Just off the interstate. You won't make it in time. We'll hold them off as long as we can, but they aren't normal."

"We'll be there in minutes. Hold on!"

I turned to the Angels in the room. All Fallen, all battle ready. Somehow, while I'd been on the phone, they'd all managed to procure swords. Luc now had two. Memphis had raided Blue's gun supply. A part of me unclenched knowing that Blue was safe in hospital.

With fierce expressions on their faces, I could only imagine what they would have looked like as part of Heaven's army.

I bent and picked up Michael's sword. I tucked my phone into the back pocket of my jeans. "It's time," I said, and they all nodded. "They are at the Damnation MC Clubhouse." Cain was a bikie. No wonder Luc was familiar with him.

The temperature dropped in the room. Memphis stepped forward, wrapping his arms around my waist. Tucking a gun into the back of my jeans, he kissed me. Gusion was next, and then Azriel.

Luc held his arms out wide. "Let's end this." Then he disappeared.

CHAPTER FORTY

We sifted into a war zone. It was the only way to explain it. People hid behind the bar, the big front double doors barricaded shut but the windows were all blown out. The clubhouse looked exactly how I thought a bikie hangout would look. A long couch and a pool table in the front room. A small bar behind which three guys in leather cuts held huge ass guns.

When we appeared behind them, a big guy with a huge orange beard spun around, giving a little girly scream. If there wasn't bullets flying and a giant gun pointed at me, I would have laughed.

"Woah! Cain called. We are here to help."

He looked at me, and then at my sword. The guys fanned out behind me, their wings spread out wide. Oh, apparently we weren't even pretending to be human now. The big guy with the beard went super pale. The guy behind him had an honest to god eyepatch.

"Cain said you were going to be trouble, but this is

fucking insane," Eyepatch said. "Cain's with the girl. Go out the back, and up the stairs."

I nodded. "I'll leave these guys with you. This is Gusion and Mephistopheles." I turned to Memphis and kissed him. "Be safe. Don't let them die. They didn't choose this war. This is my fault."

Eyepatch scoffed. "Listen here, Trouble. They came here, and tried to fuck with someone under our protection. If we didn't want it, we could have thrown Dippy under the bus. We protect our own."

I didn't have time to unpack that whole statement. "No worries, Eyepatch. So do I. And guess what? You are now officially mine."

It occurred to me that Eyepatch was actually kind of handsome. He was older, maybe early forties. But he had muscles that told me he worked out a lot, and a gruff hardness that made him appealing.

"I don't like the way you are eyeing the pirate there, Sweetheart," Gusion teased. I laughed and kissed him.

"Don't worry, Gus. I couldn't handle, Eyepatch I think."

The guy beside him, a beautiful latino man with full lips, chuckled. Red Beard just looked freaked out.

More gunfire shocked us out of our little meet and greet. "Let her through. She's with us," he yelled over his shoulder, and nodded to the door behind us.

I rushed toward the back of the room to the stairs. As I stepped through, I saw another two guys with huge shotguns behind the door jamb. One guy was wearing an honest-to-god cowboy hat.

"Ma'am," he said, tipping his hat. His eyes got wide

at the sight of Azriel, his huge sunset wings brushing the doorway.

"Hey, Cowboy." I grinned at the little guy beside him and ran up the stairs, taking them two at a time. Cowboy yelled over his shoulder, "Let her through, she's with us." Geez, how many more were there?

I answered my own question as I stepped into a room filled with about twelve more men and one pissed off looking woman. "Hey Sera. How's it going?"

I noticed Cain beside her, his face a mask of deadly calm. "We are being attacked by the fucking mob," he answered for her.

"I'm fine, except they seem to think being pregnant somehow turned me into fine china that can't hold a gun. I need a gun." She looked like she was about to cry. Hormones?

I pulled the gun from the back of my pants, and handed it to her, making Cain scowl more.

"What? Do you want her to cry? Because she's about to cry," I warned, and as expected, every single one looked horrified by the idea.

So Sera got her gun and I got to be the attention of every man in that room. Well, me and Azriel.

Whispers rang through the room. "Is that a mother-fucking angel?" someone asked.

I heard the heavy thud of a fist hitting flesh. "He's got huge ass wings. What the hell do you think he is, a friggin' fairy?" someone else answered in a heavy Irish accent.

"You know how to make an entrance," Sera said, and stood up. Every set of eyes in that room stared at her like she was about to topple over and fall on her face. That had to be annoying. "Uriel found me fast."

I rested my sword on the couch. Honestly, because I was worried I would take out someones eye, or smite someone to the bowels of Hell accidentally. Also, because the more I held it, the more I wanted to hold it, and it was giving me the jeebies. "It was my fault. I came at him too early. Blue is in hospital. He was shot," my voice cracked. "He knew I was out of Purgatory, and I guess he deduced I wouldn't have left you behind. I'm sorry." And I was. I'd hoped to keep Sera as far out of this as I could. And I definitely didn't mean to drag Cain and these guys into a war they couldn't possibly win.

"Did you bring an army?" she asked, looking at Azriel.

The room got very cold. "No, she brought the Devil," a voice said from the back of the room.

Every single person whirled around, guns raised and pointed at Luc. "Put them down, Kids. They won't do you any good here. Let me introduce myself. I am Lucifer." He pointed to Ace, who stood beside him looking like a warrior queen, her grey wings spread wide. "This is my consort, Acerezeal."

Beside Ace was Rella and her Gargoyles. "Hi, I'm Rella, Hope's twin. These guys," she pointed to Romanus and Rouen, "are here to fuck things up."

Cain looked at me. "There's two of you?" He sounded pained.

I laughed. "Would you believe I was the good twin? Besides, Rella is actually dead, and the two guys with her are Gargoyles." I looked around at the shocked expressions in the room. "You should probably suspend your disbelief for the day," I told them. "I left Memphis and Gus downstairs with Eyepatch. They probably need a hand," I told Ace and Luc, but they were both staring at Sera.

"She looks familiar. I can't quite figure out why though," Ace mumbled.

I swung toward her. "You aren't God in disguise are you, because seriously, I can't take that again."

Sera looked at me like I'd lost my mind. Actually, everyone looked at me like I'd lost my mind.

"What? No! Wait, what?" Sera shook her head. I guess that wouldn't make much sense. Plus if she was and she was knocked up by Uriel, well, that would push this day right into Jerry Springer territory.

There were shouts from downstairs, and everyone snapped into action. Rella pulled out a sword. Actually... "Hey Sis, can you grab my sword?"

Luc's eyes followed Rella as she went to grab the sword of St Michael, but it disappeared, landing at my feet. Dammit.

"What the actual hell?" Rella asked.

I waved her away. "I'll explain later, let's go."

I ran down the stairs, Azriel at my back. Everyone else was at the bottom of the stairs when we got there. Cowboy Hat was looking confused, and the little guy was looking at all the wings in the room.

"You should have stayed upstairs, Hope," Rella said. "You are a mortal playing an immortal game."

I gave her the middle finger, but it was half hearted. I knew she was right, and normally, I would have happily stayed up there, the last line of defense with Sera.

Unfortunately, someone had set me on this path, and it led straight to Uriel. "Don't worry about me. Clean up Tenebrae and back up Eyepatch."

"Who?"

But Rella wasn't confused for long, because the man in question stuck his head around the door. "They are about to break through, we need to fall back," he barked, and then stopped when he saw the rest of the people in the room.

"I brought a posse," I said, grinning at Cowboy Hat. "But you should probably fall back. This is about to get messy."

Eyepatch stared at Luc. "Lucifer."

"Judas."

I looked between the two men. Well, that's interesting. Someone was making deals with the devil, and now the name of the MC club didn't seem quite so ironic.

"Is no one going to point out the irony of there being both a Cain and a Judas in this club? A club called Damnation?" Rella said from the back, and I held in my grin. "My police sense is tingling hard right now?"

Red Beard looked at Rella. "You're a cop?"

Rella laughed at his glare. "Dude, I'm dead. You have nothing to fear from me. Though I know where you live now and I wouldn't think twice about coming around and hiding the keys to your pretty motorcycles." She winked, and Rouen chuckled.

Memphis grumbled beside me. "Fucking humans."

I reached out and grabbed his hand, giving it a squeeze.

Apparently Eyepatch, uh Judas, was getting sick of the chatter too. "Listen up. Damnation, fall back to the stairs. Hold the stairs. No one gets up to Dippy." I tried not to giggle at the fact they called Serendipity 'Dippy'.

There were nods and they moved back. I heard a loud engine revving. Gus turned to me, his brows low. "They are going to ram the doors with a car."

Well, apparently having the Angel of the Past, Present and Future was helpful friend to have in battle, because within seconds, the front end of an SUV was inside the building, knocking the bar back a few feet. It reversed back and then people were pouring through the doors. Memphis pushed me behind his back, his black wings hiding me from sight.

Uriel strolled in like he owned the place.

"Aw, it's a reunion. How's your pet human?" He asked me and I gritted my teeth. But my heart thundered. Blue was fine. He was safe in hospital. I repeated it over and over to myself.

No one answered his question. Ace, however, was not above a few barbs of her own.

"Why don't you just go home, Uriel? Oh, is it because you can't? Have you fallen, oh great and powerful Uriel? I bet your wings are the color of the bullshit that pours from your mouth," she taunted. Ace had some bite.

Uriel narrowed his eyes, and signaled with his hands. Countless Tenebrae soldiers poured into the building. Some only had a little red in their auras, and some were coated so badly that their own aura was basically gone. There was no sorting them now, as weapons started firing and bullets bounced off the angels like ping pong balls.

The Gargoyles transformed, and they were freaking terrifying. Huge and almost dragon like, and somewhat beautiful. They stood shoulder to shoulder with Rella, who looked fierce as hell as she ran into the fray, her sword swinging like a valkyrie. To the left of her, Ace looked almost bored as she mowed down the Tenebrae like they were merely ants in her way.

It was a bloody massacre, and I was glad I was hidden by Memphis' wings.

Then the other angels turned up and things went to shit.

CHAPTER FORTY-ONE

T here was six of them all up. They flanked Uriel on either side, almost perfect replicas of each other. Except a few were women. I'd never met a female angel, other than Ace. They were all perfect mannequins, impassive masks for faces. Like Azriel had been before me.

Azriel stepped forward. "Please, Brothers and Sisters, go home. There is no need for there to be a battle here to day," he implored.

One of the female angels sneered. "Traitor. As if we would ever do as you say." She looked scathingly at his wings. Oh hell no. No one talked to one of my guys like that.

"Easy," Memphis whispered at me.

Ace laughed like what she said was the most hilarious thing she'd ever heard, but at the same time, the laugh was completely humorless. It was a disconcerting noise. "Orphelia, have you seen your leaders wings lately?" The female angel, Orphelia, lowered her eyebrows, her face set in a perma-scowl.

"As if I would believe you, Demoness."

Rella let out a low whistle. "Bad call, Angel Barbie."

Ace let out a growl. "I am not a demoness. You know what, let's just kill these uppity bastards and go home. I'm missing my soap operas."

Memphis backed me up to the stairs. He turned and looked at the bikies hovering in the stairwell.

"She stays here. She dies, you all die, got it?" His midnight wings spread wide, and his face was morphed into scary mode. Unsurprisingly, the Damnation MC guys all nodded vigorously.

Memphis turned and strode back toward the group. He hefted his sword into the air and threw it like a javelin at the angel beside Uriel. The sword got him right in the chest, driving him back several feet.

It was like a starting gun had gone off as the denizens of Hell leapt forward into the flurry of white wings. Except Uriel, who stood back and let the chaos unfold. Never doing his own dirty work.

I gritted my teeth and launched forward. Judas grabbed me before I could jump that last step, pulling me back into the Damnation ranks.

"Nuh uh, Trouble. That is no place for someone without wings."

I scowled at him. "I can end this."

He shook his head, the arm he had banded around my waist never loosening. "Not yet, you can't. Gotta choose your time carefully. Running pigheaded into battle will get you killed."

I huffed but I waited. I waited as Gusion spun, slicing at an angel who stepped into the swing and slashed at his chest under his guard. I waited as Ace pinned Orphelia to the wall like a butterfly with the never ending supply of knives she seemed to have on her person. I waited as one of the Gargoyles bit an angel in half.

That one made me gag a little. By the sound of heaving behind me on the stairs, I wasn't the only one. Azriel moved with an elegant grace, still dignified in his style combat. Unlike the Fallen, who had been fighting in the gutter for millennia; they fought like they were in the pits of Hell. But Azriel and his opponent all but danced around the room, a beautiful, deadly ballet. Finally, Azriel unarmed his opponent, swooping out a foot and dropping the other angel onto his back. He jammed the two swords into his shoulders, making the angel scream. Uriel was down to three, although Gus was bleeding quite heavily. But the grin on his face assuaged my fear. He was actually having fun.

The whole time, Luc and Uriel stood and stared at each other through the chaos. Lucifer shook his head at the other Archangel. "Greed is not becoming on you, Archangel."

"I was doing the Father's work, sending sinners to Hell. Sinners like you," Uriel's lip curled in disgust.

"I must have missed the part in the bible where it said, 'Thou shalt sell innocents into slavery," he said snidely, echoing my words. "For that matter, there is no 'Thou shalt fornicate with women' either. I probably wouldn't have fallen if there had been."

"Blasphemy!" Uriel cried, surging forward and attacking Luc, his sword raised. Luc easily parried his enraged charge, but still, I found myself pulling against Judas' restraining arm. "Not yet," he murmured again. "Wait for it."

The fighting between the angels had been impressive, but the fight between Uriel and Lucifer was as awe-inspiring as it was terrifying. They moved so fast, my eyes could hardly keep up, only the sparks their swords produced when they clashed together with a terrifying strength tracking their path.

"It's time to end this," I whispered to myself, although Judas heard. He loosened the grip he had around my waist and I lifted the sword.

Then it caught on fire.

And I dropped it *because it was on fucking fire.* The flame went out as it fell to the ground. Judas snorted, and I scowled at him. I picked it back up, raising it again, and the flames ran along the blade once more. I was more prepared this time, and walked toward the fighting Archangels. As they saw the flaming sword of St Michael in my hand, Uriel's angels stilled. It wasn't in reverence, that I knew. It was probably in shock. I was wielding Heaven's most sacred artefact.

Locked in battle, Uriel didn't see the sword until I pressed the tip between his shoulder blades. The fires of heaven dripped against his skin. Unable to help himself, Uriel whirled, the blade scoring around his body, leaving a big, bloody gash. It cut through their immortal skin like butter. This sword had one purpose, and it was to deliver justice.

Uriel looked at the sword now pressed to his chest. "How is this possible?"

I shrugged. I wish I knew. Rella stepped forward. "Finish it, Hope," she yelled, urging me to avenge her.

God, I wanted to. I wanted to run the sword through his black heart. The heart that delivered misery to thousands, who was the cause of my sister's death, and my trip to Purgatory and Sera's torture. My torture. I wanted to slip the blade in and watch his soul disappear into nothingness.

But I just couldn't. I couldn't take his life, standing there as he was, his eyes wide with confusion and horror. It felt...wrong. It wasn't me. It was Luc, and Ace and Rella. They were the warriors.

I was the fixer. I gave life, I didn't take it.

I dropped the sword point to the floor. I felt like a failure, but the relief in my heart wasn't a lie.

"What are you doing?" Rella yelled, and my heart broke. I failed her.

Someone clapped from the back of the room.

Uriel's eyes went wide, and color drained from his face. He looked like he'd seen a ghost.

I spun around.

He hadn't seen a ghost. He'd seen something much worse.

The guy from the beach was there, leaning against the wall. Beside him was Michael, who was looking pointedly at the sword in my hand. I walked over quickly and handed it back to him.

"Sorry. I only borrowed it. I didn't..." I trailed off because I had no idea what was coming from my mouth.

I couldn't stop looking between the two of them. I looked back at the stairs, and realized all the Damnation boys were frozen.

The guy from the beach was still in his *Jesus is My Homeboy* shirt and torn jeans. He was smiling at me and it was all teeth and I realized I was crying a little. But not out of happiness or fear, but it was like staring at the sun.

I dropped my eyes to the floor.

"I was worried you were going to end his life for a moment there," the Beach Guy said. I couldn't think of him as God, with a big G. I was going to think of him as Beach Guy, or my brain would probably actually explode.

"I was." Ugh, wrong thing to say. "I mean, I couldn't, but a part of me really wanted to." I didn't think I made that any better.

"But you didn't, and that is what matters," Michael said softly.

Beach Guy pushed off the wall and wandered over to Luc and Uriel like had all the time in the world. Maybe he did. As he walked past, the angels dropped to their knees, even my Fallen.

Beach Guy looked over his shoulder at me. "*Your* Fallen?" He raised an eyebrow at me. Okay, so my thoughts weren't as blank to him as they were to the angels. I'd remember that. I blushed hard, and my heart hammered, but I refused to take it back. Beach Guy just laughed. "Lucifer better watch you. You hold the hearts of his entire Cadre of angels."

I shrugged. "I love Luc. I would never do anything to hurt him." I meant every word.

Beach Guy looked at Michael. "Such an extraordinary capacity for love. She loves the very Devil himself."

Michael raised his brows. "Yes, I know, Old Friend. You told me so. But I have to admit, I doubted. But you were right, she most certainly has changed things." He looked at Uriel, his face hardening. "Although, perhaps things needed to change."

The pair stopped in front of Luc and Uriel, and Uriel fell to his knees. "Father–"

The Beach Guy held up a hand, halting his words.

"Show me your wings, Uriel."

Uriel shook his head. An unbelievable power crushed the room, and I forgot how to breathe. I fell to my knees, as did everyone else in the room who wasn't already prone on the floor. All except Lucifer and Michael.

Uriel's wings became visible and spread wide. They were mottled white, with patches of brown, puce and green splattered over the white of his wings. They looked almost as if they'd grown a fungus in the fridge. They reflected the rot on his soul.

"A good analogy, Hope Jones. Your soul has begun to rot, Uriel. This child of Eve has decided to spare your immortal soul, but I am not quite so lenient." All of a sudden he didn't look like a good natured beach bum. He looked fully old testament, and fear crawled across my skin. "I banish you, Uriel, to Purgatory. May your soul never be reborn."

With that, Michael's sword came down on Uriel, cleaving him in two, his body turning to ash and sinking into the floor. Not even a speck remained within moments.

The Beach Guy was back to his natural sunny disposition. He looked at Luc, and I tensed.

"Lucifer Morningstar."

"Father." He inclined his head low.

"How is business?"

Luc smiled. "Booming as usual. Yours?"

"The same as usual, but I predict this will change very soon due to you and your seven sins. I'll see you for our chess match?"

Luc inclined his head again. "Of course."

Beach Guy turned to the rest of the angels in the room. His stare made my soul shake in terror. They disappeared one by one, hopefully back to Heaven where they belonged. He paused in front of me, looking over my shoulder at Ace, who'd moved to somehow position herself at my back, ready to whisk me from danger, even from you-know-who Himself.

"Acerezeal. It is good to see you. Do not fear, I mean your progeny no harm."

She inclined her head, but didn't move.

He shook his head in bemused exasperation. "You stole my Angel of Death, Hope Jones."

"I'm sorry, but he needed me," I explained.

"More than he needed me?" he asked. What a trick question.

"Perhaps," I answered truthfully. Ace groaned

behind me. "He had been your dealer of death for so long. He needed a chance at life."

Beach Guy reached out and touched my cheek, and the room held its collective breath. "Perhaps," he echoed. "You also killed one of my angels."

"He tortured innocent women," I protested. "He was not a good angel."

Ace kicked me in the shin. Beach Guy laughed. "No, he was not. Michael believes that he got what he deserved. I am prone to agree. But it means you'll never be in my domain. Some things are unforgivable."

I looked at all my Fallen, at Rella, at Luc and Ace. "I understand."

He looked around the room and laughed. "Maybe I should be worried? An army of loyal angels, and you even managed to sway the Right Hand of God. You setting yourself up for a management role, Hope Jones?"

I shook my head so furiously I was worried it would snap off. "No!"

Beach Guy laughed harder. "I jest. Your heart is too soft for this job anyway." He looked around the room. "Be good, Children."

Then he disappeared like he'd never been. Michael threw me a wink, and disappeared too, and the world restarted. Except it was now empty of bad guys.

I was going to pass out or throw up or something. Ace put a steadying hand on my back.

"Well done, Kid. You just absolved us all."

I let out a huge breath. We'd done it.

Judas stepped down into the room. "What the hell just happened?"

I shook my head. "Don't ask." I looked at my guys, who each looked shaken. Azriel was so grey I was worried he was going to pass out.

"Can we go home?"

I was wrapped in Gus' arms and out of there before I could even blink.

———

THREE MONTHS LATER

I woke up pressed between two angels. Today was the big day. The first batch of redeemable souls was arriving, and we were going to try our best to redeem them. Unfortunately, they wouldn't get to live out their days the way my parents did, that had been a boon especially for them, but we did get to help absolve them and send them out of Hell and up the other way. That had to be worth something, right?

Rella and her guys were running some kind of support group in Hell's palace for souls that could possibly be redeemed, those who had erred in their human life, but weren't really all that bad. Like the first two circles of hell only. It wasn't like we were letting despotic dictators out to play.

I was nervous. Playing with people's immortal souls was daunting.

I slid out from between Memphis and Gus, careful not to wake them. Stepping into the kitchen, I found

Blue reading the paper and drinking coffee, just as I knew he would be. I looked down at the ring on my finger, a blue diamond the color of Blue's eyes and worth so much money that I only ever wore it at home. I was petrified I'd lose it on the street otherwise.

Azriel emerged from his bedroom in a pair of jeans and a Harry Potter shirt. It was so cute I wanted to explode.

He leaned over and kissed me, and I stroked along his wings, making him moan against my lips. I grinned and moved toward the coffee pot.

"Ready for the big day?"

Azriel nodded. "Yes, if I don't like them, I can always just send them back."

That, in essence, was the only reason Luc had agreed to our crazy plan to start a halfway house for souls that could be saved.

I smiled so wide, I thought my face would crack. But that was what happiness did to a person; it filled you up so much that you had to let it out. "Today is going to be a good day, I can feel it."

Memphis and Gus emerged from the bedroom. Memphis was fully dressed, but Gus was completely naked.

Blue made a gagging noise. "Seriously, man. Put your dick away. No one wants to see that so early in the morning."

Well, maybe not *no one*. As if he could hear my thoughts, Gusion gave me a cheeky grin that promised all sorts of naughtiness, but went back to the room to pull on pants. Memphis kissed me deeply, and then grabbed a banana, sitting down at the breakfast bar. Gusion came back out fully dressed unfortunately. He came over, and kissed me until I saw stars. Then he took my coffee and drank half.

"Hey!"

He shrugged completely unapologetically. "Hell only has instant," he said as if that excused his caffeine thievery. I sighed, handing him the rest of my mug. "That's love right there, Pretty Girl." He gulped down the rest of my coffee and looked at Memphis. "Ready?"

Memphis nodded, and came over to kiss me good-bye. Or maybe it was good morning. Either way, he kissed me like my lips were oxygen and I was tempted to just drag them all back to bed. I briefly wondered if I could persuade Azriel to join us? Maybe Blue too, like one big happy orgy.

I shook my head. My guys were willing to share, but Blue drew the line at participating altogether. Azriel I could probably talk around eventually though. For now, we worked. I bed hopped from night to night, and everyone seemed content.

Memphis spread his wings. "Wait. I just wanted to say my parents are coming over tonight for dinner."

Azriel blanched. "What?"

Gusion laughed. "Uh oh. It'll be fine, Az. I'm sure they've forgotten all about that little thing that happened."

Azriel looked horrified. "I stabbed her in the chest. One doesn't just forget all about something like that."

I grinned. "It'll be fine. When I tell them I'm pregnant, they'll forget all about it."

Now all four guys looked shocked.

"What?"

"Did she just say-"

"You're what?"

Blue just looked stupidly proud of himself.

Yeah, today was going to be a good day.

The End

ACKNOWLEDGMENTS

So that's that. The freakin' end.

I honestly can't thank you, the reader, enough for your support. This whole ride has been amazing and terrifying and spectacular and anxiety-producing. I've learned a lot, watched the Reverse Harem sub-genre grow so fast that it blows my mind, and made some great friends and spectacular supporters.

But it is the readers that have been with me every step of the way that I owe so very, very much. The ones that encouraged me when I was just dipping my toe into this crazy community, the ones who read every single part I released and only cussed me out a little for all the cliffhangers. The ones who left such beautiful reviews that gave me the confidence to grow as an author. You know who you are, and I think you are all amazing. THANK YOU from the very bottom of my black little heart.

Stay in touch, you guys. I've got some BIG things coming out over the next few months. If you want to stay on top of my crazy release schedule, you can join my reader group on Facebook (Grace's Bookish Angels), or follow me on Instagram (@gracemcgintyauthor).

As always, there are these other options too, because I love talking to readers and I want you to be able find me if you just want to chat, or write me hate mail.

Facebook Author Page: https://www.facebook.com/GraceMcGintyAuthor/

Instagram: @gracemcgintyauthor

Website: https://gracemcgintyauthor.com

Twitter: @McgintyGrace

Email: gracemcgintyauthor@gmail.com

Turn the page for a Sneak Peek of Newly Undead in Dark River
(Dark River Days: Book One)

ABOUT THE AUTHOR

Grace McGinty is eclectic. She has worked as a choco-latier, a librarian, a forensic accountant and finally a writer. Like her professional career, the genres she writes are also eclectic. She writes romance, reverse harem romance, fantasy, contemporary young adult and new adult books.

She lives in rural Australia with her crazy family, an entire menagerie of pets, and will one day be crushed by her giant piles of books that litter every room.

The Fallen marks the end of Arcadia, Estrella and Hope's stories, but Serendipity will get her own story very soon.

Keep reading for a sneak preview at my new Reverse Harem Series, Dark River Days.

NEWLY UNDEAD IN DARK RIVER

DARK RIVER DAYS: BOOK 1

Chapter One

I woke to a rat scuttling across my chest, its tiny nose twitching as it paused to stare at me before scurrying off. Damn, I was hungry.

The fact that my initial reaction to a rat was hunger and not disgust was the first sign that something was very, very wrong. The second clue was that I was lying in a drain pipe in the middle of the night. Although it was hard to concentrate on anything but the hunger clawing at my stomach, I could hear the nocturnal animals shuffling around in the silence, smell the stale water that now soaked my clothes.

I tried to sit up and banged my head on the slimy concrete. Groaning, I rolled over and crawled my way out into the open. My body felt like I'd climbed Everest. Twice. I couldn't see my backpack anywhere. Panic began to fill my chest. Everything was in that pack. But it was pitch black, the moon not even visible behind the clouds. I became acutely aware that I was standing in the middle of the wilderness, at night, alone. I was a serial killer's wet dream right now.

I stared down the road, looking for the oncoming lights of a car or truck or something. Maybe I could hitch a ride into the nearest town. It was probably hitch-hiking that put me in this predicament to start with. My mom was going to be pissed that I'd been so irre-sponsible.

I felt dazed like I'd been tranquilized, but I patted down my clothing with sluggish movements. Nothing was torn, and all my clothes were still on. I didn't feel violated in any way. My brain was cloudy, and I tried to sift through the fog to remember why I was lying in a ditch, outside of...

I looked up at the road sign. *Welcome to Dark River.* Where the hell was Dark River?

Hunger tore at my belly again, a burning ache so painful I moaned into the darkness like a wounded animal. First, I needed to eat something. Maybe then I'd be able to work out what the hell was going on.

I stumbled down the side of the road, and I could see the muted glow of the town lights once I was over the small rise.

Electricity surged up through my chest, and the edges of my vision dimmed. The last thing I felt when my body buckled was the rough gravel scraping my cheek.

I snapped back to consciousness all at once, like when

you dream you're falling. My head felt too full, and panic was beginning to mingle with the overwhelming hunger.

I was now in town, beneath the striped awning of Bert and Beatrice's Old Fashioned Diner. How the fuck did I get here? Everything was completely blank as if someone had plucked the memory from my brain like a bad apple. A clock tower sat in the middle of town, proclaiming it to be almost midnight.

I pushed through the glass door, and a little bell tinkled above my head. The place was filled to the brim, which was unusual seeing how it was basically the middle of the night.

Every set of eyes turned to look at me, and the old guy behind the counter dropped the soda glass he was drying, the smashing sound shooting pain into my skull. I must have really looked like hell. An elderly woman bustled out of the swinging doors, which probably led to the kitchen.

"What's goin' on out..." she trailed off when she saw me standing in the doorway. She nudged the old man out of the way.

"Lass, are you feelin' alright? Bertie, get the girl a drink. The house special," she said slowly, her accent a thick Scottish brogue. "Tilda, call the Sheriff, please. Get him down here, quick smart." She was rounding the counter now. "Here, Lass, take a seat."

I took the stool she indicated obediently. She had a no-nonsense, matronly tone that soothed my panicked nerves.

"I lost my money and my passport." My voice sounded so weak that I hardly recognized it as my own.

The elderly lady just patted my shoulder.

"Not to worry, Sweet. It's on the house."

I could hear the sound of Tilda murmuring quietly into the phone down the other end of the diner.

"Yes Sheriff, just stumbled in the door. Looking like death, if you know what I mean."

The old man, Bertie I guess, slid a cardboard milk-shake cup in front of me, complete with red and white straw. It smelled so good that I fell on it like a half-starved animal. When I'd sucked down the last drop, I looked up, embarrassed.

"Sorry. I was really hungry." Bertie just took away my empty cup and put a fresh one in front of me.

"Don't worry about it, Darlin'. Have another one." I was struggling to concentrate on her words. I found it hard to concentrate on anything but the milkshake in front of me.

The bell over the door tinkled, and everyone's eyes shifted in that direction again, even mine. A tall man in a chocolate brown uniform walked into the place, and everyone started talking at once. The cacophony after the complete absence of noise was hell on my eardrums. I pushed my palms over my ears to try and muffle some of the sounds.

"Quiet!" The guy was obviously the Sheriff, judging by the way that everyone's flapping jaws snapped shut with almost perfect synchronization. Silence again. The man strode over, his every movement elegant, to where I was sitting and gaping in his direction.

The man was hot. Like, spontaneous combustion, three-alarm, call in the National Guard, hot. He had sandy brown hair and deep green eyes. The uniform hugged his muscular body. He was so attractive it made my teeth hurt. Literally.

"Ma'am, my name is Sheriff Walker Walton, do you need some help?" His deep voice was gentle, almost as if he didn't want to startle me.

"I don't know how I got here," I whispered. It was all a blank.

I'd been backpacking my way through Canada with my friends, but they had gone home last week, while I continued to travel up through Alberta by myself. I'd missed my bus to Yukon, so I'd decided to hitchhike my way through the last stretch to the border of British Columbia. After all, what's life without a little adventure? I'd been picked up by a family with teenage sons, but they'd let me off near Grande Prairie. I walked down the highway a bit more, and then poof, everything else is blank.

"Do you remember your name?" the Sheriff asked in the same soft voice.

"Mika McKellan. From Boston."

"That's good, Mika. I'd like you to come down to the station with me, so we can get this all sorted out. The town doctor will meet us there, just to check you over."

I nodded absently, and followed Sheriff Walton out of the diner, clutching my take away cup to my chest like a lifebuoy. He walked me over to the squad car, and let me sit in the passenger seat, instead of the back.

We drove in silence around the block, and I took the

town in. It was actually quite beautiful. Not the cemetery stillness of most small towns after dark. Fairy lights were strung around the town square, and people milled about. The lights were on in all the shops, and small clumps of people were talking to each other on well-lit sidewalks.

"Is there a festival going on or something?" I asked Sheriff Walton.

"Or something," he replied, letting silence fill the cab.

Within a minute, we had pulled up in front of a skinny brick building. There were shiny bars on the windows, and a police sign hanging over the front lawn.

Sheriff Walton moved around the front of the car and opened the passenger door. I heaved myself out of the seat. Moving wasn't as painful as it was when I first woke up, but I still felt sluggish.

A plain woman with sparkling eyes met us at the front door. She looked me over and then sent a pointed expression to Sheriff Walton.

"Mika, this is Doctor Alice Sommer. I'm gonna get the Doc to check you for any signs of, uh, injury."

He held open the door of the station for me, and I gave him a polite smile.

"Let's go into the conference room. We need to have a chat after the Doc has looked you over. I'll be out here doing some paperwork."

He opened the door to an interrogation room. No windows, just a metal table with two chairs. Conference room, my ass.

"Thanks, Walker. I'll give you a shout when we're done," the doctor said softly.

The door closed with a click. The doctor sat a leather doctor's bag on the metal table. "Have a seat, Miss McKellan."

"Mika."

"Okay, Mika it is. But you have to call me Alice. Now, let me have a look at you." She shone one of those penlights in my eyes, and I let out a little squeal.

"Ouch."

"Hmm, light sensitivity. You have a little bruising on your throat too." She got out a measuring instrument and measured the width of the bruise. "Anything else feel off to you?"

"Except for the starving feeling, my muscles aching, the weird blank spots and the passing out?" My sarcasm was obnoxious, but I couldn't seem to help it. "Other than all that, I'm as healthy as a horse."

The doctor clicked her tongue and wrote down the measurements. "Walker, can you get the cooler from the backseat of my car and come in here please?" She barely raised her voice, but the Sheriff must have heard because the front door of the station slammed.

"Don't worry, Mika. Your symptoms should lessen in a few days."

"Lessen?"

But the Sheriff was striding in the room, cooler in hand. Damn, he was fast.

"It's confirmed, Walker, though let's face it, it was obvious to everyone as soon as she walked through the door of the diner. You can smell it just as well as I can."

The Sheriff ran a hand down his face and sighed. "I know, but I didn't want to believe it. I didn't want to think someone we know could have done this."

What the hell were they talking about? I sniffed my armpit stealthily. I didn't think I smelled that bad, considering I'd been sleeping in a ditch. My nose twitched. A tangy metallic smell was coming from the cooler. A smell that was so familiar, but I couldn't quite put my finger on what it was.

"You know, I'm still in the room. Do you think someone could take me out to the ditch and see if I can find my wallet and my backpack? Everything I have is in that pack."

"Ditch?"

"The one I woke up in. Under the welcome sign."

The Sheriff's eyebrows knitted together, and I could basically see the cogs turning. "Sure. We'll go take a look out there first thing tomorrow night."

"Why can't we go in the morning?"

Alice laid a hand on my arm and rested her butt on the table. She was looking down at me sympathetically. In my experience, that was never a good sign.

"Mika, we have something to tell you. This is going to sound outrageous and frightening, but I want you to know that we are here for you."

My heart started to race, something in the back of my mind screamed that nothing was going to be the same again.

"Did my pet goldfish die? Are you two getting a divorce?" I deflected awkward situations with sarcasm. My therapist and I were working through it back home.

It was the Sheriff that answered. "No. Well, maybe, I don't know. I've never seen your pet goldfish, but I understand they die quite frequently." Walker ran his hand through his hair, and my hands itched to follow suit. "Look, Mika, I know this is going to sound strange, but it's our opinion that last night, you well, uh, you died."

I laughed. Maybe I'd stumbled into one of those reality TV shows. The producer was going to jump out any minute and make me sign a media release and a Non-Disclosure Agreement.

But the door never opened, and the two people opposite me never cracked a smile. "In case you guys didn't notice, I'm sitting right here, conversing with you. I haven't seen many dead people in my life, but I went to Great Aunt Milly's funeral when I was twelve, and she didn't talk back to me from the coffin."

Alice gripped my hand. There was something off-putting about a doctor holding your hand like you were about to get really bad news.

"What Walker is trying to say, Mika," they kept saying my name over and over like I'd suddenly forgotten it, "is that you are the undead. We believe you have been turned into a vampire. I should say, we *know* you've been turned into a vampire. It's the *how* that we don't understand yet."

I blinked. And then blinked again. They were actually serious. They thought I was a vampire. I'd definitely stumbled onto a TV set. It sounded like something the SyFy channel would come up with. But my heart was thudding, and I felt like I was going to throw up. It was like my body knew they weren't kidding, and it was just waiting for my mind to catch up.

"A vampire?"

Walker nodded sympathetically. "The hunger, the light sensitivity, even the blank spots, are all symptoms of the Turning."

"And you guys know this because..." No, that can't be right. My mind rebelled.

"Because we are vampires. The whole town is populated by vampires."

I stared at them dumbly, expecting something, I'm not sure what. For them to turn into bats, or broodingly sparkle in the overhead fluorescent lights. But nothing happened. They just looked like ordinary people. Not overly pale, their eyes weren't glowing red, they didn't have crooked, needle-like teeth. Nothing.

Alice had mocha-colored skin and smooth blond hair that went all the way down her back. She wasn't unearthly attractive by any means. She was pleasant and professional; exactly what you'd want in a physician. Okay, so Walker was hot, but from what I remembered of the diner, it wasn't like I'd stepped onto the stage at Milan Fashion Week or anything out of the ordinary.

"Do you have any questions?" Walker asked. Uh, yeah, I had a few. Like could he pinch me so I would wake the hell up from this bad acid trip?

"So, I'm a vampire, and you're a vampire. And she's a vampire." He nodded. "Do you, I mean I, have fangs?"

Walker bared his teeth, and there, gleaming white

against his pink lips, were two pointed fangs. They were actually quite sharp, and I wondered how he didn't cut his mouth up with them. I looked at Alice, and she too was baring her fangs, which weren't quite as long as Walker's, and sat in her mouth with more ease. I eased my tongue over my own canines and found they'd elongated. I cut my tongue on them, and the blood dripped into my mouth.

Blood.

Hunger clawed at my stomach like a ravenous beast. Suddenly, I understood what the smell coming from the cooler was.

"Please." It was a half yell, half sob, as I dived for the cooler. Walker was around the table in a flash, his arms like iron bands around my body.

"Calm down. Alice is going to get you something to eat right now." As he said it, the Doc was getting a blood bag out of the cooler, like the ones you see in hospitals. She unscrewed the cap on the tube and handed it to me.

Walker released me from his hold, and I closed off the part of my mind that was grossed out at the thought of drinking blood, and let my body take over. I sucked that baby like it was my first cocktail on Spring Break in Cabo. All that was missing was the little umbrella and the frat boys trying to convince me to come to a snow party.

All too soon, the bag was empty. "I want some more." My voice wasn't weak anymore, but it sounded slurred like I was drunk. Alice shook her head.

"With the two you had at the diner, and now this

one, you've had enough. If you gorge yourself, you'll be vomiting for the rest of the night. I'll come see you tomorrow, and we'll discuss how everything works. For the remainder of the night, you need to rest." She picked up the cooler and her doctor's bag. "Are you taking her to your place?" she asked Walker.

He nodded. "I'll find somewhere more permanent for her to live tomorrow." He walked the doctor out, leaving me alone in the windowless room.

The shock settled over me like a numbing cloak. My mind spun as I tried to process, well, everything. I placed my hand on my chest, and my heart was slowly beating in there. Somehow, that made me feel better. I may have been dead, but my heart was still beating. The illogicality of that statement was something I'd deal with another day.

Walker was suddenly back, and his warm hand was on my shoulder. "There are a lot of things we have to discuss, and we can do it here, or back at my place. I know that sounds almost creepy, but I promise you'll be safe." He shifted from foot to foot, almost uncomfortably. "You are new to this world, and I wouldn't feel right about leaving you on your own. There are rules, life or death rules that you need to know. But, if you'd like, we could do it somewhere a bit more comfortable."

I nodded absently, every warning my mother uttered about going home with strange men now defunct. What was the worst that could happen? I was already dead. Plus the guy was the sheriff of a vampire town. If I couldn't trust him, who could a girl, err vampire, trust?

We hopped back into the squad car. I looked at the

town through the window in a new light. I really studied the people, their inhuman grace, the fact that there were no children around. A guy stood on the pavement waiting to cross the road, and then magically was on the other side. I didn't even see him move in front of the car.

"Did that guy just teleport? Can we do that?" The thought was exciting. To just close my eyes and picture anywhere I wanted to be in the world, it would be amazing. Such freedom!

"I'm afraid not. He just moved really fast. As your vampirism settles into your body, you'll see him move as slow as a human. We can all move that quickly."

I was disappointed, though moving at super-speed was still pretty cool. "If we can move that fast, why the hell are we driving? Wouldn't we be wherever we are going almost instantly? Unless your house is in Alaska."

"Two reasons. Firstly, I didn't want to freak you out, plus you'll need a bit of time to get used to moving at that speed. Secondly, I enjoy the slower pace that a vehicle has to offer. Just because you can go at breakneck speed, doesn't mean you should." He sounded like my Dad teaching me to drive. Thoughts of my parents made me feel homesick.

"I need to call my parents and tell them I'm okay. Sort of."

Walker looked uncomfortable. "If you want, but just wait until tomorrow. Give everything you'll learn tonight time to process first."

He pulled up in front of a cute little whitewashed cottage, with a wrap-around porch and a perfectly manicured hedge. I looked at the man in the driver's seat and then back at the house. I saw him as the log cabin type of guy, not the gingerbread vibe that this place had going on.

I followed Walker up to the front door. I don't know when I started to think of him as Walker instead of Sheriff Walton, but it was probably around my third dirty fantasy.

When we walked in the space had a bit more of a masculine feel. Leather couches, a big-screen TV, and a scarred wooden coffee table occupied the living room. A large breakfast bar separated the living area from the kitchen, with three old diner stools tucked under the overhang.

Walker went over to the kitchen counter and poured two glasses of scotch into crystal tumblers.

"I can still drink?"

"Sure, you won't get drunk, but sometimes it's nice just to indulge in the nostalgia. You can also eat and go out in the sun. Though I wouldn't suggest going out in the daytime just yet. The increased sensitivity to light makes daylight extremely painful. It's something to work up to over time. Please, have a seat."

I walked over to the big scarred leather armchair. There was a burgundy throw rug over the arm, and I pulled it over my lap, even though I wasn't cold. The softness of the mohair was amazing. I could see the intricate pattern of the weave, the tiny flyaway fibers on each of the strands of wool. It was like my sight had become microscopic.

Walker handed me my drink and sat across from me, his elbows on his knees.

"I know this has been a lot to take in, but you have some serious decisions to make, Mika. This is a whole new world, with all new rules. Especially Dark River. We aren't your average community, as you know."

"Because everyone is the undead."

"Right, because we are all vampires. But it's not just that. Even within our own race, Dark River is rather unique. I'll explain the rules, and then it is up to you if you stay or you go. We can't keep you here against your will."

Well, that sounded ominous.

"Rule number one, there is absolutely no drinking from humans. Blood is delivered and distributed around the town by the Town Council, and no one goes hungry. The penalty is banishment from Dark River, forever."

That didn't sound so bad. It's not like I wanted to go around munching on people, giving them the hickeys from hell. I nodded for him to continue.

"Rule number two, you can never, ever, turn a human. The Town Council has decreed that the penalty for disobeying this rule is death. Because, in our eyes, turning a human is essentially murder." He looked at me imploringly. "This is what has happened to you, Mika. Someone has murdered you, and it is my job to find out who and bring them to justice. You are young, beautiful, and full of life. You should have had the opportunity to do everything you wanted to do. The opportunity to have children, get married, grow old with a loved one, live out in the light. You deserve retribution." His eyes lit up, and I don't mean sparkled with fervor, I mean literally started to glow.

"Uh, Walker, what's going on with your eyes?"

"Sorry. I didn't mean to freak you out. That sometimes happens when we get worked up. Plus I need to feed."

He walked over to the fridge and pulled out a bag of O positive. I knew it was O positive because there was a huge sticker on the side. He poured it into his tumbler on top of his Scotch. Ew.

He sat back down in front of me.

"Okay, the third rule and usually the most problematic for new vampires who want to join our community is that you must cut all ties with your old life, both for our safety and the safety of the people from before. You wouldn't know this yet, but being around humans is..." he let out a shaky sigh, "an overwhelming temptation. Especially when you are only just learning to control your new body."

I collapsed back on the couch. I'd have to cut ties with my family? Never see my mom smile again, or hear my dad tell a lame joke? Never watch my youngest brother graduate high school? Tears welled in my eyes as my death sunk in. My mind was in the denial stage of grief, apparently. I mean, I felt fine now that I'd drank that blood bag. Maybe I could go home and become a goth or something. I lived alone in my apartment, so I could keep the blood hidden.

"I know what you're thinking. Really, I do. But think about it. You will never look older than you do today. You will live hundreds, if not thousands of years. If you go home, you'll watch your parents die, and your siblings, and their children, and then their children's children. Trust me when I say that it is a soul-shattering experience to watch everyone you have ever loved whither and die." The level of pain in his eyes told me that he knew from experience.

I couldn't decide this now, I needed time to think it over.

"What if I choose to leave?"

Walker bit his lip, his fangs pressing into his full lower lip. "If you choose to leave, then you are subject to the rules of the Vampire Nation. No telling humans what you are, or revealing your nature in a way that could bring Vampires as a whole in the limelight. If you feed on humans, you must do it in a way so that they do not suspect your true nature. Which basically means that unless you have the ability to wipe memories, which some vampires do, you have to kill them and dispose of their bodies discreetly. If you break these rules, Enforcers will come, and you will die. Trust me when I say that Vampire Nation always finds out if you break the rules."

Well, okay, then.

Walker's shaggy hair slipped over his eyes, and he combed it back with his fingers. The move made his shirt pull taut against his chest, and a completely different kind of hunger overtook me. The need to lean over and rip open his shirt was almost impossible to resist.

Walker's eyes met mine, and whatever he saw in

them made him look nervous all of a sudden. He stood quickly and took a step away.

"Okay, I'll let you think it over. The guest room is the second door on the left, and the bathroom is right next door. Make yourself at home, if you need anything, just give me a yell." With that, Sheriff Walker Walton hot-footed it out of the room, faster than my eyes could follow.